PROTOGENESIS

BOOK ONE:
BEFORE THE BEGINNING

ALYSIA HELMING

"FOREVER AND TONIGHT" SONG BY MUSIC ARTIST,
KOSTAS MARTAKIS

ISBN: 978-1-61296-970-1
PUBLISHED BY BLACK ROSE WRITING
www.blackrosewriting.com

Printed in the United States of America
Suggested Retail Price (SRP) $21.95

Protogenesis is printed in Palatino Linotype
Forever and Tonight song by Greek music artist Kostas Martakis

To Hannah, my niece –
You are my original muse.
and

To the people of Greece –
May your incredible spirit persevere through it all.

PROTOGENESIS

THE PLANET GAEA

OLYMPIC GATE

MT. KOSMOS

DESALINATION PLANT

TARTARUS

SANDICANE STORM

NEW OLYMPUS

ALGAE BLOOMS

THE LONE CYPRESS TREE

REBEL DWELLINGS

OLD OLYMPUS

CAT'S EYE GATE

SCYTHIA

Map Designed by Nasia Kalokerinou of Kinari Design

www.kinaridesign.com

PREMONITION

This place feels oddly familiar. As I take in my surroundings, I recognize my childhood bedroom from the old farmhouse back in the Central Valley of California. I'm lying bundled up in my cozy bed with all my favorite stuffed animals.

Movement draws my gaze up towards the ceiling. A translucent, willowy ghost hovers above me.

It's *my mom.*

Suddenly, my stuffed animals vanish as it dawns on me that this scene is all wrong.

I cry out, "Mom, *what are you doing?!"*

My mother's ghostly image smiles at me in peaceful silence as a deep calm envelops me so completely that it stills my fears and warms my heart. Slowly, her arm swings out in a wide arc, her index finger extending towards an open window, where sheer white billowing curtains dance in the soft breeze.

I move to the window and peer outside. There, in front of me, lies a vast stretch of massive sand dunes, some as tall as skyscrapers, which sweep out as far as I can see. In the distance, a gigantic red-hued sun sinks steadily below the horizon. Across the sky directly behind me is the moon, which glows brightly as the atmosphere darkens around it.

The ruby rays of sunlight catch something massive. It looks like an enormous silver pyramid rising sharply up out of the sands, resting on the shores of a scarlet-tinged sea. I turn back towards the wispy image of my mother.

She reaches down to smooth back a lock of my hair and whispers, "No matter what happens, you are my life, my wild, wild violet-eyed love."

I listen intently and feel the strength of the love she has for me in her words. "Remember, whenever you need me, look inside yourself. For all the strength that I have, yours is infinitely more powerful. No matter what, I will be there with you...*always*."

My mother's ghost sweeps out the window up to the top of the sand dune nearest to our house. An enormous mountain lion with brilliant amber eyes roars and ambles up next to her. She jumps onto the back of the majestic creature, and together, they soar across the desert, past the smoking mouth of a simmering volcano.

Skirting the horizon, they approach a sight that takes my breath away.

A cypress tree juts out of the empty sands, standing tall and regal, all alone, an anomaly out here in the harsh, unforgiving desert. Its jagged branches frame the edges of the tree, creating a majestic silhouette against the slowly sinking red sun behind it.

A loud shriek comes from an enormous dark fortress surrounded by a deep maze of open tunnels in the ground. Massive pillars of smoke rise up from the deep crevasses etched into the land.

Darkness overtakes my mother and the mountain lion. The large, round moon projects a pale light across the landscape. Right before my eyes, the face of the moon suddenly transforms into something else...a shiny amber-colored stone that looks to me like the eye of a cat.

My mother and the giant lioness stand hidden behind the cypress tree watching as thousands of soldiers march to rhythmically beating drums. I feel my pulse quicken as I stand at the window, where I observe the hauntingly empty eyes of the men, which appear to be a disturbing shade of crimson.

The drums stop. The endless lines of vacant-eyed men halt abruptly in front of three men. All three are impeccably dressed in modern-day business suits. Two of them wear silver rings, and one wears a ring of solid gold. Most surprising, though, is their eye color, which appears to be an intense shade of purple. The trio seems incredibly out of their element, here in the harsh desert.

There is something different about the man in the middle. He is exceptionally tall, well-muscled with broad shoulders. With his imposing stature and stern demeanor, he must be their leader. His face, though, is all wrong. It's blurred, as if someone has applied an eraser to it, and shadowy, so what remains seems the emanation of pure evil. I can barely make out his shifting features, but the combined effect of it all…is terrifying. He stares with a severe grin at the mass of soldiers in front of him and lifts his hand to the sky. I can see his golden ring glistening in the moonlight. There, etched on the ring, is a twelve-point star.

In a flash, lightning bolts shoot out of his hand into the heavens. The sound of thunder vibrates the ground. The men bow down onto their knees with their eyes aimed down at the ground.

They chant, "Zeus!"

PART I: METAMORPHOSIS

"Just when the caterpillar thought the world was over,
she became a butterfly."

-Proverb, origin unknown

1 – FIRES OF LIFE

Livermore, California – Present Day – March 2016 AD

What was that?! The world steadily comes into focus and I realize that I am awake. It was only a *dream*! But the whole experience felt so incredibly real that I have to look around to make sure I'm okay. Was that *Zeus*, as in the god from the ancient myths?

But why did it all feel so *real*? Oh my, I must have fallen asleep in class!

I look around. No one seems to have noticed. Most of the kids look like zombies. There was a party last night. Some cheerleaders' parents were out of town, not that I was invited. I never am, never will be.

I sigh, content to drift back into my daydream, but a familiar image catches my eye. The canvas hanging on the wall is awash with a stunning array of vibrant greens interspersed with muted shades of red and gold, all forming the elaborate image of a tree.

Magic exists in this place. Right before my eyes, the tree seems to come to life as the intricate leaves sway to and fro, teeming with multicolored butterflies. A mystical bird is perched in the tree's branches. Like an intricate kaleidoscope, the tree changes in my mind with every twist and turn.

Usually, this image fills me with calm, as if it were an old, trusted friend; but today, something is different, as if some sort of darkness may be brewing deep within the shadows between the branches. It's like a complex paradox where nothing is as it seems.

I look down at my desk and realize that I've been doodling on my notepad. I've sketched the image of a tree, but instead of the tree that I was just admiring, something else lies beneath my pen: a much more meaningful tree to me, a cypress tree.

The tree looks like the charm on my mother's favorite necklace, one I have always loved. When I was growing up, Mom would tell me glorious stories from her youth about walking under the shade of the cypress trees, the warm sun peeking through the jagged branches, sweetly kissing her skin, filling her with happiness. At bedtime, her tales almost always centered around one special tree: an enchanted cypress tree, one that stood all alone in a friendless desert, the last of its kind. She called it the 'Lone Cypress Tree.'

Sometimes, I dream about it, like today.

Ever since I can remember, Mom has always dutifully worn this necklace, never taking it off, not even for a moment. She claims that the tree holds some special power that one day, when I'm old enough, I will fully understand. I reach up to my chest as if I expect to touch the shiny small tree charm, but all I feel is the warmth of my skin.

Just then, the voice of my fifth-period English teacher, Mrs. Dilmore, interrupts my thoughts, jarring me back to here and now.

"We were just talking about stories, creation myths, in particular – Eve being created from the rib of Adam, Aphrodite rising from the wave. Why do you think they've had such a strong influence over our cultural imagination for centuries?" She scans the room, her eyes settling on me. "Helene," she says with a smile, "any thoughts?"

She always calls on me because she knows that unlike the rest of the class, I care about my schoolwork. I need to keep my grades up for college or else meet the wrath of my overprotective mother.

I pause for a moment. I love all stories and fairy tales, but most particularly, I love mythology. In addition to the Lone Cypress Tree, my mother's incredible bedtime stories almost always included Greek, Roman and Egyptian gods and goddesses. Similar to my dream just now, her tales were so convincing that sometimes I felt sure they must be real. I'm sure this is why mythology, and particularly creation stories fascinate me. Of course, I have an answer to Mrs. Dilmore's question. I always do.

"Because even if they're fantastic and otherworldly, they delve into the most basic human question: where do we all come from?" I say, totally sure of myself.

"Excellent point, Helene," Ms. Dilmore rewards me with a smile. "And sometimes to know where we come from, or at least who we are, we have to lose a great deal first."

A few of my class-mates snicker, the usual response to my giving a correct answer. It would be nice if someone else could pipe up once in a while.

Thad Williams, a total stoner, leans over to my desk, smirking at me as he chides, "Kiss-ass!!"

I stare straight ahead and pretend I didn't hear him. It's easier to ignore idiots like him. If there is even one hint that I care at all about what he thinks, he'll just keep picking on me.

Once upon a time, I used to hang out with Thad Williams and the stoner crowd. My sophomore year in high school was tough. I went from aspiring ballerina to Goth girl dressed all in black literally overnight after a wicked dance injury. The "bad" girl in me came out with my desire to wallow in the abyss of my own despair.

Junior year, I went the opposite direction: the "good girl," star student, now wise beyond my years. The stoners weren't happy about that, I guess. My problem now is I'm not sure where I fit in. No one wants to hang out with the teacher's pet.

There are times, though, when I feel like allowing that bad girl to come back. But then I hear my mother's words, haunting me: *"Don't do it!"*

The reality with my mom, though, is that she's always meddling in my business, fussing excessively over me…to an extreme, like she's paranoid. She has some deep-seated fear that something horrible is going to happen to me. In fact, we've moved to a new house within the same city at least once per year since I was born.

I know she means well, though. Here's the thing about my mom. Whenever times get tough for us, it's her strength and perseverance that carry us through. Somehow, no matter how crazy or chaotic life seems, she has the ability to make me feel safe. The power of her words echoes through my mind: *"Strong women aren't simply born. We are forged through the fires of life."*

When I was a little girl, I'm not sure I fully understood this; but now that I am almost eighteen – almost a woman – her words make total sense and inspire me.

After class wraps up, school is out, and I board the bus to head home. Randall Sibley, a big jock with a blunt military haircut, sits next to me.

"Hey," he says, looking right at me.

"Hey." I have no idea what else to say. He's never talked to me before, so it's a little weird. He must want something. He stares out the window at the stark, flat California Tri-Valley. Not much to see, really.

"Heard you're helping out with the school newspaper," Randall says eagerly. "Listen, I'm running for class president so was thinking that you could write an article about me."

He does want something from me. But I'm not going to help him. Why would I? When has he ever given me the time of day? I respond in a clipped tone, "The article I'm writing is about ancient philosophy." I point to the book in my arm, *Philosophy Before Socrates.*

He stares as if he has no idea what I'm talking about. I'm certain he doesn't. Frowning, he shrugs, gets up, and moves back to another seat. Just another day in my incredibly exciting life. Same crap, different day.

The bus stops about ten yards from my house. As I step out onto the gravel road, I hold my arm out and wait. In less than a minute, a graceful butterfly flutters down to rest on my forearm. "Hello, my beautiful friend," I say quietly. The intricate black and orange mosaic pattern on its amazing wings mesmerizes me. This is a special butterfly – the monarch. Very soon, a swarm of these same butterflies arrive, transforming my arm into a mass of fluttering wings. I smile. This is the part of my life that I love. Every afternoon, this is our ritual.

Our home this year is a farmhouse on the outskirts of town. Rolling grape and olive orchards pepper the land around our house, but we don't farm it. We're just renting. As I open the front door, I'm greeted by our meager living room. It's a bit rustic and hip with an oversized tan cowhide sofa accented with sheep-skin pillows and a chrome-edged coffee table topped with a thick slab of obsidian. My mother has impeccable taste.

She also collects things—like cats. Not that we ever have any visitors, but the mailman once asked me, "Just how many cats do you have here?" I have no idea. We spay, neuter, feed, and house them in a makeshift shantytown made of cardboard boxes out in our yard, but more and more keep coming. My mother has become the crazy cat lady. Of course, this could be dangerous for me because I'm highly allergic to nearly all furry four-legged creatures. Mostly, our cats are feral and stay outside, so I can manage.

I catch a glimpse of myself in the mirror on the opposite wall. My brown hair is a long, frizzy mess, so today I pulled it back into a low ponytail. My hazel eyes appear alert and well rested, even behind heavy glasses. I should qualify that word *hazel*…the color of my eyes is technically hazel, but the dominant hue is violet, like the flower. Yes, I did say *violet* and not purple. I hate it when people say that my eyes are purple. No one has purple eyes unless you're a freak. I am not a freak.

The doorbell rings. As I peer outside through the screen door, I'm surprised to see two police officers standing there, a man and a woman. Hackles rise on the back of my neck in alarm. *What do the police want with me?*

When I open the door, the officers stand there, rigid and uncomfortable, eyes unblinking, arms folded across their chests. Finally, after a long, awkward silence, the woman speaks. "Helene Crawford?"

I nod.

"I'm Officer Rollins from the Livermore PD," she states in a cold, detached tone. She then points to the man, who has kind eyes. "And this is my partner, Officer Ryan. Can we come inside?"

"Sure." I nod, allowing them into our tiny foyer. "What's this about?" I ask, a little nervous.

Her grimace falls away as her demeanor noticeably softens. "I'm sorry…" she stammers.

I try to concentrate, but I'm so nervous about being questioned by the police that it's hard to focus. Why would she be sorry?

She continues. "It's your mother. There was a fire." She pauses. Her voice cracks as she speaks. "Your mother is *gone*."

2 – TRUST NO ONE

All I can do is stare. My brain tries to adjust to the sudden shock of what I think I just heard. The quiet is so extreme that I can hear the slow, steady drip of a leaky faucet somewhere upstairs.

"Wha…what did you just say?" I stammer, looking down at my hands. "What do you mean she's gone?"

This can't be right. Mom's probably just working late or out with friends. This must be some big misunderstanding. She's not really missing!

But then the officer's words replay in my mind: *"There was a fire."* It's as if someone snapped her fingers and *bam!* The stark realization hits me hard, slamming me in the chest.

"Are you saying…that…my mom…"– my voice cracks – "…is *dead*?"

A feeling of overwhelming dread consumes me. I imagine my mother, her outstretched hand and ghostly.

No….no, no, no. It can't be true. It just can't. I don't believe it.

The officer's features melt into sadness, her eyes wide and glassy, her façade of professionalism gone. No longer is this a police officer. She's now a living, breathing person, just like me. Her face is raw with emotion. She nods somberly and whispers, "Yes, I'm afraid so."

The vibrant image of my mother's warm, smiling face flashes into my vision…and then, just as fast as she appears, her features slowly fade out of view, vanishing into nothing more than a wisp of a distant memory.

"No!! There's no way she'd just leave me like this!" I shriek. *No.* Not possible. I can't believe it. Mom would not just up and leave me all alone in this world. Not my mom! She is a survivor, a warrior.

I feel as if I've just eaten a sandwich with glass in it. The shards cut into my thoughts. My stomach churns and spasms, like I want to heave. I'm no longer capable of processing anything. I've become a blubbering mess.

The female officer takes turns talking with the other officer, who has up until this point been silent. Their voices seem so far away, I can barely hear what they are saying through my sniffles.

My mind clears instantly, though, as her next words catch my attention. "After the fire died down, we found this amongst the ashes in your mother's workspace." The male officer pulls out a photo of an object that looks like a medallion, and on its face is a blue, black, and red emblem that looks like two snakes wrapped around a torch in the double helix shape of...DNA. Very strange.

My head feels fuzzy. Maybe I'm losing my mind.

"Have you ever seen this before?" he asks earnestly.

I study the medallion, but it means nothing to me, so I shake my head.

The male officer shifts awkwardly from side to side. His discomfort is clear and obvious. We're getting nowhere.

The sound of squealing tires snaps us all out of it. My nose wrinkles at the acrid stench of burning rubber. The officers seem almost as shocked as I am. Clearly, no one expected the interruption. Confusion fills their faces as the screen door opens with a swift jerk.

A seventy-something man, pasty pale with crooked, yellowing teeth, wipes sweat from his forehead with a napkin. It's not even that hot outside. From the moment when I hear his voice, I know I don't trust this guy.

His stern eyes follow me, which are in direct contrast to the forced smile on his face. Maybe it's his cheap-looking suit or his weird toupee, but all my instincts scream that this guy is not my friend. There is something seriously off about him.

"Miss Crawford," he says with a slight lisp as he shoves a dog-eared business card into my hand. "My name is Harold Avery, attorney at law." He pauses for dramatic effect. "Your mother hired me. You can call me Hal."

He snatches the medallion photo right out of the police officer's hand, catching him totally off guard. His eyes widen in shock as Hal asks, "What's this?"

"Wait...who did you say you are?" The female officer takes a moment to recover from the lawyer's abrupt rudeness, then composes herself, her professional mask returning. "Helene, can you excuse us for a moment?" she asks.

I nod. "Of course."

The two police officers pull Hal's arm and huddle in the corner with him. I hear bits and pieces of their discussion. It sounds like the female officer is talking about the medallion. She holds up her phone to show the attorney something, and now I can overhear them perfectly.

"Our research indicates that this unique helix symbol may be connected to a complex underground crime network that operates out of Athens," the officer says crisply.

"You can't believe everything you read on the Internet," says the attorney indignantly. "Most of it is just urban myth."

"Our sources are way beyond the scope of the Internet, Mr. Avery." The officer shrugs, then looks down at her watch. Hal scoffs at her with an air of annoyed indifference.

But I can't get over what I've just heard. "Wait, *Athens*? As in Greece?" I feel a chill run down my spine at the words 'underground crime network'. Are they talking about the *mafia*?

They all turn to look at me. "Relax," says Harold Avery. "There's nothing to get excited about." They turn and start talking again, voices low and urgent.

Then I hear the word "arson."

"Wait a second, what did you just say?" my attorney asks, interrupting the officer.

The officer seems annoyed but continues in a low voice. "This was likely arson. Gasoline was found on the scene. The fire erupted into an inferno at 2:33 p.m. at the lab where Diana Crawford was working. Then there was an explosion. She didn't make it out in time."

Arson? Someone did this to my mom intentionally? But why? I knew that she was working on some government-sponsored research at the Lawrence Livermore Labs, but this is crazy. Something doesn't add up.

"So, it was...*murder*? But why?"

They all turn to face me, looking surprised to still see me there.

"No one said the word *murder*, Helene," the male officer offers in an overly calm and reassuring voice. "We're still investigating all avenues."

They turn and start whispering again, but this time so softly that I can't hear them at all. Once again, I feel sadness overtake me as I long to feel my mother's arms around me. A lone tear falls down my cheek, threatening to turn me back into a blubbering mess.

"She's not coming back," I murmur softly.

I look down at my iPhone and shiver when I see the image before me. It's Mom and me. It was my sixth birthday when she surprised me with a last-minute trip to Disney Land. Like every other kid on the planet, I was ecstatic to be there. She was alive and well. We were so happy on that day.

In the photo, around her neck, is the cypress tree necklace.

I reach down to my chest as if to feel it there, but instead I feel the soft thump of my heart beating steadily beneath my hand. Then, unexpectedly, I also feel something more...

The soul bridge. Mom always told me that she would instantly know if something bad happened to me because she would feel it in the energy connected between our hearts through our invisible "bridge."

When I was in my "crazy" phase, I was out past my curfew, had a drink, and then totaled the car just down the road from our house. It was the middle of the night, and I was so tired that I left the car there and walked home. Mom had fallen asleep but claims that at the time of my accident, she popped straight up and knew exactly what had happened. She claims that she felt it all as if she were there.

Knowing this, I'm filled with a strange sense of relief as I feel her soul bridge alive and in full force. Her life's essence is there, and it's stronger than ever. Realization overtakes me.

"What if my Mom is still *alive*?" I whisper out loud.

"No, dear. I'm sorry, but that's not possible," the officer says with somber seriousness.

Have I lost it? How can I know for sure when my thoughts are spinning uncontrollably round and round in my head?

I am comforted by one simple thought: the soul bridge has never let me down before. And if it is in fact true that Mom is alive…I have no idea how, but I will do whatever it takes to find her.

The attorney cuts in. "Your mother hired me to handle her estate and to transport you to Greece where you will live with your godfather, Janus Giannopoulos."

"Wait, what?!" I ask. "There must be some mistake. I don't have a godfather, and I've never been to Greece, and neither has my mother."

I have never heard of Janus Gianno-whatever-his-name is. I have no idea what is going on across the planet, much less what is going on here. Frankly, the thought of moving anywhere at a moment's notice when my mom was alive would be *terrifying*, but to move across the world to live with someone I've never heard of before when my mother just died…?

No. My body doesn't even want to move two inches. It's as if I'm paralyzed.

Hal frowns and clears his throat. He peers down at the rain-soaked papers in his shaky hand. "Well, this is a power of attorney granting me temporary custody as your legal guardian until you arrive safely in the custody of Mr. Giannopoulos in Athens. He will be your guardian until you're twenty-one."

My mouth falls open. This can't be happening. It's *crazy*. The room feels as if it's slowly closing in on me as I consider this new information.

"You don't have any other living relatives, do you?" Hal prods me.

"No," I say quietly, "I don't."

Of course, I make no mention of my dad. That's because he was an anonymous sperm donor. Mom was all alone and wanted a baby, so here I am. The sad part is that Mom never had any brothers or sisters, and my grandparents passed away long before I was born, so it's just us…all alone. It *was* just us. A stab of pain fills my gut just thinking about this.

The male police officer grabs the tattered papers out of Hal's hand, studying them carefully. "I'm not sure about this. I don't care what paperwork you have. We can't just hand her over to you without Child Protective Services being here."

Officer Riley chimes in. "Yeah, and isn't it a little concerning for Helene to go to Greece? Isn't there a serious crisis or some sort of turmoil going on there right now?"

I don't know much about Greece, but the images I recall from the news on American TV portrayed a dismal vision of a place where the world is slowly suffocating itself with a lot of despairing and depressed people, violent protests and graffiti everywhere.

The police officers continue arguing back and forth with the lawyer. Something is off about Hal Avery. I can't imagine my mother trusting a slime-ball like him. The attorney's lips form a stern line, but before he can say another word, a loud *pop!* smacks into the front window of our house. Glass shatters as tiny particles shoot out, littering my cheek with pain.

"Get down!" I feel the female officer's arm pull me hard to the ground.

Seconds later, rapid gunfire covers the whole front of the house. My hearing is almost gone from the sound, making me dizzy. I can't see who it is.

The weight of the officer's arm across my chest seems unusually heavy. "Hey," I start but stop short when I see why. She's been shot in the head.

I hear myself scream. My mind can't register what I'm seeing. My body shudders as I turn my head and dry heave. "Oh…!"

Just as I think I'm going to pass out, a strange sense of calm comes over me as my focus sharpens. I shimmy out from underneath Officer Riley's arm and try to ignore the shock when I notice the male officer lying next to me in a heap. He's barely breathing. Another shot sails past me as it grazes the top of my ear. "Ack!!" I yell as I throw myself down onto the floor next to the officer. I try to pretend I don't feel fresh blood trickling down my cheek. If I freak out now, it will slow me down.

His eyes are fluttering as he struggles to say something. "The medallion is the key... Trrrruuussst..."– blood spurts out of his mouth as he utters a long, ragged breath – "...noooo one." His eyes roll back as he takes his last breath.

"Wait, noooo!!!" I wail. This can't be happening. All my earlier feelings about Mom being alive are gone. What did he mean about the medallion? None of it makes sense. If these are the people who caused the fire, then they are out for blood. And now, for some reason, they want me too.

As I brace for the sound of more gunfire, I'm shocked by the silence...that is, at least until I hear the ragged voice of Hal Avery talking to someone. But who? The gunman?! At the sound of his shrill chuckle, I can almost see the ugly sneer on his face.

I'm suddenly filled with a horrible sense of foreboding. The officer was right. I can't trust anyone.

Hal is facing the opposite direction from me, scanning the area for something. Me. I need to get out of here...*now!*

I pull myself up. My head throbs, and my heart races as if it's going to fly out of my chest. Every cell in my brain screams to get away. Terror threatens to overcome me, but I push it out of my mind.

I must focus or die.

Hal's shoes crack under his feet as he turns the corner towards me. I'm out of time. I sprint out of the house as fast as my legs will go, onto the gravel of the driveway. Blood pumps fiercely through my veins as panic tries to consume me. I can't look back. I run as fast as I can, running full tilt down our long, winding driveway. As I reach the main road, my ears start to ring, causing me to trip over my own feet.

I land face-down on the gravel.

I rub the side of my face. My cheek feels like it's been scraped. I think I am alone. Relief overtakes me as silence fills the space around me. Maybe Hal didn't see me or wasn't really after me. He is supposed to be a good guy, hired by my mom. Perhaps he took out the gunman.

This respite is short-lived. Boots thud nearby, crunching gravel behind me. No! I squeeze my eyes closed. My body tenses as I wait for an attack.

It never comes. I open my eyes. Standing above me is Hal Avery. But he's not looking at me. He's frowning down at something on his phone. He seems oblivious to me, as if I'm not even here. He doesn't seem anxious to leave, as if all the shooting back at the house never happened.

Hal's face is an impassive mask as he taps an icon on his phone. He takes off his jacket and throws it to the ground. Sweat rolls down his cheek and an enormous bloodstain blooms on his shirt. He's been shot. I scan the dusty road and the greenery around us for the sniper as Hal collapses onto the worn grass next to me. The coast is clear, but I'm not letting my guard down.

Hal's voice is strained but much softer, as if it's a major effort to say anything. "You…you were right about your mom…"

This is totally unexpected.

"Wha…what do you mean?"

He turns his lips up, but they quiver as he struggles for the words. "Your mother…she's alive."

"What? How?" I ask, totally stunned. My head aches. There's no way I would have ever believed this guy before, but now that he's shot and bleeding out, I reconsider my first impression of him. If he's about to die, why would he lie? But something about the sneer on his face makes me hesitate.

"I don't believe you," I say smartly, looking him square in the eyes.

"Pfft," he sputters. Slowly, he reaches into his pocket.

I draw in a breath. Does he have a gun? He removes his hand from his pocket. Whatever he has in his hand, it's too small to be a gun. He holds out his hand, palm up.

I move in closer. My mind spins when I see what it is. There in his hand is some sort of jewelry…a charm. Something about the way the light hits its tiny face makes it appear as if it the piece is glowing. I recognize it immediately.

My mother's necklace. The cypress tree.

Hal couldn't possibly have it unless...no, that's crazy. He must be telling the truth. She's alive!

A mix of euphoria and giddiness fills me. Gingerly, I take the necklace and drape it around my neck. Steady calm fills me when I place my hand over the shiny cypress tree charm just above my heart.

Maybe my mom left the necklace behind as a sign for me because she knew she was in trouble and so that I would know the truth. If so, then why? She must want me to find her, like an SOS. I think of the strange medallion – the sign of that Greek crime network. The gunman who just attacked must be with them.

Hal grunts in pain as he tries to move. The bloodstain on his shirt is growing larger. He doesn't have much time.

He looks at me through pained eyes. "I clocked the sniper, but he will come to any minute now. You have to get out of here."

"Who was he?" I ask, but Hal cuts me off.

"There's no time." His hand trembles. "You have to get away from here now." He nods towards the larger road ahead. "Just down the road, you'll see a black sedan with a driver that is waiting to take you to San Francisco International Airport. Inside, you'll find a suitcase and backpack. There you'll find money and a plane ticket that will take you to Athens." His voice cracks. "Your godfather will be waiting for you at the airport."

"But what about you?"

Hal holds up his phone. The face reads 9-1-1.

"Maybe I should just wait for the police to come?"

"No! You don't understand. These people are everywhere, even among the police. They won't expect you to go to Greece. It's the last place they will think you'll go, so it will be safe for you there."

"But how will I find my mom?"

"Your godfather will know." His voice grows urgent. "Now...*go!*"

Moments later, I find the car where a gruff driver with a stern face waits for me. After what just happened, I feel wary of him. But I have no choice. I have to get out of here. Now.

He nods in silence as he whisks me off to the airport. I see my backpack and suitcase sitting on the seat. Where did this stuff come from? My mother must have packed it and given it to Hal. But why would she take precautions like that?

Just as we're about to pass by the sign that marks the County line, a knot forms in my throat when I see the stands of the football stadium and the red and gold sign that stands on top of the large concrete building that is my school. Will I ever see this place, my friends, Ms. Dilmore, or even Randall Sibley again? I have no idea, but above all else, I am sure of one thing...

I have to find my mom, and it's not safe here anymore.

I'm going to Greece.

3 – AMERICAN GIRL

I'm standing in a long line of people, waiting to board the plane. My hands tremble as I flip through the pages of my passport, which reveals a photo of me from two years ago.

It was a bit strange when Mom went nuts with an urgent need for me to rush out to get a passport. And for no apparent reason. When I asked why, she simply said, "you never know when you'll need it."

But I'm not a baby anymore! I had enough of her usual ambiguous answers. "Why can't you just tell me the truth?! Are we going on a trip somewhere?" I inquired.

She glared at me and gave me that look. The look that means it's best if I don't ask. I was furious! How could she not tell me? But as angry as I was then, right now, I'm glad for this.

There's an annoying rustling noise behind me. As I turn to take a look, a loud sound strikes my ears...*Pop!* Instant anxiety courses through my veins. My heart quickens and body shudders as I completely forget for a minute where I am. Disoriented, I look around, taking in my surroundings. Suddenly, I'm terrified that, at any moment, the gunman will find me...and *kill* me.

"Ma'am...?" A woman's soft voice breaks my thoughts, "may I see your ticket?" As the line of people waiting behind me comes into focus, I see a boy standing there. He's crunching loudly on some chips with his mouth wide open. It's pretty disgusting! As he reaches in for another hand-full, I hear the rustling metallic sound of the bag and instantly realize that I was hallucinating.

No one is trying to kill me! Well, at least not right now.

I'm feeling a little queasy as I hand the airline attendant my ticket and breathe much more easily as I begin the walk down the long, chilled hallway that leads to the plane.

The plane slowly climbs high up into the serenity of white, wispy clouds. Here, I allow myself to fully relax as my body sinks back into the seat. Finally, I feel safe. The low hum of the engines soothes my nerves.

All the events of the past few hours come flooding back to me.

The gunman was real. My mother is alive but missing. The police are dead. The attorney, Hal Avery, is horribly wounded.

A mysterious Greek crime network wants me dead.

They likely have my mom, and now they want me. But why? I'm just some girl. It doesn't add up. And why exactly am I going to Greece, the very place where the people who want to kill me would be?

I'll admit it now. I'm filled with absolutely mind-numbing dread. I have zero control here. How can I travel all the way across the world *all alone*?

But Hal was right. I'm not safe in California. My assassins would never expect me to come to them, and this godfather whom I never knew I had before will know how I can find my mom. As we approach Athens, I look out the window and am stunned by the sight below. Clouds hover and dance gracefully over endless blue skies, a deep, vast indigo blue sea edged in turquoise and thousands of white glittering rooftops staring up at me. The mass of flat, shining roofs extends across the land as far as I can see up to the tree line of the towering majestic mountains that encircle this vast metropolis.

I am in awe.

Something warm and wet is dripping down my chin. I feel the spittle on my lower lip. Yep…I was drooling in my sleep. *Nice*. I look up to see a boy who must have been sitting in the row in front of me this whole trip gawking at me through the seats with a malicious grin on his face. Great, a witness.

I smear the slop off my lip. Who are these people on the plane with me? I look around suspiciously, slowly studying the faces near me. No one looks like a hit man, but how would I know? This bratty kid could be one of their spies.

When I step off the plane, my fears melt away. I'm greeted by bright streaming sunlight. I'm not sure if it's the ten-hour time difference or the out-of-body feeling I have, but a weird sense of euphoria hits me. It's as if I can sense that I'm closer to my mom, and once I find her, everything will be okay.

Heat warms the skin on my neck. I reach up to my chest, feeling almost as if I've been burned. There, the cypress tree necklace simmers, probably warm from the sunlight, but to me, it's as if it has come to life.

As I look around, this is completely not what I expected.

The airport is meticulously clean, and wherever I look, there are happy, smiling people greeting others with hugs and kisses. I am also surprised to see words on the signs at the airport in both Greek and English, and many local people seem to easily speak English so well.

A loud crack sounds over a loudspeaker, jarring me out of the happy place inside my thoughts. *Pop!* I cringe at the sound and cower, my ears ringing slightly as I experience sudden vertigo. The image of the gunman skirts my peripheral vision, filling me with dread. When I blink my eyes, he's gone.

Not again! This has got to stop. I feel like I'm going crazy.

A mass of people speaking different languages congregates around the twirling baggage carousel. A rainbow-hued assortment of duffel bags and suitcases is dumped from the top of a chute, colliding one on top of another, then dropping down onto the revolving conveyer belt. Judging from the avalanche of luggage, the travelers on my flight do not believe in traveling light. Of course, my overstuffed suitcase is the last off the airplane.

A loudspeaker pipes in Greek music. The sounds are subtle and exotic, a juxtaposition of old and new. The beat feels ancient, awakening something inside of me that I can't describe. An electronic ticker over-head displays the temperature, but it's in Celsius. I don't remember the conversion from science class.

As I step up to the small desk in front of the passport officer, I hope he doesn't notice that I'm not breathing. This is terrifying. He stares at my passport, pushes a button, and then turns to ask a question in Greek to some unseen person. I feel sweat pooling under my arms, sure that there is a huge stain there now. This is it! He is going to realize that I'm not supposed to be here, take me to a large jail cell, and throw away the key. Or worse than that, what if he has been hired to kill me!?

He painstakingly studies my photo. Christ, what's taking so long? Just when I feel that I can't stand it anymore, he shrugs and explains in a bored tone that I have an extra stamp on my passport now to show that I have a student visa. "Welcome to Greece." He smiles.

My heart is still pounding, but overwhelming relief floods me as I recall that I am meant to be here. I have a mission...*find Mom*. A touristy picture on the wall of the marble-columned Parthenon catches my eye, and for a moment, I think I see someone familiar there. It's a woman with long, cascading brown hair, eyes dark and defiant, holding hands with a man, smiling. But wait; she looks just like my mom. I blink and look again. It's not Mom. I must be hallucinating.

I am so totally focused on this out-of-body experience that I completely a huge puddle of slick water scattered across the floor. My white tennis shoes must have no tread left because I slip and crash down towards the floor. But I don't fall...I smack into someone, painfully bumping my head in the process. My glasses fly off my face, clattering to the ground. I'm blind without my glasses.

"Ouch!" I yelp, cradling my temple as I bend down on my knees, feeling around on the floor for my glasses. I hope that they are nearby; otherwise, I'm screwed. How can I defend myself against my pursuers when I can't see?

"Sorry!" a voice calls out to me. He sounds like a guy maybe around my age. I'm pretty sure he's not an assassin.

"With so many beautiful things to see in Greece, I'm guessing you need these?" he asks as I feel cool, hard plastic touch the inside of my palm.

My glasses! Thank god. I put them on. Much better. I can see!

As my vision clears, though, I can't believe what I see. This guy has the most stunning eyes. They're like liquid turquoise, the color of the sea.

"Uh, yeah," I stammer, suddenly shy. "Thanks."

His short, tousled dark hair and slightly unshaven olive skin present a striking contrast to those mesmerizing eyes. I'm guessing that he's about my age, but he towers over me, tall and wiry. He exudes a rare confidence for a boy in high school. Maybe he's in college. The way he runs his hand through his hair and the far away gleam in his eyes is so James Dean. His navy-blue polo shirt, pressed khaki pants, and the refined way he moves give me the impression that he must come from serious money. While he seems quite genuine, I sense something raw and untamed in this boy underneath his preppy, well-poised façade – something deep…and complicated.

"You're from America?" he asks in a smooth accent. I decide then and there that I love this Greek-English accent. It melts me.

Nothing comes out of my mouth, so I just nod like an idiot. He nods back and his warm smile captivates me. The way his gaze holds mine so completely exudes confidence. Get a hold of yourself, Helene! I would never talk to a guy like him back home, not in a million years. I'll bet all the girls fawn over him like lost puppies. Not me. Besides, I have more serious issues to deal with than to fool around with guys.

"No," I reply, "California." I'm trying to be funny.

"Oh, so California must have defected from America, then?" he smirks. So he's witty, too. There is an air of mischievous playfulness about him and an endearing crease that forms on his right cheek when he smiles, which I find absolutely enchanting. It temporarily draws me into his spell.

Suddenly, I have trouble looking directly at him. How annoying. Seriously, I can't believe that I'm behaving like this. It's as if I'm shy. God, no! This never happens! Not to me!

When I finally muster the courage to meet his eyes again, I'm startled to find him studying me. "Your eyes," he says, "they're so unusual. What is that color? Purple?"

"*Violet*," I correct him.

"Oh, I've never seen anything like them before." he says quietly, "so beautiful…"

I'm so lost in this moment that I just now notice that my backpack has fallen off and ripped. My clothes and books are splayed out all over the floor in a big mess. Ever seems to instantly know that he must have said the wrong thing because he quickly leans down, trying to help me, but I don't want him seeing my stuff – especially not my underwear! – so I grab the backpack away from him, maybe with a little too much force.

"I'm fine," I say in a clipped tone again, now fully composed. "I can take it from here, thanks."

He looks affronted, as if I've upset him, but he's not easily dissuaded, so he continues to try to help me. His persistence, despite the abrupt change in my demeanor, intrigues me.

Then something strange happens. Just as he reaches over to give me one of my books, his hand accidentally brushes mine. The hair on the back of my neck instantly prickles as a warm, tingling heat runs up my arm.

It's like…raw, pulsing electricity.

I jerk my hand swiftly back at the sensation. My eyes meet his startled gaze. He felt it too. Something deep passes between us as I stare into his eyes as if I can see deep inside his mind. There's a rare familiarity there, as if I've known this guy all my life.

The moment ends as I snap out of the fairy tale. This is so ridiculous. I'm crushing on this guy, and it makes no sense. I'm not "that girl" who fawns over guys.

I take a deep breath. *Focus, Helene.*

A woman calls out to him in a crisp accent, like she's from England or Australia. "Ever? There you are!"

The woman's regal and well coifed, her shiny blond hair brushing the tops of her shoulders. Is this his mom? "Come on. Time to go."

His face brightens at the sight of her. If this is his mom, it's clear that he loves his mother dearly. Seeing this bond between them makes me yearn for my own mom…*Mom!* I try to push the thought from my mind, afraid I might burst into tears here and now, which would be bad. It can't happen. Not in front of him.

He turns towards her, explaining, "Okay, Mom…I'm coming! I was just helping this…girl after she dropped her stuff." He points down to the scattered mess on the floor. "She's from *America*." He winks at me. Very smooth.

I roll my eyes, continuing the joke. "*California!*"

He grins with a knowing look in his eyes. "California. Yeah. Ha-ha."

If his mom catches any of our playful banter, she's not giving it away. "Oh!" She smiles briefly at me. "Years ago, way before your time, I came here from Australia, but we have relatives in California. Welcome to Greece! You're going to love it."

She looks around, concerned. "But where are your parents?"

I frown. What do I say? The officer's last words were "*Trust no one.*" While she seems incredibly nice and I'm sure she's not here to kill me, I can't tell her the truth. I need to find my godfather. "Uh, not here. I'm alone." Suddenly, I just want to leave, but she seems to want to talk more.

"Okay, but is someone meeting you here? Do you know where you're going?" she asks, eyes kind and nurturing. She seems genuinely concerned for me.

"Yes….I mean, no. Well, actually, my godfather is supposed to meet me here, but I haven't seen him yet." I look around. Where the heck is he, anyway?

Her serious brown eyes study my face. "Do you need help? I'd be happy to ask my driver to take you where you need to go."

I'm sure that he will be here soon. Of course, he will. He *has* to be. "Uh, no, that's okay."

She turns back to her son. Earlier, I thought I heard her say that his name was Ever, but I've never heard that name before, and it doesn't sound Greek. Not that I would know what typical Greek names are. Maybe I heard it wrong. Or maybe it's an Australian name. His eyes sparkle as he hands me one last book.

The woman looks suddenly worried as she notices the time on her watch. She says, "Time for us to go. *Ya sou*…Good luck!" She loops her arm in her son's and directs him away.

As they start to walk off, he suddenly turns around and waves good-bye before calling out, "Nice to meet you, *American* girl!"

I'm still trembling from the shock of the electricity that I felt with him. Then suddenly, the truth hits me. Athens is a big city. There's no way I'll see him again. A deep, aching loneliness sweeps through me as the image of him and his mother together fills me with longing.

Mom, why did you leave me all alone?

4 – THE DRIVER

I'm sad for a moment, but then I realize that I need to focus on a more pressing matter. I need to find my godfather.

I make my way over to the place where the drivers stand with their placards announcing whom they will be transporting today. I am greeted by a few cheerful souls: "*Kalispera*. Welcome to Athens." Their smooth accents and kindness are soothing, but when I don't see my name on any of the placards, I start to get anxious.

I panic. I should have let Ever's mother help me! What was I thinking? I start to cry.

One of the drivers notices and turns to me. "What's wrong? Are you okay?" he asks in English. "Don't worry! It will be fine. Listen, the person whom I was supposed to pick up is not coming after all. I can take you where you need to go." He has a kind and weathered face, as if he has spent a lot of time in the sun with laugh lines etched around his mouth and eyes. This man has smiled a lot in his life. I instantly like him.

I check the zippered pockets of the backpack for some money. Surely, Hal left me some. Of course, he would have. No luck. The pockets are empty. My tears fall even harder as I choke out the words, "But I have no cash."

"I take credit cards," he says persistently.

I shake my head. I can't even bring myself to talk for fear of bursting into tears again. I don't understand how Hal or my mother would expect me to go to Greece without any money.

The driver smiles with understanding, as if he is used to dealing with people like me. "I am sure there is money where you are going, right? You can pay me when we get there."

I am suddenly suspicious, remembering the stories that my mom used to tell me about girls who traveled alone in Europe and were kidnapped by a cab driver, then sold into slavery. Or maybe this driver is an assassin hired by that Greek 'mafia' network that has my mother!! No way…oh my God. It can't be true. How can I stay here if I live in constant fear of them?

My distrust morphs into anger. *Where the hell is my godfather?!* He is supposed to be here in person to meet me. Some guardian he is turning out to be. I can't believe my mother could leave me in his care.

Unfortunately, I have no choice. If my godfather isn't here – and clearly he is not – then taking a ride with this driver is my only option. It's either that or a take a taxi. Somehow, that seems worse. We walk over to his car and I'm pleasantly surprised to see a brand-new shiny black Mercedes. Okay, so this is not some low-end driver…probably *not* a kidnapper. Much better than a taxi.

A placard announces his name is Mr. Dimitris Paxinos, but when I call him Dimitris, he corrects me. "You don't say the *s* on the end. Just call me Dimitri. When you write it, you add the *s* on the end." Then he smiles up at me in the rearview mirror. "So where are we going?" He speaks with the same smooth, sweet Greek-English accent that I hear all around me now. I spread out in the back of the Mercedes, enjoying every minute of this luxurious experience.

I can't believe this. I don't even have my godfather's address. Even worse, I can't even remember his last name. The tears start to fall again. Dimitris points to the pocket in my backpack. "Maybe you should check the pocket in your bag." He hands me a tissue.

I take it and open the bulging pocket in the side of my bag. The first thing that pops out is a huge wad of euros, and right behind that is a slip of paper with the address and cell phone number for Mr. Janus Giannopoulos. Relief fills me swiftly. Looks like my buddy Hal came through for me after all with a small stash of cash.

Thank God. A huge smile consumes my face as I feel like reaching over the front seat to give my driver, Dimitris, a hug. I read the address out loud. "Salaminos 57 and Paramithias 15, Metaxourgeio."

Dimitris frowns, surprising me. "Metaxourgeio? You're sure?" He shakes his head as if he's uncertain about this. "How about I take you to the Plaka or near the Acropolis? There are nice hotels there."

"But this is the only address I have for my godfather," I whisper.

"Metaxourgeio is…well…" – he sighs – "…not the greatest in Athens. You're sure you want to go there?" he asks in warning. I'm not sure if it's the sweet sound of his accent, but I feel as if he sincerely cares about what happens to me.

Am I sure that I want to go there? No. I reach into my backpack and find my cell phone. Maybe I can call Janus. I try to turn on the phone, but there's no service.

I guess I have no choice. I'm going to one of Athens's worst neighborhoods…lovely. "Yes, let's go." I nod, trying to look more confident than I feel.

"Okay, then." Dimitris plugs the address into his GPS and drives me through Athens, telling me about his life. When he's not driving, he's a teacher…a high school teacher, in fact. I feel numb and sad, so I don't say much.

He tells me all about the school where he works and what the school day is like in Greece. He seems excited that I'm willing to listen to him. "I like to talk, but hardly anyone whom I drive likes to talk to me," he says. "You know, mostly wealthy tourists." Well, they're missing out. I feel like we are fast friends in just this short journey. He is my first friend in Greece.

We through the streets of Athens, passing the gorgeous architecture and ancient Greek ruins that I have seen so many times before in my textbooks, and perhaps in my dreams. He points out the Parthenon, sitting high and majestic with its grand pillars of white marble up on a hilltop off in the distance, and other sights like the Temple of Olympian Zeus, the Arch of Hadrian, and the Greek National Library.

My eyes must light up for a moment because Dimitris says, "You like mythology; I can tell."

I nod, but then the spark leaves me as this experience reminds me of Mom and her bedtime stories. She always said we'd come here…together.

Dimitris tells me how hard it is for the people of Greece to live with the financial crisis that started here eight years ago. "Most people that I know work two or three jobs just to survive, and often, with the taxes so high, even that is not enough." His expression is faraway and wistful. "But even in the face of what seems an impossible situation, I know that the Greek people will persevere. Giving up is not in our genes."

Twenty minutes later, we pull up in front of a rundown two-story building with peeling paint and neoclassical Greek architecture consisting of tall, rectangular windows. Graffiti is scribbled across the front. Once upon a time, this must have been a very nice place to be. As my friend Dimitris opens the Mercedes door for me, he seems uneasy about leaving me.

I hand him forty euros, which he hands right back to me. "Keep your money." But then he raises an eyebrow in concern. "You're sure you want me to leave you *here*?"

His eyes roam across the street to a shadowed alleyway, to where it looks like a prostitute is engaged in some sort of lewd act. This has got to be a mistake, but this is the address on the slip of paper. There's no mistake. He says, "It's usually fairly safe around here, but..." He raises his eyebrows.

After helping me haul my large suitcase up to the front door, he patiently waits for me while I ring the bell, which doesn't seem to work. I nudge the door. Slowly it cracks open, not even locked. The air is filled with a heavy stench of what must be incense mixed with...is that cat urine?! Great. I'm allergic to cats.

Dimitris holds out his hand to shake mine, but I'm so thankful for his incredible compassion that I embrace him in a desperate hug. He smiles, eyes crinkling around the edges. I can't help but feel sad that I will never see him again, my first friend in Greece. Tears threaten my eyes again, but then I remember why I'm here. Mom. She's got to be here somewhere, or at least answers are here. My resolve stiffens, and I remember that I am strong. I can do this.

As I pull back from the hug, these warm feelings disappear. Dimitris has a tattoo on the inside of his wrist – a double helix symbol with snakes wrapped around a flame. I inhale sharply. It's the same

38

symbol that was on the face of the medallion that the police found at the scene of Mom's explosion. The dying police officer's words come back to me, "the medallion is the key…"

The sign of the Greek 'mafia' network!

No! But how? He must have a gun. As my heart starts to race out of control, it dawns on me that he hasn't yet tried to kill me or made any move to do so. He must not know who I am.

I must be staring at it for a moment too long because Dimitris quickly covers his arm. I knew it! He works for them. Since I feel confident that he doesn't know who I am, I do something stupid. Curiosity takes over as I completely ignore my survival instincts and ask, "What can you tell me about the Mafia?"

His eyes grow wide. I want to kick myself. What was I thinking? I brace myself for the moment when he will pull his gun out and point it at me.

But it doesn't happen. He quickly recovers as he flashes me a wry grin, chuckling softly. "No. We don't have the Mafia here. That's in Italy."

Uh-huh, but isn't organized crime the definition of the Mafia? It can't just be in Italy. I can hear from the way he says it that he's not entirely telling me the truth. I can't leave it be.

"But that symbol…on your arm…your tattoo?" I stammer.

He sighs, thinking for a moment, but then his eyes lock on mine in all seriousness. "Yes. Many of us who work in tourism here in Greece wear this symbol. No worries."

There must be some reason he isn't telling me the truth. Maybe he's afraid for his life? He can't tell me. Yes, that must be it. Navigating this new life here in Greece is not going to be easy. It's like I'm trudging through the mud, but instead it's quicksand. At any moment, I can fall through, and who knows what is underneath? I can't wait to find my mom. Everything will be better when I find her.

He starts to turn to leave me but then stops and pulls out a business card, which describes his tutoring services.

"This is my phone number. If you need help, you call me."

Since I know he works for the people who want me dead, I don't know what to think. Is this some sort of trick? When I consider that he doesn't know who I am and that he brought me to my godfather's house refusing my money, I'm speechless at this gesture. As he lays the card in my hand, I want to caress it, to keep it safe as my only lifeline to normalcy in this scary new adventure.

"But why? Why would you be so kind to me?" I ask. "Do you give your card out to all of your passengers?"

He shrugs. "No, not at all. You...you remind me of my sister," he says in a low voice as he turns back to his car. In a second, he's gone.

5 – GODFATHER

I watch the Mercedes disappear around the corner. I look down at my trembling hand, still holding Dimitris's card. I'm still in shock that within my first two hours in Greece, I have already met a member of the Greek 'mafia' group that wants to take me out. Seriously! This is bad news. If it's this easy to cross their path here, then I'd better be careful. They must be everywhere.

What is the deal with my godfather? How could he not meet me at the airport with all that I've been through? And why is he not here waiting for me now? My face reddens in anger as my heart rate quickens. I'm already mad at him and I haven't even met him yet. Not a good sign.

Since I know my mother is alive, it should be an easy matter for my godfather to help me find her…*if* I can find him. I study the shuttered windows on the second floor of the old, crumbling building in front of me. She might even be here now. I'll bet she is.

I push the door fully open. There's no sign of anyone at all.

A strange collection of odd-sized colored jars filled with a variety of what look like herbs and dried plants fills a shelf. There is a massage table in the middle of the room next to an oversized Buddha fountain. The walls are filled with African, Chinese, and Indian art depicting different scenes of healing. It's serene. Up on a counter, there are rocks, crystals, and stones on display. I run my finger across a ledge, and ugh, it's black with dust. This place hasn't been cleaned in quite a while, if ever. My godfather must be some sort of healer, herbalist, or massage therapist. I call out his name. "Janus?" No answer.

What if something bad has happened to him? I frown as another even more disturbing theory hits me. What if my Greek assassins got to him?

As I make my way up the stairs, I hear a strange wheezing sound. The room looks like the teeny-tiny living and kitchen area of an apartment. Junk is stacked everywhere. If I thought it was dirty downstairs, this place is far worse. What a dump! The wheezing noise continues but reminds me of snoring. My eyes trace the sound to what appears to be a sleeping bag that is zipped all the way up on the floor in the middle of the room. From the outside, I can see the faint outline of a human shape, a clear indicator that someone is sleeping inside.

A cat is curled up on top, deep in slumber. My nose wrinkles in anticipation as I envision my throat closing from my cat allergy, but nothing happens. I find this odd but also an incredible relief.

Then, very carefully, I nudge the shape in the sleeping bag with my toe. The person inside begins to stir. I hear coughing, sputtering, and then cursing in what must be Greek as the sleeping bag starts to unzip. Disheveled long gray hair and a lopsided head scarf become visible as a very annoyed sixty-something man pops his head and upper body out of the sleeping bag. He glares at me, angrily rambling on in Greek, so I have no idea what he is saying. God, I hope he can understand English.

"I'm looking for Janus Giann…uh…oh, sorry! I'm not sure how to say it," I stammer, scared out of my mind. "Do you…speak English?"

He looks slightly annoyed as he straightens himself out, sitting fully upright, now almost businesslike. "Giannopoulos," he says. He sounds like he could be from New York City. His eyes narrow as he studies me with a sneer, as if I'm some sort of repulsive vermin.

His hand whips out wicked fast to the counter next to him. He's aiming a small pistol at me.

No! Not again! I freeze like a deer in the headlights as survival mode kicks into gear. Instantly, I throw my hands up in the air.

"Who are you, and how did you get into my house?" His anxiety is obvious as his voice escalates a full octave in pitch. The gun shakes in his outstretched hand.

My mouth flies open. This is shocking. How could he *not* know who I am? There must be some mistake. I stammer, "I...umm...I'm..."

"Just spit it out. I don't have all day!"

I can't think straight with the gun pointed at me. It's just too much with the sound of rapid gunfire still fresh in my ears. "Would you mind putting that away?" I ask.

"Yes, I mind," he says in a clipped, even tone, "and no, I won't."

Wow, what an endearing guy...*not!* How can he be so heartless when I've lost so much and come so far to see him? I instantly want to tell him to go to hell, but I doubt it would help, so I have no choice but to maintain my cool and try to be nice.

"I'm...Helene Crawford?" I mumble. The blank look on his face is shocking, as he clearly has no idea who I am. My patience runs out. I feel as if I'm slowly losing my mind. "You're my godfather!" I raise my voice in a fury. "My *guardian*?!"

I watch as his indifference shifts to recognition. The pistol drops out of his hand onto the floor with a thud. Anxiety overtakes his expression. His eyes widen as he asks, "Helene? No!" He twists his hands in several directions, fidgeting nervously. "You can't be here. This is not happening!"

I have no idea what to say.

He stands to his full height, which must be at least six feet. He is skinny, as if he never eats, with pale, almost translucent skin. I thought Greek men were supposed to be tan. Nope, not Janus. His eyes are a bold shade of brown and fiercely intelligent, like he is scrutinizing everything about me and not happy with what he sees. As he ties his long hair into a ponytail, his multicolored headscarf falls off, revealing a shiny bald patch, which looks strange considering that the rest of his hair is almost down to his waist.

He shakes his head in irritation. "How did you get here?"

"I...well—" I start to say, but he rudely cuts me off.

"Well, what?!" His tone grows in urgency, but I've had it with him and his obnoxious condescension. What a jerk! He can't treat me like this.

"If you would let me talk, I would tell you!" I yell right in his face.

He looks at me as if just now seeing me for the first time. "Fine."

43

"Good," I say, my arms crossed firmly. More silence.

But as I start to think through it, I can hardly get the words out. I'm choked by sadness. "The police showed up to tell me that my mom died in a fire, most likely arson…but then there was shooting. Whomever it was took out both police officers." My voice escalates in fear. "And then they tried to kill me!"

"No, no, no." Janus starts to pace. "No!"

I continue, "Thank God my mom's attorney showed up. He told me that my mom is still alive and sent me here to you, saying that I would be safe in Greece, that you would know where to find her."

"He said that she's still alive?" he asks as worry creases his forehead.

"Yes," I say blankly. "She is, right?"

"How the hell would I know?"

"But he said you would know!" I stomp my foot. "You have to know!"

I sense a growing uneasiness in him as he exclaims, "But I don't."

"But this doesn't make any sense," I say, my own anxiety mounting. "As I said before, this attorney — "

"Wait…stop!" He looks panicked, his voice quivering as he inquires, "This attorney, what did he look like? Did you notice anything strange about him?"

I try to remember. It's all so hazy now. With all the overwhelming craziness that's happened to me in the past twenty-four hours, I can barely recall anything. My mind feels numb and scattered. Really, I just wish Janus would stop interrupting me so I can concentrate.

"Everything was strange about Harold Avery. Where do I start? Repulsive breath, horrible yellowing teeth," I say, staring up at the ceiling.

"No, no, no. Not his appearance. Did you see him *do* anything strange?" Janus clarifies. He waves his hands in a sweeping motion as he speaks, revealing an overly dramatic display of some hidden angst.

"Well…" I think for a moment, but then I remember. "Actually, yes. When he first told me that my mom was still alive, I didn't believe him. But then he gave me this." I pause as I point to the shimmering charm around my neck.

"He *what*?" I almost jump out of my skin.

"Stop yelling at me already!" I can't handle this anymore.

He staggers backwards, almost knocking into a table behind him. After a moment, he grins. "You are so much like your mother. Diana was just like this with me. So darned feisty. Always raising my pulse." He visibly relaxes, his face now a mask of calm. This rapid transition from craziness to calm is unsettling to me.

"This charm…the cypress tree. My mother always wore it. She would never take it off, unless…"– my voice cracks – "unless she knew she was in trouble and wanted to send me a message."

"Or in the case that she actually is dead."

This can't be true, though. If she's truly gone, I can't deal. I want to curl up in a little ball and never wake up.

"Come on now," Janus sighs. "I didn't mean it! It's entirely possible that she's still alive!"

I shrug, completely silent. At least this slows my tears. Maybe he has some compassion in that Grinch-like heart.

"Oh gods!" he interrupts again, now pacing back and forth as he stares up at the ceiling, eyes widening as he flips open his phone and dials. "I've got to find out what happened!"

No answer. He slams the phone shut with a snap.

Janus continues to pace. "What to do?" He turns towards the window, looking outside to the street below as if he's in his own world. "This can't be happening! I have no idea how to care for a…" – he turns to sneer at me – "a kid…especially a teenage girl! Why does all the crap always fall in my lap?!"

I'm not a kid! If I'm such a burden, then why am I here? This makes no sense!

He flips around and rushes over to a drawer, from which he pulls out a bunch of mismatched papers. His muttering escalates to a frantic rant. "What about school? Where will she sleep? What will I feed her?"

At last, he sees something that shuts him up. The quiet in the room seems almost eerie as he studies the paper in his shaking hand after the chaos I've just witnessed. I just stand there, afraid to set him off again.

The silence is broken. "Okay…plan B," he says in a calm, composed voice again with that perfect American accent, as if he's known all along what to do. "Don't worry; I'm going to find out exactly what happened, and we'll figure out where Diana is."

My tears start to dry as he walks over to the wall, where a picture hangs. It's a hand-drawn image of what looks like a goddess with an oversized mountain lion. Something about the woman and the mountain lion looks oddly familiar, but I don't have a chance to see what before he yanks the painting away from the wall, revealing a safe.

"But in the meantime, you will live here with me."

Then he does something that stuns me. He's standing at least two arm lengths from the safe when he points his finger at it…and *pop!* The safe opens. But how did he do that? Was that *magic*?

As if reading my mind, he explains, "Magnetic pulse technology…but don't try it yourself. Every person has his own magnetic signature, and this lock responds to only mine."

As I peer over his shoulder into the inner recesses of the safe, I am shocked at what I see…stacks and stacks of euros, all in five-hundred denomination notes. Wow.

"This is just great!" Janus's voice is thick with sarcasm as he pulls out and shuffles through several stacks of notes. "We may have a real issue cashing these out for lower bills with the banks in disarray and the capital controls." He grumbles, "Hopefully, the school will take notes this big."

"What school?" I ask, now curious.

"Your school. You're in high school, right? We call it *Lykeio*. Diana will want you to go to the best school in Athens, where there are other English-speaking kids, of course. This would be the Athens International Academy. Most people just call it the Academy. This is where most of the elite Greek kids go, as their parents want them to learn stronger English," he says in an even voice. "I'll have to call them, but I'm sure they can make room for you."

It's a little surprising that a school as amazing as he is describing would just let me start midyear without a rigorous application process, but I keep this comment to myself.

Janus rolls his eyes. His hands shake as if he drinks too much coffee. He's starting to get pretty amped up as the conversation proceeds. "Look, you've been through a lot, but I'm not your babysitter. There are a few rules that you need to get straight if you want to live here. You sleep over there." He points animatedly over to a narrow couch in the corner next to the window. "You make your own food, wash your own dishes and clothes, and stay out of my way. My room is in there." He swings his hand in a sweeping, exaggerated gesture towards the only closed door in the place. "You are not allowed in there for *any* reason."

He pauses to catch his breath. "My shop is downstairs. You do not touch *anything* down there. If I find one thing out of place, you will find yourself working for me as slave labor until you turn twenty-one. Understand?"

I nod.

"I don't help with homework and couldn't care less about your hormone-induced urges or traumas. Don't bother me with that bullshit. Anything female-related goes in the trash. Do not clog my toilet. I don't give a flying fuck when you get home at night," he declares. I wince. "And yes, I swear like a shit-sucking sailor. I don't care. Live it up. You're only young once." He seems quite satisfied with his obnoxious speech.

He scurries over to a nearby closet and starts tossing sheets, linens, and pillows out behind him in a dramatic cascade. The safe is still open, so I sidle over to peek inside while he's distracted. Mostly, it is filled with notes, but there is something else in there. It looks like an antique version of a smart tablet. As I draw in nearer, it starts to light up as if coming alive. Suddenly, Janus is right behind me. He whips his arm out and quickly slams the safe closed.

"What was that?" I ask, eyebrow lifted.

"Nothing."

What a bad liar. What was that thing? The strangeness in his tone intrigues me.

Suddenly, a faint tremor shakes the apartment. Janus's eyes grow wide as he reaches over to catch an art piece that is falling off a shelf. As he replaces it calmly, he says simply, "Earthquake."

I raise an eyebrow at him. "Greece has earthquakes?"

"Oh yes," he says. "We are on a fault line like the San Andreas in California. You should be used to that."

Janus begins to admonish me for wearing nose and belly button rings. "Do you have any idea how much bacteria are in your nose and belly button? Those are the most concentrated places on your whole body and the worst possible places to pierce a hole in your skin. You are probably a walking infection. I'll bet you have a tattoo too."

I pull the neckline of my shirt down a bit to reveal the small tattoo of an eye.

"But, of course, you do. At least you have only one." His voice falls down an octave, his angry ranting finally fizzling out. "Although interesting choice with that eye."

"My mom picked it out for me. She said that with the symbol of the eye, she would always be able to see that I was safe." He raises his eyebrows.

Janus pulls out an old laptop and a cell phone and hands them to me. He points to the cell phone. "Use this only in case of an emergency. I do not want to see any mushy texts from any boyfriends. I will be checking."

I smirk. "Don't worry about that. I don't know anyone here, so no boyfriend."

Janus looks skeptical. "Not yet."

Then he picks up my suitcase and empties the contents onto the floor. A deep frown consumes his features as if he has just discovered something extremely offensive, such as illicit drugs. Now I see what fascinates him so much, there in his clutches. He's found my birth control pills.

"Absolutely no drugs are allowed here!" he yells.

"Janus, you have no idea what you're talking about."

He shakes his head in earnest and grabs his reading glasses, perching them on his nose. He scrunches up his face to read the label. "Birth control?"

Good. Now he's got to understand how silly he is and apologize to me, but my hopes of that are dashed when I see his face transform, gearing up for full lecture mode. Uh-oh, here we go.

"How could Diana buy into this load of crap? Birth control pills are made with synthetic hormones that are incompatible with the natural hormones in the human body. Very unhealthy!" The expression on his face shifts back to high anxiety as he continues his diatribe. "Besides, there's no reason for you to use birth control anyway. No boys are allowed in this house!"

And just like that, Janus marches my last package of birth control pills over to the bathroom, pops all the pills out of the pack, and then pours all of them into the toilet, flushing them down with a whoosh.

I scream, but I'm too late. The only thing in the toilet is the swishing water left to settle after the flush. How will I find more of these pills here in Greece? They clear up my skin and make me feel less irritable around that time of the month. I *need* my pills!

That's it! I can't take it anymore, so I burst into tears.

Janus grabs my shoulders and forces me to meet his eyes. "You need to cut the crap and stop your crying right now," he scolds me. "Nothing pisses me off more than a crybaby." Anger now boils in his eyes. "Stop. It. Now."

His total lack of empathy stuns me speechless. I wipe my eyes and glare at him.

An alarm alerts Janus, causing him to look down at his phone. "Shit. Shit. Shit."

He rushes around the room, grabbing papers off the kitchen counter. How he would know the difference between these papers and the multitude of other stacks of papers all over the place is a mystery to me. "I've got a client waiting downstairs. Gotta go. Be back in an hour." He runs down the stairs, grabbing the scarf to cover his shiny bald patch on his way out.

I pick up the thin blankets and a moldy-smelling pillow off the floor, and then sit on the ragged couch, surveying my new home. Is this what my life has come to? I'd rather live on the street than spend another second with this hateful man.

Enough is enough. I need to get out of here...*now*.

6 – BASTET

As thoughts turn round and round in my mind, a spiral staircase catches my eye outside the dirt-stained window.

I creak open the old dusty window. The staircase runs up and down the two stories of the building. As I peer upward, the sunlight blocks my view, but then I notice that the stairs seem to lead all the way up to the top, presumably to the roof.

Curiosity, coupled with my intense need to get the hell out of here, propels me forward, up and out of the window and onto the narrow spiraling stairs. As I make my way up to the top, I can't believe what I see in front of me.

The entire roof of Janus's building is covered with lush plants and trees surrounding a small, circular, wooden sundeck. Two charming chaise lounges and a sweet little table with a turquoise and white striped umbrella make me think that this little hideaway was planned well outside of Janus's influence. This looks like something my mom would do, which makes me wonder how often she visited here in the past. There's even a wicker basket filled with plush blankets. The only thing out of place is a book left out on the table titled, *The Art of Tantric Sex*. I pick it up and open it to where it's bookmarked, but I'm a little surprised when I see what's inside. *Wow*. I can feel my cheeks flush as I slam the book shut and throw it down with a thud. Janus is full of surprises.

The plants are tagged and labeled: rosemary, thyme, garlic. The smell of fresh herbs makes my mouth water and my stomach grumbles in agreement. The city is majestic from up here. The hills in the distance are covered with tiny gray and white square buildings, which seem to shimmer and twinkle in the slowly setting sun. The dimming sky creates a magnificent canvas filled with hues of magenta, violet, and amber, and I can even see the deep blue sheen of the Aegean Sea off in the distance. Church bells chime in unison all over the city. It must be the top of the hour. The sound is amazing and adds to the charm of this glorious place.

This is a special place…my new refuge…my *escape*.

I curl up on one of the chaise lounges. What do I do now? My mind spins into overdrive, so much so that the next thing I know, my eyes grow heavy…

When I open my eyes, hundreds of stars start to glitter in the darkening sky. My mind jolts back to work as I try to consider what options I might have. I consider trying to break into the safe so I can steal some money and run away…back to the United States. Almost eighteen, I'm practically an adult. But how would I survive? I could get a job, but how to avoid my pursuers? I'm guessing they won't stop until they find me. And what do they even want with me, anyway?

And what about Mom? I need to find her. I can't leave Janus now because before he turned into a complete jerk, he offered to help find out where she is. Why would he lie?

Trust no one.

I cover my ears to block the sound of the officer's voice, but he's not here. It's all in my head.

Janus can't be lying. I must believe him. The only other option is to go insane. Slowly, I make my way back down into the apartment.

"Uh, Janus?" I say, my voice soft and sugary sweet. My feet clank on the metal spiral stairway as I come in from outside to our teeny-tiny apartment. The old rusty hinges of the worn-down door creak and groan even though there is no breeze, which startles me.

An intoxicating aroma saturates the room. Rosemary, lemons, simmering meat…*yum*. My stomach grumbles in agony. All I've eaten since leaving California is a few bites of gross airplane salad.

"Huh?" Janus looks up, startled. His headscarf has fallen sideways and shifted so that half of the shiny part of his bald head is exposed. Tufts of his long, stringy gray-black hair stick out in odd directions. He's hunkered down over a plate of the delectable food that accosts my senses, holding a skewer of seasoned chicken. He flashes me a smug grin as he slowly licks the savory grease from his fingers one at a time. How fair is it for him to cook and not offer me any?

"Were you going to say something, or was there some other reason you needed to interrupt my dinner?" He smacks his lips in obvious delight as he takes another bite of chicken, which makes my mouth water with desire. This is torture.

Now that I recall his earlier rant that I'm on my own for food, it dawns on me that I have no idea how to cook anything outside of packaged microwavable food, and there's none of that here.

"Uh, yeah…I…" I stammer, stomach grumbling again. I grab my midsection to quiet the noise, wishing that my body would cooperate with my plans.

He cuts me off before I can say anything. "Would you just spit it out?" He scowls.

"Stop interrupting me!" I exclaim in frustration, but it can't be helped. He's making me crazy…again! I take a deep breath, and as I feel the calm overtake me, I start again. "Can I ask you something?"

"You already are."

"I had never heard of you before yesterday, so how can you be my godfather?" There, I said it. I asked the world's most awkward question.

He shrugs. "It's probably pretty obvious that I'm not really your godfather. Isn't that a Christian thing? I'm not a Christian, and neither was Diana. It was a convenient way, though, for you to have a 'relative' so you don't get lost in the shithole quagmire that is the US foster care system. Diana was at least smart about that."

"You sure swear a lot," I whisper, not sure that he can hear me.

"What?" he says dryly. "Oh, *I'm sorry*, but you would too if you had my life, believe me!"

"It doesn't seem that bad," I say, twisting the frizzed-out ends of my hair.

"You don't know me that well yet." Janus pulls out a tall bottle with a clear liquid inside and pours it into two shot glasses. He picks up a glass and pours it down his throat in one swift movement, shuddering and twitching as the drink consumes his body. He shoves the other shot glass full of clear liquor towards me. "Drink it."

I must be frowning because it makes him grin. "This is mastiha...a Greek aperitif derived from the mastic tree. We drink this or tsipouro to cleanse the palette before meals. You've probably heard of ouzo?"

I shake my head. Greek booze wasn't a subject that was covered in my mythology class at school.

"Okay, whatever." He shrugs. "Take it and drink it down fast. You'll feel *good*."

This stuff looks scary, but what the heck? When in Greece... I down it. Oh my! I witness my own body shuddering just as Janus's did earlier. Suddenly, the world seems not only good but...funny. *Really* funny. I laugh out loud.

The food on the stove crackles and simmers, making the succulent aroma even stronger. I don't think that I can stand it much longer as my stomach groans. Janus smirks at me. "You hungry?"

"Yes!"

His eyes sparkle, but his tone remains dry. "I suppose this one time I can relax the 'you make your own food' rule."

"Is this some kind of Greek cuisine?" I ask as I walk over to crackling chicken skewers sitting on a hot plate on the stove.

"Souvlaki," he informs me. Janus stands next to me at the stove, explaining how to prepare the meal, including the use of herbs from his rooftop garden. He seems to come to life. Note to self: Janus enjoys teaching.

When we sit down at the table, I pour him another shot of mastiha and pretend to pour one for me. "How did you know my mother, then?" I ask innocently.

He shrugs, leaning back in his chair as he licks the sauce off his fingers. "We met through common friends. Let's just say that we both have an avid interest in...Greek mythology." Janus's speech is starting to slur. "She was my client for years, back when she lived here."

"She *lived* here?" I think of the roof deck and her obvious influence there. I knew it!

"Well, yes, in this very building. My bedroom now was her room, and I slept in one of the rooms downstairs in what is now my shop. Those were the days." His eyes light up and dance in sync with the flame of the candle that flickers on the table in front of us.

Suddenly it becomes overwhelmingly apparent to me that there must be a story between my mother and Janus. "So, you and my mom were *romantic*, then? Were you…in love with her?"

Janus chokes on his food, laughing out loud. "Oh, *God* no. I'm not her type. Besides, your mother wasn't interested in men. Of course, you must have known that."

Now I'm confused. My mom wasn't a lesbian. She went out with men throughout my entire childhood. Though she did spend a lot of time with her best friend. Didn't my mother always say that anything is possible? Either way, it doesn't matter to me—but now I wonder why she felt she couldn't tell me.

Janus breaks the silence. "But then again, she wasn't really interested in women either."

What is *that* supposed to mean? So, my mother wasn't interested in *anyone*? It makes no sense. He must be getting drunk.

"Janus?"

"Hmmm?" He seems off in space, somewhere else.

"What if I told you that there's another reason that I know my mom is still alive?"

His eyes shoot open, and he sits straight up. "What?"

I decide to play it a little bit safe. "My mother and I have always had a special bond, like I can feel her in my heart. And, well, I still feel her strongly…as if I can feel her breathing inside of me. I just know she is out there somewhere…and I need to find her."

He visibly relaxes. "Ohhhh." He shrugs. "Well then, if you're so sure she is alive, where is she? Because I have a daughter to return to her in that case." He smirks, eyes sparkling.

I whisper, a bit more seriously than I would like, "The Mafia has her."

"Is that so?" A deep rumbling reverberates from Janus's chest a rich laugh that ends in a giggle. "And what makes you think such a thing?" He wipes tears from his eyes, clearly enjoying this.

"I overheard the attorney say that the fire at her labs was linked to some secret crime network in Greece. Sounds like the mafia to me" I say earnestly. "And then the shooting at the house…"

Janus fidgets with the terry cloth wristband that he always wears, now deep in thought. "Helene, the mafia, organized crime and the black markets here in Greece, are very…complicated."

"Oh, so you do have the mafia here?" I ask with an edge to my voice. "I knew it! It's not just in Italy."

He looks up with a serious expression. "Sometimes things are not what they seem. You've got to be careful asking around generically about 'the mafia.' There are immigrant gangs from a wide variety of countries and nationalities involved in many different facets of the underworld in Greece. It's a melting pot of multicultural organized crime, facilitated by Greeks. They can be dangerous if provoked, but otherwise, they leave the rest of us alone. *Do not provoke them.*"

"But how will we find my mom if we can't talk to them?"

"I have my sources," he says, "but we need to be patient. Don't do anything stupid or draw attention to ourselves. These things take time."

I'm not giving up that easily. I shudder when I imagine my mother bound, gagged and shivering on a cold cement floor at the hands of roughneck street thugs. Of course, they better watch out because my mother is like Houdini. She can outsmart any restraints. Likely she's knocked out or unconscious.

Obviously, finding help with Janus is going to be painfully slow, and this is urgent. There's no time to spare.

Perhaps more liquor for Janus is the answer. Since he's finished most of the bottle, I go across the room to the refrigerator in search of another. When I come back, he's engaged in some sort of imaginary conversation…and with whom, I'm not sure.

The only creature even remotely close by is the cat. As I get closer and go to refill Janus's glass, I see that this cat is very unusual with its long, graceful body, black rimmed amber eyes, short plush golden fur and an expressive black-tipped tail. Like a miniature mountain lion.

Janus points down at the cat earnestly. "You stay away from her, you hear me?"

The cat is staring attentively at Janus, tail swishing back and forth, one ear cocked as if listening to what he's saying. He continues his tirade. "I'm telling you, Diana would not like this one bit! Your job is to protect Helene, and that's it!"

The cat arches her back, her expression defiant. She paces before returning to sit in front of Janus. It's official: my godfather is out of his freakin' mind!

I sit back down at the table just as Janus gives the cat the evil eye. But if looks could kill, I'm afraid to say it, but the cat would be fine and Janus would be ready for his funeral. Unexpectedly, the cat jumps up on the table and nuzzles up against me, butting her head under my chin. I stroke her incredibly soft fur. Her rhythmic purring vibrates my hand. This soothing sound and her warm body nestled up against me make me feel safe, like this could be my home.

I look up to see Janus warmly smiling. It's as if he has suddenly morphed into a completely different person. There must be at least two distinct personalities residing inside of my godfather, maybe more. "You seem to like her," he says softly.

I scrunch up my face. "Actually, I'm supposed to be deathly allergic to cats, so I'm not sure how it is that we are still in the same room together right now."

"Well, it looks like you've grown out of your allergy. That happens."

"What kind of cat is this?" I ask, moving to pour him one more shot of alcohol. This one might just send him over the edge.

"I have no idea. She just showed up here on the outside stairway this morning. I tried to ignore her, but she kept sticking her paws in through the crack in the window. She's quite talkative. I had to let her in or suffer getting a noise complaint." His tone is light and easy. I can't fathom why anyone would issue a noise complaint around here with all the sirens blaring and the junkies whooping and hollering outside. But I don't buy his story. There is something very familiar between Janus and this cat.

"What's her name?" I ask.

"Did you hear a word of what I just said? She just got here. How would I know her name?" Janus gets a faraway look in his eyes, as if he is hearing a voice. "How about we call her Bastet? In ancient Egyptian mythology, a protector-warrior goddess, originally depicted as a lioness, but later as a cat. Some believe that she was a precursor to our Greek goddess Artemis."

"Okay, uh, sure," I say. I'll bet that's been her name all along. As I scratch the back of Bastet's ear, my finger grazes the edge of her collar. This isn't a typical collar. It looks like a collector's item…antique, a call back to ancient times, bronze and stately, like something out of the early nineteenth century. Extraordinary.

Janus moves over to the kitchen to the espresso machine. "Want a coffee?"

"Isn't it almost ten o'clock? I'll be up all night if I have a coffee now, especially an espresso."

"Well, that's kind of the point." Janus smirks. No wonder he's so crazy. "I don't go to bed until one or two in the morning, typically." I cannot imagine how he functions like this. "By the way, ten o'clock at night for you is twenty-two hundred for the rest of the world." He yawns and looks down at his phone. "Ah, you've got to get to sleep for your first day of school. I won't be far behind you."

He staggers over to the couch, plopping down on what is my makeshift new bed. Did he say school…*tomorrow?*

"You must mean next week?" I ask.

"Wha…?" His drooping eyes smile with his words. "Tomorrow…"

A moment later, he's out cold, mouth hanging open, breathing loudly in and out. An uneven, rasping snort almost wakes him every second or third breath.

I can't believe he expects me to start a brand-new school tomorrow! I just got here. Well, at least it would get me out of here, away from him and his craziness. His prone body is draped across the couch. Where am I supposed to sleep? The thought of my trying to sleep in Janus's bed, especially after his obnoxious lecture on how I am *never* to go into his room, freaks me out. Not an option.

Bastet rubs her long, lithe body against the refrigerator, meowing loudly. As I open the refrigerator for her, my eyes lock onto her bright golden-orange eyes. I sense panic there as her meowing grows more and more urgent. This cat is starving, but she immediately quiets down when I set a milk dish down in front of her.

Bastet quickly laps up the milk, so I pick her up, and she instantly jumps up onto my shoulders, rubbing my hair and purring loudly. This is one affectionate cat.

As I pull her down off my shoulders, suddenly I feel driven to find out more about her, so I pull out the laptop Janus gave me earlier. "Let's see what kind of cat you are," I say to her as I type in the search parameters:

domestic cat that looks like a brown and black lion

The screen fills with images of cats that look like Bastet. Aha: she's an Abyssinian. These cats are supposedly the descendants of the original domestic cats of ancient Egypt, where they were worshipped as a tribute to the goddess Bastet. Janus picked the right name. Abyssinia was once located in what is now modern-day Ethiopia. Although these cats appear to be exotic miniature mountain lions with their ticked fur and dark black markings around their eyes, they are no more related to a mountain lion than any domestic cat. Abyssinians are expensive purebred cats, which cost at the low end around US $1,200. She's royalty. What is a cat like this doing here in this dump with Janus?

My thoughts feel fuzzy and unreal. I need to get to sleep soon. Tomorrow is going to be a big day for me – first day of school. I'm kind of excited to learn more about what school is like here.

There's a pile of bedding next to the couch. This is not exactly how I envisioned my first night in my new home, with me sleeping on the hard, unforgiving floor!

I cocoon into a pile of blankets and look around drowsily. There's something smooth and shiny up on the fireplace mantel. It's a stone of some kind, a brilliant amber color with a black slash up the middle. It looks just like a… I can't seem to place where I've seen it before. Bastet jumps up onto my chest and interrupts my thoughts. Her vivid gold-orange eyes shine like a flame, and suddenly, I know what this stone looks like: a cat's-eye. This is a cat's-eye stone.

I focus on the image of the stone, imagining what it might feel like to run my fingers over its smooth, shiny surface.

Then, slowly, steadily, the stone begins to glow…brighter, more intense, brighter….

7 – THE METRO

The next morning, I wake up thinking about the cat's-eye stone. It rests up on the mantel, just a smooth stone, not glowing.

The room is filled with brilliant, streaming rays of sunlight, which, when filtered through the large dirt-encrusted window, form an array of interesting shapes and lines up on the wall behind me. Janus is gone.

Bastet springs onto the mantel. She blinks, staring out through her lashes at me, eyes sparkling with mischief. Her paw darts out and knocks the stone an inch forward.

"What are you doing?" I ask her, beginning to understand how Janus found himself engaged in conversation so easily with this animal. She's lively and playful, her tail twitching slightly as her paw zips out again. This time, she bats the stone from side to side. One more strike and it skitters off onto the floor somewhere.

"No, stop!" I recall the dream I just had about the stone. I want to pick it up and take a closer look, to feel its silky texture in the palm of my hand as I had envisioned. "Now, how will I find it?" I say to no one.

I look around through the tangle of blankets that surrounds me on the floor, and in the fold of a white sheet is the stone. I lift it up to eye level. The cat's-eye stone is inlaid into a gorgeous antique bronze charm. The color is curiously similar to the bronze hue of Bastet's collar, as if the two are meant to go together.

Thump, thump, thump. What is it that sound? I look up: Janus. He taps his foot forcefully, an aggravated assault on the wooden floor. The day has just begun, and he's already irritated with me. I am startled, and my hand drops to my side like a dead weight. The cat's-eye stone charm falls out of my hand, clatters across the rug, and rolls slowly down the hollow wood to rest somewhere out of sight. Crap!

I don't understand what is driving my sudden fascination with this stone charm. I *need* to hold it in my hand again. I also feel the strange pull to protect this stone at all costs. Something tells me that I can't let Janus know that I want it this badly…or at all.

"It's about time you wake up!"

Somewhere off in the apartment, directly behind where Janus stands rigid and glaring at me, I hear the sound of the stone roll, clink, then rattle around on the hardwood floor. Bastet's white whiskers are barely visible behind a chair as I see her golden paw shoot out as if hitting a ball into the end zone. In the next moment, the shiny amber charm clatters across the floor to the other end of the room. *Oh, Bastet!*

She peeks out at me from the corner of the chair, her golden-amber eyes filled to the brim with raw defiance. Then, a look of intelligent recognition crosses her feline face. It's almost as if she's just heard me think her name.

"Get up now! Time for school!" Janus yells. I recoil and cover my ears. I almost forgot he was standing there.

Bastet springs out from her hiding place. She across the room, headed straight for Janus. He steps aside, just avoiding her. The room is stone silent for a moment, then…*clink…clank*. The stone catapults around as Bastet bats it around like a soccer ball.

"This blasted cat is making me nuts!"

Only a moment later, calm seems to come over him, as if he's completely forgotten about the cat. Bizarre. He holds a stack of papers in his shaking hand.

"About your school. There was no time to arrange the bus for pickup today, and who knows if they will even come to this neighborhood anyway? So, you need to take the Metro there. The Academy is due east from here, but there's no direct route. These maps will show you how to get there." He drops the loose pages into my lap, jabbing his fingers into one of the maps. "I've marked your school with an X."

I nod, but I'm not listening. Bastet sits upright directly behind Janus, staring at me with keen interest. There's no sign of the stone charm anywhere. What did she do with it?

Janus backs out of the room, muttering under his breath, "That ruddy school is going to eat up all of my cash! *Really*, Diana!" It's as if he thinks my mother is here in the room with us. He stomps into his room and slams the door. I stare at the space where he was just standing. I can almost make out the trail of frenetic residue he just left behind.

I juggle the papers, trying to figure it all out. There are maps of the city and the Metro, and all the school registration forms. Most of it is in Greek.

How am I supposed to figure this out? I'm so alone in this harsh new world, and even worse, I'm afraid to go out into this strange city where crazy assassins may be lurking who-knows-where. My life is at stake.

I draw in a breath and think of Mom's vibrant green eyes, of her giving me that look, the one that means I can do this.

I smooth out the map in front of me. Janus must be the last person left on the planet who uses paper maps and schedules. He probably still has an old-fashioned answering machine with a tape recorder, too. Can I just say right now how much I *despise* paper? The piece-of-crap phone Janus gave me is for calls and texts only. No Internet, so no way to look up the route to school. I could boot up the laptop he gave me, but there's no time. Finally, after cross-referencing three maps, I figure out that I need to take two different trains on the Metro and then transfer to a separate bus line to get there. What an ordeal just to get to school!

Bastet sidles over to where I'm sitting. She nudges me insistently with her furry brown head. "All right, up and at 'em!" I say as I stroke her fur. Something about the way the sunlight shimmers off the surface of the glass lamp next to me makes me suddenly remember the stone, the cat's-eye. My desire to hold it again is back, stronger than ever. I need it. I search the floor but it seems to have disappeared.

Oh, Bastet, what did you do with it?

She shoves her head abruptly into my hand. Her tail twitches. I pat her head and thread my hand around the edges of her neck to her collar, rubbing vigorously. There, my fingers run across something cold, hard, and smooth. It's the cat's-eye charm!

The stone charm is somehow embedded now into the design of the cat's bronze collar, as if it had always been there. But how? Perhaps Janus? Not possible. He's been locked in his room for the past five minutes.

I swear that the cat's mocking me. "Oh yeah, you're really funny," I say out loud. Yes, I can definitely see why Janus was talking to Bastet earlier. Maybe he's not as nuts as I think he is.

Janus yells from the other room, "Helene, you're going to be late if you don't go *now*!!"

Argh! With no time to spare, I spring up, change, and grab a banana. I gather up all the maps and papers hastily as I head down the stairs, out the door, and onto the street.

My laptop weighs down my backpack, dragging at my shoulders. I'm wearing one of only two sets of clothes I can claim as my own, both of which Hal Avery purchased for me, probably at Walmart.

So here I stand in neon purple sweatpants and a dull blue t-shirt with the words "I Crossed the Golden Gate Bridge" splashed across the front. I may as well stand in the middle of the school stadium and yell, *"I'm American!"* While it's true that I did walk across that bridge, I don't feel like advertising it to everyone here and now. Lucky for me, I have the matching purple running jacket on over the t-shirt, but it's too small, so I can't zip it up to cover the words on the shirt. How frustrating.

The dull blue clashes with the vibrant purple pants. My long brown hair is as frizzy as ever, alive with static. I have to regularly smooth it down with water or spit. This sucks. I don't even have a hairbrush or makeup. There's also a fresh new zit on my cheek this morning, and now I have nothing to cover it up. This is *not* how any girl in her right mind would dress for the first day at a new school.

I'm standing inside the Metaxourgeio Metro station, trying to find some sort of sign. This is all Greek to me, literally. While the ticket machine is in English, I'm totally confused about what to do. I pull out a stack of euros and eye the different denominations on the bills, trying to match the numbers on the bills to those shown on the ticket machine. There is a long and very impatient line of people behind me.

"I wouldn't flash your money around here. It's not safe." My ears perk up to the sound of a gruff male voice behind me. There's a hint of that sweet Greek-English accent that I love. I'm a little nervous to turn around. I mean, what if he's trying to rob me?

Flustered, I turn to see who it is. Ummm, okay. Not a robbery, that's for sure. I try not to stare. This guy is probably a bit older than me, maybe in college. He's fairly tall, maybe five feet ten, and solid, with well-sculpted muscles visible through his fitted white shirt, which accentuates his dark tan. He has longish tousled blond hair with bright gray-green eyes and a barely visible tattoo that peeks out from the bottom of his sleeve. He wears a small gold hoop in his left ear. The crispness of his starched white shirt and creased navy pants do not reconcile with the bad boy vibe I get from him. He's a rebel in disguise.

"What? Oh!" I gush, then gape in horror as a small amount of spit flies out of my mouth, hitting him on the shoulder or...no, hopefully not on the face. *Please* tell me that he didn't notice that. He doesn't react. I cram my wad of cash deep down into my pockets and out of sight. "You speak English?"

"Yeah, I do. I'm a tourist group leader for the cruise ships." He grins confidently. The words roll smoothly off his tongue. The unique shade of his eyes captivates me, but the moment is shattered when I catch a whiff of his breath. *Yuck. He smokes.*

Right on cue, he pulls out a cigarette and lights up right in the middle of the Metro station. I look around for a no smoking sign but don't see one anywhere. I check out the people around me, and no one seems annoyed, even though they keep glaring at him. I'm not in California anymore, where we have a lot of rules against smoking in public places, which I'm starting to miss.

"Would you mind putting that out?" I ask, pointing to his cigarette with a frown. "I have asthma." Of course, I'm lying. I have never had asthma in my life, but the pungent smell of his smoky breath makes me want to gag.

It's obvious to both of us that I am full of it about the asthma. He looks down at the smoldering cigarette in his hand and then up again, as if he's trying to decide what to do next. Just then, a man behind us starts muttering something in Greek. My new "friend" and this man go back and forth heatedly. Finally, my friend turns around to face me, rolling his eyes.

"There sure have been a lot of Americans claiming to have asthma in my tour groups lately. You're from…let me guess…California?"

I squirm. "How did you know that?"

"Uh, your shirt?" He smirks.

I look down and laugh.

He continues, "Also, the tourists from California are always the first to complain about smoking as if it were the most horrible thing on the planet. But when they come to Greece, I tell them to *lighten* up…ha-ha." He laughs at his own joke. "In Greece, a lot of people smoke, and that's the way it is. If you'd rather be in America, just stay there. Don't bother to visit us here."

He still has not put out the cigarette, and I've not progressed with buying my Metro ticket, so most of the people in line behind us have now relocated to another ticket line. The two people remaining behind us clear their throats loudly in aggravation. Just then, the man who was so upset earlier taps my new tour guide friend on the back, pointing irately to a sign hanging high up from the ceiling. On the sign is a silhouette of a cigarette with a bold red line through it, the universal symbol for "No Smoking."

The irate man behind us yells at my friend, this time in English. "Hey! I said put that cigarette out *now* or I will call the Metro's security over here!"

My friend's gray-green eyes widen, then narrow as he says in an irritated voice, "Okay, fine!" He swiftly drops the cigarette onto the floor and stamps it out, folding his arms across his chest.

"So…" I raise my eyebrow as I can't help but mock him, especially after all the trouble he just gave me about the asthma. "So, yeah, I'm from California, but I live *here* now."

"Oh?" I've been upgraded in his mind from Dumb Tourist to someone worthy of his time. "Do you live here in Athens, or here in Metaxourgeio?" His sarcastic tone implies that he's sure my answer will be Athens.

"Here," I say smugly, pointing outside. "Eight blocks from here. At Salaminos."

Some man pushes us from behind, yelling at us in broken English. "Hey! Can you two lovebirds tone it down? How about letting the rest of us buy a ticket?!" I look down, embarrassed. Before I have a chance to apologize, he shoves us, forcing us out of the line.

My attractive new friend with the stinky smoke breath takes the opportunity to light up once again. Unbelievable! He leans against the wall, forming rings of smoke with his mouth as he puffs them up into the air. He obviously thinks that this is cool. *Ugh.* I catch him smirking at me, probably thinking God knows what after hearing the word *lovebirds* from that crusty old man just now. I sigh. Smoke breath or no, there is absolutely no way that a guy who looks this fine would go out with a girl who looks like me, especially on this day of all days, when I'm wearing neon purple and old stained tennis shoes. Let's also not forget my static hair and fresh zit.

"Seems like lots of people around here know English fairly well," I say to him, now trying to shift his attention away from what the old man said. I can see from here that the line in front of the ticket machine has grown much longer since we were there.

"Some do, but some don't," he states evenly as he drops his cigarette to the ground, finally smothering it out with his shoe. "I'm Nikos, by the way. We must be neighbors. My family lives in one of the apartment buildings on Salaminos right next to a weird new-age shop. You've probably seen it."

"Yeah, I have. I live there!" I declare.

Nikos must live in the old rundown apartment building with peeling paint right next door to Janus's shop. "You must be related to that crazy old medicine man, then?" he says with a wry grin.

I nod. "Yep, he's my godfather." Suddenly, I'm so relieved to meet someone in my neighborhood who's not only close to my age but also…so *hot*. Well, except for the cigarettes, of course. Not that I care to think about him or any boy like *that*, but I can't seem to help myself right now. "Nikos? Oops, I'm not supposed to say the 's' on the end, right?"

"Please call me Nick," he says sweetly. Oh, so now he's going to be nice?

"Okay, Nick. I'm Helene." I put my hand out as if to shake his. "Nice to meet you."

He moves a step backward with a frown, staring down at my hand, but then he takes it. His hand is warm and large. It's a nice handshake, but he seems uncomfortable. Maybe he's shy.

It's easy for me to see why Nick is a tour guide as he proceeds to expertly describe the Metro system and the ticket-buying process to me in intricate detail. We step back into the ticket line, he patiently helps me count out my money and insists on feeding it into the machine for me so I can buy my first Metro ticket.

"So why would you want to move to Greece? People are hurting here. Most would give their right arm to live in the US," he says vehemently. "In case you didn't notice, we're in the middle of a crisis here." His sarcastic tone and the tension in the tiny lines encircling his gray-green eyes make me think that this hits way too close to home for him.

"Well, it's not like I had a choice," I reply. He frowns and shakes his head, which makes me worry that I've said the wrong thing, so I try to backpedal. "No, I mean, if I did have a choice, of course Greece sounds like a great place to live."

His eyes light up as if this is funny. "Yeah, right. Ha-ha. You don't have to say that to make me feel better. I love living here."

I sigh a breath of relief.

"So really, why are you here?"

It's like a switch was just hit. My eyes cloud over as the image of my mom floods into my mind. The station starts to spin. It feels as if the walls are closing in on me…like I'm slowly suffocating, choking. I try to swallow, but a thick lump forms in my throat, making it hurt to talk. "I…it's…" The words won't come. A lone tear rolls down my cheek. "My mom...she's...." I stop midsentence, eyes wide and blinking. "I can't...I...." I just can't say it.

His eyes fill with concern. "Hey." He places his hand on my shoulder in a gesture of kindness, his eyes meeting mine. "No need to tell me anything. It's okay."

Just then, the fog clears, leaving almost as fast as it came. I remember now that Mom isn't really dead. She's alive. I just need to find her. "No, it's fine," I say, but my eyes dart around the room as I consider what to say next. "It's my mom. The police said that she died, but—"

He cuts me off as he takes my hand. "No, really, you don't have to."

Normally, I'd be freaked out that this complete stranger is holding my hand, but he makes me feel safe. But he's a stranger! I can't get close to him.

"No, I said its fine!" I snap, pulling my hand away.

He looks shocked, like I've slapped him. "Fine." His retort is short and icy. A moment of terse silence passes between us as stark tension fills the air.

In the next moment, though, the lines on his face visibly relax as his impassive façade seems to melt into compassion. He says, "Look, I know a thing or two about loss...but not my mom dying. *Wow*. I can't even imagine that."

He lifts his hand to push a lock of blond hair away from his face. As he lowers it, I can't help but stare at his hand. There on the inside of his wrist is the same double helix symbol with snakes wrapped around a flame tattoo that is now becoming a common theme in my life.

No, not my new friend...Nick! My head spins in a million directions as I try to wrap my mind around what this might mean.

"Nick...that tattoo...what is it?" I whisper.

He turns his wrist over, and recognition fills his eyes suddenly, as if he forgot he had it all this time. "Oh, this? I have no idea. The company I work for inked me with it when I started my job leading groups of tourists. It hurt like hell, though, like they were implanting something under my skin. I can't seem to forget that pain."

By the look on his face, I can't doubt his sincerity. He's a tour guide working for a legitimate company, not some paid hit man for the mob.

"Who do you work for?" I ask.

"I'm sure that you've never heard of him, so…" He looks down at his watch

I nod. "Probably not, so why not tell me, then?"

Nick sighs, looking around. He pulls out another cigarette and, sure enough, lights up *again*. Finally, he mutters quietly under his breath, blowing out a huge puff of smoke. "Fine. Sarantos…I work for Sarantos Enterprises."

Doesn't ring a bell. A tour guide company would not be part of some shady crime network. But then again, you never know.

"You're right, never heard of it."

His shoulders relax. I turn as a group of students rush in behind us. Something odd catches my eye. There, about five feet away from us, is a statue made of some sort of metal. Copper, maybe? That's funny, I don't remember it being there before. Even more perplexing is that it's a statue made in the image of a regular guy. Well, maybe not exactly "regular." He looks like he could be a member of a street gang around here.

"Uh, Nick?" I ask. "That statue…what is it?"

He turns to study it before saying in a bored tone, "I have no idea. Never saw it before. Must be new."

His nonchalance puts me at ease, but then I suddenly realize that I need to get to school. When I tell him that I'm going to Athens International Academy in Psychiko, he seems a bit surprised. The route that I had plotted was all wrong. He pulls out a notepad and writes out the directions, which include several transfers, then a long walk.

I look down at my watch. It's already past eight a.m., which means that I'm already late for school. I feel totally overwhelmed.

Nick tries to calm me. "It's not as bad as it looks," he says. "Besides, in the future, you can take the school bus from Syntagma Square, which isn't far from here." He seems to know a lot about the Academy and even mentions some teachers he knows there.

"Did you go there?" I ask, sure that he's now in college.

"You could say that." He smiles, but then he glances at his watch. "Time for us both to go. I'm supposed to take a bus full of tourists from a cruise ship to the National Archaeological Museum in twenty minutes."

A security guard approaches him from across the room, scowling at the smoking cigarette in his hand. "Got to go!" he exclaims.

Just as he's rushing out, he turns around one last time, now shouting over the deafening sound of the Metro station, "Hey, Helene, do you like mythology?"

"Uh, yeah!" I respond. "Why?"

"Just curious," he says, his gray-green eyes sparkling. As the bright white of his shirt disappears, I catch myself wishing he was still a student at my new school. I sure hope that I run into him again. Something tells me that I will.

A strange scraping sound makes me turn around. But there's nothing there. Bizarre.

As I make my way down the stairs and onto the train platform, I hear a shuffling sound. This time, it sounds close…too close, as if it's immediately behind me. My heart starts to race as I whirl around. Again, nothing. But then a black shadow flits across the wall next to me and then disappears. But how can that be? There is no sunlight that would generate a shadow in here.

The pulse inside my wrist is pounding so hard that I can see it pumping through my veins. Someone bumps me, pushing me hard into the wall. I feel a pinch on my right finger. *Ouch!* When I look up, I see who it is. Some washed-out, sickly looking man. His skin is translucent, like glass. I can see the greenish hue of veins dispersed over his face.

He rushes up the stairs. Just as suddenly as he appeared, he's gone. I look down at my pinched finger. What I see there stops my pulse and heart.

It's a solid silver ring with a dazzling twelve-point star on its face.

What seriously gives me pause, though, is where I've seen this star before…in my dreams. This is the same twelve-point star that I saw on the ring worn by the man with no face.

The man called Zeus.

8 – THE ACADEMY

I'll admit it…I'm freaked. I try twisting the silver ring off my finger, but it won't budge. Who was that peculiar man? I try to keep my eyes glued to the piece of paper that Nick gave me and follow the maze of trains to the proper Metro stations, but I can't help but watch my back in fear that the man may come back. I just barely make it to the bus before the doors slam shut.

After getting off the bus, I run hard for at least four blocks until I reach the wrought iron gates of a guard station. It's the school. Thank God! I'm drenched in sweat, but I can't help but smile. Finally, here, I feel safe.

The sprawling green lawns, chirping birds, and manicured gardens grant me the illusion that I could be standing in fields somewhere out in the English countryside, not here in the middle of a modern major city. Clearly, the Academy is no ordinary school.

"We aren't in Athens anymore." The words escape my lips.

I walk up the long, regal drive that seems to go on forever. The architecture is fantastic. Red Spanish-tiled yellow stucco buildings with grand pillars open onto a large circular drive. Interspersed on both sides of the driveway are lush green grass and patches of small trees where students sit with their books and laptops. I can see why Mom would want me to go here. I place my fingers on my lips in a sign of silent thanks to her.

By the time I reach the office, I've missed my first class. An uptight woman with bright pink blush and peacock-blue eye shadow takes my paperwork. She seems more than a little put off that I'm so late on my first day.

"Do you know what would happen if you were this late at a school like ours in the US?" According to her nametag, she is Bertha

Manning from New South Wales. She furrows her eyebrows in consternation as she continues her diatribe in a clipped British accent. "You would be kicked out on your ear, that's what!"

"Well, I—"

The door opens. A perky, dark-skinned girl with a long, shiny black ponytail and jangling earrings enters the office. She's wearing a well-pressed cheerleading uniform and a festive temporary tattoo on her cheek that says *AIA Chariots*.

The wicked woman from Wales's frown morphs into a full-on scowl at the sight of this girl. "Miss Mathur. What on Earth can you want this time?"

"This time? I've only been here once this morning!" The girl's jangly gold earrings sway back and forth. "Look, I just need to see today's athletic roster real quick."

Bertha rolls her eyes as if this is the most stressful thing she can imagine, then turns back to me, promptly ignoring the girl. "Alrighty then." She struggles to recall my name. "Helene, there's no way you can start classes here until you get a student tour, and since all students are currently in class—"

Just then, the perky girl pushes up to the counter. "Hello! I'm still here."

"Vanessa Mathur," – Bertha is getting mad – "you can wait your turn."

I'm fine waiting, though, and Vanessa's boldness is rubbing off on me, so I say, "Actually, she can go ahead of me."

Bertha's face turns red. "Now, Helene, I know that kind of attitude is tolerated in California, but not here!!"

Vanessa and Bertha seethe in silence until finally Vanessa shifts gears. Her voice is sweet as pie. "Ms. Manning, I would be happy to take Helene on a tour of the school if you would kindly let me see that roster *now*."

"Ah, what a great idea!" Bertha's eyes don't reach her fake smile as she turns to introduce me. "Helene, Vanessa's a senior here who came to us from Mumbai, what, two years ago?"

Vanessa agrees with a nod. "Yep."

Bertha hands the roster over to Vanessa as she continues, "Miss Mathur will be your student buddy, which means it's her responsibility to help you out for your first week here."

"You can call me Vani," she says as she looks over the roster in front of her. Satisfied, Vani shoves it sternly back across the counter to Bertha. "C'mon, let's go," she says as she leads me outside.

Once outside, Vani relaxes. "This is a great school. Don't let Bertha ruin your first day." We begin to walk the campus. Her spiel sounds as if she's done this before. "The school has over four hundred students, all from more than thirty-eight countries, including Greece. Amazing, right?"

She tells me that many of the teachers at the school are highly accomplished, published, or educated from top institutions in the United States, United Kingdom, or Greece, but most are of Greek descent. Cool.

Something about Vani puts my mind at ease. She's nice in a way that isn't too annoying. I like her. This is saying a lot because she's a cheerleader, and usually I don't like cheerleaders. This holds true for any team spirit activity. My mother would say that I'm being petty and jealous. Back in junior high, I was pretty full of myself with my success in ballet, so I thought cheerleading would be easy for me; but when I tried out for the Squad, I was laughed out of the room because my arms hyperextend and I couldn't form a proper V.

It wasn't the outright rejection that got under my skin so much; it was the laughing that did it, the high-pitched squeals of delight and obnoxious giggling directed at me as I turned beet red in front of everyone. After that tortuous experience, I immediately classified all cheerleaders, as well as any smiling, pretty or upbeat female, as "the Enemy."

The thing about Vani, though, is that she's not at all like any other cheerleader that I have ever met before.

"I was doing a stunt with my partner, Alexis, and I had to sit on his hand. Suddenly, I had to gas!" She giggles. "But we were performing at a live basketball game. There's no way out of that," she snorts, "so the only thing I can do is clench, and you know that's hard to do when you're suspended up in the air, sitting on a boy's hand."

I nod like of course I know what she's talking about, so she continues, "I couldn't hold it any longer, so..." She flashes me a devilish grin. "I let it roll right there on his hand! And do you know what that *vlaka* did?" She pauses to take a breath. "He threw me into the stands!"

I sit with my mouth gaping open, before I break into a laugh.

Vani's eyes open wide. "Can you believe what he did to me? Just look at my bruise." And there, on her upper thigh, is a large, harshly visible black and blue bruise. I am laughing so hard that I start to cry. She's so awesome. If ever there was a black sheep of the cheerleading squad, Vani is it. She even has a nose ring like mine.

We walk past an opening between two buildings, one of which has a large dome on top, and we pause to look out over a vast green field. I stop and gasp at the sight in front of us. There, standing in a cluster, is a group of guys on a sand volleyball court. Did I say *guys*? Because they look to me more like *men*, all so very tall. Serious attitude oozes from them, like they know they're cool and can have whatever they want.

They shift around with cool indifference on the white sand court under bright rays of sunshine and the deep blue sky as they listen intently to their coach. Vani doesn't even give them a second glance as she prattles on about the undefeated status of the AIA boys' varsity volleyball team. Their uniforms are decorated in the school's colors of red and gold, but they all seem larger than life to me with their olive skin, ripped muscles, and two-day stubble.

One of them tears his shirt off in anger. He turns to the coach and starts to argue with him. His taut, muscular torso glistens in the sunlight. Something about this guy seems oddly familiar to me, as if I've seen him before, but of course that's not possible.

Vani is staring too, not at all in a rush to move on yet. She lets out a sigh. "Um, yeah. So the guys here are high on hotness. This school is known for that."

"Yeah," I say, trying to sound nonchalant. "Not bad."

The coach points in our direction, and six pairs of eyes – the entire volleyball team – shift their gaze onto us. Oh no. I feel my face flush as the coach jogs across the field to where we stand. He glares first at me, then at Vani. "Is there something you need here?"

Vani explains that I'm a new student, and this is our campus tour. The coach nods and swiftly jogs back to the team, where he turns to scowl once again at the boy with the attitude. The boy's arms are crossed, but when he looks up, his eyes lock onto mine. I'm temporarily stunned by the intensity of his vibrant sea-blue eyes. He's defiant, not backing down, not for anything.

Oh God. It's Ever. From the airport. No way. He goes to school *here*?

His eyes hold mine steadily, as if deep in thought, but then, in the next moment, his whole face lights up in a warm, familiar, knowing smile. My heart feels erratic as I recall the pulse of heated electricity that I felt when he brushed my arm just yesterday at the airport.

Vani grabs my elbow, quickly ushering me back into the main building. Nothing seems to faze her. Her forehead wrinkles in a concentrated grimace as she tells me about some awful girl named Samantha. "Be sure to steer clear of her." I just nod and smile, not understanding.

Back at the office, Bertha is waiting for me, but my mind is still stuck back on the field with Ever. I know I shouldn't feel this way, but I can't wait to see him again.

"It was so awesome to meet you, Helene," Vani says. "I'm sure I'll see you around, but if you need anything, just let me know."

"How can I reach you?" I ask.

"Oh, duh. You're on Instagram, right? I can follow you."

I don't know whether my Instagram account is still active. I don't see why it wouldn't be. I reach for my phone to check, but remember that my phone is voice and text only. *Darn you, Janus.*

"Sure." I nod and wave thanks as Vani leaves.

Bertha goes over my class schedule, shows me a map of where my classes are, and gives me my locker combination. She mentions something called the siesta, a two-hour break in the middle of the day from 1:30 p.m. until 3:30 p.m. While the siesta isn't practiced in a modern city such as Athens, it is still prevalent out in the smaller villages of mainland Greece and on some of the islands.

Bertha explains that the Academy decided to adopt this tradition to not only instill some of the old Greek culture amongst the international student body, but also because studies show that people are more productive after a short midday nap. Most students utilize the siesta for lunch and to study, enjoy hobbies, or play sports, but a nap is always strongly encouraged. School resumes at 3:30 p.m., and classes end at 6:00 p.m.

"Do I have to go home for the nap?" I think of all the time it will take for me to go all the way back to Janus's on the train and bus, and then back here again.

"No, most kids have so much to do with their extracurricular activities that they stay here for the midday break."

"If no one is using the yoga studio during that time, can I use it?"

"Ah, you like yoga?" She asks.

"No. I used to be really serious about ballet before I was injured." I point down to my ankle. "Achilles injury." I pause, considering again if I should tell her more. She seems concerned, so I continue, "Sometimes, I just, uh, need to crank up the sound and *move*, even though I can't dance very well anymore."

She looks bored. "Whatever. Just be sure to turn the light off in there when you leave and pick up after yourself." At that, the bell rings, and I excuse myself.

The halls are crowded with chattering kids. I find my locker, punch in the code, and open it up. What I see on the little shelf inside my locker gives me pause as my backpack drops onto the floor with a loud thump.

Engraved on the bottom of the middle shelf is a bright yellow symbol. It's a twelve-point star—the same star symbol etched on the face of the silver ring that I can't get off my finger. Could this have something to do with Mom? During the holidays, she used to leave me clues around the house to help me find my gifts. Nothing was ever straightforward. Everything was a riddle.

My second-period class is called life sciences. What exactly is that?

Physics, chemistry, geology, biology? Or maybe social studies? Possibly a combination of all of them? Whatever it is, this is my first real class here, so I'm going to give it my best.

As I look around for an empty seat, I hear a familiar voice and instantly know where I've heard it before. It's Dimitris! The driver-who-is-also-a-teacher from the airport. What are the chances? Not only does Ever attend this school, but also, Dimitris is a teacher here. And he is not just any teacher…he's *my* teacher!

Dimitris is scolding a nerdy-looking girl with spiky red hair whose eyes look huge due to some generous use of black eyeliner. His name is written out on the board: MR. PAXINOS. I guess I can't call him by his first name. Also, who writes in chalk on a blackboard anymore?

He's upset that the girl hasn't done her homework on time. Dimitris points the girl to a seat in the back of the room. "This is your last chance. I'm *not* going to hear any more excuses from you."

A couple of kids snicker. As I survey the room, I see an empty seat, which I am pleasantly surprised is right next to my new friend Vani. Her eyes light up as we nod to each other in greeting.

Dimitris spots me and grins. "Ah, I see our new student is here. Helene, right?"

I nod. I can't believe this guy is my teacher. His being here can't be a total coincidence. He lifts his hand to write something on the board and I glimpse a flash of the double helix tattoo on the inside of his wrist again. The same company that Nick works for, Sarantos Enterprises, must employ a lot of people in Athens.

What if they hired Dimitris to spy on me…or worse, to *kill* me? But he knows where I live. Why not just take me out there? It's possible that him being my teacher is a coincidence and they don't know I'm here. Maybe the people who work for the company in tourism and teaching don't talk to the hit men? Whatever the deal, if I get to know him better, then maybe I can find out more about this Sarantos company and an idea where my mom could be.

The police officer's last words once again echo through my mind: "*Trust no one.*" While I should heed that warning, I also desperately need to trust someone besides Janus. Dimitris seems my best available option now.

Today's topic promises to be boring: geology. Dimitris writes a lot of terms I've never heard on the board, interspersing Greek words into his lecture, which throws me off. I need to learn Greek! His piece of chalk makes me squirm as it squeaks roughly against the old-fashioned chalkboard. But then I hear the words "cat's-eye stone." Suddenly, my interest is piqued.

Dimitris eyes sparkle as if alive with fire. "Of all the gemstones that exhibit cat's-eye, chrysoberyl is the best known. Chrysoberyl has the strongest and most distinct cat's-eye effect of all gemstones. Throughout history, many cultures celebrated this stone – some even used it as a currency – as they believed it to protect its wearer from evil spirits and that it held magical powers through its ability to transform energy into its best possible state, a process they called *protogenesis*."

The bell rings. Vani turns to me. "It's so cool that you are in this class."

We pause for a minute, which allows me time to muster the nerve to ask the question that's been burning inside of me this whole time. I ask, trying to be nonchalant, "So, what about Ever? What's his story?"

Vani pauses. Finally, she says, "Ever is pretty much every girl's dream, and believe me, he knows it. His father, Georgios Sarantos, owns most of Athens. You may have heard of Sarantos Enterprises?"

I pretend I've never heard of it, but inside I'm reeling. Nick said that his tattoo signified that he worked for Sarantos. The same double helix with fire symbol that Dimitris, the driver, had on his wrist. The sign of the mysterious Greek 'mafia'. Now, Ever is involved in it too? I bet he has this same tattoo. Crazy.

I feign ignorance as she continues. "Well, it's an international company here in Athens that's involved in everything like steel, shipping, real estate, banking, tourism, and probably much more. Many of us here at the Academy have rich parents, but we speak of money in terms of millions. Ever's family speaks in *billions*. He's the school's top player in volleyball and basketball as well as the lead singer for his own band. His mother, Elizabeth, was once Miss Australia."

Vani goes on. "Yeah, he used to date one of my friends, and let's just say that it ended in a very bad way." But then her voice lowers to barely an audible whisper. "And there's more. This is a rumor, but I think it's true because I heard it from my dad. Georgios Sarantos is said to be the leader of a massive underground organization known as the *Syndicate*."

"Like the mafia?" I whisper in a hushed voice.

"No." She smiles and lowers her voice so no one else can hear. "This is so much bigger than any mafia could be. In fact, the organized crime in Greece is afraid of Sarantos, almost like he's some sort of god."

Whoa. As much as I liked Ever and his mother when I met them in the airport, the fact that his dad is the leader of this mysterious organization is music to my ears. He will know where my mom is. I want to run down the hall, pull Ever out of class, and demand right now to take me to his dad.

But I can't. These are the people that want me dead. Alerting Ever now tells them loud and clear that I'm here. Not smart. I need to take my time and get to know Ever better. Of course, I don't have time. I need to find Mom now.

The rest of the morning seems slips by. I'm pleasantly surprised to have such interesting teachers in my next two classes: Language Arts with Ms. Suni from Cairo and Ancient Greek Mythology with Ms. Petraki from Athens. Then, just before lunch, I pull out the crumpled class schedule tightly wedged in my pocket and outwardly groan with dread when I see what class is staring back at me: PE.

I hate Physical Education. To start with, ball sports are usually a complete disaster for me. For some reason, it always seems that every ball is drawn like a magnet directly to the most sensitive part of my body: my chest. When I used to dance, I was flat as a pancake, so it never mattered. In fact, kids in junior high used to call me "Helene Lowlands." That's how dismally underdeveloped I was back then. But now, just two years since my dance injury, I've somehow morphed into a "woman," so to get hit there means horrific pain, which can be so bad as to cause me to double over in agony.

Today, thankfully, it appears that we aren't engaging in any sport that involves a ball. Mr. Mburu, is from Tanzania. A few of the girls in the locker room told me that he was once a lead guide for climbers to the top of Kilimanjaro, one of the seven summits of the world and the highest mountain in Africa. He's also a master in modern pankration, a Greek style of fighting. It's a combination of wrestling, kicking, and boxing. Introduced during ancient times in the Olympic games, pankration is allegedly the most original of all martial arts. I'm sure he has many talents, but what I notice the most about Mr. Mburu are his striking sky-blue eyes. His dark skin glistens as he explains that today we are practicing the art of fencing, which is another name for modern-day sword fighting.

A blond cheerleader with a fake tan, and a whole contingent of groupies following her saunters over to join the class. This girl is flawless, like there's some guy following her around with full makeup on a movie set, constantly tweaking her look with the airbrush tool in Photoshop. She's tall with long, straight, shiny golden hair, and her waist is the tiniest I have ever seen. I'm looking for a corset because she can't possibly be human at that size. All this glamour, though, is completely overshadowed by her inhospitable scowl.

This girl – I'll call her Barbie – utters the most obnoxious, bitchy, and annoyingly fake sound, which must be how she laughs. Then someone calls her name: "Samantha."

So, this is the infamous Samantha, whom I was supposed to avoid at all costs. I find myself disappointed to learn her real name because I really enjoyed calling her Barbie. Just my luck to have her here in my least favorite class.

We change into fencing attire, which includes mesh-covered protection masks, and then form a circle around Mr. Mburu. I try not to make eye contact with him, but of course, I'm called on first. As I step into the circle, Mr. Mburu asks for a volunteer to be my opponent. Samantha raises her hand. A look of glee crosses her face as she steps opposite me into the circle and assumes the proper stance.

I jab my faux sword out in front of me but am so nervous that within about ten seconds, I trip over my own feet and fall flat on my face. Samantha had nothing to do with this, of course, but she puts on quite a show after I hit the ground by overzealously stabbing me in the back several times. I feel a nasty bruise forming as I tear off my facemask.

I lie there stunned, unable to get up. I hear several snickers as others witness my hopeless humiliation and then the mocking voice of the devil herself as Samantha derides me. "So, wow!" She looks me up and down. "What's up with your purple eyes? Seriously!" Her friends giggle in that obnoxiously snarky way that makes me want to cringe. It brings back those sore memories from when the cheerleaders laughed at me during tryouts.

My eyes start to water, but I hold it in, refusing to let anyone see me cry. As I excuse myself to the bathroom, I tear off my fencing uniform and run swiftly out of class. No tears have fallen yet. *Thank God.*

A terrible sob escapes me as the floodgates open and I cry hard, now rushing down the hall as fast as I can. Just as I reach the bathroom, something gives me pause, and I look up. *It's Ever.* He's casually leaning against the doorframe of the classroom next door as if waiting for someone. Our eyes lock. He seems surprised to see me like this, like he's concerned, but doesn't know what to do.

Just then, Samantha saunters into the hallway, sidles over to Ever's right side, and whispers something in his ear. The whole time, she glares at me out of the corner of her eye. Could it be any more obvious that she is talking to him about me? She giggles.

Hello! I'm right here.

Ever smiles at Samantha and grabs her hand. The red and gold from her cheerleading outfit matches Ever's volleyball uniform perfectly. If Vani is the fun black sheep of the cheerleading squad, Samantha is the devil incarnate. Horror fills my mind as the truth quickly becomes obvious. These two are going out. Ever and Samantha, boyfriend and girlfriend.

There's no way I can handle this right now – or let's be honest, *anytime* – so I look away and run deftly into the safety of the restroom. The door slams behind me as I slump weakly into the close confines of a narrow stall. I'm so numb and my body so fiercely trembles that all I can do is stare blankly at the wall as anger and sadness consume me.

A few minutes pass, and I hear a door slam. A familiar voice, thick with a soft British accent, calls out to me. "Helene? Are you in here?"

It's Vani. She sounds so far away, but her voice is sweet and soothing to my ears. "I just bumped into Samantha in the hallway and heard about what happened in PE." I must utter some sort of response because she unlocks my stall from the outside and forces my chin up to look at her. "Look, it seems like she's got it out for you." Concern etches her kind features. "When I first started here, she gave me no end of trouble too. She acts so perfect around the teachers and administrators and her parents are such huge contributors to the school that no one believes how awful she can be. If they knew, I'm sure it wouldn't be tolerated. Don't let her get under your skin."

I can't be her next victim. No way. I recall a story from Greek mythology that Mom once told me. It was about a snobbish girl named Meropi and her holier-than-thou family, who showed no respect to anyone, much less to the gods. Meropi particularly abhorred the goddess Athena because she was terribly jealous of the exotic and unusual beauty of Athena's stunning blue eyes.

Of course, in her obnoxious and naive hubris, Meropi had no idea that Athena was a real threat until one day, Athena posed as a common girl and invited Meropi to be her guest to a festival in honor of the gods. Meropi was insulted by this invitation, so much so that she cursed Athena right to her face. Bad idea. At that moment, the goddess revealed herself and turned Meropi into an owl.

Mom's point in recounting this myth was that all things are somehow related, what goes around comes around, and if you're awful to someone else, you never know how that person might one day come back into your life. In short, always be kind to others.

Vani's face appears almost angelic to me right now, and suddenly I'm filled with an overwhelming sense of gratitude towards her. I think of all the interesting teachers and kids from so many countries here. This is a great school. Screw Samantha. I can do this. She will not ruin me. I will not only survive this...I will thrive.

But the question remains: how can a guy like Ever be with a girl like *her*?

9 – INJURY

I finally muster the courage to leave the safety of the restroom, hoping that I am alone. I scan the long, empty hallways and the rows and rows of gray lockers. The eerie absence of any sound unnerves me as the air lacks the normal bustle of the day. I'm thankful that there is absolutely no sign of anyone anywhere. It is time for siesta.

I can't stop picturing Ever, with his piercing eyes and tall, wiry frame leaning against the wall opposite me. I hate that he witnessed me in such a sorry state. I vow that I will *never* again let this happen. Not ever. What's most frustrating here is that usually I couldn't care less what anyone thinks of me, especially a guy like that, the type who has every girl in the school after him.

I can't help but second-guess myself on the earlier connection that I thought I felt with him. Most maddening of all is that I know there's no choice but for me to continue to try to get closer to him. I have to find my mother. There's no way, though, that I will do so if it requires me to sell my soul to the devil. There must be another way.

That's it. I've had it. I need to free my mind, to escape. Across the hallway, the open gym and darkened yoga studio lie empty. If I skip lunch, maybe I can slip into the yoga studio undetected for a few uninterrupted moments with just enough time to stretch. My growling stomach wages an internal war inside me, which I ignore. I need to *move*, to dance.

No one else is here. Humming, I scan my iPod song list. Sometimes I like classical ballet music, but other times, I just need to jam to something more modern, like "Animals" by Maroon 5. My mother loves that song. I dim the lights so all I can see is my silhouette in the full-length mirrors that grace all four walls of the room. I find myself a bit disturbed when I see my reflection. My body is different, now graced by the generous curves of my chest. This feels so foreign to me, so different from the look I used to have when I was a dancer. I know I need to come to terms with this, to accept myself as I have become a woman.

The bouncy hardwood floor beneath my feet feels magnificent. I plug my iPod into the overhead sound system and hit play.

As the first beats of the frenetic rhythm start, I look down at my ankle. It looks normal now, but one chilly night a few years ago, I was in Tahoe on a ski trip with my friends when I slipped on the ice and broke my ankle in two places. Even worse, I tore my Achilles tendon. The broken bones healed with no problem, but even after surgery, my Achilles never healed correctly. Just like that, my entire future in ballet was over.

I tentatively step down on it. Usually, there's a dull ache when I try to dance, but I just suffer through it because my will to move to the music is so strong that I can't stop myself. Today is no different, and here I go. The crazy, hair-flipping wild woman from the "Animals" video fills my head as my feet begin to move first as a mini-jog in place, but then sheer insanity takes over as I spin, turn, jog more, and sidestep. Next, I flip down to the floor into a tight tiger's crouch, but then spring back up with the agile deftness of a cougar.

It's all going so well that I decide to push it hard. I'm fueled by raw adrenaline. I run full tilt down the length of the yoga studio and push off into the air, fully extending my legs into a near-perfect split. As I'm on my way back down, my foot hits the floor on my bad ankle...*snap!* I hear it before I feel it, knowing instantly that this is *bad.* the pain is excruciating. I roll on my back on the floor. It feels like my calf muscle ruptured. I feel like I'm swept up in a storm of pain.

What's that? Someone is here. For a moment, I think I must be hallucinating, but then my secret observer emerges from the shadows, revealing himself.

The lights brighten, and I hear a familiar voice in that sweet accent. "Oh God! Are you okay?"

No. It's Ever. He can't see me like this. His olive skin seems to glow under the rich, deep blue of his polo shirt. His black hair is slightly tousled and wet, as if he just got out of the shower. The faint outline of his lean, wiry physique is abundantly obvious beneath his worn, rugged jeans. My heart hammers as I feel a flutter of butterflies inside. Why can't I control myself better around him? I hate not feeling in control, especially right now when I'm in such a vulnerable, compromised state.

"Let me go and get you some ice. You don't want to bruise." He runs his hand through his hair. It's like he's reviewing a mental checklist in his head. He jogs out to the gym and, less than a minute later, returns with two ice packs, a yoga bolster, and two orange pills.

I raise my eyebrows. "Advil?"

"God, no. Turmeric." His voice pitches up as he says, "Lucky for you, I have a stash of this stuff in my locker…just in case. I've pulled a muscle or two playing sports just like this, so I know what to do."

"Yeah, I heard that you play a lot of sports." He places the bolster under my leg to elevate it, carefully placing the ice under my calf. It's swelling.

"Yeah." His voice returns to normal as he quickly changes the subject. "So how long have you danced?"

"Since I was a kid. I was on my way to going professional before my injury." I look down at my ankle to show him my wicked scar. He cringes.

"Oh, that's bad," he says somberly. He looks guilty, like he knows that he shouldn't have been there watching me. "It's important to do what you love, no matter the cost." He lifts his eyes, shifting his gaze to meet mine. The sun through the skylight catches his blue eyes.

When I'm finally able to catch my breath, I feel out of sorts about this. God, he's so attractive to me that his sweetness now makes me feel even worse. Not even an hour has gone by when I vowed that I'd never let him see me be weak, and here I am at it again!

"What?" My voice is seething with venom. "While I appreciate your help, I don't appreciate your spying on me in here."

He seems genuinely surprised. "Well, I…uh…" he stammers, which I never thought possible for someone so self-assured. But then, quick as a flash, his whole demeanor shifts. When he starts again, he seems a bit put off. "Look, I had a private session with my coach in the gym a little while ago. I had just come out of the locker room when I saw you in here. And by the way, you're lucky I was nearby." His tone becomes indignant. "This is a public place. If you don't like people watching, maybe you should go somewhere else."

I'm a little shocked at his response. Just a moment ago, he was sweet as he could be, and now, it seems like he could care less about me. Like maybe he was just being nice because he felt bad about seeing me cry in the hallway earlier.

His voice grows quiet, almost down to a whisper. "My mother used to make me go to the ballet with her when I was younger, and so I grew to really appreciate it. In fact, I've taken tango, salsa, and western swing lessons. Dancers of all kinds are incredible athletes."

This confession makes him seem so incredibly charming and endearing in a sweet, old-fashioned kind of way. It's impossible to envision Ever sitting through a ballet performance and much harder still to think that he would enjoy it. And while I've been drawn in by his stark honesty, I find my mind wandering back to Samantha.

Be careful, my mind warns.

"Ummm," I stammer, "where's your girlfriend?" I imagine that if Samantha were here, Ever wouldn't be so incredibly charming.

He grins in a way that tells me he knows exactly where she is, but then he says, "Who knows?" That adorable dimple is back. "So, I had a really nasty basketball injury – tore my ACL – just over two years ago. I was out for half the season. It really pissed me off to have to sit it out, to no longer be the top player." I grow bored as he recaps the long list of sports that he plays. He sure likes to hear himself talk.

Despite my boredom with what he's saying, I can't help but be acutely aware of his alluring presence, sitting there so close to me. He smells like fresh mint with a hint of cedar and citrus, maybe. Whatever it is, wow! My heart beats so hard that I can see the vein pulsing frantically on the side of my wrist. God, I wish he didn't have a girlfriend!

I tune back in to the conversation just as he finishes recapping the stats and records he's set in basketball this past year. Obviously, he's back to number one status now despite his setback a few years ago. Unlike me. Not only have I not yet fully recovered from my previous injury, but now it's likely I won't even be able to walk without a crutch or a limp for the foreseeable future.

"Okay, seriously…is there anything that you're *not* good at?" I demand.

He scoffs a little too loudly as he answers with a wry grin, "No, not really."

He tries hard to stifle a laugh, his blue-green eyes crinkling around the edges. His laugh lines reveal a trace of that adorable dimple again. I can't help but smile. But seriously, it seems that everything comes so easily for him. I wonder, has he ever had to work hard at anything in his sheltered, perfect life? So unfair.

"Oh, goody for you, Mr. Overachiever," I say in my best pretend-frustrated voice. "Do you realize how it feels to be a mere mortal here with you, especially with my injury? I would give anything to be able to dance again."

"Well, actually, I just thought of something that is quite a challenge for me."

"Yes?" This I want to hear.

"Cleaning. I'm horrible at cleaning the house," he says his eyes sparkling with mischief. Now that's a sight I'd like to see: Ever, the golden boy holding a broom, sweeping the floor. With all his wealth, I can't imagine he's ever performed a chore in his life. Or how about scrubbing the toilet? We both laugh out loud.

Is he flirting with me? His reputation as a player shoots through my mind—and I'm not talking about sports. I hear myself whisper, "Cleaning wasn't exactly what I had in mind when I asked the question."

He steps away from me slightly, twisting a black bracelet around on his wrist. "What did you mean, then?" His blue-green eyes are wide and innocent as he meets my gaze, but I can tell there's something brewing under his smooth exterior…something deep.

"Outside of cleaning." I give him that knowing look. "Is there anything else that you're not good at? I mean, I heard that you master everything that you try, especially *girls*."

Did that really just fly out of my mouth? What is *wrong* with me?

His smile is back, the whole front row of his brilliant white teeth exposed. He's absolutely beaming. He must notice me looking at his teeth because his gaze falls to my lips. Oh no. He must think I'm staring at his mouth for *other* reasons.

Shaking his head, he asks, "And where did you hear that?"

"Around." I twist my hair with my finger, trying not to look directly at him. An awkward silence overtakes us for a moment.

He moves in closer to me and whispers into my ear. "It's true. You figured me out. I do like girls. Although I'm not sure about mastering them, because that's freaking impossible."

The hairs inside my ear tingle. I shiver.

"What? Would you prefer that I like boys?" He pulls away.

Exasperated, I turn and look him directly in the eye. "I don't really care who you like!"

"Well, clearly you do, or you wouldn't have brought it up."

His Apple watch buzzes, so he grabs his phone, quickly scanning a text message. I look away. All of a sudden, he slams his hand against the wall in anger. I can't help but turn to look at him and his phone. The message is in Greek, so I have no idea what it says.

"What is it?" I know I shouldn't ask. But how can I not?

"My dad! It's such a load of rubbish. He wants me to work with him tonight, but I promised the basketball team I'd be there later." His head is in his hands. "And the band wanted me to practice with them tonight too." Anger laces his voice now. "He wants me to be just like him. But I won't do it. This is *my* life, not *his*!"

This show of fury seems so atypical for Ever. Not that I know him well yet, but so far, he seems so composed. Except that one time I saw him arguing with his coach.

"Oh no, trouble in paradise, I see," I say quietly, and immediately regret it. Ugh, how condescending. I'm sure my life would be easier if I could just say the right thing when I'm supposed to.

"*What* did you just say?" His anger is now directed at me. But he quickly regains control of himself as if nothing is wrong. This is political prowess at its finest. He should be a politician.

"I guess I can see how you'd come to that conclusion," he says wryly, sighing.

All this banter between us has been so exhilarating that I have totally forgotten about my mission to find my mom. How could I let this happen?

Just the mention of Ever's dad triggers a typhoon of emotion in my body. I am not here to flirt, I'm here for a specific purpose. As endearing as Ever seems now, I haven't tackled the most urgent question with him. I want to scream, *"Where are you holding her?"* But I can't be that bold. I need to be stealthy about it.

"I know a little about feeling like my life is not my own," I say. "You should try moving across the world at a moment's notice to live in a foreign country with a relative you never knew you had before."

He sits silently. Finally, he reaches down to remove the ice packs from my leg and says, "Wow, no bruising at all. You might have gotten lucky on this one." He smiles as he extends his hand out to me. "Here, let me help you up."

He wraps one arm around my neck and the other around my waist. I feel that familiar jolt of raw, pulsing electricity again. The hairs on the back of my neck stand up, and a tingle runs down my spine as he pulls me up to a standing position. It takes everything I have to appear unaffected.

"Ever, where have you been?" Samantha strides into the gym. Her eyes are like evil daggers boring into Ever. "I've been looking everywhere for you!" For a moment, I actually feel sorry for him. I realize how this must look, with his arms still wrapped around me. *Oh, crap.* Her mouth drops open as she sees us together. This can't go well.

His smile is forced as he drops his arms and swiftly steps away from me. "Uh, so…Samantha, this is the new girl who just moved here from California. She injured her leg." He points down and I shift with an exaggerated limp. "Can you tell me how to say your name? Is it Helen?"

It makes me crazy that no one ever seems to be able to pronounce my name. It's not that hard. But I guess here, where English isn't everyone's first language, this should be expected.

"Helene," I say.

"Oh, like Helen of Troy," Samantha counters with a sneer.

I would take this as a complement, but from the look on her face, I know better. "No, Hel-*een*, not Helen."

"So, wow…" she looks me square in the eyes, "Are you wearing contacts? I would change them out if I were you. Purple is pretty passé"

This pushes me over some dark ledge to a breaking point that I didn't know existed. My heart feels like a hammer in my chest as I feel the heat rise in my face. I snap. "They're not purple! My eyes are violet."

Samantha laughs with a loud snort. Ever smiles with her, but the feeling doesn't seem to reach his eyes. Then he surprises us both by whispering to me, "I *like* your eyes."

She socks his arm and then swiftly directs him away from me. "We need to go…*now!*" she says as she leads him out of the gym. Just as they are about to turn the corner, Ever turns his head back towards me and winks, leaving me wonder once again what a guy like him is doing with a girl like her.

Now that I'm alone, the school feels empty, like a ghost town. As I'm still feeling frazzled from my leg injury, I hobble down the lone hallway to my locker, punch in the code, and open it up. My brain feels fuzzy, so I accidentally knock my hand softly against the side of the locker a few times to process all that has just happened. The slow, monotonous beat of my hand with the silver ring rapping against the metal of the locker mesmerizes me, fills me with a sense of calm. But what I see next completely disrupts the reverie and stops my heart.

The smooth twelve-point star symbol that is engraved into the bottom of the middle shelf of my locker is *glowing.*

10 – SECRET ROOM

I look back and forth down the hallway to make sure I'm alone. Then, slowly, tentatively, I lift my finger up to trace the lines that make up the brightly glowing yellow star.

There's a sound like old grinding gears shifting. I jump back, terrified someone will hear this incredibly loud clatter and come out of one of the classrooms. But no one does, and abruptly, the sound dies.

I peer inside the locker again. The whole back side of the locker has opened into a dark passageway. I place my hand inside and feel a cool breeze. A musty smell makes me sneeze. My head follows my hand into the dark space inside my locker, and as I look down, a red light flashes that illuminates the space below. I can see that I am standing at the top of a tunnel that drops off into a deep cavern below. A rusty old ladder hangs just under my feet.

What could be down there? I don't know, but this appears to be the only way down. What if it's a trap designed to terrorize new students? I can just see Bertha, in her hot pink blush, cackling as she watches me from afar on a hidden camera.

But I'm so curious. This mysterious star symbol keeps reappearing. It can't just be a mere coincidence! Is this a message from Mom? It could be a SOS from her. Maybe she's down there!

I look down the hallway once more to make sure that no one is around, then stiffen my resolve and step down onto the ladder. Immediately, the locker door slams shut behind me. It must be an automatic door…or maybe a ghost! My heart beats hard in my chest. I start to panic. What if the locker door won't open again and there's no other way out? I might be trapped here, never to escape. Like being buried alive!

My eyes finally adjust to the dark, which at least brings me some comfort. I breathe in deeply, regain my senses, and reach out to try the door again. It opens easily. Sweet relief courses through my veins. Thank God!

Slowly, I make my way down the tunnel shaft. A cool, musty breeze tickles my face. The rungs of the ladder are dewy. At the bottom, the red light is now distinct and brightly flashing, easily lighting the way for me to see a short hallway made of old weathered cobblestone that ends abruptly at a large, black, wooden doorway. I look around to locate the source of the breeze, and it appears that there is some sort of air shaft above jutting slightly out of the uneven stonework of the walls surrounding me.

The imposing door stands regally in front of me. Is that handprint scanner embedded into the antique wall? I press my palm firmly into the sensor. At first it doesn't work. Then I see the little twelve-point star symbol. Could my ring be some sort of key? I try my hand with the ring on my finger. *Click.* The door opens.

"Hello?" I call out as I step inside.

In front of me is a room filled with a rustic desk and old weathered books, maps, and papers stacked haphazardly across the bookshelves. I know instantly that this is my mom's secret place. *But, where is she?*

It's tiny, maybe a ten-foot square box, like a small office with a skylight high up above in the recesses of a vast cobblestone ceiling. The walls are covered with maps, newspaper articles, and mug shots of various people...and surprisingly, everything is in English, not Greek. One newspaper headline catches my eye:

Black markets consume over 50% of workforce in Athens. Is this the end of the end?

Another has a photo of a fifty-something-looking attractive man with black hair and a close-cropped beard. The description below the photo reads, *"Georgios Sarantos, CEO of Sarantos Enterprises and Billionaire Tycoon."*

This must be Ever's dad. Although father and son both are physically striking, his dad looks nothing like Ever. There's a date at the bottom of the photo: April 6, 1971. Something isn't right here. Sarantos looks like he's maybe fifty years old in this picture, which means he would be in his nineties now. Seems too old to be Ever's dad. Doesn't make sense. Nonetheless, this photo is significant for me. While I had a hunch that Sarantos was the key to finding Mom before, seeing this photo here solidifies it for me. I need to talk to this guy.

The wall is covered with images of structures that appear to be in the desert, like somewhere in the Sahara or Tunisia. One image catches my eye. It's an enormous glass pyramid whose mirrors on its vast surface reflect the image of a setting red sun. I draw in a breath as I realize that this is the same pyramid from my dreams.

What was my mother into?

I look down at my silver ring and shiver as I recall the creepy, sickly looking man with see-through skin who gave it to me in the Metro station. It was like he had some horrible disease that had sucked the life from him.

Something's gleaming on the desk in front of me. It looks like the strange, antique-looking iPad from before, the one that was in Janus's safe, but now it's safely secured inside of a petite glass box. I tap the side of the box and jump back in shock when the device lights up. A word appears on the screen: INITIALIZE.

What have I done? Could this be a bomb? I slowly lift my finger and point at the box with my index finger. *Zap!* A puff of air and a very faint, barely audible bolt of…electricity…has just flown out of my finger to the glass. The next moment, I hear a *click*, and the box opens. The device sits there within my reach. As I reach out to touch its cool metal façade, I feel compelled to pick it up…so I do. Immediately, the device completely dies, and the screen goes blank.

I look at my watch. Siesta is almost over, so I'd better get out of here. Not sure what to do, I shove the device into the back pocket of my backpack.

I shut the big wooden door, climb up the rungs of the ladder, and slowly open the locker door back into the now-darkened school hallway.

For the rest of the afternoon, I don't speak to anyone. I feel paranoid that somehow someone will know about the locker or the device, but no one even acts suspicious. Later that evening, I avoid eye contact on the Metro. I just want to get home.

The bruise on my back from fencing still hurts, as does my ankle, but this discomfort is nothing compared to the overpowering exhaustion I feel from everything that has happened. What a crazy first day of school! When I reach Janus's front door and look in my back pack for the key, I feel the cold hard metal of the iPad device. I'd better be careful with this. Since Janus had it in his safe before, he'll wonder where I got it.

That's when I see a little market on the corner. Maybe I can distract Janus from noticing that anything is off about me if I surprise him by making dinner! It would be my first Greek meal. Of course, this means I'd have to cook something besides Kraft mac and cheese.

When I go inside, I immediately regret it. The woman behind the counter only speaks Greek, so I try using hand signals to communicate. Considering I don't want to talk to anyone right now, this is torture. Finally, she throws her arms up in frustration and hands me an English cookbook. I open the book, point to whatever recipe it opens to, and she scurries off to get the ingredients.

By the time I finally make it back to Janus' place, my arms are so weak that one of the bags falls out of my grip, the contents spilling out all around me on the ground.

"For God's sake, can I get a break?!" I scream out loud.

That's when I hear footsteps behind me. My pulse quickens instantly. I don't think I can handle any more drama today. Whoever it is needs to go away. Leave me alone!

I whip around. It's Nick, my hot new friend from the Metro. He's standing there, hands behind his back, with a warm smile on his face.

"Nick...?" I stammer in surprise.

"Hey" he says as he extends one hand out. He's holding a bundle of fresh daisies, probably hand-picked from someone's garden.

"Wow," I reply. This is a surprise. "How very sweet!"

Of course, he could have handed me dead flowers and I'd be happy about it.

"Yeah," he says coyly. Is he nervous? He seems stiff, too formal. But then I find out why.

"I thought maybe…if you're free on Sunday night…that, well…maybe you would want to go out with me," he stammers, as if it were the most difficult thing he'd ever said to anyone. But then, he continues in his best tour guide voice, "I want to show you the Temple of Poseidon in Sounio. You can't get there on the Metro…and it's not every day that you get a professional guide who's willing to provide a private tour for free."

I stand there in silence, taking in his gray-green eyes for a moment. He could have asked me to go visit his sick aunt in the hospital; I was sold the minute he opened his mouth.

"Sunday, huh?" I ask hesitantly. "I don't know. I might have something important to do…like homework."

"What? You'd rather do homework than go out with me?" he asks incredulously.

I grin. "It's really *interesting* homework."

He frowns, staring down at the ground now. I guess he didn't see me smiling.

"So, okay…yes, that sounds nice," I say coyly, breaking the silence.

Nick lets out a breath, as if he had been storing it up for an hour inside his lungs. Then he starts to pull out a cigarette. I wrinkle my nose and he quickly puts it away. I'm relieved to see his usual feisty personality return when he says, "Oh yeah, I forgot how much the California girl hates smoke. I guess it is bad for my health."

"Thanks," I say, "but that's not why I don't like it. I mean, I don't want to die of lung cancer or anything, but what really bothers me is the stink breath."

"Stink breath?"

"Yeah, when you get too close to me, your breath stinks…and it's *gross*, so, like, the thought of kissing a boy who smokes is the worst for me. I mean, how does a boy who smokes go about kissing a girl who doesn't? You must have to carry around some sort of breath freshener or something." I just let it all spill out. "Or maybe you don't go out with the girls who don't smoke. That's probably more like it."

He grows quiet for a few paces. Finally, he whispers, "Wow, thanks. It really makes me feel great about myself."

Okay, now I feel like a complete jerk. I have no idea where my sudden brashness came from. I guess I needed to get it off my chest. Nick frowns, staring at the ground. I'm sure that he's going to take back his daisies and leave, but his mood quickly shifts and he seems upbeat again.

The next moment, he reaches over, grabs my hand, and pulls me in close to him. I swallow hard as a flutter of excitement travels up my spine. Is he going to kiss me, like for real? As he moves in towards my lips, I'm shocked when he skips over them to my cheeks, first kissing one and then the other. I remember now that Greek people do this in greeting or farewell with each other. I must look confused. He lifts an eyebrow and laughs.

"You just thought I was going to kiss you, like for real, didn't you?"

I shake my head in embarrassment.

"I guess my stink breath doesn't bother you as much as you thought." He smirks, shaking his head as he roars with laughter, holding his hand up. "Oh, now that is funny!"

As he starts to walk away, he yells over his shoulder to me with an eager grin, "See you on Sunday!" Then it dawns on me, hitting me hard like a brick…

Nick just asked me out, like, on a *real* date.

11 – GREEK MOTHER

Oh my god. I've only been in Greece for two days and already have a date with a Greek guy! Not just any guy either. A hot, sweet Greek guy. I really wish my mom were here right now so I could tell her, although I know exactly what she would say. Whenever I went out the first time with any boy, her usual paranoia would kick in and she'd immediately jump into the whole 'talk' about condoms and safe sex, then ask if I took my birth control. Like she thinks I'm going to jump into bed with every guy on the first date!

This is totally crazy! Why? It's not like I'm a prude, but I might technically still be a virgin. When I was a sophomore, right after I injured my ankle and couldn't dance anymore, I had a lot more time to hang out after school. That's when I went out with that stoner guy, Thad Williams. He was a bit of a rebel, but underneath that tough-guy image, Thad could be really charming. He fixed things for me and my mom around the house. He said I had a way of putting him at ease, like he felt he could be himself with me.

We went out for at least three months, so yeah, naturally, we fooled around. One night, we were hanging out with a group of kids from school out at a bonfire on a friend's farm. Thad and I had some beer, then we sneaked off to star gaze on the grass behind a large tractor. It was chilly, so we laid out a blanket. I knew what was coming next, and thought I was ready for it.

We were making out hot and heavy. He was so eager to open the condom that it ripped. "Oh crap! I'm so sorry. This sucks!" He was frustrated with himself. "And I don't have another one here. I have one in my truck. Do you mind if I go really quick and get it?"

By the time he came back, the mood for me was ruined. He was trying to be cool, but I think he was nervous too. It just got so weird, but then he had his moment, and it was over. He seemed happy, but here's the thing: there wasn't any blood. I didn't feel any pain. It's like nothing happened for me. I think he must have had too much beer, because I don't think we did it.

A few days later at school, I told him the truth about this. He insisted that I was the one who had too much beer. Of course, we did it! After that, it went from bad to worse for us. Eventually, we stopped talking altogether. It was so dumb. My mom was wondering what happened, especially when she needed Thad to move some heavy boxes for her. I told her the truth, which she was relieved to hear, but I think on some level, she missed Thad's company. After all this, I kind of gave up on guys for a while and became more interested in school. At least until now.

Here I am in Greece, on the other side of the world from the life I had in California, and something about Nick's sweet-yet-rebellious attitude reminds me of Thad. This is unsettling for me. My mind starts to spin wildly on this train of thought. I need to talk about this with someone – and not Janus - so I call Vani. Although we just met, she puts me at ease. I feel like we've known each other for a long time, so I decide to confide in her about Nick.

"Oh my God!" She sounds incredulous. "I love Nick! He used to go to our school. He's adorable."

I explain how we met and that he's my neighbor. "I think he asked me out, but I'm not sure," I tell her.

"Oh?" she asks, a little surprised.

"Well," I say, "he's a little hard to read."

"About a year ago, Nick's heart was broken...more like shredded. Who knows what he's thinking now?"

I resolve not to get too excited. My nerves are already so frazzled that I'm not sure I can talk straight, so I try not to think much more about it as the week wears on.

Sunday night finally arrives. I try to act super cool, but my confidence disappears the moment I see Nick.

He's dressed casually, in a white button-down shirt and worn jeans, his blond hair tousled with gel. His bronzed skin makes his gray-green eyes stand out in an ethereal way.

But he's on his motorcycle. My mother hates motorcycles. Presumably someone she knew was in an accident or injured somehow. She would never tell me. While she never explicitly said not to ride on one, I knew not to.

Of course, tonight, I'm so enamored with Nick's arm muscles and the tattoo peeking out of his shirtsleeve that somehow this feels different, so I eagerly say yes. I just go for it. *Sorry, Mom*!

We're about to take off when Nick looks around, flustered as if he forgot something important. "Oh, crap. I forgot my helmet! I need to run up to my place to get it. Wanna come?"

I must have a strange look on my face because he laughs. "My mom is there! Since we're neighbors, you should meet her. She will love to hear all about the girl who lives next door with the crazy old medicine man."

Only a helmet for him? What about me? I guess I'm used to the helmet laws in California. "Uh Nick, I'm not sure I want to ride a motorcycle for the first time ever without a helmet…"

His smile is wide as he starts to chuckle, "Oh, that's funny! The helmet isn't for me. It's for you!"

"Oh, then what are you…" I start, but I completely forget my train of thought when he takes my hand.

"Let's go. My house is this way," he says as he leads me over to the front door of his building and up the stairs. At the top of the first floor, he abruptly stops and begins to remove his little gold hoop earring and explains, "My mom would die if she saw this, so I have to always remember to remove it before I get home…or suffer her wrath."

I smile. "But doesn't she see the hole in your ear? It's visible from here."

"No. Well, if she does, she ignores it. Almost all my cousins have an earring, so we all play this game with our parents," he says. He smooths out his hair, then asks, "How do I look?"

I'm thinking of how to say *gorgeous* without saying it, so I settle on "great."

We step inside the apartment. The tiny living room is tastefully decorated, like something you would see inside any house in the US, except for the back wall, which is packed floor to ceiling with used furniture. The stench of cigarette smoke coats the air in the room. Someone needs to open a window.

Nearby, a forty-something, petite woman with blond highlights, too much makeup, and tired green eyes is scurrying around the kitchen, fussing over food. Quickly, I discover the source of the smoke in the room when I spy her recently consumed cigarette smoldering in the sink. Like mother, like son.

"Hey, Ma!" Nick yells over to her as she struggles with a hot baking pan that she's trying to remove from the oven. Smells like dessert. He grabs his motorcycle helmet, placing it firmly under his arm. "I'm just getting my helmet. We're headed out."

"Nikolae, don't tell me you won't be here tonight! Your aunts and uncles will be here soon for Lydia's name day party. You should be here! And by the way, where is your sister? Weren't you just for coffee with her and her friends? And why are we speaking English?"

Then, when she sees me, her face falls flat. "Oh. Who's this?"

"Oh, Mama, this is Helene." His mom watches me carefully. She doesn't like me. Nick must notice the awkward pause between us as he explains, "She's our neighbor. She just moved in next door with the crazy old man Janus. Remember, I told you about her and you said to bring her by sometime."

Relief sweeps over her face as she rushes over. "Ahh, our neighbor! Helen, did you say?"

"Hel-een," I correct her.

"So nice to meet you, Heleen-a. You'll have to come over another time when things here aren't so hectic." She's trying to be nice, but for some reason, this is difficult for her. She sweeps away, bustling back into the kitchen.

"Lydia?" I ask innocently as I turn towards Nick.

"My sister," he explains simply as he points over to a photo of a smiling young girl with short, curly black hair and dark eyes.

"Name day for Greeks is like a birthday, but it's even more

important. Everyone's name has a particular date assigned to it, like today, March 27, which is the name day every year for all girls named Lydia. This is a big deal because all of the girls in a Greek family with the name Lydia will celebrate together on this day."

Nick's mom yells out loudly in Greek. Nick fires back at her, also in Greek. His expression is rigid with displeasure.

They stare each other down in a silent stalemate. His mom nods sternly at Nick. Nick, with both arms crossed over his chest, nods back. After a long moment, she sighs loudly, raising her eyebrow at him. This must be some sort of secret code because Nick swiftly takes my arm and leads me out of the apartment, down the stairs, and outside to the sidewalk. The whole time, he's apologetic, trying to make me feel better.

"Your mother doesn't like me," I say.

"That's not true!" he exclaims. A moment later, though, he says, "It's not that she doesn't like you. She doesn't like any girl who isn't Greek for me."

"What?" I ask.

"My parents are very traditional. If I even breathe a word to a non-Greek girl, my mom starts ruminating about this maybe being the one, the girl I'm going to marry. She kind of freaks out about it. But times have changed. People our age are much more open-minded, especially in bigger cities like Athens. Anyway, it's okay to date someone casually without it automatically leading to happily ever after."

Wait, is he talking about marriage…already? I mean, we've only just met! Seems a little soon. I know the culture is different here, but there's no way I'm going to think, speak, or hear about weddings at my age.

Also concerning, he just said he would never marry a girl who isn't Greek. Not that I should care, since I'm not even his girlfriend. More importantly, I have some pretty heavy stuff going on in my life right now. But what if I do want to date him? What then? We pause in front of Janus's shop, leaning side by side against the outside wall. Our arms almost touch as we look out into the street.

Next to us is Nick's motorcycle. I run my fingers along the length of the bike in admiration. It looks expensive. He must notice because he says, "It's the one thing that I wasn't willing to give up."

"Oh," I say, trying to act casual, "what do you mean?"

He shrugs, quickly changing the subject when he asks, "Do you know anything about Sounio or the Temple of Poseidon?"

Since I love mythology and history, of course I know something about them! But mostly, I love the sound of his voice when he goes into tour guide mode, so I pretend that I don't know very much.

Just as I'm sure he's going to tell me something of interest about this place, he surprises me with, "Good. You will be *amazed* by what I show you. I can guarantee that."

12 – TEMPLE OF POSEIDON

What could that mean? While I'm sure that the Temple of Poseidon is impressive, I can't imagine that I will be *that* amazed. But he did just entice my curiosity.

"Time to go," he says as he hands me his helmet.

"Where's yours?" I ask, even more curious than before.

He mounts the motorcycle and replies in a gruff voice, "It's a long story. Tell you later?"

He's already revving up his motorcycle, so we can barely hear each other talk. I sense that there's a lot involved in that story, so I decide to drop it for now. I shrug and jump on behind him, wrapping my arms around his firm torso. Almost immediately, I'm both terrified and exhilarated by this. I'm riding on a motorcycle! I can only imagine what Mom would say right now.

Athens is vibrant this evening. The oncoming night is warm and humid as the breeze tickles my skin, making me feel so full of life. My hands hold Nick close around his chest and there, under his thin white flowing shirt, I sense his heart beating strongly, steadily, which fills me with calm. This guy could ruin me if I let him. But that's not going to happen. I try to tell myself that we're just two friends going out for some fun.

We drive down a long stretch of Poseidonos Avenue with the beach and coast on our right. Seagulls fly overhead as if to follow hot on our trail, spying on us from their vantage point high above us. The highway slowly narrows to a meandering road through the Athens Riviera. I see a sign that reads "Vouliagmeni." When we stop at a light, Nick points over to the grand Mediterranean homes with barrel tile roofs gracing the sides of the parkway, explaining that many Greek celebrities and wealthy vacationers live here.

I can smell the decadent aroma of slow-roasted fish. We pass through the Greek countryside, a blur of lush green trees and plants interspersed with flowers in red, gold, and bright pink. The turquoise sea strokes the shore with lapping waves in front of umbrellas and beach chairs.

As Nick takes off from the light, the wind grows stronger, and the road narrows even further. Here, the vegetation grows sparse and rocky, and while the area appears abandoned and desolate, it is also hauntingly beautiful as the sun gradually sinks down into the horizon beyond it. The blue sky above the mountains begins to darken, slowly and surely, and we continue onward, wind licking our faces as the moon starts to show its glorious face. I feel so alive here, my arms wrapped around Nick, his warmth a contrast to the vigor of the strengthening wind.

Finally, the bike slows to a stop at the top of a hill, and there, slightly lit up but still in the distance in front of us, is the Temple of Poseidon. Nick stows my helmet and grabs my hand firmly, leading me up the path, past the gift shop, bathrooms, and café, which are all closed now, and up to the hill where the ruins lie.

"Where is everyone?" I ask him.

"Well, technically, it's closed for the night," he says. "Shhh…look." He motions silently to where a guard is slumped over his chair, snoring in a deep slumber.

"So, we're breaking and entering at a historic site?" I ask.

"Something like that."

"But can't you lose your tourist leader license?"

"Probably," he says, "but I come up here at night all the time, and it's rare that anyone is here during this time of year. Once the summer is here, though, that will be a different story."

"You're such a rebel," I say, smiling. God, I *love* this about him.

He scales the fence, then grabs my hand to help me over to the other side. As we reach the crest of the hill, I am absolutely stunned by the sight in front of me. A gigantic harvest moon provides the perfect backlight for the incredible grandeur of the Temple of Poseidon. The weathered white marble pillars appear to shoot out of the ground as if it's on fire. Off in the distance, the light dances across soft waves, onto the beaches and over jagged rocky islands jutting out of the sea. It's spectacular.

Nick shares the history of this place. His eyes light up with excitement as he recounts the tale. "Around the fifteenth century BCE, the people of Athens had to pay a blood tax, which was a sacrifice of fourteen young girls and boys to the dreaded Minotaur. Theseus, the son of King Aegeas, enraged by this atrocity, sailed to Crete to kill the Minotaur and end the sacrifice. When he returned from battle, Theseus told his father that he would display a white sail if he killed the beast or a black sail if he did not. When Theseus returned after slaying the Minotaur, he forgot to change his sail to white. King Aegeas, in his overwhelming anguish, jumped from these cliffs in Cape Sounio, killing himself. This is how the Aegean Sea got its name."

I love watching him tell the story. He emanates warmth and kindness. And there's just something so enchanting about how the r's roll off his tongue when he speaks. I swear that I could listen to him all day and never tire. Of course, all his sweetness is oddly juxtaposed with his wild side. He's a nice guy in a bad boy body.

"That's pretty dramatic," I say.

"Yeah, drama is a key component to any great Greek tragedy," he says. His eyes gloss over. "I come here sometimes when I need to get away and think," he says softly. "Go ahead and look around," he says, seeming more than fine to let me venture off on my own while he enjoys a moment of peace to himself. "I can join you in a minute."

I maneuver carefully around to the side of the temple that is closest to the edge of the cliff, which juts dramatically down into the sweeping sea below. A bunch of rocks here look like the perfect place to sit.

Just then, up on the smooth white marble, under the towering pillars highlighted by the giant harvest moon, I see an odd shape in the moonlight: half of a man's head phasing in and out…and then his body flickers on and off, glowing against the darkened sky. A chill runs up my arm.

Even though the whole image of the man is unclear, his face is anxious, as if I've caught him by surprise. A minute of silence passes between us. Finally, the image of the man speaks. "Who…are you?"

And just as quickly as it appeared, the image and sounds vanish, as if they were never there.

I'm so shocked, I can't believe my eyes or my ears. I recognize this ghost from the dream that I had about the gods. This man was the spitting image of one of the three purple-eyed men out in the desert…not the leader, but one of the other two.

Next to me, a lighted sign catches my eye: "Temple of Poseidon." The two gods next in importance after Zeus were his brothers, Hades and Poseidon. So this "ghost" must have been Poseidon.

I pace back and forth. Oddly enough, this ghost wasn't at all what I would have expected if he in fact was a god from the legends of the past. He wasn't at all imposing, aggressive, or larger than life, and from the look of the suit he wore, he could have been someone's dad on his way to the office in this day and age, not five thousand years ago. Whatever the case, I need to ask Nick about this. If it's true that he comes here a lot, then I'll bet he's seen the apparition too.

I make my way back over to where Nick is perched on a rock, staring off into the distance. The glittering lights of a nearby town dance on the surface of his eyes, bringing them to life like a flame flickering in a soft breeze. I stop dead in my tracks. Holy crap, I'm terrified to ask him about this, but he must know something. "Hey, Nick?"

"Yeah?" He looks startled for a moment as I interrupt his concentrated reverie. After a short pause, he smiles sweetly at me, patting the spot on the rock next to him. "Come here," he says. I sit down on the rock, then inch over so we're touching shoulders. He wraps his arm around my shoulder.

"We need to talk," I start, running my hand nervously through my hair. I'm so totally freaked about this, I can't hold it inside anymore. I feel as if I've been holding my breath this whole time. It just flies out of my mouth. "Have you ever noticed anything supernatural up here…like ghosts? Do you believe in that sort of thing?"

His gray-green eyes grow serious, then narrow. "Uh...no." He rolls his eyes as if he's irritated by my ignorance. "Anything that isn't verifiable by science is a load of crap."

"What?" I ask incredulously. His reaction seems so extreme. I didn't expect such vehement opposition from him and erroneously assumed that he would be more open-minded.

"You heard me," he reaffirms, arms crossed stubbornly in front of him.

I'm not giving up that easily. "Fine, but will you just hear me out on something? Please?" I plead.

He lifts his eyebrow in that same defiant expression that he gave his mother earlier. This is not going well, but I'm not backing down.

"I think I just saw a... ghost up inside the temple," I whisper.

His body tenses up as his eyes widen in disbelief. We stare at each other in silence, when all of a sudden, the tension melts into a smile as a deep, rumbling sound erupts from his chest. He's laughing at me! "Oh, okay, I get it now. You're being metaphorical. Many tourists claim to experience the 'vision' of Poseidon here. It's just the lights playing tricks on your mind. Happens all the time."

My shoulders tense up. While it's entirely possible that it was, in fact, just a trick of the lights, I also know that I saw what I saw. On the other hand, I don't want to ruin this date, or whatever it is, with Nick. Probably best to play it safe, let him feel that he's right this time. "Uh, yeah, probably so," I say.

He must notice my discomfort because he moves in closer to me again. "Don't worry," he says, now so close that I feel the heat emanate from his body. He continues, "You're not crazy. I thought you were going to talk about Ouija boards or something hacked like that."

"Good!" I say, clearly relieved, trying to catch my breath. "Although I have to say that you were right when you said I'd be totally amazed tonight."

He reaches over to take my hand into his. There, as he shifts his wrist to the side, I can't help but stare at the double helix tattoo of Sarantos that I've grown so accustomed to, but something about this symbol concerns me. "Uh, Nick?"

"Yeah?" He smiles sweetly at me.

"You know how you said before that you work for Sarantos Enterprises?" I stammer.

His eyes grow wary again. "Yes?"

"I told you that I hadn't heard of Sarantos before, but the truth is, I know about him now." I say. "And what I don't understand is why you would want to work for someone like that."

"I'll tell you why." His voice is filled with anguish and contempt. "The government marched in with their tax collectors and shut down my dad's business, claiming he owed back taxes. But my dad, he's always been honest. He paid all his taxes. But the tax collectors didn't see it that way. They froze all his assets, destroying his thirty-year-old business. My whole world was turned upside down. We lost *everything*."

"That's awful!" I say. My heart aches for him.

"Yeah," he says with a sigh. "All of the kids in my family had to quit school to go to work because my dad was blacklisted. No one would hire him."

I had no idea that when he talked of not giving up his motorcycle earlier that his situation was this extreme, but he still has not exactly answered my question of why he has to work for Sarantos. "But why Sarantos? Isn't he involved in organized crime?"

Nick looks up at me, incredulous. "Really, that's what you think?" He brushes his hair back from his face. "You don't understand anything! Sarantos runs the black markets. A lot of hardworking people work for cash because they can't live on their income after paying a huge amount of taxes. And because we can't take much money out of the bank, we horde whatever cash we get."

It's a relief to hear that Sarantos isn't completely Satan, especially when I think of Ever. "Yeah, well, I met his wife, who seems really nice. His son, Ever, goes to my school. He seems okay, too…a little full of himself, but I guess Sarantos can't be all bad with a family like that," I say.

At this, Nick drops my hand like a lead weight. "You met Ever?" His gaze grows melancholy. "Of course, you did. Why am I surprised?" He turns to me, voice low and urgent. "You need to know something about Ever. He's bad news. Believe me. That's all I'm going to say about it."

First his extreme reaction to my question about ghosts, and now he's flipping out about Ever. There's more to Nick than I thought. Although this isn't the first time that I have been warned about Ever.

"Okay, fine," I say, holding my hands up in resignation. We sit quietly on the rocks next to the cliff. The seaside towns stretch out across the peninsula far off into the distance. The strain I felt from Nick a moment ago seems to lift. Sitting so high atop the cliff, we spot a patch of soft, shimmering sand on a small, intimate beach below us. Since it's late, no one is out.

"So, you should know that in most parts of Europe, it's safe to take it all off at the beach." He says this in his best matter-of-fact tourist guide voice.

"Really...*everything*?" I stammer, slightly flushed.

He smiles warmly, clearly enjoying my reaction. "Well, no, not *everything*. I mean, you can't take off the bottoms," he chuckles. "We are open here about a lot of things, but not *that* open."

I laugh. "Well, thanks for clearing that up for me, but in America, nice girls don't take off their tops in public."

"In case you didn't notice, you aren't in America anymore. And since you live here, you should embrace our freedom from those silly puritan restrictions." He smirks.

"Oh, really?" The moonlight reflects off his eyes. He doesn't seem to know that he's attractive, which is both rare and charming.

The ride back towards Metaxourgeio is quiet, smooth, and peaceful as I allow my body to melt into the smooth muscles of Nick's back. When we arrive back at our neighborhood, as if out of nowhere he says, "So I've decided to quit smoking."

I guess my "stink breath" tirade must have gotten to him. "What? When?"

Nick turns his head to look at me, a gleam in his eye. "I have my reasons."

"Oh?"

"Well, I don't want to limit my dating prospects to only girls who smoke…and I *definitely* don't want anyone thinking that I have stink breath."

"Oh God! I feel like a jerk for making you feel bad about that the other day. I'm not sure what got into me," I say in apology.

"It's fine," He says in a small voice. We stare in silence across the street at the dilapidated building covered with graffiti and a couple of homeless people arguing in Greek over the contents of a withered paper sack. I like the comfort of not necessarily having to say something to Nick at every moment. It's rare to find someone with whom silence feels so easy.

"So, I need some motivation to get through the week without smoking," he says, looking off in the distance. "What do you think it should be? Is there something you could do or give up for the week with me, like a dare, maybe?"

I try to think about something that would be terrifying for me to do or to give up, but I feel I've been through so much in this past week that there's nothing left to offer.

"Like Lent?" I ask, joking a bit. But then something he said a moment ago brings a thought to mind. About my 'silly puritan restrictions'. There's something liberating about being in a foreign country where the rules in the United States don't apply. Suddenly, I'm dying to try something new…and *forbidden.* "I'll go topless at the beach," I declare.

Is the rebel in Nick somehow bringing out some sort of inner vixen in me? Or perhaps the fact that my mother is missing and the Syndicate is after me is suddenly making me delirious, contemplating things I would never have dreamt of doing before, not in a million years?

"What? No…wait…" he shakes his head, but I cut him off.

"Yeah, if you quit smoking for five days straight, I'll do it." I say. I think we're both a bit startled by my sudden boldness.

"I don't know…" he says, running his hand nervously through his hair. "What I said before was…"

"What? I thought this was 'normal' here?" I challenge him.

"Well that's not exactly what…" he's trying to back pedal on what he said before. Where did his confidence go? But then, his eyes light up in defiance. "Okay, fine."

"Fine what?" I ask, goading him.

"Fine, it's a deal," he declares, now completely sure of himself.

He agreed to that way too easily. That's when it hits me what I just committed to. He's going to see me half-naked! Of course, this is what he must have wanted all along. No wonder he conceded to the dare so fast.

"You tricked me into offering this!" I say. "Somehow, you planted the idea in my head, and…"

"No, I did not!" he seems affronted. "You had the idea!"

It's true. He's right. Somehow, I have boxed myself into this silly dare. But I'm not one to back out of anything. What am I afraid of any way? This is something that is normal in Europe! The only reason it's a big deal is that it is new for me. Maybe I can do it under certain conditions. "Fine, it's a dare…," I declare, "but only if I do it at night when no one can see me."

"Fair enough," he seems a little surprised, but also relieved, like he doesn't want another confrontation with me. "It's settled then. We have a deal."

13 – CLARKE'S THIRD LAW

It's getting late. Even though there were plenty of opportunities for Nick to make a move, he hasn't yet, so I'm feeling a bit confused about his intentions with me. Back at his apartment, he was talking about marriage, and now…nothing?

"Hey…" his voice is soft like velvet, as he turns towards me. "What are you thinking about?"

"Uh, nothing…"

"You sure?" he says as he wraps his arms around my waist, drawing me in so close that we're staring at each other's lips. It takes my breath away. Everything around us seems to freeze, suspending time. My heart quickens in anticipation of what is coming next. He's moving in closer…then closer…then…

Stink breath. I step backward.

Nick's face falls and grows red. He throws his hands up in exasperation. "You've got to be kidding me! I brushed my teeth like five times!" He frowns, brow furrowed in frustration.

I nod silently, not knowing what to say, feeling horribly guilty. I just so totally ruined the moment, screwed up big time.

His frown deepens as he stares at the ground. "Uh, I should get going."

This is bad. I've got to do or say something quick to salvage this.

"Hey," I stammer, "I didn't—"

He cuts me off, his eyes cool and indifferent. "No, it's fine. Besides, I wasn't actually going to…." But he doesn't finish. He looks out to the street and steps away.

I touch his arm and offer, "Wait…since you showed me where you live before, maybe you should come upstairs to my place?"

He regards me carefully. "It's really getting—"

I cut him off. "But you could meet my crazy godfather." I give him a genuine smile. "I know you want to."

He doesn't budge. I'm sure he's going to say no, but then as his eyes greet mine, a cautious smile slowly forms as he says, "Uh, okay."

I sigh. Crisis averted, at least for now.

As I lead him inside the dark shop and up the stairs to the apartment, I'm counting on Janus being asleep by now. But as we enter the apartment, not only is Janus wide awake, he's sitting at the kitchen table, snorting some sort of white powdery substance up his nose.

Is that *cocaine*?! Seriously?

I try to reconcile Janus's obsessive health-crazed habits with this sight in front of me. At least this might explain some of his bizarre mood swings, but with all his preaching about health and wellness, what a hypocrite!

Nick raises an eyebrow as he takes in the scene. I shake my head at him with a look that says I will explain this later. God only knows what he's thinking now. Of course, I have no idea how to explain it. Maybe "My godfather is a cokehead"? This night is turning out to be a total disaster.

Janus unapologetically wipes his nose. Instead of being defensive, embarrassed, apologetic, or demonstrating any sort of reaction, he acts like snorting drugs is a normal part of life for him. As I start to ask about it, his eyes grow wild, and he turns the tables on me.. "I told you…no boys allowed here!!"

Nick's face falls. This isn't going to be a friendly introduction. He starts to back away towards the open doorway and surprises me with a knowing look. "Consider us even now. My mom is totally nuts too. You saw that." He grins. "I'm looking forward to our dare. See you in five days…next Friday! I'm counting on you!"

My eyes widen. The Dare. I forgot all about it. Five days seems so far away considering all that has happened to me in the past two! For now, I'm just psyched that Nick wants to see me again after the stink breath almost-kiss.

He barely makes it out into the hallway when Janus grows irate, yelling at the top of his lungs, "You need to get out…*now!*"

He slams the door in Nick's face with a violent thud.

Just because Janus is a drug addict does not mean that he can treat people badly, especially not my friends. "Hey!" I scream. "Nick's not just any boy; he's our neighbor! He was coming up here because he wanted to meet you. Do you have to be so awful to everyone?"

"I'm not awful to *everyone*." Janus straightens his head scarf, suddenly appearing calm and serene, like Oprah. "Obviously, you haven't attended one of my yoga classes yet, or you would know that." It drives me crazy that he can shift his mood on a dime like that. I literally never know which side of Janus I'm going to see.

"I was pleasantly surprised to come in tonight to see that you went grocery shopping." His expression is easy, almost smiling, if that's even possible. "And what's this?" He picks up a book in his hand. "It looks like you bought a Greek cookbook?"

I forgot all about my shopping adventure the other day.

I was going to make Janus dinner! Was trying to distract him about the iPad device. No need for that now, but it might be good for me to cook something before the food goes bad. Even though it's late now, I can hear my stomach grumbling. During my date with Nick, we forgot to eat! I grab the cookbook out of Janus's trembling hand.

His mood makes a sudden, dramatic shift again as his eyes narrow in suspicion. "But here's what doesn't quite compute for me, Helene. Where did you get the money to buy this stuff?" His voice grows harsh and stern. "You broke into my safe, didn't you?"

I wanted to do something nice for him, and this is how he acts? Unbelievable! I'm not about to let him treat me like this, so I try to ignore him. I leaf through the cookbook, to the page marked with the recipe I selected when I was at the corner market, and am pleasantly surprised that it only takes a few minutes to prepare. The recipe reads, "seared *glossa ntakos*." It's a white, flat fish with chopped tomatoes and onions served over barley rusks. I start to busy myself by pulling the ingredients out onto the countertop.

"You didn't answer my question!" Still mute, I unwrap the fresh fish, not making eye contract. He grabs my arm. "I expect you to pay attention when I'm talking to you!"

This sets me off. As the queen of confrontation, I've never been good at ignoring anyone, ever. I lose it entirely as I wrench my arm out of Janus's fierce grip, raising my voice to him. "I was trying to make you dinner, to do something nice for you for once!" My eyes grow wide, upset. "You wanna know how I got the money?" I challenge him. "That attorney, Harold Avery, left me some money in the pocket of my backpack. It was only a little bit, but it's certainly more than you've ever given me!"

The frantic chaos that consumes Janus's eyes suddenly fades out, and now I see something I didn't think possible...he looks *sorry*. He holds his hands up. "Look, I..." his eyes fill with compassion. "I'm just not used to anyone ever doing anything for me. In all of my years living here, no one, not even your mother, has made dinner for me. I guess I have a hard time seeing the good in people, always assuming the worst."

This is a shock. I can't imagine that my mother would not want to cook for Janus. She made me food all the time. While this doesn't add up for me, something in Janus's pained expression makes my heart reach out to him. I want to believe everything he says. My face softens as I offer, "Well, okay. Look, why don't you let me cook for you?"

Janus softens into a little boy. It's unexpected, quite disconcerting. I continue with a disclaimer. "I have to warn you, though; this is my first time attempting Greek cuisine, so I'm not sure how it will turn out. Usually, I only know how to boil water or use the microwave."

We both chuckle for a moment; then he studies the recipe. After a moment, when he speaks, his voice is encouraging. "Incidentally, I haven't eaten yet, so I'm rather looking forward to it."

The fish has been thawing. I unwrap it, set it aside, and start chopping tomatoes. Janus says, "So here's the deal. I haven't seen your mother in twenty-one years. From what I recall, Diana didn't have a uterus, so I'm not sure how you came about." He quirks an eyebrow at me. "Adoption?"

I shake my head.

"Immaculate conception?"

I laugh. "No, silly, I'm the product of in-vitro fertilization, with assistance from a sperm donor and a surrogate."

"Oh yes, silly me, of course I should have guessed that," he says with an edge. "Well, that's a real mouthful. Your mother told you all about it, then?" He is incredulous.

I nod enthusiastically. "Well, yes. She was a firm believer in telling the truth, no matter what."

He nods as if he agrees with me, but his eyes betray him, like perhaps he knows something that I don't. Maybe she didn't tell me everything.

A thought suddenly crosses my mind. "Janus, it was nice of you to just go along with the godfather story for my benefit. But *why* would you do that for me?"

"Oh, I'm not doing it for you," he says wistfully. "Diana was very…special. I would do anything that she asked of me."

"Oh," I say. He told me before that they weren't romantic, and I've just heard that she never cooked for him when she lived here. Weird. "So just how special was my mom to you, then?" I try my best at a joke. "I saw your book about tantric sex, you know. What exactly is that?"

"That is my private business!" he says tersely.

Oh no, now he's going to get all worked up again. I try to keep my expression neutral, but suddenly I feel the burning urge to crack up and laugh hard. I fight this impulse for as long as I can, but then I can't hold it any longer, so I burst out in loud obnoxious laughter right in his face.

"You're making fun of me, you smug brat!" He looks spurned, as I've clearly caught him on a sensitive topic.

Suddenly, Bastet leaps up onto Janus's lap, tail curved up behind her, twitching directly into his face. He yelps and grabs the cat around her torso and tosses her down on the floor. "Damn cat!"

I see the amber cat's-eye stone on the front of Bastet's collar. Janus continues on and on about how the cat is such a bother. She's always mocking him. But then, the cat's-eye stone starts to glow. I squeeze my eyes shut. When I open them again, the stone looks normal. What is going on here?

This makes me recall something even more disturbing: the ghost of Poseidon. I know that Nick said it was just my mind playing tricks on me, but it still felt incredibly real to me. "Janus, do you believe in ghosts?"

He stops admonishing the poor cat. Bastet's expression is one of relief, as if she understood exactly what he was saying that whole time. Not possible, of course. "No...well..." he starts, but he's suddenly deep in thought as he uncharacteristically weighs his next words carefully. "Why do you ask?"

"I think I saw one tonight," I whisper.

"Where?" Janus asks, although he doesn't seem surprised in the least.

"At the Temple of Poseidon," I say as I finish simmering the fish, setting it aside on the stove. Next, I begin to set the food on the plates. "I thought I was going insane. Nick told me that it was just the light playing tricks on me."

Janus frowns. "So, you were on a date with him. I knew it!!" But then, his eyes soften, crinkling around the edges. "No, really, I don't think you're crazy. But also, I don't think you can just blame it on the light either. Many things are not what they seem."

He seems to use that expression a lot, and it's starting to get on my nerves. Why doesn't he just say what he means? Not only did he not answer my question, but he just raised more for me.

He continues, "Have you ever heard of Clarke's Third Law?"

I shake my head.

"Futurist and writer Sir Arthur C. Clarke says, 'Any sufficiently advanced technology is indistinguishable from magic.' I believe this explains most supernatural phenomena."

"But how...?" I start to say, but then stop short when I notice that one of the terry cloth wristbands that Janus always wears has fallen down his arm. On his wrist in plain sight is the double helix DNA snakes tattoo.

"No," I stammer, taking a step backward in panic. Suddenly, I feel faint, like I need to sit down. I turn the knobs on the stove to off and then fall onto the seat of the chair. "You…you work for Sarantos!"

Janus twists the band back up and over the tattoo, covering it, then holds his hands up in defense. "Now, wait just a minute…"

"No! You need to tell me what is going on right now!!" I say, my voice growing in intensity. "Is this why I'm in Greece?"

Janus fidgets with his wristband, deep in thought. "As I told you before, the black markets here are very…complicated."

"You mean the *Syndicate*?" I stand up and slam a plate down hard onto the counter.

"You know about the Syndicate?" His expression grows serious, as he sits down on the chair. "OK, fine. Half of Greece works for Sarantos, Helene. There's no way around it. He has his hands in everything, all the way up into the farthest reaches of government here. How do you think I can afford to live in this house? You think my holistic business funds this place? No!"

My mind starts to spin. This makes me wonder what exactly Janus is doing for Sarantos if not the wellness stuff. Dealing drugs? Cocaine? I'm not ready to talk about this now, though. There are much more pressing matters to deal with here.

"But he tried to kill me!" I scream.

"No, Helene. There's no way that was Sarantos. For God's sake, he doesn't *kill* people."

"Who hired that gunman then?"

He shakes his head, not saying anything.

I throw my hands up into the air. "Never mind!"

There's no time for this. What I want is plain and simple. "Where is my mom, Janus?! If you work for Sarantos, then you must know where she is." My eyes fill with tears as I plead, "Just tell me!!"

"The woman you knew as your mom is dead, Helene!" His eyes are wild, yet cold as he utters these horrible, harsh words that cut into my heart, ripping open fresh wounds. "Stop this crazy talk. I know it's hard, but she's gone. Stop looking for her!"

Janus storms out of the room, leaving me torn to pieces. The tears fall hard, streaming down my cheeks as I stare down at my first Greek cooking creation, unable to eat, not even hungry anymore. How could

Janus be so uncaring, so awful to take away all my hope about Mom? Why is he now saying she's dead when before he pledged to look for her? He's lying; that's why. Now that I know he works for Sarantos, I understand exactly why he doesn't want me to look for her.

I reach down to my heart and feel the jagged border of the cypress tree, her pendant, and then the smooth metal of the ring with the twelve-point star, the ring that led me to Mom's secret room. I know she's alive. It's up to me to find her.

As I sit there feeling hopeless, I force myself to take a bite of the fish. Not bad. But then when I look up, something peculiar catches my eye. Up on the wall, hanging in front of Janus's safe, is the black pencil drawing of what looks like one of the Greek goddesses that I noticed before. The goddess is a fiercely beautiful young woman with long, cascading brown hair, eyes dark and defiant, holding a magnificent bow and arrow. But there's something oddly familiar about her. She looks so much like… I shake my head, saying to myself, "No, it can't be." I can't believe what I'm thinking. "My mother."

But what comes next, really makes me pause. My hand-drawn mother's mouth turns up into a smile! But when I look again, her mouth is back to the thin, serious line it was before. I must be hallucinating! Now, as I walk up closer to the picture, I can see the image much more clearly now.

This time, it is obvious. She's winking at me.

14 - THROUGH THE LOOKING GLASS

I jump back in shock, squeezing my eyes shut in panic. This can't be real! Slowly, I crack one eye open at a time and peer out to take another look at the picture. But now Mom is gone. The goddess is back. Not my mother.

My left "logical" brain kicks in, and I realize that I'm probably being a bit dramatic. I inhale…exhale…in and out, then finally calm down enough to think this through a bit more. I've heard that sometimes people who are dealing with extreme grief and loss think they see the person they've lost, so likely, this is my mind trying to cope with my grief. If that's true, is it possible that it's just my imagination that tells me my mother is still alive? Janus may be right. What if Mom really is gone?

My eyes begin to water, fogging up my glasses, as sadness consumes me. I can't think straight. But something is blocking the path under my feet. It's my backpack! I kick it hard. There's something solid in the side pocket. I reach inside.

My insides churn when I see it: the strange iPad from Mom's secret room.

I'm so overwhelmed with anxiety that I slam the iPad hard against the wall, but I don't hear the telltale shatter or crunching sound that should occur with so much impact. When I pick up the iPad to inspect the damage, I find nothing. Not even a scratch.

This iPad must be immensely important to Janus. First, it was locked away in his safe, and then, days later, someone moved it to the secret room under the school, where it was safely protected inside the glass box.

But how, and who moved it? I can't imagine anyone coming through my locker to access the secret room. There must be another entrance.

I need to hide it someplace safe for now, at least until I can return it to the secret room. While I might have returned it to Janus before, now that I know he works for Sarantos, he can't be trusted. I'm not sure why, but I feel strongly that no one can know that I have the iPad. I should protect it at all costs.

I can't think of any place in the apartment where Janus won't find it, though. This is so frustrating! The only thing that is truly mine here is my suitcase, which is shoved under the side table, overflowing with clothes, next to the couch that is my bed. Who knows if Janus will snoop there? I don't know after he rummaged through my things and tossed out my birth control pills on my first day here.

Bastet jumps onto my lap, then springs down on the top of the suitcase, flexing her claws on its side.

"You need a scratching post!" I exclaim.

She seems to enjoy herself as she kneads her claws back and forth, purring loudly. But this joy swiftly shifts to alarm as her claw catches on a seam. When I try to help her, I spot a hidden zipper in the seam of the suitcase that I hadn't seen before. A concealed pocket. The perfect hiding place.

Bastet's claw breaks free. She steps aside, regarding me carefully. It's almost as if she's fully aware of everything and has carefully orchestrated this turn of events. I wrap the iPad in a shirt and shove it inside the hidden pocket. Then I get ready for bed and fall asleep.

A grinding, grating sound wakes me up. I hear Janus's dusty old grandfather clock, slow and steady like a heartbeat. I look up at the clock face, which is backlit to cast an eerie glow and long shadows across the room. Then I see the time. I sigh. It's 3:00 a.m. *Argh*. I hate waking up at this hour because going back to sleep seems impossible. Then, the entire next day, it's like I'm comatose.

The noise is back, so I switch on the lamp. Bastet furiously scratches and claws at the door that leads downstairs, suddenly urgent to go out. While I love Bastet, there are times when having a pet is a chore, and this is one of those times.

I open the door and Bastet darts downstairs to Janus's forbidden shop. I creep down the stairs and almost run smack into an overflowing bin that is filled with faceless handwoven dolls. *Creepy*. I wonder what Janus does with these? Voodoo?

With only the faint light of the street outside shining in through the dusty front windows, I carefully sidestep the bin, only to knock the side of my ankle into some other unseen item on the floor. Where's Bastet?

I hear scratching. There she is! She's worked herself into a frenzy, scratching frantically at a tiny crack at the base of the bookshelf. I point my index finger at the narrow crack in the bookcase.

Zap! A bolt of electricity flies out of my finger, just like when I was in the secret room. The next moment, I hear a *click*, and out pops a quarter-sized tray from the side of the bookcase. I can barely make out anything in the faint light, but when I get close enough, I'm stunned to see the now-familiar symbol of the twelve-point star, identical to the symbol in my locker that led to the secret room under the school. Of course! My ring is the key!

Excited, I stick my ring finger out and press it firmly into the little tray. At first, nothing happens. Then, about ten seconds later, I hear another *click*. The bookcase creaks open. It's a doorway.

"Hello?" I call out and proceed inside. No answer. Thankfully, there is a light switch to my right on the wall, which I flip on. A dimly lit gray stone stairway winds down in front of me, off to some distant place beyond my sight.

I fly down the stairs, Bastet at my heels, padding noiselessly behind me.

At the bottom of the stairs, drab cement walls surround me to form a perfectly square windowless room, maybe twenty-five feet in both length and width, topped with a low-beamed ceiling. The floor looks like it's made of dirt, but then I realize it's cement covered in a fine layer of dust. It's as if no one has been here in a very long time. All the furniture and other items are draped in old white sheets. It looks like a roomful of ghosts.

I yank a musty sheet down from a tall bookcase that stands up against the wall, packed with old, worn, yellowed books. Every book is about Greek mythology. One of my favorite topics! I'm giddy. The titles cover the well-known deities such as Athena, Zeus, and Poseidon, but also some I've never heard of before, such as Epimetheus. I brush the dust off the cover, open it to the first page and read:

"Epimetheus ("hindsight") was the twin brother of Prometheus ("foresight"), a pair of gods called the Titans who acted as patron-gods of mankind. Epimetheus, depicted as foolish and malleable, accepted the gift of Pandora from the gods that unleashed all evils unto the world. Conversely, Prometheus was depicted as clever and defiant, and was sentenced to eternal torture by Zeus for stealing fire for the humans."

In my excitement, I bump up against a large painting hanging on the wall, which I can't see because it's draped in a filthy gray sheet. I take a step back, but a piece of the sheet catches on my hand. It falls swiftly to the floor in one fluid movement, exposing what's underneath.

It's an enormous rectangular mirror. The highly polished marble-framed mirror stretches from the floor almost all the way to the ceiling and is maybe five feet wide. It's not the incredible size that gives me pause, though, but the ornate frame that surrounds it. The glossy marble is edged in a magnificent gold-braided trim embossed in an intricate pattern, reminiscent of ancient craftsmanship. This relic is so elaborate and detailed, it makes the mirror look like a grand antique that must be worth a lot. I'm surprised that Janus hasn't sold it. Perhaps if he peddled all this stuff, he could stop pushing drugs, or whatever he does for Sarantos.

I catch my reflection in the mirror and I'm struck by how ordinary I look. My thick, square glasses so totally overwhelm my face that my violet eyes appear way too small in comparison. My dark brown hair is a little frizzy from sleeping on it. I'm wearing a flowery night shirt that drapes down to the middle of my thighs.

The top of the mirror, where the gold braid decorum seems much more intricate, is inlaid with a gorgeous amber-colored stone. As I try to get a closer look at it, I first stand on my tiptoes, but then I drag over a wooden chair to stand on. The shiny stone feels cool and smooth under my fingers as I trace a stark black line down its amber face. I realize with delight that I've seen something similar recently. "Ah, it's the cat's-eye stone again," I mutter softly to myself.

I'm startled out of my reverie by the sound of pattering little feet. It's Bastet. She strides purposefully forward as her long, lithe body jogs gracefully up to the base of the mirror. Her tail forms a question mark with a twitch at the top as her bright golden eyes greet me eagerly.

"What on earth are you up to this time?" I ask as I step off the chair and scoop her up. She starts purring wildly, rubbing her ear affectionately against my hand.

Just then, the cat's-eye stone at the top of the mirror starts to glow, casting an eerie light throughout the small room. It brightens gradually before erupting into a dazzling blue light. Bastet drops down to the ground with a thump as I step back on the chair with startled amazement. Tentatively, I reach up to touch the glowing blue light, which immediately grows warm to the touch, forcing me to pull my hand away in surprise. Bastet starts pacing back and forth anxiously.

A low humming sound fills the room, and the mirror starts to vibrate. Its face transforms into a brilliant blue sheen that looks like a free-flowing waterfall. Entranced, I touch the shimmering, water-like substance that coats the mirror.

Slowly, my fingers extend forward, attracted as if by a magnet. First my fingers, then my hand pass through, but I feel nothing but pleasant warmth, as if the sun is shining down on me during a bright, cheery day. I can't stop there. I'm consumed with terror as my face passes through the mirror.

Washed-out sands extend up to what look like war-torn ancient ruins. Something like the Parthenon, but out in the desert. What is this place? Wherever this is, it is clear as day to me. I swiftly withdraw my head from the mirror, back into the safety of the room.

"Meeeoooooowww!" It's Bastet at my feet. The cat's-eye stone attached to her collar is glowing brightly. She twitches her tail once as if to tell me something important. The black-tipped end of her tail extends my line of sight back to the top of the mirror, where the stone glows with equal intensity.

"So...*you*...you are doing this?" I exclaim, astounded.

Yes! I hear a voice sing in my head. Wait...did I just hear the cat talk to me?

Bastet leaps past me into this strange new world. "Bastet, wait!!" I yell over the hum, but she doesn't seem to hear me.

I reach steadily through the shimmering surface of the glass. There's no stopping the forward momentum as I'm completely sucked inside. My vision starts to spin out of control as the world around me swirls into a spectacular blur of colors and lights, all racing forward to merge dynamically into the epicenter of a massive vortex.

Darkness swallows me whole.

For a moment, I can't see anything. As my vision starts to come back into focus, everything is blurry. My heart beats furiously. Suddenly, the world in front of me clears, and I take in the image of crumbling ruins half-buried in vast desert sands that surround me.

Oh my god. I've been here before. It's the place from my dreams. My mother's words echo through my mind: *Anything is possible.*

I look around but see no sign of Bastet. My ears pick up a soft shuffling noise to my left. I whip my head around and suck in a breath at the sight in front of me.

An oversized mountain lion, as large as a tiger, is sitting on the sand directly in front of me, staring me down with intense amber eyes. My body feels paralyzed, frozen in place. The giant lion roars, instantly severing the icy stillness between us. I start to shake...violently. I am too terrified to move, so I hold my concentration and continue to stare at the lion.

Suddenly, the lion gets up and saunters closer to my frozen body. He's so close to me that I can smell the large cat's breath on my face. It smells like...wait, is that *cat food* on his breath?

Just as I'm sure that I'm going to be eaten, the massive lion slurps a big sloppy, wet kiss across my face. *Ugh.* My cheek is dripping with saliva, rubbed raw by the lion's enormous tongue, which was rough like sandpaper. Next, he brings his face up under my hand, rubbing back and forth. It's almost as if he wants me to pet him...like a house cat! I allow my hand to fall onto the lion's soft head. He moves his head around in circles on my hand as if with affection, and a low thrumming sound begins. Is this lion *purring*?

I scratch the big cat's ears. More purring, but much louder this time.

I search the lion's startling amber eyes and recognize him as the mountain lion from my dreams. Suddenly, I recall my mother also from the dreams, and hope fills me that maybe she will show up here too.

I scan the big cat's strong body and don't see any male parts there. I whisper, "You're a *lioness*." As I stroke her ear, I feel the cool metal edge of something under my hand...a collar! This cat belongs to someone. But then I recognize this collar. It's the same ancient, bronze finish with the cat's-eye charm embedded in the center that belongs to...

"Bastet, is that you?" I ask incredulously.

The enormous lioness utters a small sound, barely audible, then lifts her tail up, forming the sign of the question mark that I've become so familiar with.

"It *is* you!"

She nudges her head under my hand for another pet. Convinced I'm still in a dream, I just go with it. This is so totally cool!

Now that I know that Bastet is here as a fearsome lioness who can protect me, I'm filled with courage. I decide to explore this strange new land. We're standing in front of an arched gateway in some sort of large open-air structure, perhaps the size of a football field. It looks like the Colosseum in Rome, but rather than being constructed from stone, the building's materials appear to be rusted-out steel, as if this was once a modern building of some type.

The arched gateway, which was the doorway that brought me here, has the same ornate stone inlaid at the top, which now glows a bright blue similar to the stone at the top of the mirror on the other side. The sheet of water hums softly behind it. Sandy dunes cover the floor of the vast room, so we trek across it to the other side to find another arched open-air passage that leads outside.

It's the same vast desert landscape from my dream, but this time, I see the extensive abandoned ruins of an old city. A swift wind whips my hair across my face as I take in the sight.

At one time, this city must have been the size of Manhattan. Jagged remains of rusted-out skyscrapers, now partially engulfed by light brown sand dunes, dot the surface. The skies are filled with what look like dark, menacing clouds, which partially obscure a giant red sun. Angry lightning bolts strike the vast dunes as they disappear into the horizon where an enormous smoking volcano rises out of the sands.

Just outside the entrance to the gateway that we passed through, we come across a rusted sign that is half-buried in the sand. It squeaks back and forth on its hinges in the gusty wind. As the sand blows fiercely in my eyes, I can barely make out a printed word on the sign, but I don't recognize the language. It looks to me like some strange dialect of ancient Greek.

My head starts to throb which makes me wince in confusion and pain. When I open my eyes, the sign now clearly reads, "OLYMPUS." Of course, I've heard of this place. Olympus is the city of the gods.

But this can't be the glorious and ancient city of Olympus! Where are the grand pillars and other hallmarks of traditional Greek architecture? This place looks like the apocalypse hit a modern city maybe a hundred years ago leaving it utterly abandoned and decimated in ruins.

A loud cracking noise comes from beneath me. The earth starts rumbling, shaking violently. Fear passes over the features of my giant lioness. I glance back across the large open-air room to the arched gateway that leads back home. There, the bright blue waterfall starts to shimmer and fade, pulsing and flickering. Bastet's amber eyes meet mine, and I know instantly that we should go back...*now*.

We run full speed towards the flickering blue light. Bastet leaps through the shimmering surface of the gateway. Fear and adrenaline propel me forward as I follow her through to the other side. My world fades to black as my vision is lost. I'm falling…and falling…then nothing.

I'm back in Janus's basement. As I turn to look towards the mirror behind me, the shimmering blue substance shifts and transforms instantly back to solid mirrored glass. The humming sound halts.

Beneath my feet is Bastet, lying sprawled out on the floor in front of the mirror, sleeping soundly as if deep in a dream. There is no sign of the mountain lioness. The room is quiet, as if nothing ever happened.

I touch my face. My glasses have fallen off! I feel around on the ground. When I don't find them, I panic. Now what will I do?

The shiny stone on Bastet's collar catches my eye. It dawns on me that I can see just fine. The room…the mirror…the sleeping cat at my feet…they appear crystal clear to me!

I don't need my glasses anymore.

15 – TRANSFORMATION

I take in the room around me. What was dull and muted before now appears vibrant and bold. The change is more than just the clarity that comes from wearing glasses. Every color and hue looks brilliant and ethereal in a way I never thought possible.

The caution and fear that consumed me before seems so very far away, like a distant memory. As if someone else had been living my life for me.

My body is stiff and sore, as if someone has beaten me all over with a large bat. Every muscle in my body cries out in agony as I crouch on my knees and try to stand up. I have no idea how I can go to school today like this; the pain is almost unbearable. If it weren't for my pristine eyesight and renewed zest for life, I would be seriously worried about myself right now.

Bastet jumps up and nuzzles my knees, so now I have no choice but to stand up. Painstakingly, I get up and slowly turn around. I glance at myself in the mirror for a split second, sure that I must look as horrible as feel.

"Wait…what?" I stop and look at the person in the mirror staring back at me. Without my glasses, my violet eyes look much larger and more vibrant. My lashes are long and curly. My face has always been blemished and scarred from old breakouts, but now, all the scars are gone. My skin looks so clear and luminous that I can't even see any pores. In fact, my whole body appears visibly darker with a rich tan, smooth as honey.

There are other changes as well. My jeans are now too short, as if I've grown an inch or two, and they're loose around the waist. The material of my shirt drapes over my body, accentuating my curves. It's not like I'm super skinny now, but I flex my bicep and am pleasantly surprised to see a sculpted, lean muscle there. I feel strong and fit, like I could really kick some ass.

My hair is a lush and shiny rich chocolate brown, which hangs long and straight almost down to my waist. *Who is this person in the mirror?* Honestly, I kind of miss the freckles on my nose and can't believe my pierced ears have closed up, but I won't complain too much about it!

"How is this possible?" I wonder.

Since there is no way the deserted city of Olympus could be real, I must still be inside my dream. I'm probably upstairs resting on the couch, and the mirror and the basement are part of the dream. In the morning, I'm sure I'll wake up and it will be as if none of this ever happened.

I'm suddenly startled out of my thoughts when I hear a noise. *Croak!* Bastet's eyes grow wide and her ears perk up as the sound transforms to a squeak and then a low groan. I hear footsteps, like someone is coming down the stairs. It must be Janus! What am I going to do? I look around the room. There's no place to hide.

It's clear now that I can't confide in Janus about anything. He's been lying to me, feeding me only bits and pieces of information when it suits his needs. I can't trust him.

I shudder when I think of what he will do to me if he finds me down here. My heart thumps hard in my chest as I recall the overzealous fire that so totally consumed Janus when he told me that his shop was off limits. It was as if he was possessed. I have to get out of here!

Thump...pause....*thump*...pause... My whole body tenses up.

The sound stops. I'm afraid to move, paralyzed in fear, but the next sound is much further away, like it's the croaking floorboards of the room upstairs. Bastet's expression tells me that all is okay. Her ears and face completely relax, and she starts to lick her paws. I sigh in relief as I realize that no one is coming.

Now what? It's obvious that someone is walking around in the room above us. Somehow, I've got to get out of here undetected. Slowly but surely, Bastet and I creep up the steps, careful not to make any noise.

When we reach the top, I push on the door, and it starts to crack open. To my horror, it starts to groan…but then it stops, like it's stuck. There must be something wedged behind the door. As I reach inside to figure out what is causing the jam, I try shoving the door open further and am greeted with a loud grunt.

As I try to peek through the crack, I can't see much, but I can hear. From where I stand, it sounds like a hundred voices are harmonizing in unison. "Ommmm…."

It sounds like there's choir practice going on. The door starts to slowly crack open, but only an inch more. I think I can see a shock of red hair on the floor. Then as the door opens all the way, the owner of the red hair becomes visible. It's a man. He grimaces slightly as he rubs his head, so I'm pretty sure that I hit him with the door. I would feel sorry about this, but I'm totally distracted by a prolific variety of nose hairs that peek out of his bulbous nose.

No sign of Janus. Inside the shop, almost every possible square inch is filled with people from all walks of life suspended in a wide variety of outrageous poses. The room is so packed that I can't see a way through to get up to the apartment.

I didn't think it was possible for anything to surprise me anymore here, but this…well, it's *bizarre*. Up on the counter, a wrinkled old woman with wiry gray hair balances the whole weight of her body on her forearms with her body and legs suspended overhead, contorted into a strange alien shape. The man with the nose hairs is now twisted into a wacked-out position that looks as if maybe he's trying to do the splits, but one leg is bent in the wrong direction.

I close the bookcase/basement door. As I turn the corner, there, front and center and on a raised platform, is Janus, sitting upright with his legs crossed, eyes closed, and facing away from me. I expel a sigh of relief when I realize that he can't see me. I should be able to easily sneak past without his knowing.

This must be some sort of séance or yoga. Janus continues chanting in Greek, and the room is perfectly still. No one is moving, which makes me think that this must be something else, like meditation. They chant again, but much longer this time. "Oooooouuuuummmmm…"

All of a sudden, Janus grows quiet, and his eyes snap open. He speaks in a very slow, melodic, sing-song voice. "Ah, Helene." He closes his eyes again as if to continue his practice. His voice is now almost a whisper. "Please, come join us."

I'm terrified. How does he know that I'm here? I have no idea, but I can't allow him to notice the changes in me, or he will know that I've been up to something.

No one looks up at me. I'm overwhelmed by the pungent stench of sweaty bodies. Someone here has some pretty serious body odor. Time for me to get out of here. I tiptoe across the various bodies, trying not to hit anyone on my way. In some places, there isn't even room for the width of the toe of my shoe, so I have to leap over people for a few feet here and there just to get to the next open space.

I've almost made it to the stairway leading up to our apartment when Janus whips around and resumes his serene whispering, sing-song voice, now addressing the whole room in English. "Children of the ancient peoples of Greece, thank you for your time today." He bends in a dramatic bow. "Namaste." Heads bob in silent thanks as he continues. "I will be performing energy work in the Tranquility Room of the villa now. In case anyone is interested, please join me." What? I had no idea that we have a "Tranquility Room" here or that this building is called a "villa."

I study Janus for a minute. Who the heck is this guy? There is such a vast difference in Janus's persona in front of these people compared to his crazy outburst yesterday. Today, he seems so Oprah…so *calm*…so oddly pleasant that I don't even recognize him.

Before he shifts his attention over to the energy work in the mysterious Tranquility Room, Janus nods at me, trying to get my attention. "Ummm, Helene?"

I'm just about to reach the stairs but stop short. I won't turn around. "Yeah?"

"Where are your glasses?" All traces of Oprah seem to vanish for the moment.

I panic, then blurt out, "Contacts," and rush up the stairs and into the apartment.

Fast as can be, I throw on some clothes, grab my backpack, and head out and down the spiral stairway to the street below. Through the dingy windows, I see Janus looking around for me as people approach him inside his shop.

On my way to school, one thing is abundantly apparent to me. The mirror has affected me, and somehow, I know that my life will never be the same. But what if it wasn't a dream? What if it was real? Just as I hop onto the school bus at Syntagma Square, I pinch myself. *Ouch!* The sharp pain tells my mind that I am not dreaming.

***

Something big is brewing at the Academy today. Several girls whisper in hushed tones, stifling giggles as I pass by them in the hallway, outside on the school grounds, and even in the classrooms. What on Earth could they be talking about? I know that the spring dance was just announced, which is like the prom here, but how can a silly dance be the source of so much drama?

Ever and his buddies are striding down the hall in my direction, and amazingly, Samantha's not hanging on his arm as usual. Today it's just him surrounded by his friends, who I'm sure are all popular super-athletes. Right now, Ever's friends razz him about something, all laughing hysterically, but he looks only slightly peeved.

I wonder what happened to Samantha? I conjure scenarios that must have led to her ultimate demise, each more outrageous and ghastly than the last, so much so that I'm not paying attention to where I'm going.

I snap out of my daydream just in time to see that I am headed straight for Ever. Just as I'm about to collide with him, I gasp in embarrassment when at the last second, I shift to the side, barely avoiding him, but my hand swings and unintentionally grazes his. I feel my whole arm tingle as his eyes open wide in surprise. I want to crawl into a small hole and stay there, but he doesn't even look up as he continues down the hall in the opposite direction.

Of course, curiosity gets the better of me, so I stop and whip around. Ever and all his friends stand there, leaning against the lockers. He's staring directly at me. It appears that he's listening to his friends, but his sparkling blue eyes bore into mine, and I know that he's thinking about me…but this time, I feel something new. He's not studying me in the usual way, but rather, there's a perplexed look on his face as if he's confused about something. Heat rushes up my neck and into my face, so I turn back around and practically run down the hallway into my next class.

Vani waits for me inside but does a double take when she sees me. "Holy sweet Jesus, Helene, what happened?" She takes my arm to spin me around. "Because…oh…wow…you look fabulous."

I pause for a moment, trying to think of what to say as I suddenly remember the change in my appearance. "Juice fast," I say quickly, hoping to change the subject.

Still scrutinizing me, she says, "So Janus must have finally splurged to get you some contacts. It's about time." Then she scrunches up her face. "Oh no."

"What?" I ask, worried.

"Looks like we need to go shopping. You need new clothes." She points at my legs. "Your jeans are too short." Then she laughs. "Weren't you just wearing them on Friday?"

I blurt out the first thing that comes to mind. "Oh yeah, I washed them in hot water. I hate it when they shrink like that."

Vani gives me a knowing look. "Of course. It's the worst!"

Just then, Dimitris – I mean Mr. Paxinos – clears his throat, which means it's time to quiet down and start class. Almost immediately, my mind is swept away into reflecting on the fantastical place on the other side of the mirror. Part of me still does not believe that it could have been real, that it was nothing more than a spectacular dream. As I glance down at my tanned arm and flawless skin, I know better.

I snap out of it when some of his words catch my attention… "Renowned Princeton philosopher David K. Lewis postulated that the Greek gods were real in another dimension."

I listen intently as Dimitris continues, "Lewis postulated the theory of *modal realism*, which is the idea that alternate dimensions, or universes, exist that are similar to ours but experience a different reality. Critics don't take this theory too seriously, though, because the rules of quantum mechanics as we know them would not allow passage between different dimensions, so it's impossible to prove."

My mother was completely obsessed with anything 'quantum'. Not that I understood most of it, but I remember her telling me about this place in Switzerland that had something to do with other dimensions.

What was the name of that place? Curiosity is killing me! I have to know. To my left, I see Vani's phone sitting out on her desk.

"I need your phone," I whisper to her.

She raises an eyebrow at me, but then passes the phone over to me under the desk. Dimitris continues his talk at the front of the room, oblivious to this. Under the desk, I type in the words: "**Switzerland alternate universe**".

A long list pops up regarding an organization called CERN. They specialize in nuclear research and invented a machine called a particle accelerator that is used to detect and possibly create mini black holes. One headline reads: "**CERN's Large Hadron Collider could prove parallel universes exist, say researchers...**"

This is significant. I need to find out more. Now.

"Dimi...oh, I mean Mr. Paxinos!" I say out loud.

All eyes in the room shift to me.

"Helene, yes?" Dimitris asks. He seems surprised at my sudden outburst.

"Are you talking about parallel universes?" I ask, looking around. For a moment, the room is completely silent. Time and space seem to halt.

A look of whimsical delight fills Dimitris expression, while he gathers his thoughts.

I glance down again at Vani's phone, where I see the words: "**hidden doorways...portals...bridge to multiple universes...**" The eerie blue light of the mirror in my godfather's basement comes to mind. Could it be so?

"What about a portal?" I ask.

Dimitris eyes grow wide. He breaks the silence with a slight shuffle of his shoe. "How very astute, Helene. Yes, but portals theoretically can exist only where all realties are identical in both content and kind, meaning they must share the same physical properties and space-time continuum. Lewis was talking about universes where the realities are different in content but not kind." A sparkle fills his eyes. "Keep in mind that all of this is just theory until proven or disproven."

The bell rings. As everyone gathers up their stuff, Dimitris catches my arm. "Helene, where did you hear about parallel universes and portals?"

I sigh. I can't exactly tell him I was using Vani's phone during class. "Uh, I read it somewhere. My mom is really into this kind of stuff."

Dimitris grins, his whole face lighting up in interest. "Yes, of course. Impressive." As I turn to leave, his next words stop me in my tracks. "You know, the great Greek philosopher Plato also wrote of the existence of a parallel world."

The squeaking sign with the worn-away word OLYMPUS on its face flashes through my mind. A chill runs up my spine as I turn around to respond. But Dimitris is gone. That's weird. He was just right here. There was nowhere for him to go.

Out in the hallway, I realize with dread that my next class is my least favorite – P.E. The dread turns to outright anguish when I hear the obnoxious sound of Samantha's laugh behind me. Just as I'm about to dash away, I hear her grating voice. "Oh, okay. Now, this is funny. What the hell happened to you, Helene?"

This time she has no trouble getting my name right. My usual fear of Samantha seems to have disappeared after my recent visit to a supposed parallel universe. In fact, I'm eager to confront her, to have some fun with her so I make up the most outrageous thing I can think of.

"Lipo," I say with a mischievous smirk.

From across the hall, I hear a laugh. Someone else is listening. It's Ever. He's trying very hard not to crack up. He seems to know that I'm completely making this up, like he's in on my little joke. Not surprising, really. I mean, it's not like I was overweight before, but now I'm more toned. Besides, how would a poor girl from Metaxourgeio like me suddenly afford an expensive cosmetic procedure like liposuction?

A look of recognition floods Samantha's face. "Yes, of course. My mom had it done last year. Where did you go to get it done? Dr. Sampros is the best in Athens. But wait…" She stops with a finger on her chin. "That doesn't explain your eyes."

Clearly on a roll now, I go with it and say, "LASIK."

Ever can't hold it in any longer and laughs out loud.

"Well, you sure had a busy weekend." Samantha studies me appraisingly, totally ignoring Ever. "But you really should have planned the post-op better. Those clothes look totally ridiculous on you."

"Yeah, well maybe I should hire you to be my personal shopper," I say boldly. I don't care anymore what she thinks.

She's dumbfounded, like no one has ever dared to make her the butt of a joke before. Ever laughs again. Not a normal laugh. A loud, bellowing laugh.

This is clearly too much for her. "Enough, Ever! Now you're laughing at me?!" Infuriated, she runs into the gym, scowling. While I'm glad, I'm also pleasantly surprised that Ever was taking my side with her. What was *that* about?

I relish my moment of triumph until it dawns on me that it's time for PE class. Samantha will be there, surrounded by her friends. A hostile environment for me, especially since I know we're supposed to be fencing. I'm not super-excited to suffer through the expected humiliation that is sure to ensue here yet again today.

When I get to class, of course, I am picked first…and once again, I must face Samantha. As I stare out at her from across the mat, I should be shaking with fear, but I'm not. When I pick up the sword, it feels light in my hands, as if it weighs nothing.

As soon as the joust starts, we go a round or two – stab, swing, and lunge – back and forth several times. Fear of the humiliation that I felt with Samantha hits me, making my legs seize up, so I stumble. I hear Samantha snicker as she turns towards her obnoxious friends, as if she's taking a bow for the crowd. Big mistake.

I experience a surge of immense strength as the vision of me as a powerful and seasoned warrior consumes my mind. I'm perfectly calm, almost Zen, as if nothing can faze me. Where is this coming from? I don't know, but I let it engulf me. With a single flick of my sword, I fling aside Samantha's with ease, then thrust mine towards her with all my weight, causing her to stumble, back up, trip, and fall to the floor, painfully knocking the wind out of her.

Only slightly winded, I stand over her body splayed on the floor with my sword pointed at her neck. Suddenly, it hits me what I've just done, and I'm stunned. I almost tear up and cry in gratitude.

As Samantha recovers, she is outraged, huffing and cursing under her breath. "Get off me! It doesn't matter what you change. You'll always be a loser!"

I don't care what she says now. I know who the winner is, and so does everyone else. Finally, I remove my sword and let her stand.

But she's not finished with me yet. She calls out to the surrounding crowd, "I think this was a fluke win. I think Helene should fight someone else, like…" – her eyes are alive with vengeance as she nods toward the boys across the gym – "…like a boy!"

The girls, mostly her obnoxious friends, cheer all around me.

Samantha flips her blond hair, looking at me with a malicious grin. "Helene, I dare you to fight Ever Sarantos!"

Silence falls across the crowd as they stand staring at me with their mouths hanging open. Samantha slinks back into the crowd of girls.

Before I have any chance to react, the teacher's assistant calls over to Mr. Mburu, who is busy with the boys across the gym. "Mburu! Can you send Ever Sarantos over here? We need a more 'worthy' opponent for Helene Crawford."

A look of admiration comes over Mr. Mburu's face. This must be quite surprising given my total lack of skills before. He yells over to the boys, "Sarantos. Come over here."

Ever jogs past me to assume the proper starting position. He whispers just so I can hear it, "I can make this easy for you."

Oh no. What if Samantha was right and that was just a fluke? I shift the weight of the sword in my hand and the serene calm that came over me before returns.

I can do this.

"No need," I retort. Ever raises an eyebrow in surprise but also seems intrigued and maybe a little perplexed. I don't need his sympathy. I have otherworldly power on my side, of which he is not aware.

Ever dons his mask, and we begin. I expertly move my sword in and out, rolling once and doing a standing backflip to avoid his attack.

Ever pauses and looks at me as if for the first time. "Wow."

He lunges forward in a deft move. I expertly block him, pushing his sword back at him, then whip my sword out to the left and smack him on the side of his torso. His eyes widen in shock. He's clearly starting to realize that he has underestimated me. His eyes narrow as he begins to fight me for real. He turns and stabs with expert precision, but even so, I gracefully thwart him at every turn. Just as our dance harmonizes to the crescendo, I see something that stops my heart.

There's a twelve-point yellow-gold star tattooed on the inside of his wrist. It looks like an exact match to the symbol that is on the shelf of my locker, the one that opened the door to my mom's secret lair. It's just like the star on my silver ring, the same ring that the god Zeus was wearing in my dream.

I start to panic. I tear my helmet off and hyperventilate. I hear the teacher yelling at me to keep it on, but Ever follows suit and tears his off too, probably to see more clearly why I am so upset.

Now both winded and sweating, I jump backwards with all my strength, kick out at him, and knock him flat on his back. The opposing force propels me forward, sending my body sprawling out over Ever's heaving chest. My legs pin him down firmly on either side of his body, which is laid flat on the ground. My face is so close to his now that my senses are overwhelmed by his scent – a seductive blend of cedar and citrus mixed with sweat – and it's totally intoxicating. Oh my. What am I doing here?

The point of my sword lightly touches his neck.

"Impressive," he whispers in my ear. I try to maintain an impassive façade, but I can't help but feel overwhelmed by the euphoric sensation of his very muscular body below mine. Adrenaline pulses through my body, making me feel incredibly triumphant in this win.

I feel something poking into my leg. Curious, I look down, but see only Ever's legs and nothing else. It must be something inside his pocket…a key chain…a wallet?

My mind spins out of control as it dawns on me that what I feel strong and firm against my thigh is a part of Ever…a very *private* part of him. I flush about five shades of deep crimson.

I jump up as if I've just been stung by a bee. Frantically, I tear off the rest of my fencing gear as if ridding myself of some awful bug crawling on me. Unwilling and unable to make eye contact, I rush off, pushing through the wall of girls surrounding us, and sink down to my knees near the wall, chest heaving.

I'm terrified that Ever will come after me, but there is no sign of him as class continues. Why exactly am I so upset? Shouldn't I be happy that he was aroused by me? Perhaps I might feel differently if it had happened in a less public place, and definitely not in front of his girlfriend. As I think about that look on his face, with his lips so close to mine, I can't help but want more. I need to see him again.

The thought that tickles the back of my mind, though, is frustration that I've made exactly zero progress in finding out any information from Ever about my mom. How is it that whenever I'm around him, I completely forget all about my critically urgent mission?

What is wrong with me? I've got to focus harder and get the job done.

I will, Mom. I promise.

***

At siesta, many kids are out attending a rally downtown. The school grounds are eerily quiet, so I sprawl out with my laptop under my favorite palm tree, which stands grand and stately, directly in the center of the square surrounded by school buildings. I should be studying for an upcoming physics test because I'm way behind the other kids since I just moved here.

I'm scanning my Instagram account when I see a notification. A request to follow me. When I look to see who it's from, I'm startled to see who it is…Ever Sarantos.

Oh. I sigh and frown as I glare down at his smiling profile picture, his gorgeous sea-blue eyes staring back at me. As I think about what happened earlier, I can't help but smile.

"So, are you going to let me follow you or not?" His voice swiftly jars me out of my thoughts. I lift my eyes, and there he is…Ever.

He stands there with a warm knowing smile, leaning up against my favorite tree, holding his iPhone out in front of him. His rugged tan is unusually vibrant next to the bright sky-blue of his button-down shirt. His brilliant eyes are energized and magnetic. My heart hammers in my chest as I feel the usual flutter of butterflies…and something else…inside.

"What?" I stammer. My face is most definitely flushed.

"On Instagram. I just followed you." he smirks, looking down at his iPhone and then back up at me. "So…are you going to accept me and follow me back, or not?"

I look down as if I'm thinking it through even though I already know the answer. Of course, I click "accept." His breathes out like he's *relieved.* Was he really concerned that I wouldn't want him to follow me on Instagram?

He looks down at my ankle. "Oh, it looks like you're fully recovered now," he says sweetly. His incredible eyes draw me in as he studies me. "By the way, I noticed that you look…different."

I play it safe with, "Yeah, right. Well, I've been working out…Pilates."

"Uh-huh, sure you have." His eyes light up with mischief. My heart rate skitters. He's not buying my story even for a second.

"You must have it all figured out, then," I goad him.

"Not entirely," he says in a smug voice, so darned certain of himself. Makes me nuts. "But it's only a matter of time, and I will."

"Keep telling yourself that," I say, matching his arrogance. "I'll be laughing the whole time while you guess."

"I like a challenge." His eyes flicker as if they are on fire, then simmer down as he sits down on the grass next to me. "You're incredible with a sword. Remind me not to make you mad. Where did you train?"

"I watch a lot of Star Wars," I laugh.

"I was kind of surprised, because Samantha told me she won so easily before..." he says wistfully, "but clearly, she was lying. She doesn't want me talking to you."

"Oh...?" I ask, but then it dawns on me that she's not here with him.

"So, where is she?" I ask, suddenly wishing that I didn't have to suffer through being so close to him. His presence is unsettling and exhilarating.

"What?" he asks as if I interrupted from some deep thought. "Who?"

"Ummm, your girlfriend, Samantha?"

"Oh yeah. Her."

"So?" I stare straight ahead, willing myself not to look at him. His nonchalance about Samantha leads me to believe that something is awry.

"We broke up." His voice is uncaring, monotone.

"What? Why?" I ask.

His voice is playful. "Not sure that's any of your business."

"Fine. Never mind." I shove my laptop into my backpack.

"Wait." He grabs my arm. An electric pulse shoots through me as my cheeks flush a hot red. I feel conflicted as I look up into his mesmerizing eyes. God, he makes me crazy! I want to like him so badly. I still can't believe he and Samantha are over.

"Samantha broke up with *me*," he says intently. He looks down at his hands. "I told her that I was thinking about someone else…a girl."

Of course! That's exactly what I'd expect. He's always thinking of another girl. He can't commit to anyone because there's always a prettier, more perfect girl out there…and they all want him, so why not? His gaze is intense as it meets mine, and then he breaks into a warm, sweet smile. Does he have to look at me like that?

"What girl?" I whisper, afraid to hear the answer.

His gaze falls to my lips, his voice soft and quiet now. "Isn't it obvious? You must know."

This is going too far, getting out of hand. He can't just treat me like all the other girls. I'm not falling for it.

"This has got to be a joke," I say, frowning.

Ever looks hurt as he says softly, "I assure you, it's *not* a joke."

My gaze falls to his hand, which is still resting firmly on my arm. It's all too much for me. I need to go, but as I twist my arm away, his wrist turns over, fully exposing the twelve-point star tattoo that I saw when we were sparring earlier.

The same symbol that opened my locker to my mother's secret room. My need to depart is suddenly overcome by an overwhelming need to understand what it means.

"When did you get this?" I run my finger across the length of his wrist. He shudders slightly at my touch. I must affect him as much as he does me.

His expression grows solemn. "I don't know, but my mother told me that one day when I was in kindergarten, I came home from school and there it was. No one at school knew how I got it. This star symbol resembles the Vergina Sun, which is the sign of the Greek First Army, the highest form of the Hellenic Army, and represents their determination, strength, and will. Like the Green Berets or the Navy SEALs in the States, they are called upon to perform the toughest duties here in the armed forces. My grandfather served in the First Army, so my mother believed that somehow it came from him."

"Your grandfather?" I ask, perplexed. "How could he give you a tattoo in kindergarten?"

145

"I don't exactly know since he died when I was young, but like my father, his influence was far reaching and significant. He and my dad shared many traits, even appearance. Some say he looked almost identical to my dad at the same age." Ever says this with his usual air of confidence. Suddenly, the photo of the younger Sarantos on the wall of my mom's secret room from 1971 makes more sense.

A sense of urgency overtakes me. Mom can't wait. "I need to meet your dad."

He breathes in deeply. "Why?"

Shoot. He's skeptical. He's used to everyone wanting something from him, probably using him to get close to his dad. Me and my big mouth. I may have just ruined any chance to ever meet Georgios Sarantos now. I need to cut my losses, at least for the moment.

Twisting my arm away, I say abruptly, "Never mind. I need to go."

As I leave Ever behind, I turn one last time to glance his way and see something wholly unexpected in him: *uncertainty.*

16 – THE DARE

On my way home from school, my thoughts are all over the place. I struggle for control. I can't let Ever get to me like this or let anyone distract me from my mission to find my mom.

For a girl like me, who has always needed to be in control, these feelings are both foreign and terrifying. Makes me crazy. Never in a million years would I have imagined myself with someone like Ever. He's frustrating, adorable, and arrogant all at once. And just so…well, it's all a bit too much for me. I feel like running away and never talking to him again.

On the other hand, I'm upset that I had to be so obvious about so urgently needing to meet his dad. *Why* did I do that? Of course, I know why. I've now been here in Athens for over a week and made almost no progress on finding my mother. I shouldn't be upset about being too forthright. If anything, I need to be more aggressive with my efforts. What if it's too late now for Mom? And all because I didn't do enough?

I touch the cypress tree necklace, which stills my mind and calms my heart. I hear my mother's words: "Keep your eye on the dream." In this case, the dream is my mother. I won't stop until I know she's okay, even if it means scaring off Ever Sarantos. Surely there are other ways to meet his dad.

Somehow, the rest of the week passes by quickly, although I find myself increasingly nervous as I travel to and from school every day. More than a few times, I feel as if someone is following me, that I'm being watched, but when I turn to see who is there, I'm alone. Only shadows lurk around me. Sometimes, they seem so dark and menacing, like something evil is at work. I'm probably just being paranoid.

I manage to easily fend off a few snarky comments about my "enhanced" appearance and avoid any close encounters with Ever. I must admit that it's been incredibly difficult to get him out of my mind. When the end of the week arrives, I feel almost elated to have escaped any major incidents. Since I moved here to Athens, my life has been so chaotic, there's been no chance to feel grounded, and that makes it difficult to know how I feel about anyone, including Ever.

On my way home from school on Friday night, I turn the corner to my street, and all my thoughts about Ever are blown to bits when I see Nick standing there. His bronze skin glows under the muted streetlights. He's leaning up against the side of Janus's house next to his motorcycle. As I approach him, his eyes light up in anticipation.

What's this about? Whatever it is, it's a welcome diversion. While Ever makes me feel totally out of control, Nick feels safe and comfortable, which is a bit of a paradox considering that when I first met him, I thought he was the ultimate rebel. Underneath it all, Nick has a sweet, calm, and gentle nature, whereas Ever's disarming, defiant, and ever-changing persona makes it hard for me to feel at peace with him. Often in life, things are not what they seem.

I think back to when I last saw Nick. The Temple of Poseidon and the moonlit beach below fill my mind, and suddenly it all comes flooding back. I remember now! Today is day five of my dare with him.

I was kind of hoping that he would cheat on his no-smoking promise so that I wouldn't have to live up to my end of the bargain. Even though it was my idea, I'm not exactly as excited about it now that I'm so confused as about what he wants with me. His mixed messages make me nuts.

It's just before sunset, so it must be almost seven o'clock. Right on time. He holds out his helmet to me and says, "You ready?"

"Uh, yeah, but I wasn't really sure you were coming," I say wryly.

His eyes open wide as if he's just seen a ghost, and for a nonbeliever like Nick, that would be a big deal. "Helene," he says as if in shock, "when did you start to speak Greek?"

I stop short, biting my lip, not understanding what he's talking about. "You're not making sense, Nick."

"You're speaking flawless Greek right now," he says in astonishment.

"Nick, if I'm speaking to you in Greek, then why are you answering me in English?"

"I'm not," he says slowly. "I am speaking Greek, Helene."

My mouth hangs open in shock as I try to comprehend exactly what he is saying. I'm fluent in Greek? When did this happen?

"Okay. Can you speak in English?" I ask tentatively, testing the waters.

"Yes," he says tersely. "This is English."

It's as if I can't tell the difference between English or Greek. Total *insanity*. Somehow, I speak the language as needed without thinking about it, as if an automatic translator has been installed in my brain. But how can this be?

This must be yet another facet of the change in me after going to that place beyond the mirror…to *Olympus*. But was I speaking Greek at school this whole week? No one said anything about it. Ever definitely would have noticed. One thing, though, is for certain…there's absolutely no way that I can explain this to Nick, especially given his total animosity towards anything mystical when we were at the Temple of Poseidon.

"What the heck is going on, Helene?" He seems almost angry at me now.

"What do you mean?"

"You look like a freaking movie star." He continues, "I'm worried about you. Are you doing…coke…like your godfather? If yes, I know someone who can help."

"What? No!"

"And suddenly you're fluent in Greek too? There's no way you could have picked up the language that fast."

"I…I don't know," I stammer. The truth is that I am all out of smart explanations. I feel as if I've reached a solid brick wall at the end of an alley with nowhere to go. "I woke up like this."

He eyes me skeptically. "Uh-huh. That's nuts! You can't just wake up like this."

My eyes begin to water as panic fills my head. I should just cut my losses and leave him here on the street. "I did, Nick. I swear!"

He just shakes his head like he's sure I'm lying.

I can't stay here and take any more of this. I'm finally being honest here, and he's being a complete jerk. "Look, I'm really tired. I had to stay up late with extra homework, so maybe we should just do this another night," I say, completely deflated. I start to turn towards the door to Janus's shop.

"No, wait!" Nick practically shouts at me. Startled, I feel as if I jump out of my skin. He continues, this time in a much softer tone. "I'm not really buying it, but let's just talk about this another time. It was darned near impossible for me to quit smoking this past five days. You have to come with me." His eyes are pleading. "*Please.*"

"What do you mean you aren't buying it?" I ask, annoyed.

"Forget I said that!" he says, "Look, you've been through a lot. I know that. Be with me tonight." His voice is so low it's like a whisper. His thoughtful, round eyes melt my anger away.

"You sure you didn't cheat?" I tease him. "I know what kind of willpower it must take for a chain smoker to quit, even for a week."

He looks incredulous. "What? I'm not a chain smoker! You know that, right?"

I smirk, not responding.

"Well, I'm not. I only smoked like three or four cigarettes a day," he says.

"That's *all*?" I say, eyes wide. I am so enjoying this. "Uh-huh, right."

"Yes!" he says anxiously, but then he must see the teasing in my eyes because he visibly relaxes and grins. "You're giving me crap, aren't you?"

"Yep." I smile.

Just then, I hear Janus coming down the outside spiral stairway towards us. He must have been up on the roof deck. *Argh.* After Nick's reaction to my altered appearance, there's no way I'm taking it tonight from Janus too. I've got to get out of here.

"Nick, let's go," I say urgently, grabbing his arm.

"Wha...?" He must see the alarm in my eyes because he stops short.

We hear the shuffling *clang, clank* of Janus's shoes as he makes his way down the metal stairs. He calls out in a shrill voice, "Helene! Before you go, we need to talk!"

No way is that happening. "We have to go *now*!" I raise my voice.

Nick nods, steps onto the bike, and guns the motor. *Vrrooommm!*

"Helene!" Janus yells over the rumbling engine.

I shove Nick's helmet on my head and leap onto the bike behind him, hugging his back tightly. Our tires squeal as we peel off into the night. I wrinkle my nose at the foul smell of burnt rubber that fills the air around us.

"Woo hoo!" I yell in delight. Nick grins, his face filled with triumph. This act of outright rebellion is exactly what makes his world go round.

As I rest the length of my torso on his back, I feel the stir of something in me with his rock-hard body so close to mine. We drive through the narrow streets of Athens, through some side streets, flea markets bustling in busy fury on either side, the succulent aromas of herb-roasted lamb and chicken tantalizing my senses.

The wind blows against my skin, sending chills under my shirt as it flies out behind me. Nick curves around a bend and starts up a steep hill. The city's lights start twinkling subtly as the sun starts to set off towards the horizon, a majestic swath of orange streaks across the sky all around us. We continue to climb up higher and higher, the street winding through a thick pine forest. The breeze is slightly colder here, making me hug Nick's back even more to stay warm. He doesn't seem to mind.

As we approach an area about midway from the top, there's a parking lot with a hot dog stand, but it's vacant. This is not a typical tourist area. Nick stops the bike near the edge of the hill near a low stone wall. The orange of the slowly descending sun is now fading to a menagerie of tendrils shooting out in varying hues of red, pink, and purple. I pull the helmet off my head, sure that my hair is a total mess. There's not a whole lot I can do about that, though, so I decide not to worry about it.

"Where are we?" I ask in a hushed voice. I experience a feeling of utter peace and awe at the sight of the miraculous view from this amazing place.

"Lycabettus Hill," Nick says in his tour guide voice. He tells me about the crumbling old white church at the top of the hill called St. George; the Agioi Isidori, which is another tiny church built into the hillside; and the Lycabettus Theater, where plays and concerts are performed.

The setting sun is visible in the reflection of Nick's gray-green eyes as he stares off in the distance. He continues in a serious tone. "Athena wanted her temple on the Acropolis to be much higher, closer to the sky. One night, while she was in the middle of moving a huge rock to the Acropolis, two black birds brought her bad news about an urgent issue. In her haste, she accidentally dropped the rock here in this very spot – and that's how Lycabettus Hill came about." He points. "See down there, on that hill? That's the Parthenon and the Acropolis. And that's the Temple of Zeus."

It all looks so tiny from up here. I can't believe that the little white-pillared structure on the top of the tiny hill is the Parthenon. It looked so grand and majestic from the ground when we rode past through the streets of Athens earlier.

This bird's-eye view of these ancient archaeological wonders makes me think of that magical place through the mirror…the vast desert sands of Olympus. It feels strange to think that I was just there. Since Nick purports to believe only in ideas backed by science, perhaps he will know something about parallel universes and Plato's theory about another parallel world.

"Nick?" I ask.

"Yeah?" he replies.

"Have you heard about CERN and their research where they are trying to poke through the fabric of our universe to try to reach into another one? I think I heard they are trying to build a bridge or a portal between the two realities. Do you know what I'm talking about?"

His eyes light up slightly as if he's intrigued. "Maybe," he says quietly.

"I also heard a theory that if in fact this other universe could exist, perhaps the gods could be real there. Have you heard that?"

"Uh, no." All the interest he showed just a moment ago shuts down. His face is now completely impassive and cold. "C'mon, Helene! The gods aren't real. Now you sound like those wacked-out pagans your godfather hangs out with. Seriously! That's crazy talk."

We sit there on the stone ledge in silence for a moment. I shudder as I feel the chill from the updraft of wind traversing swiftly up the hill. Nick must sense this because he moves closer, wrapping his arms around me, which feels nice. Is he going to make a move or what? Is this a date, or are we just friends? This ambiguity is making me crazy.

His blond hair is swept back from his face as the wind blows softly. "Let's go and get some dinner." He gets up and turns towards the hot dog stand, which is the only sign of life here in the middle of this vacant parking lot. "Hope you're hungry. These are the best dogs in town."

The thought of a nice juicy hot dog makes me long for lazy summer days growing up in California, going with my mom to Giants Stadium.

"You look disappointed," he says softly.

"Me? No, I love hot dogs. Janus would never approve, though," I say. I can just envision the sneer forming on Janus's face at the sight of a hot dog.

"Well then, I say let's eat a lot of hot dogs!" Nick beams.

We walk over and peruse the wide variety of toppings for hot dogs. I'm impressed. And of course, they have French fries, which I have seen everywhere here. Unlike in the States, the fries taste like real potatoes, and they're probably fried in virgin olive oil. I tell the street vendor what I want. Nick pulls out a wad of euros to pay.

"This week when I didn't see you for a while, I thought about coming over to take a yoga class from your crazy old man." Nick's eyes shine as he bites down on his hot dog.

"Even before your five days was up?"

"Well, yeah. When I reached day two, I needed a little encouragement to get me through it. I almost gave up...almost!" His expression is animated, full of life. "But also, since I'm not in school anymore, it's not exactly easy to make new friends in the tourism business. Everyone you meet is a new face."

"And maybe...I just wanted to see you again. I missed you," he says wistfully.

"Even though I'm not Greek?"

He smiles mischievously. "Especially since you aren't Greek."

"You're such a rebel," I say.

"Yep. Always."

I tell Nick about my victory over Samantha. I can tell he hates her. His expression is visibly pained when I talk about the awful humiliation that I felt during my first fencing experience with her. He tells me that Samantha acts that way only when she senses competition.

I am flabbergasted. "But why would I be competition for her?"

Nick throws his arms up. "You really need to ask that?"

I shrug.

He smiles wryly. "Nope, sorry." He says playfully, "There's no way I'm saying anything because we'd have to resume our earlier conversation about your...appearance. Is that what you want?"

"No!" I exclaim. He's right. Best to drop the subject. "So, what's next?" I ask.

"What? This isn't enough?" He smiles. His white teeth are visible in the darkening evening. I'm happy to not hear him mention the beach. Maybe he forgot about our bet, or maybe the whole thing was a joke after all.

Nick's eyes come alive. "Actually, I do believe that it's time to go to the beach. Nice and dark...just like we discussed." He raises his eyebrows mischievously.

Oh yeah. The Dare. Some of the excitement that I felt from when I first thought of it returns. It's no big deal to take your top off at the beach here. Everyone does it.

He discards the hot dog wrappers, takes one last swig of water, and then hands me the helmet. Time to get back on the bike.

I welcome the heat from his body as we follow the long, winding road down to the streets of Athens. On the way down, the sparkling lights of this vast metropolis glisten in the darkness of night. The city is alive with people out mingling in the streets, the smells of roasted meats and noises of people dining in outdoor cafés near the road. As we hit the coast, I hear the sounds of cawing seagulls and smell the salt water in the air. A soft mist caresses my face as we pull into a parking lot.

Smiling, Nick leads me down to a beach in Varkiza, where the path is now only dimly lit by the nearby parking lot lights. The beach is gorgeous at night. A soft warm breeze flows over my skin. A crescent moon sits alight above the crashing waves of the sea directly in front of us. I continue to follow Nick's gray silhouette until we stop very close to the surf. Surveying the beach, we are for the most part alone. Another couple is sitting on the sand, but it is so far down the beach that I can't see them clearly. We both sit down on the beach, staring out at the calm surf, when Nick produces a wine bottle and two glasses. Where was he hiding these? I didn't feel them on him when we were riding on the bike. Suddenly, this is starting to feel like a date.

After pouring the wine, Nick hands me a glass. "Time to celebrate. I have officially been smoke-free for five days."

"*Yamas!* And so now what?" I ask as we clink our glasses in a toast and take a sip.

"What do you mean?" he asks, perplexed. He's staring at my lips. Uh, that wasn't what I meant.

I decide humor is in order here. "Are you planning to continue this smoke-free trend or to now go back to life with the stink breath?" I chide.

"No, not that." He frowns, then blows his breath right in my face. "How does it smell now?" He's laughing at me. The smell of his breath is sweet and minty with a hint of the wine we are drinking. Very nice…exhilarating.

The look on Nick's face right now reminds me of his expression earlier when he handed me his helmet just as we were taking off on his motorcycle earlier...his lone helmet.

Why not two helmets? Is his safety less important than mine? Not that I mind the look of the wind flowing effortlessly through his hair.

"Why is it that I am always the one to wear your helmet?" I ask, "I mean, is there a law here in Greece that only girls are supposed to wear helmets and not boys? That seems awfully sexist if true. Really!"

Nick's eyes grow wide as he chuckles, which grows into a full-on hearty laugh.

"What?" I ask, wondering what about what I've said could possibly be so funny.

"Well, so, remember when I told you that my family had to...downsize? We gave up everything," he says with a sigh, lifting his hand up to brush his blond hair back from his face as he continues. "I felt like I was being really selfish to keep my bike, but I needed it to keep my sanity. Also, it helps to get me to my job, which provides for my whole family, so I guess that's how I justify it to myself without feeling too guilty. But I did have to give up everything else, including my second helmet." He seems relieved to confess this to me. "And after my girlfriend left me, I didn't think I had any reason to keep it...until now."

Nick's face looks pained and hurt. But wait, what was that last part? Is he thinking that I am his next girlfriend? *Wow.*

I can't help but ask him about it. "Uh, Nick?"

"Yeah?" He turns his face towards me, once again staring at my lips.

I know I shouldn't ruin this moment, but here it goes. "Your girlfriend..." I say, looking out into the distance.

"*Ex*-girlfriend. Yeah...Melina," he says in an icy, cold tone. His gaze is still focused on my mouth, which makes me shift my body nervously.

"What happened with that?" I ask. His hesitation and vagueness make me want to know more.

Nick drops his arm from around my shoulders. His voice grows tense, and his hands clench. "We were pretty serious for about two years, at least until she ripped my heart out. Right after I had to quit school, she ran off with my best friend." His face reddens in anger, but a deep sadness is also evident in his pained expression. "Don't even get me started about him. That *malaka*! It was all over after that. She moved away, and I no longer speak to him."

I can't think of any words to express how hearing this makes me feel for Nick.

The silence is broken when he pulls away. "I wish I had a blanket for you, but there was no room on my bike," he says sweetly.

We share a moment of easy silence. I feel the tension rise as he moves over, very close to me and takes my hand again. His fingers softly caress my hand, slowly tracing circles on the surface of my palm. The sensation sends chills tingling up my arm, igniting heat somewhere deep inside of me.

"Getting cold?" he asks softly.

All I can do is nod, my gaze now locked onto his. Slowly, he moves in very close and brushes his lips against mine.

"Oh...I guess I am," I whisper.

He cups my chin as he moves in again. This time his lips find mine in a slow, sweet, kiss. I feel the tension leave my body in surrender as we continue...slow and steady...his tongue finding mine...in this tantalizing dance. When we finally pull away, I'm breathless. He grabs my hand, now kissing each finger. His eyes are filled with so much adoration that it makes me blush.

The glistening moonlight dances over the lapping waves of the sea in front of us. Of all the boys I've kissed, this felt as if it were my first *real* kiss. So, this is what cloud nine feels like. I never want it to end.

Then Nick pushes back, looking down at the ground. "Look, Helene, I have a confession. You won't be happy about this, but I need to get it off my chest."

Part of me wants him to declare his undying love for me, but I know that would be hasty and is definitely not happening.

Nick downs his whole glass of wine. "I lied to you about something. Well, it was kind of teasing...but no, well, it was a trick...a lie…not a nice thing to do." He looks out towards the softly lapping waves. "The girls here don't really take their tops off at the beaches in Athens. There are a few nudist beaches, but it's not a common thing here. It is sometimes something that people do on some of the Greek islands…but not here. So, don't feel like you need to…disrobe just because of our dare."

This display of innocence and overwhelming honesty makes me want him even more.

Suddenly I want more than ever to hold up my end of the dare. If he's trying reverse psychology on me…well, it's worked.

I start by taking my jacket off. He looks at me, mouth gaping open in shock. "Wha…?"

"A dare is a dare. You held up your end of the bargain, so…" I start unbuttoning my shirt, which makes his eyes grow wide. As he stares at me, I feel a flush rise in my cheeks.

It does help that we are on a mostly deserted beach in the darkness, with only the moonlight casting its spell on us in such a spectacular setting. The image of the crescent moon shines in his eyes, giving them depth. I sense him holding his breath in anticipation.

I drop my shirt, then pull off my bra straps…and throw it down onto the sand. My heaving chest shines naked and exposed in the rays of the soft moonlight. I extend my arms out in glee. "See? No big deal!" I yell, laughing.

But Nick isn't laughing. His mouth falls open in shock, and a look of consternation consumes his face. This is not the reaction I was expecting. I realize too late that I shouldn't have done this. I hastily gather up my clothes, pull on my bra and shirt, and cover everything up.

Nick's arms are crossed in clear discomfort. He looks as if he's just eaten something unsavory and has sudden indigestion.

"What? What's wrong?" I ask, trembling and terrified at what his response will be.

He is quiet and contemplative, sinking to sit on the beach, staring solemnly out over the crashing waves.

This silence makes me feel exposed, betrayed…angry. "You

should be careful what you ask for!" I exclaim, my voice irate. But my anger turns quickly to shame. "There's something wrong with me, right?! Look, I know that I'm not perfect—"

Nick cuts me off, still looking off in the distance. "No, that's definitely not the problem."

"Then what!? What is it?"

As he turns to look at me, his eyes immediately fall to my lips. "The problem is..." He turns away uncomfortably. "Nothing. There's no problem. We should probably get home."

The whole way home, there is an awkward silence between us. Nick's body, once relaxed and fluid, is now stiff and rigid as I hold onto him on the back of the bike. When we get back to the apartment, I try breaking the ice by congratulating him again on his quitting smoking.

He avoids eye contact, nodding thanks, and departs quickly without a word.

What just happened here?

17 – PROPHECY

Saturday and most of Sunday passes by with no word from Nick. Why did I have to go and do such an idiotic thing? Nick was trying to tell me *not* to take my top off, and then I had to go ahead and do it anyway. What was wrong with me?

Still, it was *his* dare, after all. He was the one who teased me, "lied" was the exact word he used. He asked for this, and now he can't handle it. So how is it fair that it's now *my* problem?

I like Nick…that's how. I like him *a lot.*

My mind swirls with elation at the memory of us sitting on the beach under the magic of the moonlight…and oh, that *kiss.* I want to feel like that again. My heart aches. I miss Nick.

My hand hovers over my phone. Maybe I should just call him. At least then I'd know where things stand, and I wouldn't have to waste any more effort worrying about him.

But then my mother's words echo through my mind: "Girls don't call boys." I had argued vehemently with her that this view was sexist and old-fashioned. Modern women should be able to do exactly as men do, right? Wrong. Mom always had a way of making her point so that no one could argue with her. Her argument centered on the evolution of our species and animal behavior. At the pinnacle of the hunt, men need to experience the thrill of the chase, and in this case, I am the prey. And as much as it bothers me, I see her point. If he's not calling, texting, e-mailing – whatever the communication – there's something wrong. The hunt is not in play.

"Oh, Mom, how I wish you were here with me," I whisper to myself.

My head aches and my temples throb. I'm in so much pain that I don't even care about avoiding Janus anymore. Besides, it's probably about time to face the music, time that we talk. I'm tired of trying to forestall the inevitable.

And I need help for this pain.

I start down the stairs to Janus's shop to see if he has some holistic headache remedy. Even though it's late, he must be down there since I don't see him in the apartment or hear him up on the roof. He literally never leaves this house. I have no idea how he buys groceries. It must be when I am away at school.

The shop is full of Janus's usual cast of characters. I see lots of familiar faces from yoga, acupuncture, and who knows what else Janus does. In the middle of the shop, they all sit quietly in a circle of chairs, listening intently to something that Janus is saying. His voice is patient and quiet. Must be Oprah mode today...thank God.

It looks like this could be a self-help group or, knowing Janus, some sort of séance. He holds up a book, and everyone bobs their heads up and down in excitement. Maybe it's a book club meeting.

As I attempt to walk past the group, Janus's eyes catch mine. *Argh.* Even though I need to face him, I was hoping to do it alone. First, his eyes narrow as if he's just tasted something unsavory. But then, just a few moments later, his eyes light up as if he's happy to see me. Inviting me to join the group, he assumes his sing-song voice. "Helene, come on over. I want you to meet some of my friends."

Like I have a choice. I try to talk my way out of it anyway. "I have a really bad headache. Do you have anything I can take?"

I hear a lot of snickers around the circle. Some of them stare at me with a little too much intensity, like they've never seen a teenager before.

"It's better to suffer through the pain so you know what true pleasure feels like," says the redheaded nose-hair guy whom I hit with the hidden door the other day when I was trying to escape from the basement. Everyone nods in unison.

Janus smiles with a gleam in his eye. "He's right, Helene. Besides, with the new improved you, pain medication shouldn't be necessary."

What is that supposed to mean? He must know about the mirror!

Begrudgingly, I sit down in the only empty chair next to a woman with a rainbow scarf covering her head. I assume that they're all speaking in Greek, but I have no idea because both English and Greek are now completely interchangeable in my head.

Janus walks over to me and whispers in my ear with a sneer, "Have you been snooping around my shop?"

His tone becomes menacing, accusatory. "I think you've done something that you shouldn't have. You know what I'm saying? I know you do."

I just shrug, totally mute. There's no way I'm admitting anything right now.

This just angers Janus. He raises his voice. "You're going to tell me everything, understand? I'm not—"

"Hey, Janus?" nose-hair guy abruptly interrupts. "We need to get started."

Janus's demeanor completely shifts back to pure calm. He uses a little mallet to ignite a small tabletop gong, and the group chants, "Do as you will, but harm none." I notice now that there's a small altar in the center of our circle covered with statues and figurines. It looks like all the key ancient gods are there. Dried flowers and the multicolored faceless dolls I saw before are scattered on the altar. What is going on here?

A knocking sound interrupts the group, and through the glass I see Nick standing there. He's looking down at his hands as if he's deep in thought over something important. His pressed white polo shirt looks bright against his olive skin, and he's wearing his usual khakis from work. His blond hair is slicked back in a tidy way. He's quite handsome all cleaned up. His gray-green eyes light up when I wave him inside.

As quietly as possible, I leave the inner circle of the quietly chanting group to join Nick near the door.

"Hey," he says quietly.

"Hi," I say with a smile. I twist my hands nervously.

I glance over my shoulder and see Janus frowning at Nick. Nick isn't exactly smiling back at Janus either.

"I just wanted to apologize about the other night," Nick whispers.

"Oh?" I stare straight ahead, making him wait.

The look in his eyes seems genuine, like he's really sorry. "Look, it's all my fault. I asked you to do that, but then when it happened, I didn't know what to do. I panicked."

I nod and smile as if to say it was fine when I see Nick's ears perk up as if he just heard something scandalous.

Rainbow-scarf woman is holding up a book titled *Before the Beginning: The Primeval Gods*. A woman with long gray hair and a ring in her nose asks with an empty, vacant look in her eyes, "Uh, April, is this like the primordial deities, similar to the creation story in Genesis and the Torah?"

April rolls her eyes as if the answer should be obvious. "Well, yes, Cindy, we're talking about the building blocks of the original creation story, which are earth, air, sea, sky, fresh water, underworld, darkness, night, light, day, procreation, and time. The primordial gods represented each of these basic elements in ancient mythology."

Nose-hair guy gets excited. "The Protogenoi!"

Cindy's eyes grow wide. "Like the Prophecy!"

What prophecy?

Janus is suddenly nervous. I can sense it when his eyes meet mine. "Let's stick to the book, okay? We're not talking about the Prophecy here."

April cuts in, ignoring Janus. "Yes, the Prophecy! The Protogena will be born from the virgin goddess to one day save all worlds."

The room erupts in applause, which stops when they chant, "Glory to the Protogena."

Next to me, I hear Nick utter under his breath, "Seriously? Is this some sort of religious worship of the…gods? Holy crap. I knew it! Your godfather is a pagan!"

April clears her throat, looking directly at Nick. "I heard that."

Nick's eyes grow wide in surprise, then narrow at her.

Janus, clearly irritated, glares at Nick, then sneers at me. "Helene, I told you, no boys allowed in here!"

"I was just leaving," Nick says in a tight, controlled voice. This can't be good. So much for his apology. A look of distress passes over his features as he turns to me and whispers, "Helene, you don't buy into any of this, do you?"

"What? No." I shrug.

"I need to go," he says.

"Okay. Sorry you came?" I ask tentatively.

"Yes…no. I mean, no. I…" He looks frustrated. "Well, I'm glad that I saw you tonight, but that's all I can say here."

Nick disappears through the glass door and off into the night. I'm glad he apologized, but where does this leave us now? Better or worse?

As I come back to the group, Janus announces that we will be hosting another guest here at the villa for the next few days. "Everyone, please meet Thomas," Janus says with a warm smile.

An odd-looking boy, maybe seven or eight years old, sits quietly in the chair that I was just occupying, looking down at the floor. Thomas is odd mostly because of the strange color of his eyes. They are pure silver. His skin is very pale, almost translucent, and his hair is blindingly white.

Janus explains that Thomas will be staying with us for a couple of days. I have a zillion questions, such as where in our teeny-tiny little apartment will Thomas sleep? Better not be on my couch.

"Thomas will be staying in the Tranquility Room, so it won't be available for the next few days," Janus states. Groans fill the room. The rainbow-scarf woman and nose-hair guy exchange disappointed looks.

Janus sounds the mini-gong. Everyone starts to disperse. Just then, a mysterious businesswoman, impeccably dressed in high heels and fashionable suit, pushes the front door open. April and Cindy's eyes light up at the sight of her. The group greets the woman as if they all know her.

Janus and the woman talk in the corner of the room. It's a heated discussion, motioning over and over to where Thomas sits. I overhear the woman say, "I am certain that Georgios will welcome him with open arms into his home. There won't be any problems."

Janus whispers, "Ah, but Aliki, are you sure that the police will not catch wind of it?"

The woman assures Janus that the proper people have been paid to keep this quiet.

What is going on here? Could this be *child trafficking*?

After Aliki leaves, the whole shop is eerily quiet. Janus scurries back to the Tranquility Room with Thomas to settle him in for the night. After a moment, Janus comes back into the room.

"Janus?" I ask. "What is going on here? Are you...engaged in...illegal activity here?!"

"You've got to keep Thomas's presence here an absolute secret," he says urgently. His eyes are tired. "There's nothing to worry about, Helene. This is a humanitarian effort, and we are the good guys. The government here is good at some things but very bad at others. Some things need to be handled outside of their purview, and this is one of them. I told you before, it's all very complicated."

I hold my breath listening to this as absolutely none of it makes any sense. I'm not sure I buy it, but on the other hand, it doesn't sound like a story he could easily make up on the fly either.

Janus sits down on a tattered old sofa, twisting his wristband that he always wears round and round in a swift, monotonous motion. He explains that the boy is an orphan from one of the neighboring countries and that he has no home. Janus sometimes helps to locate homes for these refugee orphans. "Haven't you heard about the refugee crisis here, Helene? So many people are in dire need. I'm doing my part to help."

I need more answers.

"Who was that woman? And why was she so concerned about the police not getting involved with Thomas?"

Janus looks surprised. "Oh, you heard that?"

I nod. "Yes, and I also heard her talk about Georgios. Are we talking about Georgios Sarantos?"

"You know that I work for Sarantos. That's no secret." Janus explains that the woman, Aliki, is the personal assistant to Georgios Sarantos. The police cannot be involved because most levels of government are corrupt and can't be trusted. Sarantos is the good guy.

He is planning to adopt Thomas in a few days.

Still, it feels like Janus is telling me only part of the story. I'm so tired of his lies and confused about whom I can trust. What if Janus is one of the bad guys?

"Speaking of Sarantos, I want to meet him," I say boldly.

Janus's eyes grow wide in surprise. He twists his terry cloth wristband around a couple of times before responding. "Absolutely not. You're not allowed."

"Why am I not allowed?" Suddenly I'm distracted. I hear a low, continuous beep like an alarm coming from up in our apartment.

Janus's eyes grow wide in suspicion. "What is that?" he asks.

At first, I'm not sure, but then I think I know where the beeping is coming from. My stomach churns, making a loud sound like hunger pains. But really, I'm suddenly terrified. It's got to be the strange iPad! I need to stall Janus long enough to disable it.

"It's just my alarm," I stammer, already heading for the stairs. I race upstairs and pull my old, ratty suitcase out from where it was hidden under the end table. Carefully, I unzip the secret compartment where I last hid the iPad.

I feel around and breathe a sigh of relief as I sense the cool metal cover of the iPad under my fingers. As I pull it out, I hit a button on the side, trying to turn off the beeping sound. Something works because a moment later, the sound stops.

I sigh in relief. But then, not even a second later, strange words in an unfamiliar language and a perplexing image flash onto the screen. The image appears to be two planets joined by what looks like a connecting tube. I'm not sure what it could be. Possibly a wormhole?

Just then, recognition hits me hard. It's a portal bridging two planets located in two different realities or universes.

In a split second, the words appear easily to me in English:

Gate construction commencing in 30 seconds.

No, this can't be right. How can I stop this thing?! I smack the iPad on the couch. Nothing. Next, a countdown starts on the screen...30, 29, 28...

What is this thing doing? Clearly, it is counting down to

something. "Gate construction"…what can that mean? I don't know, but whatever it is, I've got to stop it.

I hear Janus's bedroom door creak open, then the sound of mumbling, as if he's still engaged in some pretend but heated conversation with someone. Bastet wedges her body through the crack.

I'm totally freaked as it dawns on me that I'm running out of options and time.

What to do?!

18 – GAEA

I totally panic. 24…23…22… I hit the red button on top. The countdown continues. 20…19…18… An awful thought hits me. What if this is a bomb?! *Oh my God!* 7…6…5…4… I slam it hard on the wall. *Smack!*

The device beeps, then shuts down. The words appear: Gate construction aborted. Suddenly, the screen goes blank.

I fall to my knees as overwhelming relief floods me. I praise God, the universe, the gods, or whomever will listen to my gratitude. *Thank you!*

The beeping sound must have alerted Janus that something is awry because he's in quite the turbulent mood when he rushes into the room. "What the *hell* is going on here?"

"Uh, nothing." I quickly stash the iPad device behind me before he has a chance to notice.

Janus's eyes grow erratic as he frantically looks everywhere for Bastet. "Where are you hiding, obnoxious cat? This is all your fault. *All* of it!!" He starts pulling the pillows off the couch, which is peculiar because I don't see how it's even possible for Bastet to hide under there. "You've got to stop your meddling!" he screams, but there's no sign of the cat. She's gone. I can't say that I blame her.

"Um, Janus," I say meekly, not wanting to set him off further. "I don't think Bastet is here. She must have gone outside."

Suddenly, he stops, eyes wide and frozen in place. His scarf is lopsided, exposing the shiny bald patch on the top of his head. Time stands still as we stare at each other in absolute, eerie silence. What can this mean? Dr. Jekyll, Mr. Hyde, Oprah, or something else?

"You've been in the basement!" he shrieks, so loud that I jump out of my skin.

"No!" I yell back. But then I realize that I'm not supposed to know about the basement. Time to fake him out. "Wait…what basement? You have a basement here?"

Janus frowns as his face starts to grow that deep red color that tells me he's going to totally lose it. He's not buying it. "You know all about the basement. I'm sure of it."

"Even if I did – which I do not – but if I did, what are you so worried about, Janus? Are you hiding something down there?" I say with a confident sneer.

His eyes light up, ablaze with fury, but then a moment later, something dawns on him. As if none of this has just happened, his face completely relaxes. He shifts his scarf back onto the top of his head, turns on his heel, and enters his room, slamming the door behind him.

That was close! I still feel the residue of his chaotic energy here in the room with me. Adrenaline surges through my veins, like I just jumped out of a plane.

I sit down on the couch-that-is-my-bed, numb over what happened earlier with the strange iPad device. The stark image of the planets connected by some sort of bridge between them fills my mind. Gate construction…the countdown…to what?

The realization of what this means hits me like a brick. My heart rate quickens. The iPad device must have been trying to create a new "gate," like a portal between our universe and some other reality. OMG.

Back at school, I remember reading on the Internet that there was some huge controversy with that organization in Switzerland – CERN. Some people were concerned that they could possibly create a black hole with their nuclear Hadron collider, one that could swallow up the Earth and maybe the entire solar system. Some fringe groups even filed a lawsuit claiming that CERN could potentially open a portal to another world and allow demons to come here.

It's not CERN they need to worry about; it's me with my iPad device!

My hand is shaking. I might have just now caused some sort of

Armageddon…and for what? None of this helps me find Mom!

Enough of this screwing around. This iPad device is going back to school tomorrow. I'll never look at it or touch it again.

I feel a soft brush against my leg. It's Bastet. "You are trouble, girl!"

Her mischievous smirk is back.

"Why does Janus dislike you so much?"

She kneads her paws on the ratty couch, ripping the soft cloth with her claws. Her tail forms a question mark before she plops down on my lap. Oh, to be a cat…what a life!

Janus's wacky reactions to Bastet give me pause. Now more than ever, I'm sure that I can't trust him. It feels as if there's something more going on here.

Wait a second. Since I found this odd iPad device in my mom's secret room under the school, could it somehow lead me to her? Could the alarm on the device be some sort of hidden message from her, or maybe even a call for help?

I feel a surge of heat on my chest. It's Mom's cypress tree charm. An intense pulsing fills my heart. I feel compelled to go back through the mirror, to that other place…to "Olympus." It's as if the soul bridge between my mother and me – that invisible energy force that tells me she is still alive – tugs at my heart, urging me to act now. It's as if she's calling me to go to back there.

I tiptoe down the stairs to the shop and hold my finger out to trigger the basement door open. But it won't budge. Crap! Janus did this. He changed the lock, and now I can't go back there even if I wanted to. Depression hits me as I slump to the floor in defeat.

Suddenly, the red light on top of the device starts to flash again. Not again! I start to panic, but then I notice that, this time, the screen remains blank…until a remarkable thing happens.

Another source of low red light starts to flash on and off.

It's coming from the bookshelf-that-is-the-door to the basement. An idea comes to me to touch the light on the device to the light on the door.

Instantly, the flashing lights cease…and *click!* I'm inside.

Glee fills me as I run down the stairs, flip on the lights, and peer inside. My moment of triumph, though, is short lived when I see the grand mirror, but it's covered by a white sheet. Janus must have done this, too. Of course, he did.

I yank on the corner, and the sheet falls to the ground in one fell swoop. But the mirror is just a mirror. I knock on the glass, and nothing happens. I sigh in annoyed frustration, pacing around to check the back and the sides and then again to the front. Nothing.

I know why! Bastet didn't follow me down here. Where did she go? I thought she was right behind me. Frustrated, I start to worry that the place beyond the mirror might not really exist, that I must be freakin' nuts, when I notice that the heat is rapidly rising in the room. I hear the pitter-patter of Bastet's paw pads as she runs down the stairs.

I look up to study my reflection and notice that the cat's-eye stone at the top of the mirror is starting to glow, casting the same eerie bioluminescent blue light that I remembered from the last time I was here. The waterlike look of the mirror starts to fade, which prods me to jump through. Just like last time, my vision starts to spin as the world around me swirls into a magnificent blur of colors and lights, all racing forward to merge dynamically into the epicenter of a massive vortex.

When I open my eyes, there are two wide-eyed kids staring down at me. The boy and girl are maybe eleven or twelve, with skin of rich ebony. Their faces are wary and parched as they stand there holding gas masks in their gloved hands. The boy has a fresh scar on his cheek, as if he's recently been in a fight. They're wearing some serious desert survival gear. Every so often, they place a breathing ventilator over their mouths to take a breath.

The stare down continues as I attempt to stand, dusting off my body from the arduous journey. I feel a sharp pain in my side. The boy has stabbed me with what looks like a red-tipped spear.

"Hey!" I raise my voice. "That hurts." It barely sticks into my skin, so I pull it out and throw it on the ground. "Who are you?" I ask, irritated.

"You first!" the boy yells as he retrieves his spear.

"Yeah!" says the girl. Remarkably, we all seem to speak the same language. That, or it could be like Greek, where I somehow have the ability to understand them. Who knows?

Standing up to my full height, I tower over them. "I'm Helene. I came from there," I say, pointing back to the glowing portal.

"Yeah, we saw it," the boy says. His voice is laced with sarcasm.

The girl chimes in. "We've never seen a Dreg come through the Gate backwards before."

"*Dreg*?" I ask.

"Anyone who comes here to Gaea from the other side is a Dreg," the boy says firmly.

"Gaea?" I ask, puzzled.

"Yeah." His face is shrouded in apprehension. "You came from Earth." He waves his arms in an arc around him. "This planet...this is Gaea."

The girl seems calm. She looks at me, pointing behind us to where my behemoth lioness sits, and asks, "Is that your animal?"

Bastet glares intensely at the girl as fire dances in her stunning amber eyes.

I nod. "Yeah."

The kids look at each other Almost instantly, relief passes between them.

"I am Xonos." The boy steps up, then points to the girl. "And this is my sister, Serina. He points through the gaps in the crumbling stone open-air structure that we stand in, out to the far reaches of the desert, where the skies are consumed with raging fierce clouds of red dust slowly spinning counterclockwise as it crawls across the sand dunes towards a vast mountain on the horizon. It looks like a hurricane but out on the desert instead of over water.

"That's a sandicane." The boy's expression is grim. "It's headed this way. We don't want to get caught in it. We have to leave now." Xonos nods, then turns towards the Gate, which somehow has gone dormant, just a blank wall. "Turn it back on! You're going back!"

"I don't know how," I stammer, perplexed, as I look around for

Bastet. She's nowhere to be seen.

The ground starts to shake. The kids scream in fear as they point outside. "Look!"

Directly outside the door of the structure we stand in, the earth cracks open to form a large fissure, from which an enormous creature rises up. The beast looks like a wing-less cross between a dragon and a snake, with dark brown scales and blazing red eyes. Jagged horns cover the top of its head and grow smaller as they run down the spine of its snake-like body. It roars in fury as fire blazes from its mouth. The land churns and quakes as the creature snakes in and out of newly formed cracks in the sand directly in front of us. Just as the beast almost reaches the door to our structure, I spot what looks like a tiny man riding on the back of the beast. I point at him.

The kids yell, "Drakon rider!"

The giant beast roars one last time and plummets back into the depths of the dark crevasse. The land grows quiet and silent.

"What was that?" I ask, breathless.

"Drakon," Serina says with passion. "The riders guide them to break up and loosen the land and rocks with the fire from their mouths. Then the miners come in and take out the lumite. This mining is why this planet and others nearby are worthless desert wastelands."

We walk over to the edge of the crevasse that is quickly filling with sand. Directly in front of us is a large, smoldering, luminous white rock. Xonos points to it. "This is lumite, the primary source of power for the city of the gods, New Olympus." He points somewhere far off in the distance to where I can barely see a massive shiny silver pyramid jutting out of the desert sand.

"So, you're telling me that the gods from the old myths are real?"

The kids look at me, astonished, and say together, "What myths?"

"You know, the myths about the gods?" I say.

The kids look confused, but then Xonos says incredulously, "Oh, so you think that the gods are like characters in a fairy tale or something?"

Serina smirks. "I sure wish that were true! Then we could close the book and be rid of them, those yikkers!"

"But you can't because they're immortal, right?" I ask intently.

"Immortal?" she asks as if she doesn't understand what I mean.

"Yeah." I explain, "You know, like they live forever, can't be killed."

The kids exchange glances, then burst into laughter.

"Oh, they can die," Xonos corrects me. "In the old days, there were many more of what you think of as gods, but now only a few are left."

Something bothers me about this. If these "gods" can die and are not immortal, then how is it that thousands of years later, they are still alive? Time must move here at a much slower pace than in our universe.

The whistling winds of the sandicane are fast approaching. As we turn back towards the door to the structure where the Gate is, Bastet comes bounding around the corner, rushing past me towards the Gate. A harsh gust of wind sweeps past us, stirring up the sand. I feel the impact. *Whack!* I've been hit by something hard. Teetering and off balance, I slam against the side of the structure and onto my butt. That hurt!

"Are you okay?" I hear Xonos ask with genuine concern.

As I sit up, my ribs smart in pain. Not a good sign.

Some tumbling debris lies on the sand next to me. With the ferocious wind whipping my hair into my eyes and face, I can barely see it. I grab it, crawling on my belly through the sand. The kids follow behind me. We barely make it through the door into the structure. Sweat drips down my face as we stop to rest next to the Gate.

Bastet's cat's-eye charm is glowing brightly. The shimmery blue surface of the Gate looks alive in its bioluminescent splendor, all ready for me to go back to Earth.

The debris next to me look like a branch from a living tree. I'm surprised to see any sign of green plant life out here in this wasteland. The tree must be nearby if its branch is here now. It's not likely that the branch could tumble that far, even with the intense winds here.

This branch is odd. It's covered with symbols, as if they were carved with a knife but by different people, like graffiti. As I run my fingers over these symbols, I can feel my necklace getting warmer. I look down, and as I touch my mother's cypress tree pendant, it begins to glow.

"Hey, where did this come from?" I ask the kids. Something about these symbols seems eerily familiar to me, as if I've seen them somewhere before, but I can't recall where.

The kids tell me about the legend of the Last Standing Tree, which supposedly exists somewhere on Gaea. "But no one knows where it is. It's a mystery," Serina says with wide, innocent eyes.

"I don't think it's real," says Xonos in an edgy voice.

Hearing this brings to mind my mom. When I was growing up, she would tell me stories about an enchanted cypress tree, one that stood all alone in a friendless desert, the last of its kind.

"What are these carvings?" I ask, curious, still feeling the warmth on my chest. The howling of the wind is starting to reach the interior of the structure. I know there's no time for this, but I've got to know.

Xonos's eyes grow wide at the stirring sand around us. "We have to go." He motions to Serina, who places a full mask on her face. Just before Xonos starts to place the mask over his face, he becomes irate. "Helene, you won't survive the storm. You have to go back through the gate…*now!*"

A bizarre, soothing calm comes over me. Something about the warmth of the tree on my neck and this tree branch under my fingers makes me hesitate. I can't go back now.

"No!" I yell back. "I want to know more about this tree."

They both ignore me, shaking their heads through their masks.

Urgent, overzealous need overtakes me, so I grab Xonos's arm in desperation. Before I know what's happening, though, he forces me backwards, pushing me through the Gate. I hear Bastet roar behind me as I free-fall through space into nothingness…

19 - OLYMPUS ARCH

The cold, hard floor of the basement feels harsh under my aching body. I grunt as I turn my body over, my ribs smarting in pain. My headache is back too. It must be almost time for me to go to school, but I can't imagine going like this. Maybe I will call in sick.

I look around the room for Bastet, but there's no sign of her. What if she didn't make it back and she's stuck on Gaea? That would be bad. I'm not worried about Bastet being there alone because she seems more than capable of fending for herself there. But how will I get back?

My cell phone starts to beep. Crap! It's my alarm. Time to get up. Even more than before, I want to call in sick. I totally would except for my urgent need to get rid of the strange iPad device. It must go back to the secret room under the school...now.

Because I'm already running late, I skip my usual bus pickup and take a cab to within a few blocks of the school entrance. I just finish paying the driver when I hear a weird scraping noise somewhere behind me.

The sound is strangely familiar to me, but I don't know why. I halt and listen.

The sound stops.

Okay, that's *creepy*.

I start to walk again.

Scrape...shuffle...scrape.

A memory floods my mind. I flip around.

There's nothing there but my shadow stretching long across the sidewalk in the early morning sunlight. A throng of tourists stands on the sidewalk across the street taking photos of an average-looking building.

There's enough people here that I'm not that scared…not like before when that washed-out, sickly looking man at the Metro station was following me and gave me the ring!

I start walking again, but this time, I watch my shadow move behind me from the corner of my eye. Just then, a much larger shadow emerges from mine.

Shuffle… scrape…

I whip around to face my perpetrator. Instantly, I recognize this pasty-pale seventy-something man with disgusting yellow teeth and wearing a crappy suit: my mom's attorney, Harold "Hal"' Avery!

I open my mouth. "Hal…"

Before I can finish, a horde of tourists crosses the street and swallows him up right before my eyes.

Where did he go? I search the crowd, but there's no sign of him. I blink my eyes a few times. But he's not there. *Gone.*

At school, I stifle a yawn as I plop my stuff down next to my desk and take a seat in mythology class. Our teacher, Ms. Petraki, who stands at least a whole head shorter than me, speaks in a squeaky voice as she hands me my corrected book report. For once there are no red marks on the page.

The chair next to me sits vacant. Usually a quiet, dark-haired girl named Anya sits there, but she's out today, which is weird because I heard that she holds the class record for perfect attendance. I feel a tap on my shoulder. It's Vani. Her usual perkiness is somewhat muted today, as if she's deep in serious thought.

"First Sonia, then Philippos, and now Anya's not here?" Vani's voice is breathy, like she's winded. "It's weird."

"Yeah, really. What's going on with them?" I ask, curiosity suddenly overtaking me.

"No one knows. I tried calling Sonia yesterday and no answer. I've asked around to see what I could find out, where she could be. I made Alexis go to her house. He knocked on the door, but no one was there. It's like she's just vanished into thin air."

I shudder. "That is strange!"

"Now, with Anya out – and you know she's never absent – I know something's going on," Vani says. "And I'm going to find out what it is."

Vani and I stare at the vacant seat just behind me on Vani's left. That seat belongs to Samantha.

"By the way, where is...our favorite person today?" I say, suddenly curious.

Vani shrugs, raising an eyebrow. "Don't know."

It's horrible of me, I know, but for a split second, I feel happy as I fantasize that whatever is going on with the others has also happened to Samantha, that she might be gone for good and never bother me again.

Ms. Petraki doesn't seem to notice us talking as she walks the aisles, still handing out the reports, bending over occasionally to whisper into a student's ear.

"One more thing," Vani says, making me turn to face her.

"Yes?"

"I absolutely cannot stand it one more moment." She looks exasperated. "I mean, *really*, you can't continue to wear these blousy clothes. Time to upgrade."

I look down and see what she means. The long, flowery shirt that I'm wearing with black leggings flows around my body like a giant tent. It looks a little silly and doesn't complement my new physique at all.

"What do you have in mind?" I ask.

"Shopping with me this weekend," she says with a gleam in her eye.

"Uh, I'm not sure about that," I say hesitantly. "I don't have any money except the tiny amount that Janus gives me whenever he feels like it."

Vani quirks her eyebrow at me as if confused. Ms. Petraki's squeaky voice takes over with the day's lesson. "Let's talk about it later," I say. I can tell Vani has no concept of what it's like to not have endless funds available for shopping whenever she wants.

"You at least need a decent dress for the dance!"

"Oh, I'm *not* going," I whisper. I can't even begin to verbalize the reasons why not. Let's see...my dead mom is alive and I need to find her. Oh, and as if that weren't enough, no one has asked me to go to the dance. And since it's only a week away, I'm sure it's not going to happen now. It's too late.

Vani forms a *W* with her fingers and mouths the word *whatever.*

The class is discussing ancient Greek mythology. Ms. Petraki draws a flowchart on the dry erase board that defines the twelve key Greek gods and goddesses and their relationships: first Zeus, Poseidon, and Hades, and then the other eight – Hera, Athena, Artemis, Apollo, Hermes, Hestia, Demeter, Aphrodite, and Ares.

Suddenly, something distracts Ms. Petraki, which causes her to stop short. She looks down in confusion at something on her laptop. Eyes wide, she rushes over to turn on a large computer monitor on the wall. As she flips it on, the screen blares with breaking news:

A group of mountain climbers have accidentally discovered the ruins of what looks like an ancient archway in a cave on a plateau near the summit of Mytikas Peak on Greece's highest mountain, Mount Olympus. This is an incredible archaeological discovery for historians. Initial estimations place its construction around the second millennium BCE.

My heart stops. This "ruin" looks almost identical to the Gate on Gaea...*my* Gate. The hieroglyphs, or more likely logograms, etched into the top of this Gate appear to be in some unknown ancient writing system, presumably some precursor to ancient Greek. Maybe like Linear A? If so, this is exciting. Some argue that deciphering Linear A holds the answers to the origins of early civilization.

Ms. Petraki freezes the screen to pause on a picture of the Gate with the logograms displayed clearly. Giddy with excitement, she turns to the class, still looking down at her laptop from time to time as she reads the news to us. "Experts from all over the world are gathering together in an effort to understand this incredible discovery. They are calling this treasure the Olympus Arch."

I glance down at the mythology workbook on my desk. When I look up again, I gasp in surprise. What appeared as ancient logograms just a moment ago now become visible to me as words: **Only one of the lumite may pass.**

I must have said it out loud because Ms. Petraki responds, "I'm sorry, but Helene, what did you just say?"

All eyes are suddenly on me as I'm singled out in front of the class. I croak, "I think it says, 'Only one of the lumite may pass.'"

The whole class stares at me like I am a complete idiot. Ms. Petraki laughs and says, "So you can read unknown ancient words, then? Nice try."

But there's more. On both sides of the arch, I can now clearly see twelve symbols, six on each side. I recognize them immediately. These are the same symbols that were etched into the tree branch on Gaea.

As the teacher continues the lecture, she asks us to open our workbooks to page fifteen, so I do. There, right beneath my eyes, one of the symbols appears…the hearth.

This is the sign of the goddess Hestia!

Excited at this revelation, I eagerly flip through the workbook. Page after page show another god or goddess and the symbols that typically represent them in mythology. A lightning bolt for Zeus. An owl for Athena. A dove for Aphrodite. A bow and arrow for Artemis. A lyre for Apollo. A hearth for Hestia. A trident for Poseidon. A sword for Ares. A hammer for Hephaestus. A winged shoe for Hermes. A peacock feather for Hera. A grain cob for Demeter. A helm for Hades.

The gods and goddesses of Olympus!

Something is strange about this. I can't quite figure out why. My thoughts shift back to the image of the tree branch sitting in my arms and the eerie glowing of my mother's cypress tree necklace. Why would it glow? Maybe I was imagining it.

The bell rings and class is over, but the teacher asks me to stay behind. She's quiet for a moment, then asks, "Helene, what is *lumite*?"

"Um…" I start to tell her that it is a mineral that is mined on another planet called Gaea, but then I realize that Ms. Petraki might think that I'm insane. No one knows about Gaea here, so I quickly backtrack. "I mean, never mind. I just made it up."

Ms. Petraki's face drops in frustration. She must have wanted to know. Maybe she had heard of it somewhere before. Then she says something interesting. "I've been to that cave on that plateau before and have never seen anything like this there. Many people have been there. I wonder how those climbers suddenly 'discovered' it? Very odd."

PART II: SYNCHRONICITY

"Every heart sings a song, incomplete, until another heart whispers back."

—Plato

Old Olympus designed by Nasia Kalokerinou of Kinari Design
www.kinaridesign.com

20 - BALLERINA

The startling discovery at Mount Olympus leads to more questions. If the gods from our myths are in fact real people and their symbols are carved into the stone of this Olympus Arch gateway, is it possible that this is how they came to Earth thousands of years ago? If so, then one very important question remains:

If, as Xonos and Serina said, the gods are not immortal, then how are they still alive on Gaea after so much time has passed?

I don't get it.

My mind spins. I look down at my watch: time for lunch and siesta. I make my way to the cafeteria. The gymnasium is completely dark. It looks like the yoga studio is not in use. A perfect time to dance. The sudden urge to *move* once again comes over me. I haven't been in here since the last time I danced, when I injured myself and Ever came to my rescue. Was that just last week? It feels as if months have gone by since I first arrived here in Athens and started school.

Someone flips the lights on, flooding the gym with bright light, and a group of boys charges inside. Looks like basketball practice. The noise level rises in the gym as the boys pass the ball back and forth and then start running laps around the perimeter. Disappointment hits me hard. There's no way I can dance in here with all these boys watching.

I look down at my leg that I injured and study it carefully. Slowly, I gingerly step down onto it. I feel nothing...no twinge...no dull ache. I run my finger across the place where my old scar resides but then quickly pull my hand back when I realize that there's nothing there. My scar is gone. God, this is exciting! My body tingles in anticipation. My need to dance is so overwhelming now that I no longer care who is watching me. Nothing can stop me.

Nothing, that is, until I see Ever Sarantos saunter into the gym. What is he doing here?

I feel the heat rise inside as my frustration grows. Why does he have to show up every time I want to dance? The coach marches over to him, clearly upset, probably because he's late to practice.

As I close the door to the yoga studio and look out to the gym through the windows, I see Ever gaze in my direction. His eyes light up when he notices me, a huge smile crossing his face. He must know that I'm in here to dance because he nods in encouragement before turning back to his practice.

Standing at half court, he effortlessly shoots the ball with one hand. The ball travels through the air in a high arc, then *swoosh*…it travels swiftly through the basket and down to the floor. He turns my way with a satisfied grin, then winks at me, like he was showing off and wanted me to see how amazing he is. Everything always seems so effortless for him.

But then he points to the empty studio and holds his arms up like he's trying to be a ballerina, then nods as if this is his way of letting me know that he's on my side. He wants to see me try again…to dance.

This is all the encouragement I need. No longer do I feel fear, pain, or anxiety about anyone watching. It's time to fly high and free as a bird, to soar through the boundaries that constrained me before, to dance again…for real this time.

Humming softly, I scan my iPod song list. Some unseen force moves me to stop at one of my favorite ballets ever – Prokofiev's *Romeo and Juliet*. I dim the lights so all I can see is my silhouette in the full-length mirrors that grace all four walls of the room. Delight etches my face when I see the bouncy wooden floor beneath my feet. I strip off my oversized flower shirt down to my camisole and leggings, plug in my iPod into the overhead sound system, and hit play.

The deep sound of the viola fills the room, then the strings of the violin begin with a slow, soft vibrato that awakens something inside of me, an inner energy deep down in my core. I reach for the barre on the wall and find myself startled by my image – long, lean legs, thin waist and torso, strong wiry arms. My body is no longer that of a ballet dancer since I have curves now. I feel so strong and alive, vibrant and beautiful. At long last, I'm comfortable with the girl who stares back at me in the mirror.

The high arch of my foot extends to a perfect point down to the end of my toes. I sweep my leg back up into a graceful attitude, and using my hand to hold my leg up, I extend it out into a perfect split with my back arched. This is shocking, as I am more limber now than ever before, even when I danced several hours every day.

Absolutely amazing.

I lift and extend my leg out in front of my body and lay it flat up on the barre, and as I gracefully stretch my body down over it, my back flattens to lie completely on top of my raised leg. The bold sound of the clarinets begin, which is my cue that it's time to let go…to live in the moment…to dance the famous balcony scene that I know so well in my heart.

The first beats of the flute call out, and suddenly I'm transported back in time. I envision myself back on stage at the War Memorial for the San Francisco Ballet Student Showcase.

I'm up on a balcony staring out at an empty stage, visualizing my long, sheer skirt billowing in an artificial breeze. My hand cups my cheek as I gaze with a faraway gaze into the blackness of a fairy-tale night…and then I see him, my imagined Romeo, as he sweeps into my view, and I will myself to become Juliet.

My world shifts to one where I absolutely adore him. I'm consumed with utter and desperate love, the kind that I would die for. As the music pulses, my breath hitches in my chest when I see my Romeo run to me. Giddiness fills my whole being as I run to him. And he sweeps me away into the most incredible dance of my life. He spins me towards him, and I feel the softness of his face warm against my cheek as we waltz together in effortless grace.

As I arch my back and swing my leg up behind me into a dramatic arabesque, I imagine him lifting me high overhead, swinging me down into a graceful arc, ending on my toes. My body moves effortlessly as I wrap my arms around my imaginary Romeo.

Only he's no longer imaginary.

In the low light of the yoga room, I see the dark silhouette of a beautiful man standing in front of me…

Ever.

I'm so swept up in the moment, in the fantasy of this dance, that Ever becomes Romeo for me. In the splendor of the dance, I completely give myself to him, and in this moment, I feel so alive. As the music draws to its end, I feel the perfect center of gravity when I turn in a pirouette once…twice…three…and four times, ending in a gorgeous arch of my body in magical alignment with his.

My real-life Romeo silently pulls me up. Moving slowly behind me, his hands encircle my waist as he draws me in close against his muscular frame.

Oh my. His breath is hot on my neck just under my ear, sending shivers up and down my neck and spine. "That was amazing," he whispers. "You're amazing."

I'm still partially lost in the fantasy of the dance, but a real tear streams down my face. I begin to cry for real. I imagine Romeo in the story leaving me now. As I feel him start to pull away, my body screams, *Don't leave me!*

The music ends. I collapse on the floor, panting and sweating in elation as I envision the applause from my imaginary audience.

A sound startles me. As I slowly come out of my trance, I look over and see Ever standing there, concern filling his sea-green eyes. He's worried about me.

I sniffle and wipe the tears from my eyes. I'm sure I look like a mess.

"Are…you okay?" he asks hesitantly. His smile is warm but slightly worried.

"Yes, of course!" I stammer, struggling to catch my breath. "I'm fine."

"Okay, good." His eyes are wide as if he's perplexed, thinking about something. He walks over to the other side of the room and comes back a moment later with a tissue. "Here."

After I wipe my tears away, Ever extends his hand to help me up.

"How did you get in here? You were…playing basketball," I whisper. I feel so totally exposed, as if he just read my diary and now knows all my innermost secrets, my walls torn down in one fell swoop.

Totally unacceptable.

"Are you…upset?" he asks in surprise. "You look angry."

"When I dance, I let my imagination take over, as if I'm not really here in this room. It's like a fantasy for me. You being here was …unexpected."

In front of us, the entire gymnasium is illuminated through a long row of windows. The scene before us sharpens into pristine focus when I notice that the entire basketball team is cheering with applause at us, whooping and hollering. Some are laughing.

I turn about five shades of red.

"See? They enjoyed your performance," Ever says with a smirk, pulling me up to my feet. "Time to own it. Take a bow."

Still blushing, I only slightly acknowledge this is happening with a little wave to the crowd. I hear the loud ruckus of the boys' stomping feet on the indoor bleachers. While I'm annoyed, part of me is pleased that they liked my performance.

Ever grins, clearly happy as we walk out together through the throng of rowdy basketball players, past his coach, who stands glowering at us with his arms crossed. "Sarantos, I need you back here ASAP!"

"Five minutes!" Ever scoffs indignantly.

The coach shakes his head. "I'm watching the clock."

As we walk out into the hallway, I pull my sheer flowery shirt back on over my head. Ever turns on the charm as he smiles sweetly at me. He seems a little too confident, as if he's up to something.

"So…you're going to the spring dance with me, right?"

Wait…*what* did he just say? I halt in the middle of the hall. The corridor is bustling with kids coming and going to their classes.

The dance, with *him*?

I should be ecstatic, but instead I'm confused. The nonchalant way that he asked the question was so arrogant, so presumptive. He must think that he's my Romeo in real life now, that I'm going to fawn over him like all the other girls. He thinks he knows all about me, who I am, but he has no idea.

"Dance? I don't recall you asking me to go."

"Well, I am now."

Backing up, I shake my head at him. "You really are something, you know that?"

He smirks. "You didn't say no."

"Definitely no!" I say in a mocking tone, shaking my head. We turn and walk outside onto the grass and into the bright, sunny afternoon.

I hear Ever say, "Great! See you there next Saturday at eight, just after the band gets warmed up."

I pretend not to hear him as I walk straight ahead and across the circle driveway in front of the school. How could he not hear me say no just now?

Shouldn't it have felt more special when he asked me to the dance? It's as if he expects me to meet him there. This is a formal dance. He should pick me up at my house. I start to ruminate about this. Perhaps he's just asking me to go as his friend. That's how it seems. I bet he would pick up Samantha in a Rolls Royce.

I'm overcome with disappointment. I don't want to go as his friend! Despite the long trail of girls who follow him everywhere, I can't shake the feeling that he's special to me, maybe meant to be something more, especially after he became the Romeo to my Juliet just now in the studio. Not "just friends"!

Besides, I'm frustrated that I've made very little progress in my search for Mom. Why not?! I came to Greece to find her, and for what? I feel like I've been spinning my wheels, getting nowhere. Too many distractions. That settles it. I'm not going to the dance. *No matter what.*

A big shiny black Mercedes squeals to a halt next to us. Alarm fills me for a second, but when the driver's window inches down, I hear a familiar voice call out, "Ever! We need to go now. There's an urgent matter with your mother."

I instantly know that voice, that smooth Greek-English accent. It's the driver who saved me at the airport when I first arrived in Athens, my first friend in Greece, and now my science teacher. Dimitris.

"Mr. Paxinos?" I say, not able to help myself. "Shouldn't you be in class? Working? Science is my next class."

Dimitris turns to look at me, but he's clearly in a hurry, so he responds in a cool, clipped, professional tone. "I *am* working. There's no time to explain now, but I'm not teaching here anymore. I work exclusively for the Sarantos family now."

This is sad. I have grown so fond of him as my teacher. I can't imagine this wonderful, kind man not sharing all his knowledge and warmth with us in class.

"No!" I exclaim in frustration. My head is starting to ache, so I rub my temples.

Ever nods to Dimitris. "What's this about?"

The light fades from Dimitris's eyes as if there's no life there for a moment. "Your mother, she's horribly sick. We have to go to the hospital *now*."

Ever sinks down into the backseat in silence. I watch his usual mask of overconfidence rapidly descend into vulnerability as he grapples with what is happening. It's obvious how much his mother means to him. He loves her dearly. His face is filled with anguish, worry, and fear.

I remember feeling this way just a few weeks ago when the police officer told me the horrible news about my mother's death. And now, even though I know she's alive, I *still* feel it. It tears me up to see Ever like this. My heart goes out to him.

"Helene," he says quietly. "Come with me. *Please.* I can't do this alone."

21 – THE SYNDICATE

I can't say no to Ever. He needs me.

"Of course," I say as I sink down into the soft leather seat next to him. He grabs my hand, holding it tightly.

"Thank you," he says softly, squeezing my hand.

He gazes out the car window. As we drive through the city at maximum speed, the bustling street life in Athens swirls by us as it quickly morphs into a gray, muddied canvas interspersed with splashes of color. The outside world seems so very far away from us right now.

Before we know it, we arrive at Evaggelismos Hospital and rush inside. Once there, we check in at the front desk and are quickly ushered to a special waiting area for friends and family.

As we step inside, Ever's dad and his newly adopted brother, Thomas, are waiting for us. My heart rate goes haywire when it dawns on me that I'm here in the same room as the notorious Georgios Sarantos...the man who tried to kill me.

Both he and Thomas look exhausted and sad, but something about Thomas is different now. His skin and hair are noticeably darker, and his eyes appear to be light brown now instead of the silver-gray color from before. Strange.

While I try not to, I can't help but stare at Georgios Sarantos. The pictures do not do him justice. He is just as ridiculously handsome as Ever but in a more sophisticated and mature way, appearing regal and powerful with his piercing brilliantly blue eyes; short, curly dark hair; and manicured beard. And while I know that now is not the time for it, I sense that before this day is done, I will have my chance to ask where my mom is. Georgios Sarantos will know the truth, and he's going to tell me about it. I just know it.

At first, I'm a little nervous by the presence of the two bodyguards standing near the doorway, dressed in plain black suits and staring straight ahead as if they are mannequins. But I know better. One of them is Dimitris, and I know that he's not a mannequin. At least I'm comforted that he's here in case Sarantos decides to take me out here and now. Dimitris wouldn't let that happen. Neither would Ever.

"Dad? This is my friend, Helene Crawford."

I cringe at the word "friend," my earlier suspicions now confirmed.

When Ever's father looks up at me, his eyes open wide as if he's just seen a ghost. "Oh," he says, drawing in his breath. In the next second, his demeanor shifts back into almost perfect normalcy, as if I'm nothing special. But I know what I just saw in his eyes. He knows who I am.

"*Kalispera*," he says politely, extending his enormous hand to shake mine. "Thanks for being here with us."

Before I can respond, a doctor with a clipboard steps into the room. "Sarantos?" He makes eye contact with Ever's dad, who nods. "Please step over to room two."

The doctor steps aside as the nurse guides us into the room. Ever's mother appears to be sleeping. Incredibly beautiful before, now her face is blotchy and sunken. Her shiny blond hair is pulled back, appearing in this light as a stark shade of white.

Ever rushes over to her side. "Mama..." Eyes wide and unblinking, he holds her hand almost desperately, as if he can heal her now with his love. Seeing him here so much like a child, so innocent, ignites my nurturing side. It makes my heart ache. I feel so overwhelmingly sad for him.

Ever sniffles, and then he's sobbing. As he looks up at me with a puffy, tear-streaked face, I pull him close into a warm embrace. He holds me tight, his fear and anguish so deep. I find myself stunned to see him like this, so vulnerable and different from the person who I thought he was. The extreme confidence he normally shows to the world is completely gone. He is so distraught, he doesn't even try to hide his raw sadness from me. After a moment, his body slows, the sobbing stops, and his tears dry.

I pull back and gaze into Ever's eyes. "I only met your mom that one time, but if she's as strong-willed as you, she'll pull through this." After crying, his irises appear almost liquid, assuming an incredible shade of vibrant turquoise. While always some shade of blue, it's as if the color of his eyes adapts to how he's feeling. Just like mine. A chameleon. He nods solemnly, forming a half smile. Maybe it's helping at least a little bit for me to be here with him.

Just then, an attractive brunette woman abruptly rushes in and wraps her arms around Ever's dad. "Georgios, I came as fast as I could."

Georgios stands to his full height, which must be over six and a half feet, takes the woman's hand, and pulls her in close. It's disturbingly obvious that something romantic is going on between these two.

All of a sudden, monitors go off, beeping like crazy, and I notice that Ever's mother is awake. Her eyes are filled with pain and alarm as she struggles, almost convulsing as she shakes her head, trying to sit up. Even as sick as she is, she's going crazy. It's not hard to guess why.

Ever's eyes light up at the sight of her awake. "Mom!"

A nurse yells, "Sedate her!" A team of people rush into the room and inject something into her IV. Ever's mother instantly falls back deep into sleep.

"*No!!*" Ever yells at the nurses as he slams his hand hard on the table next to the bed.

His dad rushes over to him. "Ever, calm down. It's probably just a severe case of the flu. All she needs is rest. I'm sure she'll be fine."

Ever whips around to face his dad, anger boiling over to irate, heated fury. "This is all *your* fault, Dad!" He points over to the brunette woman, standing there with her mouth hanging open. "You brought *her* here! How could you do that? And right in front of Mom while she's sick?" The tears start to fall down his cheeks again. "How could you?"

Georgios is not taking this treatment from his son. "I said calm down, Ever. *Now!*" He gestures to the brunette woman and Thomas. "Nadia, can you take Thomas outside and wait for me in the car? I need to sort this out."

The woman, Nadia, is clearly concerned, but she nods. The stoic bodyguard who is not Dimitris leads her and Thomas out the door.

"Please excuse us for a moment," Georgios says to me as he and Ever step to the other side of the room.

It's as if a super-volcano just exploded. Their arugment goes back and forth intensely. They glare at each other in stubborn silence until finally Ever slumps down into a chair, presumably in defeat. My heart aches for him.

Georgios Sarantos strides over and turns his attention to me.

"I know…I mean I knew your mother. You look so much like her." He appears sad but then grins with a nostalgic look in his intelligent blue eyes. "Diana was one heck of a woman, that's for sure. She will be missed."

What? I am stunned. This isn't what I would expect to hear from a major crime boss, and most definitely not from the one who is responsible for my mother's disappearance and for hiring the gunman who tried to *kill* me.

Ever is silent. His eyes dart first to me, then back to his dad. Clearly, he's as surprised by his dad's fond recollection of my mother as I am.

Despite this, I'm convinced that Georgios must know where she is. Since I need to find out, the fear of his killing me now doesn't seem to matter. I can't stop myself from blurting out, "I know she's not dead."

"You think so? Well, then, perhaps there is hope after all. Best of luck with that." He turns to leave, but I'm not finished with this conversation yet. He's not getting off the hook that easily.

"I heard that this group like the mafia in Greece was behind her disappearance. The *Syndicate*. Would you happen to know anything about that?"

He says nothing.

Anxiety about my mom threatens to overwhelm me. Fueled by the angst generated earlier from the conflict between Ever and his dad, I feel totally uninhibited, free to finally ask whatever I need to ask.

"*Where is she?* You must know."

Ever looks up in alarm, staring at both of us in shock, as if I've betrayed him by not telling him about my mom before. It pains him; I can tell.

Georgios runs his fingers nervously through his hair, then looks at me...and laughs loudly. Not just a regular laugh, but a hearty, deep, throaty laugh. "You are so much like your mother...so much fire, passion." He smiles wistfully. "It was part of what I loved about her so much. Of course, she was not the least bit interested in me, though."

I stammer, "You...you *loved* my mother?"

"Bloody hell!" Ever scoffs loudly.

Georgios explains how he had courted Diana many years ago, way before my time and his marriage to Ever's mother, Elizabeth. Diana was his first love. But it wasn't meant to be, as she did not return his affections.

"So...the *mafia*?" he says, smirking. Then he laughs again. "Most of the Greek mafia is gone, as everyone of such influence has been arrested. And the way that you said the word *Syndicate*...sorry, it's just so funny to hear it said with so much venom, as if it is hell and I am the devil who rules it."

Ever hides his head in his hands, clearly upset.

"But you tried to kill me!"

Sarantos is shocked. "What?!" He seems offended, but then he starts to chuckle. "I don't kill people!" A mask of seriousness falls over his features. "While I dabble in the black market here in Greece, I assure you that the government is intimately aware of my business operations and activities, legal or not. In fact, the government relies on me to do my part to keep the markets rolling. It is not my fault that they can't collect their tax payments. No one wants to see the funds going to pay down the ridiculous amount of debt this country is in. I am just a necessary cog in a broken system."

Ever cuts in. "Sweet Jesus, Dad...really?"

Georgios ignores him, still focusing on me. "Believe it or not, I'm not the bad guy here. My mission is to help the hardworking people of Greece, especially those from the now nonexistent middle class, who are the victims of a broken system. My wealth is anonymously funneled into nonprofit efforts such as setting up refugee camps or providing food and shelter for those who need it. I work extraordinarily hard to allow the lower classes to keep as much of their hard-earned money as possible. I give them work, the kind of work that feeds their families and allows them to avoid these ridiculous taxes so they can survive in these hard times. You may call it the black market or the Syndicate…but I call it survival."

Georgios watches the nurses and hospital personnel scurry by. "I'm just as curious about your mother's whereabouts as you are. One thing I know for sure, though, is that if Diana doesn't want to be found, you won't find her."

It so deflating to finally be here talking to the one man who I was so sure could help me, now only to find out *nothing*. He doesn't seem to know any more than I do. But one thing is for certain…finally someone besides Hal Avery is admitting that my mother might be alive somewhere and not dead, that she may have willingly disappeared. But *why*? Why would she leave her only daughter – *me* – behind like that?

Georgios breaks my train of thought. "Well, my car awaits. Nice to finally meet you, Helene. Perhaps you will let me know when you find your mother. I would really love to see her again." He turns on his heel to head outside, but just as he reaches the door, he looks my way one last time. "A few words of caution. If you are anything like your mother, you're stubborn and reckless." His tone is terse and abrupt. "Don't do anything foolish. Stay put and out of trouble. *Understand?*"

22 – ROCK STAR

Stubborn and reckless? Is that what he thinks of my mother? If so, he's all wrong. *Adaptable* and *vigilant* are much better words to describe her. He obviously doesn't know her as well as he thinks.

Something is gnawing at the back of my mind. For Sarantos to know that my mom is still alive, he must have either seen her recently or heard affirmation from someone else. There's more to this story than he's told me.

Ever sits next to me, his dark hair disheveled and spiked out in several directions. He stares straight ahead in awkward silence. His eyes are tired and red rimmed, but in this dire state, somehow he's even more attractive to me.

We are both in shock, but I know already that I'm in big trouble with Ever. I can only imagine how this whole thing looked to him, like I used him. Maybe I did.

I try to explain. "I'm sorry, I—"

He cuts me off. "No. It's just…" He pauses, taking a moment to study his hands. When he looks up again, his eyes are alive with fire. He's angry. His hands shake as he struggles to find the words he wants to say.

"Why didn't you tell me the truth about your mom?!"

I knew he was upset, but not like this. An aura of fury fills the space between us.

The truth is that I can't remember why I didn't tell him. I'm still so dazed from that talk with his dad, the illustrious Georgios Sarantos, that I can't even think straight. What a bizarre and surreal experience.

He raises his voice. "You don't trust me!"

"No, that's not it." Then I remember something. "Okay, well, actually, I'm not sure how to say this without you getting mad at me…"

"I'm already mad!" Ever exclaims.

"Okay, fine!" I say, frustrated with him. I take a deep breath before continuing. "You're right. I don't trust you. I barely know you."

"What?!" He's totally dumbfounded, as if no one has said this to him before.

"I…I just moved here – to a new country where I have no one – because I thought that my mom died in a fire, and then, some mafia hit man tried to kill me!"

"But my dad's not with the mafia!!" Ever shouts.

"How would I have known that?!" I raise my voice. Tears well up in my eyes, but I won't let myself cry. Not now. "When I found out there's a chance that she could be alive, that she might be here in Athens, perhaps held captive by the mafia, or the Syndicate, I did what I had to. I won't stop until I find her, even if it means you won't like me anymore!"

I can see the turmoil of feelings stir as the tension slowly leaves his face. I feel my heart rate slow as I catch my breath. Some unspoken understanding passes between us.

His voice is sweet and somber as he breaks the quiet. "I will *always* understand when it comes to family. You know what mine means to me. I can't bear to think about life without my mom." His voice cracks as the liquid turquoise consumes his eyes once more. He looks over to the window where his mother is sleeping peacefully. "I can only imagine how horrible it has been for you to be without her, to not know where she is and go through all that craziness by yourself."

All the angst I felt only a moment ago crumbles. I stare at Ever, eyes wide, brimming with tears. I'm about to break down and cry for real when he pulls me in close to a tight hug. Warmth fills me as I inhale his sweet scent. For a moment, I wish that I could rest here in his arms like this forever.

I draw in a breath as he steps back and looks in my eyes. I see something new in his. It's as if all that anger tore us apart, only to bring us back now closer.

I don't know why, but my stomach flutters as if a million

butterflies swarm there. It makes me want to run somewhere far, far away and hide. My mind is a messy jumble.

I feel raw and exposed here with Ever now, so instead of enjoying the sweetness of this moment, I say something stupid. "How could you possibly understand anything about my life when you have it so easy?"

His eyes grow wide in shock, incredulous. "Why would you say that?" He shakes his head and sighs loudly before his eyes lock onto mine again. "Unbelievable!" He slams his hand down on the table, making me want to jump out of my seat.

"Why does everyone think that I'm just some spoiled rich kid? Like my life is so perfect?" He stands and begins to pace. "I've been working since I was twelve for my dad's company, which everyone thinks is mostly a front for the Syndicate, doing grunt work that I hate because he has this crazy vision that I will someday take over his empire, which I have absolutely *zero* interest in. In fact, I really feel sorry for the girl who wants to be with me for my money."

"I don't care about your money!" I say, but it's as if he doesn't hear. He's on a roll. Clearly, I've hit his emotional hot button. "Because after this shithole economy eats up all the profit from my dad's business or whenever he gets shot dead by one of the street gangs, I will be left with *nothing*. Heck, maybe they will shoot me too. But none of that matters anyway, because..." – he stops for a moment to catch his breath and collect his thoughts, then continues a little more slowly now – "...because my plan after high school is to move away to Los Angeles with my band where we can jam, go to the beach, and play volleyball." His eyes light up in excitement. "And maybe someday I'll be a famous rock star!"

Ever captivates me when he talks about his passions. I feel drawn in and swept away into his vision for the future, as if we're on a road trip and he's taking me along for the ride.

"Rock star?" I ask. Not that this is that surprising. He is the lead singer for a rock band at our school, after all. But Los Angeles? I tease him a little. "I know you sing with your band, but are you any good?"

"Any good?" he says with intense fervor as if it were the most ridiculous question I could ask. The recessed lighting above reflects onto the surface of his eyes, making them appear almost gray-blue now. "You've obviously never seen me perform before!"

I love how strongly Ever emphasizes certain vowels when he's truly excited – so much passion in his words, which, coupled with his sweet Greek accent, fans the flames inside me. I'm entranced.

"True, but…" I say playfully.

"I have something special in mind for you at the dance – a song that I wrote. You have to hear it."

Not the dance again! He didn't hear me say no before, or perhaps he ignored it.

Wait, did he just say that he wrote a song…for me? I must not have heard him correctly. This must be a mistake. I was *not* going with him before, mostly because I was hurt that he wanted to go as "friends," but now my willpower wavers. He's staring into my eyes with so much…what is it? Adoration. The flutter in my stomach returns. I *want* to go with him. I can't help it.

Then the voice of reason fills my head. Even if this is something more than friends, I can't go with him, or anyone, for that matter. Above all else, I need to spend my time looking for my mom.

"Uh, about the dance. I…uh…well…" I say as my eyes rove around the room. I can't bring myself to look directly at Ever.

"Yes?" he says. Maybe I see just a hint of doubt cross his features, but in a flash, it's gone.

"I won't be here, so…"

"What?" His expression is incredulous. "You can't miss the dance! Whatever it is, reschedule. Really, no one misses the spring dance. Of course you're going!"

I still can't look at him, so I sigh and remain completely silent. I won't win this with him. He's very convincing. I'll have to bow out later somehow. Maybe he can sing his song for some other girl since I highly doubt that he wrote it just for me. I bet that he wrote this song a long time ago and now recycles it over and over to sing to unsuspecting girls when he wants to win them over.

The nurse enters the room and closes the curtain. "Time's up."

"We have to go now?" Ever says. "But we just got here."

A look of mild annoyance comes across the nurse as she looks down at the clipboard. "Your mother will be asleep for at least the next twelve hours. We have your cell number in case anything changes. We'll let you know."

Ever is not happy about this. He clearly doesn't want to leave his mother's side. But the nurse is ready for us to go. Her tone is clipped as she says, "Your mother will want you to go out and live your life while we assess her situation. Now, run along."

They stare at each other for a bit before Ever takes my hand to lead me out. As we leave the waiting area in the hospital and go down the front steps to the street, I see the hint of a shadow standing nearby.

"Your bodyguard?" I ask, already knowing the answer.

"Yeah. It's your buddy Dimitris," he says with a grin.

The shadow turns human and steps out into the light of the streetlamps. It's almost dark now as the sun has just set below the horizon. Ever nods to Dimitris curtly, but Dimitris stares straight ahead, stoic like a statue.

"Dimitris?" I ask. I'm not used to seeing him like this. No reaction. I can't keep myself from walking up to him, where I stand on my tiptoes to reach his eye level, trying to make him acknowledge me.

"Why did you quit teaching?" I ask, trying to rouse him from his mute stance.

A smile flashes across his face, but he won't look at me. His ability to ignore me is quite impressive.

"Really? You can't talk to me? That seems a bit extreme," I say.

Finally, he chuckles and relaxes, making eye contact. His voice is low and hushed, as if this discussion is completely forbidden. "I'm not supposed to talk to anyone outside of my immediate charge." His eyes dart over to Ever.

Ever scoffs. "Like I care! C'mon, Dimitris, stop being silly."

Dimitris sighs, then visibly relaxes. "Ah, well. We can't always follow the rules." He grins, pulls out a cigarette, and lights it up before continuing. "I had to quit teaching because Sarantos hired me full time." His eyes are intense.

"I can't believe you gave up doing what you love. You were such a great teacher!" I say incredulously.

"I was working only four hours a day with the teaching, not enough to provide for my family. And trying to manage driving around that schedule was impossible. Besides, Sarantos pays so well. It's a great opportunity for me and an honor to work for him," he says firmly.

"And *me*," Ever says with a grin.

Dimitris rolls his eyes. "Yes, of course. I always enjoy a good challenge."

My stomach growls. Suddenly, I realize that we haven't eaten in hours. Ever must be starving. I turn to him and say, "You should eat."

His eyes light up slightly, and he nods. "Uh, yeah. I probably should," he says pensively. "You need to eat too, right? I know just the place."

Wait a second. Is he asking me out?

23 – AGORA

Just breathe, Helene! It's not a real date, just two friends hanging out. Ever's being nice, showing me around Athens because his mom is sick and mine is missing, so we have a lot in common. That's all it is. So much has happened tonight that instead of trying to control the situation, I decide to just relax and go with it.

It's already dark. We walk in the crisp, cool air for a while until we reach a cobblestone alley. A throng of tourists rushes past us. We walk up a long road, then down through a narrow alley, and come out into a large square.

"This is Monastiraki Square," Ever announces. A stately white stone Greek church with a domed bell tower stands in the middle of the square. The bells are ringing gladly, as if to announce the glory of life as another hour in time begins. Instantly, I feel transported back to a time when life was very different here...back to Byzantine times. Some things were simpler then, but most were much more trying, even compared to the current crisis.

We walk up some stairs and stop at a café built into the side of the hill. High up on the hill above rests the Parthenon, fully lit up in all its splendor. On the steps are cushions where people sit and dine with little footstools that serve as tables. At least twenty cats of every size and color wander from table to table in search of food scraps.

Ever says, "Most people say that the cats are the real owners of this place."

"It certainly seems that way," I say. I take in a deep breath, expecting the usual allergic reaction...but it's not there. Of course not. The Gate must have healed that too. "You like cats, then?" I ask.

"Ummm, no. Felines are too unpredictable, like women," he says playfully. "Dogs are much more reliable." He holds up his iPhone. Lit up in full color is a photo of Ever and a golden-colored dog with an adorable wrinkled face.

"Your dog?" I ask, "What's his name?"

"Hampos," He says, eyes dancing.

"But reliable can be monotonous," I say, teasing him. "Wouldn't you prefer unpredictable to boring?"

His eyes light up as he nods. "If for a woman, maybe." His tone is mischievous. "But for a cat, never."

The café owner beams when he sees Ever. He opens the door wide in welcome, patting Ever warmly on the back as if they are old friends. I haven't even had the chance to order when he places a stout-looking black coffee down in front of me. I frown when I notice that there's no cream nearby.

"Where's the cream?" I ask, perplexed.

Ever grins. "I take it that you haven't had real Greek coffee before. No one puts cream in Greek coffee. It detracts from the experience of savoring it." He picks up the cup in front of him and sips it slowly, his smile drawn in deep satisfaction as he gazes at me over his cup. Some of his earlier sadness must be back because his eyes take on a deep turquoise cast, the color that sweeps me away to another place, somewhere far away and blissful.

"What is it?" he asks.

Realizing that I must look ridiculous right now gawking at him like a doe-eyed puppy, I pick up my cup of coffee and take a sip. It's bitter and harsh. My whole face wrinkles in disgust. "Ugh, no," I say as I briskly set the cup down on the table.

He laughs as if he were expecting my reaction. "Well, I guess it's a bit of an acquired taste...but you had to try it. Everyone must try Greek coffee."

I see Dimitris standing by the door, trying not to smile at us. I'll bet he's seen a lot in his line of work, but I almost feel as if he's watching my back as much as he is Ever's.

Ever asks the café owner to bring me an espresso instead.

"Decaf," I correct him.

Ever gapes at me. "Decaf? Seriously? No one orders decaf

espresso. I'll bet he doesn't even have it."

The café owner shrugs as he explains to Ever that of course he has decaf espresso. The tourists from America order it all the time.

"See?" I say. "And since I am from America, I should be allowed a little break here. I would like to get to sleep at some point tonight. An espresso at this hour would keep me up all night."

Smiling, Ever shrugs in defeat. "Fair enough, American girl."

The café owner comes back. Ever turns to me. "Want dessert?"

"What? Oh, why not?" I sigh as it dawns on me that in only a few days, I will be eighteen. "My birthday is this Sunday."

Ever looks surprised. "You're an Aries?"

"Yep," I'm glad he's into astrology.

"Let's pretend your birthday is today," he says. He orders his favorite dessert, something called mosaiko, and his favorite Greek wine for us.

"We can drink wine?" I ask incredulously.

"I'm eighteen," he smiles. "But also, no one really cares about the drinking age here."

Ever goes on to tell me about his life, about how he can't recall any part of his life before he was around eight years old. "Perhaps it was so bad that I blocked it out. I don't know," he says softly, looking down at his hands.

He talks about how angry he is with his father so obviously cheating on his mom, how awful that is. "I am so sick of it, of all the pain it has caused my mom all these years, that I have taken a vow that when the time comes, I will never cheat on my wife."

This is hard to believe given all the talk at school about his being a major player. "Well, that's hardly the image you have, you know," I challenge.

"Yes, you've said that before. But sometimes things are not as they seem," he says seriously. The trace of sadness and vulnerability that I saw in him earlier at the hospital is evident once again.

The dessert arrives. I've never seen anything like it before. At first glance, it looks like a mosaic tile. Upon closer inspection, though, it's a chocolate cake randomly interspersed with tiny light-colored biscuits, like a work of art. A candle burns brightly in the middle for me. "Happy birthday," he says sweetly.

As we eat the cake and sip the wine under the stars, Ever reveals more about his life to me. Maybe it's because of our confrontation at the hospital about my mom, but I've not seen him so open in this way before…and it's refreshing. He's animated, using his hands as he talks, deeply engaged in this conversation, here and now. I feel a little guilty that I'm not sharing equally with him. I am blown away and still in shock about so many things today that I just sit and listen quietly, laughing and smiling, just allowing myself to enjoy being here so relaxed and free with him.

Just then, Ever's expression grows serious, as if he's going to tell me something of grave importance. "One thing you should know. My sign…I'm a Sagittarius." He says this in a serious voice, as if it's a big deal. I'm not sure what is so worrisome about this. Concern shrouds his face as he continues, "I have trouble with Aries. Once I dated a girl who was an Aries, and it was like we were speaking different languages. Like I would say something and she would completely take it the wrong way."

"Oh, really?" I suddenly hear my mother's voice in my head when we used to talk about men and astrology. My mom religiously followed her horoscope but also regularly shared her rather animated observations about men with me. "What you're talking about, isn't that true for all men and women? You know, like Mars and Venus?"

Ever smiles, nodding. "Well, yes, but this was different…more difficult than usual."

I tell him that my mother is also a Sagittarius. She once told me that both of our signs are Fire, which signifies energy, but her sign is aligned with the goddess Artemis, and my sign, Aries, is aligned with the goddess Athena. Artemis and Athena were both strong, intelligent, and brave, but even though they approached life in different ways, they always had a strong sense of shared purpose.

Ever is keenly interested. I'm surprised that he's so open-minded about this. I wonder if he is also open enough to believe in the supernatural. I'm not sure I should ask him, though, especially as I've been shot down so many times by Nick over this.

"What's your rising sign?" In astrology, the sun sign determines general personality, but the rising sign, or moon sign, dictates inner emotions and mood. The two together create the full picture of a person.

"Gemini!" he says.

"Oh no, not Gemini!" I tease. I quote my mother: "The Twins. Anything with two heads is a monster!"

We laugh at this together.

"I'm not a monster!" He points to his teeth. "See? No oversized, pointy teeth!"

"That's a vampire, not a monster!"

"Monsters have pointy teeth!" He beams.

"No," I playfully challenge him, "I don't think so."

"Vampires have fangs, not teeth." He smiles but then looks away in awkward shyness, face slightly reddened. Is he blushing?

My senses grow dull from the wine, so I finally muster the courage to ask Ever about things of a more "mystical" nature. I desperately need to be heard by someone who believes, who can at least relate a little bit to my bizarre life beyond the Gate.

"Do you believe in the supernatural?" I whisper the question, bracing myself for the usual backlash that I'm used to with Nick.

Ever's eyes turn a bold, royal blue. What can this mean? He's going to laugh at me. I'm sure of it. I look away, irritated with myself for even bringing it up.

But then he surprises me with his response. "Of course."

"What?" I say in shock. "You do?!"

"Well, yes," he says. "While I'm deeply spiritual and my religion is Greek Orthodox, that doesn't preclude me from believing that there is more to the universe than just us. But I don't believe that the mystical and science are mutually exclusive. Albert Einstein said it best: 'The more I study science, the more I believe in God.'"

"Oh, wow," I say in awe of his intelligent mind. I knew that he was deep, but this is wholly unexpected.

Ever suddenly glances down at his watch. "It's getting late. Can you stay out a little bit more? I want to show you something…unusual. Something that I think you will especially appreciate." The look in his eyes means there's no way I can possibly say no.

We leave the café and take a walk outside in the odd quiet of what is usually a very busy and alive city at this time of night. We stroll on a barely lit wide stone pathway in the darkness. To our right, the Parthenon is still lit up in all its majestic splendor on the hillside next to us.

A variety of street vendors line the walkway here, which seems like a favorite place for tourists to visit. Tourism, which is the primary source of income for so many people, seems to be thriving, even though I know that many people here are suffering with the financial crisis. I wonder what life must be like for all the people nearby, unsure of how they will make ends meet or how long the crisis will last.

It seems so wrong, so unjust, but nonetheless, I can't seem to not enjoy myself here with Ever right now. He's so infectious in a debonair and extraordinarily charming way, which makes me feel like all the ugliness is not even happening, like we are off in another time and place.

"Of course, I'm sure you've visited the Parthenon," he says, staring up at the stately white marble pillars lit up like it's on fire above us.

"Uh, no," I stammer. "Actually, I haven't."

"What? You must go. It's…well, it's spectacular."

"Isn't it usually packed with tourists, though? Doesn't that kind of take away from the splendor of it all?" I ask.

Ever seems almost offended by this. "Yes, it's usually packed, so you have to know when to go. Sunset…go just as the sun is setting, just as the sky is turning pink. All the tourists from the cruise ships are gone, and there are very few people left. The energy there at that time is…startling, a sight to behold."

As we approach a vendor display, a naked statue as tall as my leg catches my eye. I stop, suddenly startled.

"Whoa, hold on," I say as I stare up at the statue and then back at

Ever. "Oh my. You look almost identical to the god in this statue. Hermes, right?"

Ever grins. "Yeah, but…" He looks down to the lower portion of the statue. "While I'm flattered to be told that I resemble a Greek god – who was a major stud, by the way – I'm not sure that I look *identical* to this statue." He's pointing to where a large part of the male anatomy is missing, as if it has been sawed off with a chisel.

Ever tells me the story of how in Roman times, the people believed that Hermes brought good luck to the home. Because of this, most households displayed a statue of this god in front of their house. Over several centuries, Christianity became the predominant religion here, and the church started covering the private parts of the Greek gods – Hermes included – with leaves.

Ever's expression grows animated. "And then, around 1500, the pope decided that covering the private parts wasn't enough, so he ordered them all to be cut off!"

"Oh no," I say, grimacing. "Poor Hermes!"

Fascinated now, I continue to study Ever in comparison to the statue. "Well, I guess you don't look *exactly* like him. He has blond hair, after all, but your hair is dark brown."

Perplexed, he says, "Hermes had blond hair?"

"Well, yeah. Everyone knows that the Greek gods had blond hair and blue eyes."

He laughs. "Now *that* is a myth that I'm sure most Americans perpetuate." Continuing, he says, "If the gods were real – and I don't believe that they were – then no one has any evidence that this guy in the statue had blond hair or what his eye or skin color really was." He stifles a laugh as a playful smile covers his face. "The other possibility, which I'm sure is hard for you to believe," – he gives me a huge, smug grin – "is that I might not be a real Greek god after all."

He's so full of himself. I need to put a stop to this…*now*.

I punch his arm. "Unbelievable! I did *not* say that you were a real Greek god. This is all going to your head. I said that you looked a bit like this statue, and that's it."

"Ouch!" He rubs his arm where I hit him. "I believe the word you used was *identical*."

"No, I did not."

"Whatever," he says, crossing his arms.

All of a sudden, a policeman steps out onto the pavement. My pulse rises when I see his oversized gun, riot gear, and bulletproof vest. Dimitris steps up to the policeman and whispers something in his ear, which causes the policeman to step aside, almost as if bored.

Ever explains that the Sarantos name has far-reaching tentacles that touch all aspects of Greek society. He nods to Dimitris, and as if he can automatically read Ever's mind, his bodyguard lifts his gun and unlatches a rope that blocks an entrance that clearly says, "Ancient Agora Excavations – Do Not Enter – Staff Only."

"The public doesn't have access to most of the underground artifacts at this site," he explains.

"Right. This must be the world-famous archaeological site, the birthplace of democracy," I say, intrigued.

The artifacts here are vast and amazing, but according to Ever, there is much more below ground than the general public knows about or has access to.

Dimitris comes back to Ever's side and quietly tells him, "I phoned ahead to the general manager, and he has made arrangements with the head archaeologist there. We will meet his assistant."

When we arrive at the entrance, a trembling young man with heavy black glasses leads us down into the depths of the excavation and flips on a bright overhead light that bathes the room in brilliance. Dimitris stands near the entrance. The assistant hands Ever a digital key and then leaves us. Deep within the excavation, long rows of shelves filled with dusty artifacts line the stone path where we walk.

"Come over here and look at this, Helene," Ever says. We are moving towards the center of the room, where an aged, weathered book rests inside a glass square box. "This is one of the oldest versions of Hesiod's *Theogonia*," he says with an air of reverence. "It was printed during the thirteenth century when the first books were printed. Hesiod's poems have been passed down orally since first composed around 700 BC. It's usually stored in the Blegen Library downtown, but it's here for the time being. You know what it's about, right?"

"Of course!" I say as my eyes light up with excitement. "The poems describe the creation and lineage of the gods."

"Yes, and allegedly, the poems were a gift given to Hesiod by the Muses." He stares into my eyes a bit longer than usual. "Are you ready?"

I nod. But seriously, what could he possibly show me now that is all that remarkable after all that I've seen before?

Ever inserts the digital key into the stone column that holds the glass box, and slowly, the glass sides of the box drop into hidden crevasses within the stone column below. Next he places his right hand directly on top of the book. I stare in awe as the stone tablet begins to glow a faint golden hue. The longer Ever's hand rests there, the brighter the glow grows.

"Here, you try," Ever says. This text is several hundred years old, so I'm more than a little concerned about what my hand touching it could do to it, but Ever doesn't seem concerned in the least. Slowly…gingerly…I place my hand beside his. The book lights up, now blazing into a brilliant inferno.

"Whoa," I say, mesmerized at the sight and feeling that burns inside me. This is truly amazing, almost as incredible as seeing Poseidon's ghost at Sounio. Ever shifts his hand now to cover mine. The intensity of the energy magnifies, ejecting an aura of a rainbow of colors that bounce across the walls. Intense tingles run up my arm and into my spine, causing me to pull my hand away in shock.

"I knew that I felt this energy with you that very first day you knocked into me at the airport, the first day that I saw you," Ever says quietly.

I don't know what to say. It's all too much. I'm getting creeped out.

I ask Ever, "When did you discover that you could do this?"

His expression is filled with wonder. "I was here on a private tour for my eighteenth birthday with legendary archaeologist John Camp. When it happened, he was as shocked as I was, but we agreed to keep it a secret. Ever since then, the book has remained here."

While it makes sense that my hand could light up the tablet because a lot of bizarre stuff has happened to me since I went through the Gate, how is Ever able to do this? Is it possible that he has been through the Gate, too? The bold yellow star tattooed on his wrist comes to mind, and since Janus works for Ever's father, it wouldn't be a stretch for him to visit the basement and the mirror over there.

Whatever the case, I now know that there is much more to Ever than meets the eye. I hate being direct, but I need to know if he has been through the Gate or at least knows *something* about it. I don't want to be all alone in this.

I ask playfully, "Maybe you have special powers, like a superhero? Been to any faraway lands lately?"

"Ha-ha. Very funny!" He doesn't take the bait but then says, "Well, actually, when I was six, I thought I was Superman." His eyes sparkle. "It was great until I jumped off the roof of our house into the backyard pool. I almost hit the pavement!" He chuckles to himself. "I guess I'm only human after all."

This wasn't exactly what I had in mind, but it's incredibly endearing. I can imagine how adorable he was as a kid dressed as Superman.

So, I guess he doesn't know. I must be all alone in this.

I'm the only one who knows about the Gate.

24 – THE MAFIA

"Are we done here? Ready to go?" Dimitris works his magic, and we are back on the pavement walking under the mystical Parthenon once again. We stroll in silence, enjoying the cooler nighttime air. The peaceful ambiance is shattered, though, by the shrill beep of Ever's Apple watch.

He glances at it but doesn't react. His expression is totally stoic, as if it were nothing. But then, in the next moment, he stops walking and turns to me, saying, "Something came up. I have to go."

He steps aside, leaving me standing there all alone. I shiver as I realize that I didn't bring a coat. Ever doesn't seem to notice. He pulls Dimitris over into an urgent huddle. They talk back and forth, and while I strain to hear what they are saying, I can't. Dimitris shakes his head as Ever throws his hands in the air.

Ever turns back to me. "Helene, can you make it home on your own?"

The intensity in his eyes compels me to answer fast. "Uh, sure," I say.

Ever steps up, reaching his arms out to me as if in apology. "I asked Dimitris if he could take you home, but he insists that he has to stay with me. It's like a matter of national security or something that I not be left alone. Seriously! You sure you're okay?"

I shrug as if it's no big deal. "Of course! I take the Metro all the time." But the truth is that it *is* a big deal. It's not cool for him to suddenly leave so abruptly without any explanation whatsoever after all we've shared tonight. The good news is that I'm not as worried about my life being at stake after meeting his dad.

Dimitris waves at me to get my attention. "Yiannis will be here shortly. He can take you home," he says, voice laced with concern for me.

I nod to him in thanks, but honestly, I know I can get home okay on my own. That's not the issue here.

Just then, Ever pulls me into a tight hug, and almost instantly, all bad thoughts disappear. He whispers softly into my ear, "In Greece, friends don't shake hands. This is what we do." He kisses both of my cheeks before pulling away with an adorable smile. The Greek kiss.

I stare at his lips, willing him to kiss me there, like for real...and *oh*, I want him to. I feel the heat stir inside of me. He smiles and moves in closer. I close my eyes and tilt my head back, anticipating the feel of him. And then, *nothing*. Frustrated, I open my eyes to see him push back from me. He looks away for a minute, then takes my hand. He laughs as he squeezes my hand gently. "And here's a handshake for you, American girl."

I'm stunned for a moment. What just happened? I feel the sting of rejection. This might be funny under different circumstances, but here and now, I feel such a jumble of emotions, I don't know how to react. I just stand there staring at him, speechless.

God, how could I be so stupid?

The car's engine rumbles loudly behind us. Dimitris is waiting for Ever. Time for him to go. Just when I think he's leaving, he moves in very close to me, almost brushing the bottom edge of my ear with his lips. I feel the heat of his breath there as a fierce shiver starts at the top of my neck and travels down through my spine, unleashing a flurry of tiny, tingling bumps that totally consume my body.

He whispers softly, "See you at the dance."

My breath is shallow as I struggle to breathe, lost in the bliss of it all. My voice is breathy as I mutter, "Yessss." Then I realize what he just said. "Wait...*no!*" My eyes open wide in protest. "I told you, I won't be in tow—"

Before I can finish, he places his finger on my mouth. "Shhhh." He grins as if he thinks I'm playing some sort of game with him. And then, before I can respond, he squeezes my arm and jumps into the back of the waiting Mercedes, the door slamming behind him.

As the dark car speeds away, I overhear Dimitris talking on his phone from inside. I hear him say, "She's leaving…"

But who is he talking to? Must be the driver Dimitris mentioned before…Yiannis.

As I watch the Mercedes fade into the night, I'm relieved to see the bright lights of the nearest Metro station nearby. After a few minutes of waiting, I start to get cold, so I don't feel like waiting around for Yiannis. I make my way onto the train, and before I know it, I'm back in Metaxourgeio. Now, only eight blocks to walk home.

Finally, I let myself reflect on what just happened. I feel my face grow hot as I realize that something was off with Ever. That whole exit was all wrong!

Why didn't he kiss me? I blow on my hand to check my breath. Smells okay. But then it hits me. That text! It must have been from a girl he's seeing. His exact words were, "Something came up." Another girl. Maybe Samantha. This must be why he introduced me to his dad as his "friend." He's back together with her, but she's not able to go to the dance.

Since he needs a date, Ever asked me to go as his friends. That's why he didn't kiss me! All that has happened tonight, while it seemed magical and wildly romantic to me, was just his way of trying to make me feel better. The almost-kiss, his abrupt departure with no explanation, his expectation that I should meet him at the dance…all of it was designed to send me the message, *Let's just be friends.*

A dull ache seizes my chest at the thought of this. I don't know how or what or why, but somehow, I was starting to *feel* something for him, which makes this situation so much worse.

Perhaps he can take some other "friend" to the dance! That's an *awesome* plan. Makes it so much easier since I'm not going, especially not with *him.*

I'm so deep in my thoughts that I'm not paying attention to where I'm walking. It's completely dark outside…like, scary dark. The moon and stars are completely shrouded by coastal fog tonight, and there is a biting wind that chills me to my core.

I walk past a man conversing with an imaginary person in a frantic and angry voice. Just around the corner, I pass by a dark alley when suddenly I hear what sounds like breaking glass. I whip around to locate the source of the sound, but no one is there. Now I think I'm going crazy...that is, until I see a dark form emerge from the shadows, a man dressed entirely in black.

His bloated body is covered head to toe with tattoos. He grins, exposing crooked, disgusting yellow-brown teeth. He murmurs something unintelligible. His accent sounds guttural, almost feral to me. I scan the area around us and wince as I realize that we are completely alone.

The next words out of his mouth stop me dead in my tracks. "Ah, sweet girl. Come here. I won't hurt you. I hear you've been asking about the Mafia. Well, here we are."

Panic and adrenaline fill me. I launch into a run in the opposite direction and unfortunately end up in the alley. I yell out in frustration as I reach a brick wall. It's a dead end. Two more hideous men wait for me there. They look hungry. Either I'm about to get mugged, or someone sent them here. Sarantos. He must not have liked my asking about my mom and sent these thugs to take me back to him...or worse. Maybe he wants me dead. But I can't think of that. I need to stay calm and be smart, which feels impossible because I can't seem to quiet my erratic pulse.

Tattoo guy grabs my backpack and tears it open, exposing my laptop, which clatters to the ground. He grabs the laptop, switches it on, and gives his friends the thumbs-up. Next he searches my pack and pulls out a ten euro note but then glares at me harshly as if he can't believe that this is all the cash I have.

"Such a pretty girl." He comes closer and closer to me, stopping only a foot away. "I wonder what you look like under this." He strokes the hem of my shirt with his dirt-encrusted finger. "Hmmm..."

Panic surges into terror, and some unseen force suddenly kicks into gear as my hands clench into fists and I assume a classic fighting stance. I experience the same surge of immense strength I felt when I was fencing with Ever. A powerful vision of me as a seasoned warrior consumes my mind. I let it engulf me.

Ugly tattoo guy grabs my arm…*big mistake*. My free arm whips up at incredible speed and easily chops down on his hand, causing him to yelp in agony. In a split second, I spin and smack him hard in the head with a graceful kick. He's knocked out, sprawled on the ground with blood on his lip. The two other hoodlums back away in fear at what they just witnessed, but I rush at them. Holding both my arms out, I simultaneously punch them both, first in the stomach and then in the face. Now they too are out cold.

Surveying the scene, I roll tattoo guy over and turn his wrist, expecting to see the usual blue-black helix DNA tattoo that I've been certain is a sign of the Syndicate. But it's not there. This guy must be from one of the local mafia street gangs. I'm not going to wait around to find out which one.

I'm about to retrieve my laptop and backpack when I see two stone life-sized statues in front of me. I'm certain they weren't there just a moment ago. They look identical to the two guys I just knocked down. I rub my eyes, not believing what I'm seeing, but when I open them, the two statues have somehow morphed into real men. My heart rate rises as they start inching forward, coming at me with knives. I run down the alley to head out.

Just as I'm a few feet away from the street, someone new comes into view – my mom's attorney, Harold "Hal" Avery!

Sweet relief fills me. He slowly moves in towards me from the street, hands out with a smile on his face. He's here to help me. "Hal…" I start. "You're still alive!"

"Yes," he says, still smiling. However, his grin doesn't reach his eyes as I notice his pasty, balding head is dripping with sweat. Something is off. Just like how I felt back in California when I first met him, my instincts scream in warning. But he must be here to help me! He works for my mom!

Hal's expression suddenly morphs into an ugly sneer as he says, "Unfortunately, so are you."

"Wha…what do you mean?" I ask, stepping back from him.

"We brought you here to lead us to the Gate," he scoffs, "but all you've done since you've been in Greece is behave like a stupid girl, following these boys around like a lost puppy."

I shake my head at this. He has it all wrong. I'm not the one following the boys. They are chasing *me*. And they are not "boys." Seriously. They're *guys*. But what he said before that is what shocks me. Hal works for the mafia? The mafia wants to find the Gate? They know about Gaea?

"But you were shot!" My mind spins through the scene in California.

"We had to stage that. It was the only way you'd believe me." Hal's face is a mask of cruelty as he laughs. "We should have known that your mother would never tell you where it was. You're worthless."

He starts to move towards me and pulls out a knife. But I'm not concerned. Hal is no match for me. In fact, I'm looking forward to wasting him after all he's put me through. This is going to be fun.

Raw adrenaline and sheer power pulse through my veins as I whip up my leg into a roundhouse kick, knocking Hal square in those disgusting crooked yellow teeth. No loss there. I must be a bit too distracted by my fight with Hal because I don't even notice that at least four more scraggly thugs have just materialized out of the shadows. How did I not see them before? Then, the four suddenly become ten.

I feel the harsh blow before I see it coming. Someone hits me hard with insane strength, bringing me to my knees. I hold the back of my head as the world spins out of control. What happened to my awesome super fighting power?

As my vision clears, an apparition materializes in front of me. My heart stops midbeat. Another ghost. But not like Poseidon. This ghost's image appears crisp and crystal clear, and he's meticulously dressed head to toe in high-end fashion, like he should be in *GQ*. His dark hair whips around while his black trench coat floats out behind him, as if he's caught somewhere in a slight breeze, but there's no airflow here. It must be coming from somewhere else.

The ghost pulls off his gloves and speaks. "I'm Ares."

Ares, as in the god? My mouth hangs open in awe.

"You know who I am?" he asks in a haughty voice.

"Of course," I stammer.

"I know what you're thinking. God of War? Silly, weak human...you know nothing. I'm the commanding officer of Zeus' First Army, the Vorlage." He talks down to me like I'm a complete idiot. "You do know who Zeus is, right?"

"Uh, yeah," I whisper in disbelief. "B...but how are you here?"

He sneers at me as if the answer is totally obvious, but he's not telling me. "You haven't figured it out, have you?" He scoffs. "Do you even know who you are?"

What is he talking about? "Of course I do. I'm Helene Crawford," I say.

Ares eyes me, smirking, then swiftly turns to Hal Avery, who is still profusely bleeding from when I crushed his teeth earlier. Hal whispers something in a hushed tone that only the two of them can hear. Ares turns back to me. The way the light above shines on his eyes, it's as if they are dancing with delight. "So, it's true. You don't know. Your mother didn't tell you, did she?"

Ares knows my mom? What does she have to do with Gaea? The legend of the Last Standing Tree comes to mind...of the carvings of the gods on the branch and how her necklace glowed when I touched them. Since Mom once lived with Janus and he clearly knows about the mirror, it's entirely possible that she's been there before. Maybe I was wrong before. Could the Last Standing Tree be one and the same as my mother's Lone Cypress Tree?

My God. Yes!

If that's true...is it possible that Mom is on Gaea now?

Ares clearly enjoys the intrigue of playing this guessing game with me, but I need to play it cool and act as if this doesn't mean anything to me. I don't want to say anything that could possibly hurt my mom. I shrug. "I don't know what you're talking about, so why don't you just tell me?"

Ares motions to tattoo guy, who kicks me hard in the back, knocking me flat on the ground. Satisfied with my pain, Ares tells me, "Since you've not led us to the Gate, Zeus ordered your immediate execution. I am quite happy to oblige."

Tattoo guy is driving his boot into the back of my neck, which forces my face right into the ground. I can barely breathe. Zeus wants to kill me? But why?! This can't be how my life is supposed to end after all that has happened! I'm in total shock. My first thought is that this is all a big mistake. They have the wrong girl. But deep down, I know that there's no error. I've heard about this Prophecy before, and somehow, it's about me and my mom. Clearly, I'm not dealing with the local mafia here.

Then a horrible thought hits me. Zeus must have my mom.

"My mom," I command. "Take me to her."

Ares's eyes grow wide in surprise. "We don't have her. She escaped—" He stops short, as if he shouldn't have told me. I'm both relieved and sad at the news that my mother isn't with Zeus. But how can I save her if I can't find her? Perhaps Sarantos was right about her not wanting to be found. But that makes no sense. She would never intentionally leave me. Even if she's not with Zeus, she could still be on Gaea. The Last Standing Tree is the key. I need to go there and find it.

Ares seems to enjoy debate. Maybe there's a way to talk my way out of this. Maybe he would be open to a negotiation. I whip my head backwards, hitting tattoo guy's foot with so much violence that I hear his bones snap. He screams in agony. While he's distracted, I lift his body high above me and slam him hard against the brick wall. His body hits with a crack, knocking him unconscious.

The remaining nine thugs start moving in towards me when Ares yells, "Halt!" They all freeze in place, completely motionless. As I stand to face Ares, he chuckles.

I shut him down when I say, "Look, Ares, maybe I can make you a deal."

He raises a mocking eyebrow. "Really? I don't 'deal' with mortals."

I try to distract him enough with our conversation that I can make a run for it...through his apparition. I doubt there's any substance to this "ghost."

I goad him by saying, "What makes you so sure that I'm a mortal?"

For a moment, Ares converses with someone I can't see before returning to our conversation. "Fair point." His answer surprises me. Is there a possibility that I could be immortal? Serina and Xonos said that the gods can die. They're just mortals, so why would I be immortal? Weird.

I need to get out of here, so I continue to talk. "How about this? I promise not to go back to Gaea if you'll just let me go."

The smug, delighted look that he had before is suddenly gone. "What do you mean? You've been to Gaea?"

We stare at each other in astonishment. He doesn't know that I was in Gaea? Then why was he talking about the Gate like I already know what it is? He tricked me!

Just then, we're startled by a loud yell, "*Helene!!*"

I turn to see who is there. *Nick*. I sigh in overwhelming relief at the sight of him, so grateful that I rush up and throw my arms around him, taking him by surprise. "Nick, *thank God* you're here!" I say in half-crazed giddiness.

Ares screams, "Resume!" The thugs immediately come back to life. Suddenly, it doesn't seem so great to have Nick here. He could get hurt or worse. Tattoo guy and Hal Avery lead the group of thugs as they start to move in towards us. As I turn back towards Ares, he's gone. Vanished.

The thugs seem temporarily lost, unsure what to do without their leader, so we use this confusion to attack. I've never seen Nick fight before, but he surprises me with his deft skill as he picks up a long pipe and takes down two thugs in one hit. Feeling confident that Nick can handle himself, I launch into the rest of the clan. Before we know it, the ground is littered with bodies. God, I hope we didn't kill anyone!

Nick lies on his side, his body bloodied and bruised. Fear fills me as I run over to him. I pray that he's okay. I don't know what I would do if he were seriously injured while trying to save me.

He has no idea what he's up against.

25 – MIRACLE

Nick groans as he slowly turns over and attempts to stand. His gray-green eyes suddenly come alive with concern. "I told you not to mess with the street gangs! You sought them out, and they came for you." His voice fills with anxiety. He's upset with me. "And how are you able to fight like this? I've been around the block a time or two and have *never* seen anyone fight like that."

I'm so entirely exhausted now that I can't even come up with a good story for him. I just stand there with a stupid look on my face. I feel completely shaken up by his attitude towards me, so I lash out. "What do you care what happens to me?" I scream.

"Because!" His eyes widen in fury. "You're important to me!"

All my fear, confusion, and anger melt into nothingness…and then I start to cry.

"Hey…" His tone shifts to worry as he strokes my hair. "Look, I just want to know the truth. What's going on with you?"

It's my turn to yell as I wail, "I don't know…about anything! I'm scared. *Please,* Nick, you have to believe me."

I'm delirious as tears begin to fall down my cheeks. He hands me a tissue when I snuffle. He must feel some compassion because he reaches his arms around me and pulls me in close. I sense the warmth of his firm body against mine as he whispers in my ear, "Hey, look." He guides my chin up to look into his gray-green eyes. "We can talk about this later. Let me get you home. There's a huge gash on your forehead."

I look down and gasp when I see my shirt torn and covered with bright red blood…*my* blood. He rips off a strip of his t-shirt and wraps it around my head to stop the bleeding. "I don't want to hear about you going out at night all alone again. Understand?"

"I can go out and do as I want, when I want!" I declare. Nick can't dictate my life. He may care about me, but he's being a bit overly concerned here. He reminds me a little of my mother when she's scared and tries to control every aspect of my life. Way too overprotective. On the other hand, while I'm not sure that I can handle being babied by Nick, he fills me with such a sweet sense of calm. I feel safe with him. Such a contrast from Ever, who makes me feel wild and alive but *frustrated.*

"Fine!" he raises his voice. "Right now, we need help. You're bleeding."

We walk arm in arm across the street. When we reach the front door and discover it locked, Nick shakes his head, swearing under his breath. "Shit! What now?" he asks.

My head hurts a little, but not as bad as before.

"Let's go up on the roof," I say. He helps me quietly up the outside spiral stairway, careful to not awaken Janus. When we reach the top, we step onto the roof. There, I feel my breath catch in my chest as I stare up. Above us is a vast darkened sky lit up faintly with millions and millions of shimmering stars. The layer of fog that covered Athens earlier now hovers off to our right where the mountains meet the sea. Towards the coast sits the moon, now much smaller in this later hour of the evening.

Nick grabs a blanket and throws it over a lounge chair, where he sits with his legs out in front of him, slightly parted. He motions for me to sit with him, so I sink down onto the lounge chair, lying face up with my back to him. He wraps his arms and the blanket around me as we snuggle and enjoy the solace of this beautiful place and the twinkling stars above.

"I'll bet you believe in ghosts now, right?" I ask. There's no way he can deny the clear vision of Ares earlier.

"Why would I? You know my thoughts on that topic," he declares, using the skeptical, annoyed tone that he usually gets when we talk about this.

"So, you didn't see the ghost tonight, then?" I whisper mostly to myself. "Argh!" I bury my head in my hands, totally frustrated. How could he not have seen Ares? He was right there!

Nick doesn't at all get why I'm upset, but he wraps his arms tighter around me. I should be careful about how much I confide in Nick about Gaea or my transformation. He's not going to understand.

"So…your insane ninja skills…where did that come from?" He seems so genuinely interested that I feel a little guilty I have to lie to him.

"My mom wanted me to be able to defend myself," I start. So far, all true, but then I continue, "So I took tae kwon do and eventually got my black belt." I think he believes me. "See? You don't have to worry so much about me. I'm fine."

"Okay, but just promise me you'll stay away from street gangs and the mafia!" he says insistently.

I sigh. Luckily, I couldn't care less about the mafia now because I know that they can't help me with my mom, so it's an easy promise to make. "Fine. I promise."

Nick turns me towards him, the moonlight reflecting off his gray-green eyes. "So…isn't there something that you're supposed to ask me about?"

I have absolutely no idea what he's talking about. "What?" I stammer. "Can you give me a clue?"

He grins. "You know, like something that might be going on at school on Saturday night?"

Oh, the dance. Vani must have talked to Nick. They're friends, after all. The problem is that I'm not going to be here on Saturday.

"Oh yeah. But…well…" I start to turn him down, but now that I've been attacked and almost captured by a Greek god, I suddenly feel desperate for a normal life. Nick did just save my life! Mom would forgive me for one night of peace. She would want this for me.

Suddenly, it dawns on me that Nick is expecting *me* to ask him to the dance. Something about this role reversal feels all wrong to me, so even if I wanted to go with him, I would never ask him. That's his job. "Nope, I can't do it. You're the boy. You're supposed to do the asking."

"But it's your school and your dance," he jests. "I can't ask you to *your* dance."

I sock him softly on the arm. "Well then, I just won't go at all if you can't just ask me."

We grin at each other, beaming at the ridiculousness of this situation. He's not going to ask me, but I'm definitely not asking him. So how do we do this, then?

Then, amazingly...*finally*...he breaks the impasse by getting down on one knee. He takes my hand up to his mouth, kisses it, and asks, "Will you *please* go with me to *your* dance?"

I want to say yes, but I can't. I'm thinking about Ever. This day has been so crazy that he seems so far away and surreal now, but I can't escape the memories of the sorrow in his liquid turquoise eyes, his magnetic charm, and the insane tingling sensation I experience every time he is near me. He bared his soul, sharing so many personal, intimate aspects of his life with me in such a short time that I couldn't help but fall a little for him.

Of course, all of this is hard to reconcile with his hasty departure and that text, most likely from another girl. My heart lurches as I relive the sting of rejection from his "almost-kiss." I intrigue Ever only when he can't have me, but as soon as I show interest, he discards me like some old toy he doesn't want to play with anymore.

Besides, I clearly told him no when he asked me to the dance, so I can't help it if he doesn't listen. He'll be fine. I've made my choice. I'm going to the dance with Nick.

I smile and say softly, "Yes."

"Good...because I wasn't leaving until you said yes, no matter what was required. Be ready at 19:00 Saturday."

"You're picking me up?" I ask, envisioning Nick whisking me off to the dance in my gorgeous dress on the back of his motorcycle. My hair would be a total mess from his helmet. "But how? Not on the motorcycle..."

"No! Of course not." He smiles sweetly. "I have a few tricks up my sleeve."

We cuddle up on the lounge chair, the sounds of the city surrounding us in the oncoming night as I rest my head on his chest, listening to the slow, steady beat of his heart. I touch the spot on my head where the blood was before, and I don't feel anything there. It's like Nick's sweetness has somehow cured me. His gorgeous gray-green eyes glisten under the soft moonlight as he slowly lifts my mouth to his. We start kissing, gently and sweetly.

The moment is shattered when suddenly the door to the roof flies open with a loud crash. There stands Janus, headscarf crooked, with his watering can sloshing liquid all over the wooden roof deck. What is he doing? I mean, who waters his garden in the middle of the night? Janus, that's who. His vivid brown eyes grow wide as they lock onto Nick's. *Not good.*

"I told you…no boys sleep over at this house!" Janus has reached a whole new level of crazy as his eyes grow maniacal. "Not on a school night…and *especially*…not him!" He jabs his finger at Nick in a dramatic sweeping motion.

Janus must notice that my head is injured. He swiftly marches over and rips the strip of cloth from my head. "That's a nasty cut, Helene." Then he turns to Nick. "What the hell happened?"

Nick tells Janus what he witnessed with the fighting and my getting roughed up, but he leaves out the part about us fighting ten thugs who all belong to a local mafia street gang.

Janus is irate, unleashing his fury at me. "Helene, you've got to pay more attention to your surroundings around here! I warned you about this. It's dangerous here at night." He pushes Nick towards the edge of the roof while in the middle of his rant. "But you never listen to a word I say. It's like I'm not even here, like I'm not even alive. This is all a crock of God-damned teenage bullshit!"

I turn to see that Nick has safely escaped Janus's continued tirade by jumping over the side of the roof and down the outside stairway. No!

Janus grabs my arm and leads me swiftly down the stairs and into the kitchen, where he opens a cabinet and pulls out some sort of new age healing concoction. He grabs my forehead to examine my cut. I hear a sharp intake of his breath, which makes me nervous that the laceration must be much worse than I suspected. He hands me a small hand mirror.

I glance at my image. The gash is *gone*. Feeling faint, I struggle to remain standing as it fully sinks in that my head is completely devoid of any cuts or imperfections whatsoever. I have miraculously healed in less than thirty minutes.

Remarkably, Janus doesn't even appear surprised. Why not? He just shakes his head at me and slams the door as he heads into his room.

One thing is for certain. The stakes have been raised. This is so much bigger than a local mafia street gang. There are people here on Earth working for the gods, and they want me dead.

26 – SCYTHIA

I feel paralyzed. I rack my brain, trying to figure out what is going on. Why would Zeus want to kill me? If not because I went through the portal to Gaea, then why? Some essential piece of the puzzle is missing. Zeus shouldn't care about me or my mother. We're just regular people from Earth. But I know too much now to trick myself into believing that story any further. Ares mentioned the Prophecy, which I've heard before from Janus and his band of weirdo friends. The key to it all is my mom.

The bloody ripped cloth that Nick placed around my head lies on the ground. I touch my head. I can't believe this super healing ability. I've experienced so much change since I went through the portal. It has made me into a much more powerful, capable version of myself. Suddenly, I'm filled with intense gratitude for this strength. It makes me realize that I can sit here and cower in fear, or I can go and do something about it. I've been given these powers for a reason. Both Sarantos and Ares all but confirmed that my mom is alive. I've got to get back to Gaea to find out more.

Suddenly, a terrifying thought hits me. If my mom escaped Zeus in the fire, then he must be looking for her too. Once again, I feel warmth on my chest, but this time, I feel a strange pulsing on my neck…the cypress tree necklace. Somehow, I know that the tree on Gaea is my next step in finding Mom, but how to find it? The answers are in Gaea. I need to go back through the Gate.

There's a problem with this, though. I need Bastet and the stone on her collar. Panic fills me: I don't remember her coming back through the Gate with me. I can't think like this. She must be here somewhere! I'm going to find her.

As I make my way upstairs, our apartment is completely dark. I can hear the soft snoring of Janus sleeping in the other room. I slowly close his door to keep from waking him. Softly, I call out for the cat. "Bastet! Where are you?" Frantically, I look everywhere I can think of…behind the furniture, in the cabinets. I fear that I'm making way too much noise, but there's no sign of the cat anywhere! All my hopes are dashed. I sink down into the couch depressed, in total despair. Maybe she truly is trapped on Gaea. My eyes fill with tears.

Wait—a soft scratching sound is coming from Janus's room. As I move close to his bedroom door, the sound grows louder, like someone is directly opposite me on the other side. Suddenly, an orange paw shoots out towards me from underneath the door, then swiftly disappears. It's Bastet! Janus must have locked her in there to keep her from me. Relief floods me at the sight of her, but the thought of Janus locking her away is awful.

I try the door handle, slowly turning it to avoid any noise, but it's locked! Crap, now how will I get Bastet out of there? I pace back and forth, thinking through my options. There are none. I guess I'll have to wait until tomorrow. *Argh!* I throw my hands up in the direction of the door. In my mind, I envision the door opening…and then, miraculously, *click!* The door does open, and Bastet trots out with a smug, satisfied look on her face.

In a flash, she shoots past me, running at full tilt out of the apartment and down the stairs. I sprint fast to keep up with her. As if reading my mind, she's heading for the bookcase that is the secret door to the basement. Effortlessly, I disable the lock, and we head down into the basement. There, lying in wait for us, is the mirror. Its surface is already enabled to the magnificent blue shimmering surface that has become so familiar to us. Without even turning to look back at me, Bastet leaps through the Gate. I follow close behind her.

My vision starts to spin as the world around me swirls into the blur of colors and lights, all racing forward to merge dynamically into the epicenter of the now-familiar vortex. But instead of passing out like before, I walk smack into a pale, white-haired, silver-eyed boy, maybe eight or nine years old. He looks a lot like Thomas. Upon impact, we both tumble back onto the soft, sandy ground on the Gaea side of the Gate.

Bastet, my mountain lioness, is crouched low next to the boy, hissing. We're standing on the hot sand, facing the vast stretches of desert, which we can easily see through large gaps in the crumbling stone open-air structure. Long ago, the roof must have caved in here because the edges of this place are littered with scattered tiles. Far off in the distance, another sandicane with gale-force winds swirls in colossal fury. An imposing man dressed in harsh desert gear and a gas mask pokes a lit-up spear into my side. The pain is far worse than Xonos's spear last time.

In an instant, I grab the white-haired boy's shirt, pull him in front of me, and wrap one hand around his neck, holding him as my hostage. Bastet roars in a murderous fury. Her voice echoes throughout the enclosed area, causing the walls to shake and shudder. Ancient décor crumbles from the stone arch above the Gate.

"I don't want to hurt him!" I yell at the man who just tried to attack me. The white-haired boy trembles in fear under the weight of my hand. "Stand down!" I yell.

I can feel the man's intensity through the eye shields of his gas mask, but he says nothing. It's a standoff. His arm muscles ripple. He yanks off his gas mask and scowls. He takes a moment to study me before his scowl relaxes into a wry grin. He says, "Impossible. You're a Dreg!"

As my vision clears, I'm greeted by the image of Serina and Xonos, standing off in the background, grinning ear to ear. We study each other for a moment in curiosity but then visibly relax as I release my hold on the boy.

The man takes a raspy breath through a ventilator. His voice is incredulous as he asks, "You…you can breathe here?"

Serina interrupts, "Yeah, she so totally can!"

"Serina, no!!" Xonos socks her on the arm, annoyed. The man looks from one kid to the next, shaking his head as if they are in some sort of trouble. Xonos puts his hands out. "I swear, we've never seen her before. Not ever."

Serina comes to my rescue. "Yes we have! Xonos?"

His eyes grow livid, and incredulous. "Serina! Use your brain!"

The man takes off his gas mask and flashes me a smug, knowing look, then asks, "How many times have you been here?"

Something about his face makes me want to immediately tell the truth. There's no messing around with this guy. "Twice," I say, trying to sound confident. If I have any hope of finding my mom, I need to play ball…and win.

The man frowns at the twins, raising his eyebrow in shrewd silence. They shrug, trying to feign innocence. Xonos turns his back to us, lip jutted out in a full pout.

The man sighs as he stands to his full height. "Well, that's just great." He extends his arm towards me in a friendly gesture. "I'm Minios. These two kids are in my charge. I have been training Serina and Xonos to someday guard this Gate. We were just preparing for their coming-of-age ceremony, which will happen today." Minios's expression is reproachful and irritated. "Clearly they aren't ready for such an important responsibility yet, since I've heard nothing about your being here before now. May I ask how you came across this Gate…from Earth? Where was Janus?" His voice is laced with frustrated annoyance at the mention of Janus.

I explain that Janus is my godfather and that my cat, Bastet, has a cat's-eye stone on her collar that activates and opens the Gate.

Minios and the twins jump back in amazement, as if this is the most incredible thing that they've ever heard before. "Ah, yes, of course, Bastet," Minios says as he glares into the giant cat's amber eyes. "I should have known *you* were behind this!"

Bastet stands to her full height and roars.

"You don't scare me, old girl!" He shakes his head, laughing at her. Bastet paces back and forth, clearly annoyed with him, but then settles back down on the hot sand.

Minios turns back to me. "I'm guessing that Janus doesn't know that you're here. We have a strict code that forbids anyone to ever allow a Dreg to pass to here from Earth. I would have heard about that for sure." He taps his ear twice, then says, "I need to let him know immediately."

He knows Janus? I feel sweat on my palms, and my heart quickens with fear.

Minios taps his ear again in frustration. *"Blasted Drakon dung!* Too much static!" He turns back to me. "There's only one thing to do, then. You have to go back."

No! I can't go back now. I need to find Mom. Time is of the essence.

"Wait!" I startle them. "I need to find the Lone Cypress Tree."

The kids look at each other as Minios begins to chuckle. "Oh, is that so? An urban myth. A fairy tale. It doesn't exist."

Serina pipes up. "That's not true! Athena knows where it is!"

"Athena?" I ask. Finally, a lead. She will know where Mom is. I need to meet her.

"Serina, no!" Minios scolds her, then turns to me, hands out as if to apologize. "Look, Athena tells these kids many stories at bedtime, so they believe this stuff, but honestly…"

Just like my mom. She used to tell me similar stories when I was a child. This is the key. It's got to be. I feel the cool silver of the ring that sits on my finger. My mind spins with possibilities. I point to the strange white-haired boy cowering in the corner. "Who is he?"

Minios looks skeptical for a moment. "Janus hasn't told you?"

I nod and explain, "He said that he was helping refugee orphans in Greece."

Xonos clears his throat while Minios grins. "I'm guessing you don't buy that story now, eh?" He laughs. "So I'm sure you've gathered that Janus, like me, is a Gatekeeper?" I nod in agreement. He explains that the white-haired children are from Zeus's pyramid city, New Olympus, where they are regularly abused or tortured, often for sport.

"We funnel the kids out, and Janus finds families that are willing and able to adopt the children on Earth. It's a way we can make a difference here, slow and steady, one child at a time," Minios explains. His voice is full of meaning and purpose.

Finally, it feels like someone is telling me the truth! While this is refreshing, I'm disturbed that Janus has kept so much from me and lied to me about Thomas. What other tall tales has he told me? I knew I couldn't trust him. Something still bothers me about all this. It feels like child trafficking. "But aren't you taking these kids away from their parents and homes?" I ask.

"No. In New Olympus, the children are taken away from their biological parents when they are only a year old and raised together in group facilities until they come of age at thirteen," Minios explains.

This makes some sense, but I'm losing patience. I need them to take me to see Athena.

Suddenly, I feel the tip of Minios's spear under my hand, lifting it up towards him. His eyes grow wide in quiet contemplation as he studies the silver ring on my finger. After a moment, he whispers as if awestruck, "The ring of Artemis. You…this is very unexpected. Athena will want to know." His expression shifts as he becomes distracted by the incoming dust storm. "We need to leave soon or risk getting swallowed up by that storm."

Suddenly, a loud screeching noise pierces my ears. A horn sounds. Minios and the kids exchange horrified looks.

"What's that?" I ask, sure that I don't want to know the answer.

"Cyclops," Minios says harshly. "Shhhh!"

Directly in front of us, two oversized shadows pass by us.

"Quick, let's hide!" he whispers as he ushers us across the sandy structure to where some old shelving units sit toppled over and half buried in the sand. We peer through the old rusted metal slats, watching in horror as the shadows suddenly materialize into rugged one-eyed monsters. Upon closer look, though, I see that they're wearing heavy, oversized black gas masks with a large red roving mechanical eye in the center and a strip of black hair covering the top like a Mohawk. I can hear their ragged breathing as they shuffle with a limp and rest directly in front of the Gate.

"They must be here to hide from the storm," Minios says sternly.

"Who are they?" I ask.

"Cyclops. Desert nomads. Most are survivors of the Gaean plague, called the Scourge, which destroyed their eyesight and minds, then drove them mad."

Through the holes in the structure, we can see the dust storm fast approaching. In the distance, multicolored bolts of lightning strike in brilliant flashes of green, red, and purple, which is incredibly beautiful in an eerie, dangerous kind of way. Minios taps his earpiece again. "Still no communication!" He slams his hand on his head, totally frustrated.

The Cyclops closest to us whips his head around in our direction. His large red eye roves around the structure as if he's scanning for predators, or worse, prey. Then suddenly, his mechanical eye stops, frozen in place, aimed at the structure where we're hiding. I feel a shock of adrenaline as he hoists a massive rusted weapon in front of him and starts shuffling towards us.

He's almost to the edge of the shelving unit when Bastet jumps out, stopping the Cyclops dead in his tracks. She roars.

A violent flash of lightning shoots past my face.

Minios turns to me and the kids. "Time to *move!*"

Bastet remains behind to fight as the other Cyclops joins his friend. I'm horribly concerned for her, but there's no time to think. We've got to get out of here.

As we rush through the crumbling vestiges of the old city, I'm surprised to see a compact desert blimp hidden here, lying in wait for us. Its massive camouflaged sails rise high up into the sky, like a sailboat for the air. We leap on board.

"Wait!" I cry. "We can't leave Bastet!"

Minios frowns and shakes his head. "I'm sorry, but we have no choice." He maneuvers the controls, and the blimp starts to pull away from the surface. We're five, then ten meters away. The image of Bastet dead at the hands of those monsters fills my mind. No!!

Suddenly, just off in the distance near where we departed, I see her. The two Cyclops are hot on her tail as lightning bolts streak past her, barely missing their mark.

"There's no way she can make it! We're too far away!" I cry.

Then, almost as if in slow motion, Bastet leaps across the incredible distance between us. I can barely breathe as I watch her body sail over the vast desert sands. Next I hear the scratch of her claws, then the thud of her landing on the balcony of the blimp as it rushes away. Overwhelming relief rushes through me as I run over, wrap my arms around Bastet, and kiss her fur. "You made it!!"

As the fierce winds swiftly carry us across the vast desert sands, Minios explains that Gaea's main power source, lumite, is inaccessible to anyone outside of Zeus's pyramid city, so they must rely on the sun, water, or wind. "While you on Earth treat renewable energy like it's a hip fad, here it is all we have to survive. We make it work because we must. Of course, it also makes the air easy to breathe where we live." He points to his mask. "No need for extra oxygen there."

We barely stay ahead of the massive storm as it licks the back of the blimp, causing us to shudder and sway. My stomach feels queasy, as if I'm going to heave at any moment, so I place my head between my knees. While this is uncomfortable for me, I'm totally ecstatic to be going with Minios and the kids. Finally, the chance I've been waiting for!

Peaceful calm falls over the blimp, and I feel the heat of the hot red sun on my back. We grind to a halt. Slowly, I lift my head and open my eyes. Here in the middle of the vast desert sands, the blimp has docked on the edge of a gigantic hole in the ground. The mouth of the cavern is at least the size of a football field. I feel I've seen something like this before somewhere on Earth. That's it: It's a cave in the rainforests of Mexico: *the Cave of Swallows.*

"Welcome to our city, which we call Scythia," Minios sighs as we both take in the sight of this amazing place. "Home to the Prometheans."

"As in Prometheus, the god?" I challenge him. "I thought he died after he risked everything to bring fire to humans."

"Your stories about the gods on Earth, what you call 'mythology,' are grounded in reality but are only partially true." He nods, smiling. "Prometheus is very much alive but not here…on Earth."

A huge crowd has assembled around the edges of the mouth of the cavern, looking down into the dark depths of the immense crater. Minios leads me through the mass of people, shoving through the crowd to reach the front and edge. The twins and white-haired boy are whisked away.

I'm afraid of heights, but I can't help from peering over the edge. My heart beats out of control, and I'm dizzy with vertigo. Directly beneath my feet, there's a vertical drop of at least a thousand feet that ends abruptly at the cavern's floor below. Incredibly, there are modern-looking dwellings built into the sides of the cavern, spiraling all the way down to the bottom, like a contemporary metropolis contained inside the walls of a cave.

I step backward. The crowd around me is growing antsy, ready for the action to start. Then, I see the twins standing on a platform that juts out over the cavern's edge. It's a horrifying sight. They are wearing what look like space suits. They look scared, yet somehow also incredibly excited.

Minios explains, "This is the twins' thirteenth birthday, which marks their passage into adulthood in Scythia. They must complete their coming-of-age ceremony by passing a test that requires them to jump into the mouth of the cavern with only a small parachute on their backs, then safely land on the cave's floor almost sixty stories down."

The crowd begins a countdown: 10...9...8... The twins exchange nervous glances. The counting continues: 3...2...1... The crowd goes crazy, clapping and cheering in anticipation. Then the twins make their jump.

I can't look. But before I know it, it's over. A raucous roar echoes from the cavern. I finally allow myself to peek through my fingers to see what's going on. The twins have landed at the bottom, and a mass of people is swarming them in celebration.

Exciting as this seems, it feels to me like a delay for my mission. There's no time for me to party! I need to find my mom. But where is Athena? I need to get down to the bottom of that cavern and find her, but how? All around me, the people who rim the edge of the cavern shuffle forward, slowly and methodically in a long single file towards the double doors of a high-speed elevator that transports them down to the cave's floor.

As I contemplate how I'm going to cut in ahead of these people, my eyes are greeted by a startling image: Bastet is standing precariously on the edge of the same platform from which the twins just jumped. She peers down over the edge.

Suddenly, I hear a voice, clear as day, inside my head that says, *"One day, someone will die doing this."*

I look around. Minios is gone. So, who said that?

Bastet roars, shaking her fur and body. Her amber eyes grow wide. I hear the voice again. *"Don't worry. This is easy for me!"*

I'm either totally insane or Bastet just spoke to me. Well, actually, I know the truth. It's just time I acknowledge it. I'm not nuts.

Without warning, Bastet leaps off the edge. I watch in horror as her strong, graceful body hurtles at incredible speed sixty stories down through the depths of the cave. If I wasn't shocked before, now I am!

The shuffling crowd abruptly halts. An eerie silence consumes everything as the mass of people standing near me peer over the edge to witness Bastet's insanity. I watch apprehensively as her body soars with effortless grace, landing firm and steady on her paw pads with almost no discernible sound. The crowd at the bottom of the cavern seems hushed in awe as they start to move in around her to form a tight circle. The mass parts as a stunning blond woman steps inside the circle and reaches her hand out to pat Bastet affectionately on the head as if they are old friends.

"Athena." I hear Bastet's voice in my head again. *"This is Athena."*

Suddenly, the woman looks up towards me. Our eyes lock. Another voice fills my mind…one I don't recognize: *"Hello."*

Athena can talk to me inside my head too? I must be dreaming.

"It's not a dream. Come on down." I hear the voice again. It's velvety soft, so persuasive that it makes me powerless to resist her. I feel my feet moving closer…and closer to the edge…so close that I almost lose my footing. My mind feels woozy, but adrenaline surges through my veins as I realize what Athena wants me to do.

I hear the voice again, so soft, so convincing. *"Trust me. Jump."*

I shriek inside my mind, *"No!!"* But it's as if I've lost control over my body. My heart beats wildly as I feel one foot move forward. My mind reels.

Athena's voice is firm and awesome as it echoes through my mind. *"Your physical transformation is just the beginning. Your true metamorphosis must come from within. Believe you can, and you will. Now, JUMP!"*

Slowly, I raise a foot...and step over the edge into the void.

27 - ARTEMIS

I plunge downward, arms flailing in an insane free fall as I plummet to the ground. Gravity takes over as my stomach lurches up into my throat, forcing me to scream at the top of my lungs.

I watch in horror as the tiny people on the cavern floor below grow larger and larger. I grab at my sides, my back, anything that might be a parachute, but then I remember: I don't have one! I must have had a heart attack and died because everything has just shifted to slow motion. I feel totally surreal and out of body, like I'm floating or it's happening to someone else. In the next second, my survival instinct kicks in. Gut-wrenching terror hits as I watch the ground approaching closer and closer and...

This is it. I'm going to die!

I squeeze my eyes shut, and my body goes tense and rigid as I brace myself for the impact. When I don't feel it, I make the mistake of opening my eyes. There, right in front of my face, I see the ground, so close. I close my eyes again as a door in the cavern floor slides open beneath me....and *slam!* My body hits hard. *Crack!* Mind-blowing pain surges through me. All my bones must be broken. But how am I still alive?! I bounce off a spongy soft surface, then slide down and down, until finally I land on a tarp that feels springy like a trampoline. My world swiftly fades to darkness.

Some time must have passed when I finally crack open my eyes. Slowly, I refocus. I'm still alive! But where am I? Still lying on the tarp, I see that I'm in the middle of what looks like an enormous underground chamber. Just adjacent to me is a colossal marble statue, beautifully sculpted into the likeness of a gorgeous woman with long, flowing, wavy hair. She is holding a magnificent bow. The look on her face is fierce and courageous. Next to her is the likeness of an oversized mountain lion, staring ahead in fearless audacity.

Instantly, I recognize them both...my mom and Bastet.

I gasp at the sight of them. Just then, the real Bastet steps out from behind the shadows to stand next to her own statue. She utters a loud, ferocious roar. At the bottom of the statue, I read the words "Our Beloved Artemis."

My mother is Artemis.

Oh my God! My breathing is shallow, so I feel like I'm hyperventilating. I wrap my arms around my fluttering stomach as the pieces fall in place. Of course! It's as if I've known this all along and am finally able to acknowledge the truth. I know who I am now...the daughter of a goddess.

"You figured it out." I hear that voice in my head again. Athena.

As she steps into the light, I take in the sight of her. She's unusually tall, with a long, regal neck and smooth, perfect skin. Her striking blond hair is pulled away from her face in a severe ponytail.

Most exceptional are her piercing blue eyes, which draw me in and totally captivate me. I'm fully entranced by the montage of varying shades of blue that I see in her eyes, gradually building from the darkest navy in the center to the lightest sky blue, all rimmed in a ring of radiant gold. The effect is limitless and breathtaking, like an infinite geothermal spring.

Athena breaks the silence and speaks out loud. "Welcome to Scythia. This is your mother's chamber." Bastet nudges her large head into Athena's hand. "Of course, you already know her lioness." They stare at each other as if they are secretly conversing...and most likely, they are. Something bothers me, though, about Bastet.

"I don't remember any of the myths describing Artemis with a cat or a lioness. I thought her preferred companion was a stag or a dog?" I ask, perplexed.

Athena lifts her chin back and laughs. "Smart girl! You're right. Keep in mind, though, that all 'mythology' as you know it on Earth occurred over thousands of years, shifting from storytelling to written form. All of it, however, came to a big, grinding halt when the Olympic Gate, a portal on a plateau near the summit of Mount

Olympus, destabilized and collapsed on itself." Her voice is alive with excitement. "All of the 'gods' that you know from your beloved stories were attending an event over here on Gaea, so when the Gate fell, we were trapped here and unable to return to Earth. This is the reason that all of your epic tales about us on Earth have so many variations and different endings."

The image of the archaeologists' recent discovery of the Olympic Arch gateway with the logograms and twelve symbols of the gods on the plateau in northern Greece comes to mind. But what does this have to do with my mom and Bastet?

Almost as if she can read my mind, Athena is two steps ahead of me. She continues, "Think about how much time has passed since then – thousands of Earth years. A lot can happen, and change, in that time, including your mother's animal companion. She has had many through the years, but Bastet has been here the longest. She's a goddess in her own right."

I recall what I can about the goddess Bastet from Egyptian mythology. She was the protector goddess who, through the ascension of many legends, assumed the likeness of either a cat or...a lioness. Bastet is a real goddess. Of course! Why not?

"Exactly," says Athena. Apparently, she can read my mind. "All mythology throughout Europe, the Middle East, Scandinavia, and the Far East originates with us, all starting around four thousand years ago. That's a long story for another time and place."

Athena moves in close to me and picks up my hand to inspect my ring. "This belongs to your mother. Each point on this star represents the twelve ruling gods who make up the Council of Twelve. You should wear it on your left hand, as from now on, it is your legacy. It has some interesting, uh, properties that you will discover over time."

"'Gods'?" I ask. "Why do you call them that if they can die? Don't they have to be immortal to be considered gods?"

Athena grins. "Well, they are immortal...in a way."

"In a way?" I ask, perplexed.

"When the time is right, you'll understand."

But I want to know now. Why should I have to wait? Wait for

what? When the time is right? How frustrating!

I stroke the engraved image of the star on the silver face of my ring. A moment later, I feel heat emanate from my chest. As I touch the warmth there, my fingers brush the smooth, shiny surface of the cypress tree pendant. Instantly, the image of my mother's smiling face flashes through my mind, and I remember why I'm here. I still need to find her. Athena must know something.

Once again, she's ahead of me. She says in a stern voice, "Now that you know your mother's identity, isn't it enough? Why worry about her? She'll be fine. You need to worry about yourself."

This is not what I need to hear. "You don't understand. I've been searching for her since the...accident. I'm not giving up now! I have to find her!"

Athena's eyes light up. "Ah, yes! You are your mother's daughter after all."

"Where is the Lone Cypress Tree, Athena? At least you can tell me that!" I plead, tiring of this silly charade. Why can't anyone just be honest with me? Just tell me the truth!

"The truth is that no one really knows where it is. Most consider it a fool's legend, but if it does exist, then the only way to find it would be to use the Catalyst, which unfortunately is hidden somewhere far away on Earth." Athena's mesmerizing multicolored eyes seem to glisten as she speaks.

"The Catalyst?" I ask, annoyed at yet another obstacle that stands in the way of finding my mother. I roll my eyes.

Athena narrows her eyes and answers, "Really, it's not that hard. Stop being so whiny. I always told your mother not to baby you so much, that she was making you weak. Fine, I'll tell you about the Catalyst. Why not?"

God, what a b-i-t-c-...

"I heard that!" she screams at me. "You want to know or not?"

Crap, I have to be nice, even inside my own head. Something about this seems so very wrong, like a massive invasion of my privacy.

"You'll get over it," she says with a condescending smile. "The

Catalyst is a quantum destabilizer, the only one of its kind. It was originally created by Atlas to pierce a wormhole through the fabric that exists between our universe and yours, bridging Gaea and Earth. It looks a bit like what you call a smart tablet – a handheld device – but it's so much more than that! Your primitive iPad can't construct a Gate!"

An image of the ancient-looking iPad device from the secret room under the school comes to mind. Athena's eyes widen with alarm. "You've seen it! But how…how did you get into the Stronghold?"

I need to totally clear my mind while I'm here. I can't allow her to see any more of my thoughts. If she won't be completely transparent with me, then I'm sure as heck not telling her anything else.

"That's more like it!" She's happy with me, which is totally disconcerting. "Own up to the strong woman you are! It's essential that you understand one very important thing about the Catalyst." The limitless essence of her eyes bores into my soul. "Zeus must never get his hands on the Catalyst, or it will be the end of life on Earth as we know it."

"I don't understand. Why can't he just create a new Catalyst?" I ask.

"Atlas is dead. No one else knows how it works. Prometheus stole it from Zeus just before he escaped to Earth, and ever since then, Zeus has been desperate to find it."

Dire fear seizes my mind, but I fight the urge to think more about the Catalyst. I can't know anything about it. Athena eyes me with suspicion when suddenly an apparition appears…of Janus.

His face is wild, frantic. "Athena, we've got a problem. It's Helene. She's gone!"

Athena starts to chuckle, which works Janus into a panic. His face turns red, filling with rage. "This is not a joke!"

"Uh, Janus?" she says as her eyes rove over to where I'm standing. His gaze follows hers. He blinks a few times.

I give Janus a little wave. He shakes his head at me in utter disbelief. "Goddammit! But…*how*?"

I can't say that I'm surprised by his reaction, but I am perplexed as to how Janus, or the *image* of Janus, is here right now. I decide to offer him a deal. "I'll tell you how I got here if you explain to me how you are here now when we all know that you are physically on Earth."

Janus grows stone cold and silent. He and Athena exchange looks. After a moment, he nods and then proceeds, his tone thick with sarcasm. "Fine. But you first. How did you get through the Gate?"

I scratch behind Bastet's ear, place my finger on the cat's-eye stone on her collar, then ask, "Recognize this?"

In a split second, Janus has completely lost his mind, hopping around like a possessed madman. "You! But how?" he exclaims as his eyes settle on Bastet. "I knew it! This is all your doing! I should never have allowed you in my house!"

I move myself in front of Bastet as if to protect her from his childish tirade. Athena comes to her rescue. "Careful now, Janus…"

He ignores her, eyes wild and intense, as he continues, "Bastet's collar doesn't explain how you broke in through the basement door! I placed a magnetic signature enhanced force field around that door," he pauses, deep in thought. "There are only two people capable of breaking it…me and…"

Recognition crosses his face. "Oh yes…*you*. The Prophecy…you've been through Protogenesis." He catches a glimpse of my ring. "The ring of Artemis," he says with an air of reverence. "Of course you can break the force field. It would be easy for you."

"She is my mother, after all," I say quietly. Then I ask, "Protogenesis?" I feel I've heard this somewhere before, maybe in science class with Dimitris, something about a myth of the power of the cat's-eye stone.

Athena cuts in. "Protogenesis occurs when any living thing passes through a portal, or 'Gate' like ours, which alters DNA at the molecular level to its best possible state. Like a butterfly emerging from its cocoon, the transformation from Protogenesis can be drastic and life changing, although for most, the change is subtle."

"I knew you had been through the Gate! I just didn't know how!" Janus exclaims heatedly.

Well, at least now I know there's a reason for my enhanced

abilities. Still, I need to know what's going on. "Okay, so we had a deal. Your turn to tell me how it is that you are here right now."

Janus sighs, recomposing himself as his eyes flit over to where Athena stands. She nods in somber silence. And then…he starts to laugh. He knocks the side of his head a couple of times, grabs his earlobe, and twists it until a small earpiece falls out onto the floor. It looks like a tiny hearing aid possibly, but something that fits only into the inside of the ear, completely invisible to the outside world.

His laughing subsides as he reaches down to hold up the earbud. "Do you believe in ghosts?"

I decide to humor him. "Uh, yeah. In fact, I saw one recently at the Temple of Poseidon."

"Oh, you did, did you?" Janus says, relishing my lack of knowledge here. Athena gives him the evil eye, but he continues his mischief. I start to get annoyed with him when he opens a drawer and picks up an electronic-looking device about the size of a toaster and launches into lecture mode. "So, most supernatural behavior on Earth, including 'ghosts' and 'spirits,' are created by this or a similar device – Orion's Key. It's a quantum destabilizer, which creates a mini-black hole between universes."

Sounds familiar. I can't help but interrupt him. "Like the Catalyst?" I ask.

Janus raises his eyebrow at Athena, who just nods at him. He crosses his arms, then continues in a less animated voice. "Yes, but the Catalyst creates an actual wormhole, either a temporary or permanent Gate, between realities. Orion's Key and others like it can be used only to create the image of a person, like a hologram, if on the high setting, or if used on the low setting, it can be used to spy on another universe."

He holds up the earbud again. "This hearing device is connected to Orion's Key and enables me to communicate regularly with Athena. I just tug on my ear, and it activates the device. She can hear everything I say and anything within about fifty feet of where I stand."

This explains a lot about Janus's bizarre behavior. All those times I thought he was hearing voices and hallucinating, he was communicating with Athena here on Gaea.

Athena smiles at me. "Sometimes Janus is really crazy, Helene. Those are the times when I want to kill him. Right, Janus?"

He shakes his head, muttering under his breath. "Okay! That's it. This lesson is over!" Before Athena or I can say anything more, Janus's image vanishes.

Athena shrugs. "I was done with him anyway." I think she must be done talking to me as well because she starts to turn as if to leave me here. She lifts her hand to head, as if deep in thought, then turns back to me. "I heard about your little fight with Ares. Congratulations on your victory."

"Thank you," I reply. For some reason, her validation of my survival, as if it were some sort of sport, seems off. For God's sake, my life was at stake! "I was a little surprised that he didn't know that I had been to Gaea."

"*What* did you just say?" Her face fills with worry, but her voice is laced with fire. "Please tell me that you didn't tell him about the Cat's-Eye Gate!!"

"No, I didn't. I only said that I had been to Gaea. That's all."

Athena sighs in relief, but concern still fills her voice. "Well, that's good, but you must understand why he can't know that you've been to Gaea, right? Zeus is razor sharp and will easily connect the dots that another Gate exists."

This can't be all my fault! I'm not going to be made to feel guilty when no one has bothered to tell me anything until now. "He already knows. Isn't it obvious to Zeus and his thugs on Earth that Gaean kids are disappearing from New Olympus and then showing up on Earth?"

Athena's eyes widen, but her face relaxes into a wide smile. "Oh my, you're a spirited girl! Excellent analysis. There might be hope for you yet." She winks at me.

Was that a compliment or an insult? God, I hate her right now, but it's as if I love to hate her. She's so *frustrating*...just like someone else I know back on Earth.

"Besides, Hal Avery told me that the reason they wanted me to come to Greece was to lead them to the Gate," I tell her.

"Hal Avery?" Athena's eyes grow wide. I think I've surprised her.

When I describe him to her, she gives me a grin before explaining, "Just to clarify, Zeus's spies on Earth, including your friend Hal Avery, aren't 'thugs.' They're Vorlage, Zeus's royal army of protectors and spies. On Gaea, they are gold-plated cybernetic droids or automatons. What you see on Earth is what was left of the old guard from ancient times. They are humans whose genetic memories have been passed down from generation to generation, originating from a time before the Gate collapsed."

This explains why it was so easy to wipe them out when they attacked me earlier tonight. Athena smiles in agreement. "Well, it's getting late. You should sleep." She points to a large, plush bed nearby, and before I know it, she's gone.

I sit down on the bed and sock a pillow in angst. After all the effort that it took for me to finally come here to Scythia and meet Athena, how is it that I've made so little progress?! It's clear that neither Athena nor Janus wants me to find my mother. But why not? I don't care what they say…or don't say. I'm not giving up my search.

It dawns on me that I'm not tired. Today I learned one very important piece of intel. I already possess the secret to finding the location of the cypress tree…the Catalyst. Unfortunately, I'll have to go to Earth to get it. Maybe I should look around here. Perhaps I can find some clue on Gaea that will lead me to the Lone Cypress Tree so I don't have to go back.

Feeling restless, I wander over to the door and crack it open. No guards. I hear a sound behind me, then a nudge under my hand. My lioness. "Sorry, Bastet. I need to look around here, and you're sure to be noticed."

"No problem." I hear her voice in my head as she nudges my hand one more time. Then she jumps up onto the bed. So much for my sleeping there. *"I can move when you return!"* she jokes.

"It's fine," I say, laughing with her.

Quiet as I can be, I make my way out into the empty hallway.

Scattered voices fill the space around me as I wander past several closed doorways – most likely apartments. I'm about to turn the corner when I recognize the sound of Athena's familiar velvety-smooth voice. I wonder whom she's talking to. A brusque male voice whispers softly, but it sounds a lot like Minios. Something tells me that this is a conversation I need to hear. Hopefully, Athena can't hear my thoughts right now, or she'll know I'm here.

As I move in closer, I hear both of their voices clearly. Minios whispers urgently, "It's confirmed. Someone has activated the Catalyst. This is *bad*. And if you and I know this, then surely Prometheus will know. Even worse, Zeus will be alerted, which no doubt will ignite a major manhunt."

Athena's voice is icy and hard, ruthless. "You're sure? It doesn't make sense. No one knows about the Stronghold....Oh." She stops.

"What is it?" Minios asks urgently.

"I know who it is," she says in an irritated voice.

"Do we need to alert Prometheus?" he asks her.

"Absolutely not!" Athena replies adamantly. "I'll take care of it. Don't worry. Everything is fine. There's no way Zeus will find it."

My heart pounds. She knows that I have it! I take a deep breath and try to slow my thoughts to sharpen my memory. Now I remember! When she read my thoughts earlier, she saw my vision of the Catalyst inside my mother's secret room – inside the glass case – but not that I have it in my possession. Good.

I'm torn about the Catalyst. On one hand, I feel horribly guilty about fiddling with it and taking it away from the Stronghold. I'm filled with remorse as I recall the moment when the crazy iPad device was counting down to Gate construction. Now that I fully understand what that means, I'm terrified about what could have happened. A new Gate. Catastrophe. Armageddon. On the other hand, now that I know that the Catalyst is the only way to find the cypress tree, I feel compelled to keep it so I can find my mom.

I rush back down the hall to my room. Bastet is waiting there for me, as if she already knows that I need her. *"I'm being totally selfish about keeping the Catalyst, right?"* I ask Bastet in my mind.

"No! I want to find your mom too." She glowers at me, her amber eyes blazing.

It's a relief to be able to talk to someone about all this craziness, even if she is a cat. I'm not alone in this journey. Like my mother, Bastet truly has my back.

We need to get out of here, and quick. Athena will be on her way back here at any minute. Bastet explains what she knows about how to escape. Once out in the open desert, she can take me back to the Gate. "But how?" I ask.

"You can ride on my back," she says, *"like a horse...only I'm much more fun."*

We sneak out and make our way together down the hallway. A small boy suddenly opens his door, and as we pass him, he calls out in surprise, "Your lion is so..." He's going to give us away! Somewhere around the corner, I hear footsteps approaching, then that same terse cold tone again...Athena. She's almost here. How can we get past her?

Suddenly, Bastet leaps past the boy, through the door, and into his apartment. Smart lioness! I follow her inside and shove the door closed behind us, just in time to avoid Athena. The boy is ecstatic to have Bastet here with him, so much so that he doesn't want us to leave. I can tell that Bastet is disturbed by his cries behind us as we take off.

Luckily, we make our way up the high-speed elevator and out into the open desert without incident. Unfortunately, though, we have no choice but to skirt the edges of the sandicane for us to reach the Gate anytime soon. If we don't go now, we could be stuck here until morning, at which point we would be forced to face Athena's harsh inquisition. That would be bad considering she can read my mind.

Sand crystals whip past us in menacing fury as the sandstorm reaches the edge of the ruins of the old city. How are we going to get through this mayhem? There's no easy way to get back to the Gate.

The only way is through the heart of the storm.

28 – THWARTED

Thousands of tiny grains of sand sting my face. I can barely see Bastet as I grasp onto her body. We trudge through the sand, which is now almost knee high. Just when I think it can't get any worse, thunder rumbles, the ground shakes, and then *crack!* A flash of red lightning strikes a couple of yards from us. A few seconds later, *splat!* A green bolt hits so close that it singes some of Bastet's fur, stopping us cold in our tracks. We huddle close, moving down to the ground to avoid the lightning, but because the sand is gusting over us, we can't lie here long or we'll risk being buried alive.

Just when I'm sure that it's all over for us, I hear Bastet's voice inside my head. *"Look…over there!"* She turns her head to the left, where there's an indentation in the side of a sand dune. It could be an entrance to a hidden cave, now visible after the harsh wind scattered the sands in the storm.

"But we could get trapped in there!" I say to her, concerned.

"It may be our only option," she pleads. *"We can't find your mom if we're dead!"*

She's right. We have no choice.

It takes all our strength and resolve, but we plod on, one foot in front of the next until we reach the dark, cool solitude of the cave. Once inside, we both collapse onto the ground, gasping desperately as we struggle to inhale the fresh air here. My body is numb and shaky, completely exhausted. All I want to do is lie here and rest, but as my eyes begin to adjust to the darkness, I notice that there's a light further down inside the cavern. "Bastet, do you see that?" I ask her.

"Well, yes. There are some benefits to being a cat. I can see in the dark. Come on, I will guide you," she says.

I grasp her collar so I don't lose her. Soon, the light grows brighter, and my eyes adjust enough to see that we are inside some sort of modern subway station that looks like the Metro in Greece but is much more sophisticated. Except for the echo of my shoes, an eerie silence fills the space, making it feel as if it had been abandoned long ago. "What is this place?" I ask as my voice reverberates through the tunnels ahead of us.

Bastet seems happy to tell me what she knows. *"This was once a hyperloop maglev train tunnel system, something like a subway on Earth but much faster. In the old days, at the height of Gaea's glory, this was a magnificent city...the original Olympus. It was much larger and more advanced than any of Earth's modern cities are now. Gaea was several thousand years ahead of Earth in terms of technology by then. Sadly, over the span of thousands of years, after climate change and the Scourge, the great city fell into the ruins that you see now."*

This makes sense considering what Athena told me about the "gods" from Gaea.

The tunnel ahead splits. Which way to go? The tunnel to our right has some sort of writing on the wall, like graffiti. It makes me feel as if I'm back in Athens for a moment.

Bastet's voice echoes through my mind. *"Cyclops. We must go left."*

A shiver runs through my spine at the mention of those monsters.

Suddenly, a loud clanging sound farther down the tunnel forces us to halt. Bastet and I exchange a worried glance, then sprint as fast as we can down the tunnel on the left. A stairway leads up. I follow Bastet up, slow and steady, but almost pass out when we reach the top, that is, until I see what waits for us there: the crumbling ruins that surround the Gate.

We shield our eyes as the cat's-eye stone works its magic, and the brilliant shimmering surface that is now so familiar to me returns to its usual splendor. Sweet relief. We're going home!

Bastet and I race forward, leaping through the Gate's iridescent surface. I feel my feet slam down on the basement floor even before I know I've made it back. The room spins for a moment, then slows to a stop. I slowly open my eyes and inhale deeply to breathe in the fresh, uncontaminated air of Earth. We made it!

But my elation is short-lived.

"Helene!" Janus yells so loud in my ear that it makes me jump. "You have two seconds to give me that collar. One…two…"

I stand in shock from our near-death experience in the sandicane. It's like jumping on an airplane in Antarctica and landing immediately in the Bahamas – surreal and unsettling.

Janus eyes me with skepticism, eyes narrowed, taking in my image. Head to toe, Bastet and I are completely covered in sand.

I pick Bastet up and stroke her back as her tail swings up into a graceful arc. I'm surprised that I haven't heard anything from her since we got back. Perhaps she can't get into my head here as she can on Gaea.

"You have no idea how much trouble you've caused!" Janus paces back and forth, then swings back around to me. "Prometheus is going to kill me!!"

"I keep hearing about the amazing Prometheus. But, where is he?" I ask.

Janus appears startled. "Ah, yes. Of course, you know. He's been in hiding since he fled Gaea to Earth. He manages the rebellion from afar, someplace safe."

"That seems a bit of a cop-out, if you ask me," I say. If anyone knows where my mom is, Prometheus probably would.

"You have no idea what you're talking about," Janus says defiantly. "He's only reason you're still alive, so I'd be careful what you say about him!"

This is ridiculous! It's not right that this supposed god, Prometheus, is too chicken to show his face while the rest of us fight for our lives. The only reason I'm still alive is that I've fought hard for myself, not him!

Bastet leaps out of my arms onto the floor. When she lands, her bright orange gaze locks onto Janus's serious eyes. A few seconds pass between them in silence, and then he completely flips out. His hand trembles as he points at her. "You! I should lock you away until the end of time!" He reaches down to grab her, but Bastet shimmies out of his grasp, sidles through his legs, and sprints swiftly up the stairs.

Janus runs after her and screams, "You can't escape me!"

A moment later, I hear the pitter-patter of her paw pads as she scurries back down the stairs with Janus close on her heels, yelling obscenities as he chases her. Her eyes are wide in terror when he reaches out to grab her again. Unfortunately, this time he's successful. He pulls her flailing body into his arms.

Claws fully extended, she swipes her paw across his face, drawing a trail of blood. He screams and drops her to the floor with a thud. "Okay, that's enough!" he yells, looking at both of us. His voice softens, but only slightly. "Here's how this is going to go. Helene, I need you to pick up that cat and hand me her collar...*now!*"

"But you told me I wouldn't get in trouble."

"You're not in trouble...yet!" He taps his foot. "I don't have all day! The collar?"

"I'm not even sure she'll give it to me," I say.

"She will. Do it *now!*"

I shrug and walk over to Bastet. When I lean down, I kiss her on the nose. "Sorry, girl!" But then I whisper close into her ear, "We'll find a way to get it back." She licks my nose. Gingerly, I unclasp and release the collar from her neck, then step back and hand it to Janus.

Bastet and I follow Janus as he stomps up the steps and into our apartment, the whole time carrying on like a crazy man. "I'm taking this away, hiding it a place safe from *both* of you!" He steps over to the picture on the wall, flips it to the side, then opens the safe with a zap of his finger and tosses the collar inside.

Not even a moment later, he whips around to me. "Now, give me the Catalyst! I know you have it."

Athena! She must have told him about me immediately after my conversation with her. I knew it! But there's no way I'm giving him the Catalyst. I need it to guide me to the cypress tree, my only lead to finding Mom. Since Janus so easily lies to me, I don't feel a shred of guilt about lying to him now.

"I don't have it," I say in my most confident voice.

"Athena thinks you've been playing around with it in the Stronghold," he says with wild eyes. "If anything happens to it, I'm going to find out. And when that happens, screw the Prophecy! You'll be responsible for the end of life as we know it here on Earth, you hear?"

Janus marches over to the refrigerator, grabs some glasses, and pours us some wine. Wait, what?! The end of the world? Suddenly, I wish I could just give the Catalyst back and be done with it! But what exactly is this Prophecy? Ares mentioned it when my life was at stake. I don't understand what it has to do with me. I drop down into a kitchen chair and take a sip of the wine. *Ugh.* This is not as good as the wine I had with Ever. "Tell me about the Prophecy. What's this about, Janus?" I demand. "No one will tell me what it is. It's about me, right? I have a right to know. My life is at stake!"

Janus backs away and for once is at a loss for words. He shakes his head, arms extended out, then says, "I can't tell you. That's your mother's job, not mine!!"

"So, now you're admitting she's alive?" I ask, incredulous.

His eyes shift. "Actually, I meant to say that she was supposed to tell you...before she died." He looks down at his shoes in awkward silence, but it's too late. He's been caught in his own lie. Time to confront him. I'm sick and tired of his lies. It's not right.

"You've known all along that my mom was alive! Why didn't you tell me? Why?" I crumple into the back of the chair. My heart feels crushed as a wave of emotions hit me hard. I feel betrayed and angry. How could he keep this from me?!

Janus sits in the chair next to me and touches my arm to comfort me. "It was all for your own good, for your protection. It's dangerous for you to know too much before you're ready. One day, when the time is right, your mother will tell you everything. Then this will all make perfect sense."

"Oh, so you must be talking about my mother who is supposed to be *dead*?" I say, my voice dripping with sarcasm. "I think you need to rethink your logic. How am I supposed to protect myself from Ares if I get attacked again if I know nothing about what I'm up against?"

"That won't happen again," he says quietly. "The guard we assigned arrived too late that night, but—"

"I don't care!" My voice rises. "If you can't tell me anything about the Prophecy, then how about the Lone Cypress Tree? I know this tree is the key to my finding Mom. If I can just go back to Gaea and find it…"

Janus starts to laugh. "Are you nuts? There's absolutely no way you're going back to Gaea!"

The ground shakes beneath our feet. A rumbling tremor travels through the whole building. "No, no, no! This is not good…not good at all!" His lips quirk in agitation as his intensity grows. "Do you feel that?! That's the Gate! When both you and Bastet pass through it together, you make it unstable! You're going to cause it to collapse, just like the Olympic Gate!"

"Whatever!" I yell. "It's not fair for you to keep my mother from me. It's wrong!"

"You don't understand. Your mother doesn't want to be found. There are important reasons for all of it. It's imperative that we keep you safe. Trust me on this."

Of course, he's lying again. There's no way my mother would be hiding from me. She would never leave me like that! But a trace of doubt seeps into my head, and suddenly my eyes well up with tears.

I look down at my phone and see the date. Saturday. *What?* No. There's no way that can be right. If it is, then I have been in Gaea for five days and missed almost a whole week of school.

"Janus, ummm, what day is it today?" I ask sullenly, wiping tears from my eyes.

"Saturday," he says evenly. "I had to lie to the school for you. Told them you were sick."

As I listen to his tirade, my thoughts wander off, and then realization hits me. "The dance…is tonight," I whisper, my voice wavering in a panic.

"Well, there's no way you're going! It's not safe. I can't let you out of my sight."

"But you don't understand! I promised Nick that I would go!" I erupt. The intensity of the last four days is now completely overwhelming to me.

Janus frowns, a crease forming on his brow. "You're going with *him*!? Then definitely no."

It's not fair. I turn eighteen tomorrow. Janus has no right to suddenly act like my guardian. This is the most horrible day ever. I'm not allowed to go to the dance, Janus has taken away the collar and my only way to get back to Gaea, and now I'm afraid that my mother doesn't even want me to find her.

"I hate you!" I slam the door and run downstairs into Janus's shop. Anger surges through my veins. Just for once, I wish more than anything that I could live a normal life and go to the dance just like any other girl.

My thoughts are interrupted by a soft rapping sound. I look up and am startled to see Nick staring through the glass door at me. What's he doing here? When I open the door, he asks me if I'm all ready for tonight.

Before I can even say anything, Janus comes stomping down the hollow wooden steps in a rage, then yells at Nick, "She's not going!"

Nick's face grows ashen. "What? But I've been planning this all week."

"Life sucks sometimes," Janus says. "You'll get over it. Now, run along!"

But Nick isn't backing down so easily. "Look old man, you can't…"

Their voices escalate into a yelling match, which abruptly comes to an end when Janus forces Nick out the door. It is bad enough that he won't let me go to the dance, but now he's going to completely sever any chance for me to go out with Nick ever again.

"You're ruining my whole life!" I yell at Janus, then run outside after Nick. I've got to salvage this. What to do? An image of my mom fills my head. She would want me to go tonight no matter what. I have an idea.

"Nick, wait!" I call out after him. He halts in his tracks and turns to me. His look is apprehensive. "Listen, I don't care what Janus says," I say. "I'm going to the dance with you. I'll sneak out…whatever it takes. Can you meet me there?"

Nick is disappointed. "This is so *not* cool. I was planning to pick you up and take you to a nice dinner." He shrugs, looking up to the ceiling. "I had something really special planned. There's something, uh, *important* that I need to ask you."

"Can't you just ask me now?" It must be something significant because he's not making eye contact. Something is different about him. "What is it?" I ask, suddenly nervous.

"Do you think you could be happy with me?" he asks tentatively.

That's a strange question. I answer, perplexed, "Of course I'm happy with you!"

"No," he says, sighing heavily. "I mean...what I meant was...would you want to go out with me, like, you know...*seriously*?"

"What?" I step back.

"You know, like you could be my..." he stammers, "...girlfriend."

I had an idea about this, but well, since I'm not Greek, I wasn't sure. He is a rebel after all. Maybe it's about time he breaks this rule. This is a lot to process, so all I can think to say is, "Oh!"

A look of pained frustration comes over Nick. "Well, if you're going to be like that, then I don't know."

"Oh no," I say, "I didn't mean to sound like that. It's just...well, I'm kind of in shock because I wasn't expecting it."

"Oh," he says, relieved. "So that was a yes, as in you want to?"

The street life around us seems to freeze in time as I gaze into his endless gray-green eyes. I don't want to freak him out further, but I can't do this right now.

"I'm not sure I can be who you want me to be. My mother is missing, maybe dead. I just moved around the world to stay with a crazy godfather I didn't know I had, and someone wants me dead. I come with a lot of baggage...warning labels."

It's not as if I'm lying. I'm not exactly an expert at serious relationships, so to add that to the stress of trying to find Mom is just too much, too crazy.

"You mean the kind that say, 'Treat gently. Handle with care'?" Nick's strong arms surround me in an embrace. He takes a step back, peering deep into my eyes. "I can do that. We can take this as slowly as you want. All I ask is to be with you and to have the privilege of showing you my masterful dance moves later."

"Masterful dance moves?" I ask, unable to resist smiling.

He nods and spins me around into a dip. "Oh yes. You, Miss Ballerina, aren't the only one around here with some killer footwork."

"I believe you," I say, laughing. It feels good to joke around for just a moment. I'm a normal girl whose biggest problem is what to wear to the dance.

I watch as Nick walks back to his apartment, and I allow my mind to drift off somewhere far away as I consider it all. So much has happened this week. Somehow, I thought I would have plenty of time to talk to Ever, to explain why I was going to the dance with Nick, but how could I have known that I would be in Gaea for a whole week?

Ever. In my heart, I'm torn. Every time I'm with him, I experience something so intensely deep. It's raw and primal, as if I've known him beyond this life, maybe in a past life, and it's terrifying. If I let myself be swept away by him, I'm not sure I'd ever recover. He might push me over the edge, and how could I help Mom then? Besides, it seems that my feelings are one-sided. All we'll ever be is friends. I'm not sure I can do it.

I look at my watch. I need to call Ever to try to explain. My heart trembles and my breathing grows shallow as I pick up my phone to dial his number. The phone rings a few times. I almost hang up, when I hear his cheery voice on the other end...but it's his voice mail. What to say? I don't know.

"Ummm, hi. It's me. Look, when you asked me to the dance that first time, I said no because, honestly, I thought I would be out of town looking for my mom, but...I didn't leave town after all, and...well, now it's all screwed up, complicated. So, since I'm sure that you already have another date by now, I've made plans with a..." – I pause for a moment, not sure what to say about Nick – "...*friend* to take me."

At least tried to let him know, even though my excuse feels hollow and flimsy. Anyway, he'll be the hot commodity at the dance and won't even notice that I'm there.

I try to envision Nick all dressed up for the dance, but then it dawns on me that he may not be able to afford a nice suit. I don't care. He could be dressed in nothing but torn-up jean shorts and a tight t-shirt and look amazing. Better yet, how about no shirt? *Yes!* A part of me hopes that he will do just that.

The grandfather clock chimes heartily to announce that yet another hour has passed. I'd better hurry up and get ready! Just then, a startling reality hits me. What will I wear tonight?

Crap. I don't have a dress!

29 – THE DANCE

I take a deep breath. It's all relative. Seriously, I just found out that my mom is Artemis! Who gives a crap about a silly dress? I can figure this out.

I make an emergency call to Vani. She's going to be mad that I've been out all week and am just now calling her. I can only imagine what she'll do when I call to beg for her help at the last minute before the dance. Hopefully, she's in her usual cheerful mood today.

She picks up on the first ring.

"You know how much I love you, right?" I say.

"Cut the crap, Helene. Where have you been?"

"I've been sick!" I say, pretending to cough.

I'm expecting her to give me more trouble, but instead, it's as if she expected this. "Yeah, half the school is out with some sort of weird bug. It's crazy! But you're okay, right?" she asks, concerned.

"Well, yes and no. The illness is gone, but I had no time to shop for a dress this week! I'm supposed to meet Nick in a few hours for the dance. Please, can you help? I need a dress."

Vani is totally incredulous. "God, Helene! This is crazy!"

"I can wear anything, really," I tell her. "It doesn't have to be super fancy."

"The dress is easy," she says with confidence. I can feel her grinning through the phone. "What is totally insane is you not calling to tell me that Nick asked you to the dance! I don't care how sick you are. You can pick up the phone!" She's pissed at me, rightfully so, but I can't get upset because I know that I had a very good reason for not calling her. I was in another universe talking to Athena!

"Of course, I already knew about Nick. He asked for my help, so I told him to ask you to the dance."

"I thought that might be the case," I say. She always has my back.

I hear her rustling something in the background. "Well, lucky for you, I spent most of today at Celia Kritharioti's boutique in Golden Hall."

"*Who*?"

"Uh, she's like one of the most exciting Greek designers in Athens," Vani exclaims. "Anyway, I couldn't decide what I liked best, so I bought three gowns. You and I are about the same size now, right?"

Thankfully, yes. I explain my predicament. I'll have to sneak out to go to the dance. There's no way for Nick to pick me up here. He's meeting me later.

"I don't get it," Vani sighs. "Why is Janus being such a turd?"

"I don't know," I say in frustration.

She's quiet for a bit, probably considering my options. Finally, she sighs again. "Fine. Just figure out how to get over here, and I'll take care of the rest."

I locate Janus's stash of cash in the tin can hidden on the top shelf of the kitchen cabinet, and twenty minutes later, I make my way over to Vani's house via taxi. She looks amazing in a full-length emerald green dress that drapes elegantly around her slight frame.

She ushers me into her room and takes over. She hands me dresses and makes me try on shoes, all the while doing my hair and makeup. She chatters on about nail polish colors and Spanx. All this fussing is giving me a headache.

Just when I think I can't stand it any longer, I turn and catch my reflection in the full-length mirror. I barely recognize myself in this gorgeous crimson full-length gown. *Wow.*

I barely have time to admire Vani's handiwork when her phone rings. She lifts her eyebrow, deeply engrossed in her call. "Yeah, uh-huh…" After a few minutes, she covers the phone with her hand, turns to me, and says, "It's Nick. He's running a little late, so he'll meet us there." She touches my arm in concern. "Look, just be careful with him. He's had a hard time over the past year. You know, his heart was brutally broken over a year ago."

I sigh. "Yeah, he told me the whole story, including how his best friend betrayed him."

"Ah, well, then I'm sure you understand why it's such a huge deal for him to take you to the dance at the school where all of that awfulness happened," she says, her expression serious and pained. "He hasn't been back to the Academy since he was forced to drop out."

"Yeah," I tell her, "don't worry. We agreed to take things slow. We're cool."

"Good!" she says as if relieved, but then she looks at her watch. "Alexis should be downstairs with the limo. Ready?"

The drive is short. We step out of the limo and it's clear that Athens International Academy has spared no expense in creating a truly spectacular experience for us tonight. Lining the walkway is a long azure-blue carpet edged in white – the national colors of Greece – that stretches through the entryway and into the main gymnasium. The principal announces each person as we arrive like we are celebrities attending the Oscars.

Then it's my turn. As I stride down the "blue carpet," I catch my reflection in the mirrors that cover the walls around the entryway. I barely recognize myself. It is almost otherworldly. My dark hair is long and shiny, hanging down my back like a curtain, swept up and away from my face, which accentuates my eyes and lashes, making me appear doe-eyed, exotic, and glamorous.

And the dress...oh my! Bold crimson silk accentuates my smooth, sun-kissed skin as the gown plunges down from my neckline, forming a deep V that ends at my waist, where the fitted silky fabric hugs me like a glove, only to then sweep out and cascade fluently down to the floor. Sheer elegance. Like a movie star It all feels so surreal, almost overwhelming. Is this really me?

I feel as if all eyes are on me as I take in the incredible décor. The entire interior of the gymnasium has been transformed back in time to a much earlier era in Athens's history, decorated with a potpourri of banners displaying majestic ancient Greek temples made from white marble and cobblestone streets lined with tall cypress trees. In the true spirit of ancient Greece, a female musician dressed in a tunic, called *hitonas*, plays the lute, or *laouto*, an instrument that sounds so distinctly Greek to me. When I hear the musician's fingers touch the different strings, I hear an echo in my heart. It takes me back to when I first arrived here, when it sounded so foreign, so exotic. But now that I live here, it feels very familiar, as if it has become a part of me.

A whole crowd of people swarm around us, but after saying hello, I'm growing anxious to find Nick, so I move away from the group to look around. There's no sign of him yet. Remarkably, there's no sign of Ever either. Distracted and alone, I look to the stage, where the band is gearing up to play soon. Suddenly, the music starts, the lights grow dim, and the crowd goes crazy. What is all this madness about? Then suddenly, the lead singer appears.

My heart leaps when I see Ever saunter onto the stage. Of course, I knew I would see him tonight, but nothing has prepared me for how I feel seeing him here like this. He's truly a sight to behold up there on stage with his dark tousled hair, smooth tan, and intense sea-blue eyes, all dressed up in an extremely expensive designer suit – like a real rock star.

I can't wait to hear Ever's voice. I've never heard him sing before, and suddenly I want to. I don't think he's seen me yet, so I try to hide within the mass of single girls who swarm near the front of the stage. Nick's still not here yet, so I don't feel totally guilty about this.

Ever signals to his band, then starts to sing. It's a deeply emotional and seductive ballad. The melodic sound of an instrument called the *oud* subtly juxtaposed with the rhythm of this unbelievably passionate song stokes a long-lost fire within me. The raw fervor and melancholy in his voice moves me somewhere deep inside, almost to tears.

All eyes are fixed on Ever as his rich, silky voice resonates through the gym, mesmerizing the swaying crowd.

And we chameleons who fall in love with light…
Fallen in love with forever.

Suddenly, his blue eyes meet mine. His lips brush the microphone. *Oh God.* Goose bumps form on my neck, running down my spine in little rivers.

I can't seem to break the connection between us. A subtle attraction radiates from Ever on the stage to me in my heart, back and forth throughout the song. His voice reverberates through my soul as he sings,

I want you now, don't you see?
Burn your boundaries and come with me.

It's as if I can sense everything he's feeling with each beat of the music, as if we have become part of the melody itself. It makes me want to move...to dance. The ballerina in me yearns to come alive. I can't help myself.

I want forever and this night.
Eternity begins tonight; come hold me tight.

Then it hits me. This is the song he wrote for me. I didn't believe it before, but now I'm sure of it. I'm filled with such a tremendous flood of emotion towards him that I can barely contain myself.

A tiny voice inside me can't believe that Ever feels this way about me. I thought he just wanted to be friends. He's performing, as an actor does! This emotion can't be for me. But then again, I know the truth. It's not just an act. There's no denying it.

He *cares* about me.

As the song draws to a close, the magic of the spell is abruptly broken. Ever's focus is pulled to the frenzied mass of girls waving at him. His charisma is infectious as more people crowd up to the front, bumping and smacking into each other, all trying to get closer to him. It's madness! This is exactly why I can't be with him.

I feel a tug on my arm. Nick. His hand falls down my arm to my hand, where he strokes the inside of my fingers, which instantly brings me back to the here and now. He whisks me away from the stage, off to the side. As his adoring gray-green eyes take in the sight of me, an enormous smile grows on his face. I've never seen him like this, so elegant and posh with his light brown hair slicked back, wearing a dark, expensive suit. His bronzed skin appears vibrant under a crisp white shirt, which falls open at the neck. I can't even believe this is Nick.

"Hi," he says shyly. Then he leans over, nuzzles my ear, and whispers, "You're stunning."

"Thanks," I say, smiling sweetly. "You don't look so bad yourself." I give him a playful wink. "Where did you get the suit, *GQ*?"

"Nooo," he says with a laugh. "This is a relic from the old days, from when I was able to afford to go to Athens International Academy."

"Oh yeah," I say. Maybe I shouldn't have asked him about it. "Well, I'm glad you can still put it to good use."

The DJ takes over from Ever's band, and the music shifts to hits from America. Nick moves his arms around my waist, holding me in close as we sway back and forth to the sound, touching cheeks in silence. I inhale, filling my senses with his sweet minty lemon scent. The hairs on my neck tingle from being so close to him. Vani and Alexis come over to join us. We laugh and all dance together.

I'm glad that Nick's here with me, but part of me aches for – I hate to say it – Ever. That song still haunts my heart, and I can't stop thinking about him. I'm so confused. Looking around, I don't see Samantha, which confirms my earlier suspicions that Ever asked me to the dance only because she couldn't go. I was so sure my feelings were one-sided, that this was completely platonic. The longing in Ever's eyes and the surge of emotion in his song, which he said he wrote just for me, tells a different story. I'm afraid to look up because I might see him. Of course, I'm sure he got the voice mail, so…

I feel a tap on my back. It's *him*.

He's not happy. I immediately tense up. If he was interested in being more than friends with me, then I know this can't go well. I should have made sure to reach him in real time to explain before now.

Ever's eyes narrow as he takes in the sight of Vani, Alexis…and then Nick.

"Did…did you get my voice mail?" I stammer breathlessly.

"What voice mail?" His voice is tight as he pulls out his phone, then nods tersely when he sees the missed call from me.

Nick pushes around me and says, "What's going on?" Suddenly, he sees Ever. His face grows ashen, as if someone has shot him.

Ever and Nick glare at each other. Hot rage and seething, pent-up anger boil between them. The music stops, and suddenly, all eyes are on us. Everyone is gawking in strained silence. I just stand there, completely numb, frozen in place like a deer in the headlights. This can't end well for anyone.

Vani stares at us in silence, mouth gaping open in shock.

After an eternity of this concentrated staredown, Nick finally speaks. His voice is cold, cutting like ice. "Helene?" He pulls me in close to him as if to protect me, ironically, from Ever.

"Don't tell me that you're here with…*Nick*?" Ever's voice cuts me like a razor. "Unbelievable!" He laughs in a mocking voice.

Nick frowns, interrupting gruffly in a tight, hostile voice. "What do you care who she's with?"

Ever is incredulous. "She didn't tell you? She's supposed to be here with me tonight. Tell him, Helene."

I want to explain, anything, but what can I say? "If you recall, when you asked me to go to the dance, I said no."

Ever shakes his head.

I continue, "In the voice mail that you didn't hear, I told you that I was coming with a friend!"

Nick's eyes grow wide as pain fills his face. "Oh, so now I'm just a friend?"

Instantly, pain, anger, hurt, and frustration consume Ever all at once. In the next moment, though, the tables turn on me when he comes back with, "I've clearly underestimated you, Helene." He flashes me a wry smile. "Don't worry. It won't happen again."

I stare at him in shock. *What?* His eyes are cold and impassive, completely void of emotion, as if he doesn't know me. The thought of Ever being so dismissive, so angry at me – and that I might deserve it – hurts me so deeply that it burns me down to the core. The memory of his words from that song consumes my mind and scalds my soul. He thinks I did this on purpose?

Nick turns all his attention to Ever, now completely ignoring me. "I'd say it's more than poetic justice that she's with me and not you! You're nothing but a lying rat who has no trouble stealing his best friend's girl." Nick's face grows hot and red. "You *so* deserve this!"

Ever doesn't back down. "I would be very careful what you say, Niko. My father owns the tour operator that you work for…and since you're nothing more than a high school dropout, you're lucky to even have a job like that. *Extremely* lucky."

That was low. I knew that Ever could be cold at times, but this is merciless. Deep-seated distress fills me as I try to imagine how Nick must feel right now. The crowd surrounding us starts to whisper, which makes matters worse.

Nick's face reddens in fury. His fists are clenched. "Fine. Go cry to your daddy! He'll fix everything for you like he always does when you mess up! You weren't man enough then with Melina. Why should you be less of a *malaka* now?"

I stand there in stunned silence as it dawns on me what this is about. Melina. All the stories that Nick and Vani told me. Ever is the childhood friend who stole Nick's girlfriend. Oh God.

Ever steps away from Nick with a smirk on his face. His tone is dry yet mocking. "Look, Niko, I didn't steal Melina. She made her own decisions. She just wasn't into you. It's not my fault that she liked me more than you."

Nick's face contorts, bright red with emotion now.

Ever.and Nick exchange glowering stares. But then, slowly but surely, I catch a glimpse of what they must have been like back when they used to be friends…*best* friends.

Ever's voice grows quiet. "You know she was a gold-digger, right, Nick? She didn't care about either of us. We were just means to an end."

"No!" Nick yells so loud that it pierces my ears.

"It's true," Ever says. "You were like a brother to me. But none of it even mattered after that…all of it gone. Poof! All over some stupid girl!"

Nick's whole body shakes, but he starts to back away. "But I *loved* her!"

Ever has his hands out in consolation, trying to explain further. "I'm sorry about that, I truly am, but she lied to us. She told me that you guys broke up and that you wanted me to go out with her."

"Wha…?" Nick looks incredulous, eyes wide. "No!"

I'm worried that Nick might take a swing at Ever, so finally I step in between them with my arms out. "Stop it! That's enough."

Nick shakes his head in anger at Ever, eyes alive and daring. "This isn't over!"

I guide Nick by the arm to a table to cool off. I'm so consumed with soothing him that I barely hear it when Ever shifts his anger to me. "Speaking of girls," he says with exaggerated vehemence, "watch out for her!" Before I can even utter a word, Ever turns on his heel and stalks off across the dance floor.

Shaking my head, I turn my attention back to Nick, who looks so wounded that it makes my heart hurt. "So he's made a play for you, then," he whispers. "Don't try to hide it. He clearly thought you were here for him, but *why*?"

I shrug, looking away. What can I say? Clearly, I have handled all of this in the worst possible way.

Then, I see Samantha. Far off on the other side of the gymnasium, I watch Ever walk over and pull her away from her date. They start to dance, slow and close. It's painfully obvious to me now just how often Ever gets his way.

I try to explain to Nick, "He asked me to the dance two weeks ago, but I said no. In fact, I said, 'Definitely no,' but it's as if he wasn't able to hear me or something."

"I should have known that he would go for you." Nick seethes. "Of course he would."

Just then, the band starts playing again as Ever jumps up on stage. This time, he sings a song in Greek, his voice laced with passion and anger as his intense blue-green eyes bore into mine. The words in this song cut into me like a knife.

"*Oute Ikseres…*"

As I glance to my right, I can see that Nick is uncomfortable, and not surprisingly, he's starting to get upset. It's too much for him. And really, it's too much for me. Nick turns to me, shaking my shoulder. "Helene! Just tell me the truth. Would you rather have come here tonight with him?"

I shake my head no, but the pull of Ever's pained, sultry voice keeps me from forming any words. My mind says no, but my heart is moving somewhere else, to a place my mind should not go with Ever. I shake my head in an attempt to break the spell.

"Let's get out of here!" Nick says, clearly upset.

"Okay," I agree. We barely even say good-bye to Vani and Alexis as we hastily depart out the back door, not looking back. The sound of Ever's voice still haunts me as if I can still hear him, but now off in the distance.

Vani's limo whisks us over to Janus's place. The whole ride back, Nick barely looks at me, so I don't look at him. Both of us sit awkwardly in unnatural silence. It's so strained that I don't even care about facing the wrath of Janus when I get home.

When we finally arrive back in Metaxourgeio, the night is shrouded in an eerie hush, almost as if the city knows that something is amiss between us. A wave of disruptive energy seems to emanate from Nick, so much so that I'm afraid he's just going to leave me at the doorstep, never to talk to me again. So when Nick turns to leave just as I knew he would, I try to stop him.

"Wait. Nick. Please don't go," I plead.

A moment of silence passes between us. Remarkably, Janus is nowhere in sight, and for once, it seems we have the whole place to ourselves. Normally, this would be perfect, but tonight, well, things are not going well. Not at all.

Finally, Nick breaks his silence. "I know there's something between you and Ever. That was *very clear* tonight. And I won't allow myself to be caught in the crossfire of an impossible situation again. *Never* again."

He turns slightly toward me, his face an impassive mask that I don't recognize. I just want one last glimpse of him...*my* Nick. I glimpse a flash of the helix tattoo on his wrist, and the image of my mother fills my head.

I snap out of my angst. All this craziness tonight pales in comparison to what I've been through these past weeks. Seriously!

My mom is a goddess. Artemis, goddess of the hunt, animals, and the environment, and protector of young girls. As much as I like both Nick and Ever, this conflict from their past is not my issue.

With these thoughts, I'm not sure what to say to Nick, so I stand there staring at him, eyes unblinking.

He looks at his watch and frowns. His voice is strained and tight. "It's getting late. I need to go."

As I watch him leave, my heart is sad, but I hope in time he'll realize that his issue is with Ever, not me. Perhaps he just needs to be alone to process all of tonight's craziness, but in my heart, I know the truth. He is upset...*with me*. I hurt him. And the worst part of it is that I have no idea what I could have done differently.

How is his past with Ever...with Melina...*my* fault?

30 – MIRAGE

Bastet jumps up onto my lap and nudges my chin to comfort me. The haunting melody of Ever's song plays over and over in my head. I attempt to block the sound from my mind, but the cry of the clarinet won't leave me alone. I catch a glimpse of the photo next to my bed: my mom's smiling face. Her valiant voice echoes through my mind, reinforcing my thoughts about Ever and Nick.

"Time to refocus, Helene. Remember what's important."

She's right. Enough is enough. Back to business. I need to use the Catalyst to find the Lone Cypress Tree and get that collar back so I can go to Gaea to find Mom. There's no more time to waste! I remember now where Janus hid the collar. The safe! If I can break the basement door lock, why not the safe's too? Hope fills me as I rush over to the wall, push the picture to the side, and point my left finger with the silver ring directly at the safe. *Zap!*

It opens.

Adrenaline pulses through my veins as I shove the stacks of euros to the side, searching the expanse of the inside of the safe. There's no sign of the collar! Janus must have known I would be able to get in here, so he moved it. *Argh!* Now how will I get back to Gaea?

I realize I'm completely exhausted. I can't think anymore. I strip off my dress, careful to hang it up nicely for Vani, throw on my PJs, and crash onto the couch. The next thing I know, my eyelids grow heavy, and my breathing slows and I'm out cold.

I dream that I am in Gaea. I am alone in the desert, walking unsteadily in the hot sand, with the giant red sun shining above and no water. My skin feels burning hot, my mouth is parched, and my tongue is swollen with thirst. I walk up a large sand dune but am unsure of my destination. The sun is starting to drop to the horizon, indicating that early evening is here. My feet are searing even through the soles of my shoes, which feel like they are melting into my feet. One foot plods on slowly in front of the other.

As I reach the top of the tall dune, I look out over the vast plateau, and something strange catches my eye. At the bottom of the dune I see what appears to be a mini-oasis with a sparkling pond glistening under the red sun and a copse of silver-colored palm trees. The water looks so inviting with its translucent clarity. *This must be a mirage*. But then I remind myself that it must be a dream. "Of course it is," I whisper.

I tear down the dune in a full run, oblivious to my body's pains, stripping off most of my clothes, and I throw my body full force into the sparkling water. "It's real!" I squeal with delight. Lapping up the water in earnest, I am suddenly so thankful for my dream taking this turn for the better.

I hear movement behind me. Turning slowly towards the sound, I'm surprised to see another mirage. Standing under the shade of a silver palm tree is Nick, his brawny, powerful body dressed only in shorts.

"May I join you?" he asks, smiling.

Excited to see him standing there, so vibrant and healthy, the fibers of his muscles virile and strong, I rush out of the water and throw my arms around his neck in a fierce hug. I'm happy that he seems to be over what happened at the dance.

"Nick, it's good to see you," I say earnestly. His gorgeous eyes melt me as he slowly lifts my mouth to his. We start kissing, gentle and sweet.

Then something shifts and changes in his energy. As his kisses grow more and more urgent, I sense heat growing deep inside of me. His passion turns raw and unabashed, as if fire from a dragon has been unleashed. This doesn't feel like the Nick I know…but not that I mind.

Feeling a little overwhelmed by the sudden transformation, I pull back to look at him. As our eyes meet, I see intense hunger and desire, but the exquisite sea-blue eyes staring back at me do not belong to

Nick.

They belong to *Ever*.

Suddenly, I'm consumed by the memory of these same eyes locked onto mine, of him singing to me that hauntingly romantic melody at the dance, his ever-changing demeanor exposed for the world to hear in the song that he wrote just for me.

Like a chameleon, I'm changing in your eyes.

Ever is my real-life chameleon. I'm paralyzed, unable to move.

"What…what are *you* doing here?" I stammer as I struggle backwards, tripping on the sand. The sun is now setting, casting images of the giant red sun with hues of pink, purple, and yellow into Ever's hungry eyes. He is dressed in nothing but a loincloth, like one would imagine a Greek god would wear. He looks majestic with his tan, muscular chest oiled to a brilliant sheen.

"Relax. This is a dream, remember? You can trust me here," he says calmly.

"Hermes?" I ask tentatively. Of course, I know that this is Ever, but it's a dream, so what fun it is to tease him, especially with him wearing a loincloth of all things.

"No! Not Hermes. Don't you recognize me?" he says in a small, disappointed voice. But then he looks down at himself. "Oh, I guess I can see how you'd think Hermes. Ha!"

"*Ever?*" I whisper hoarsely.

He nods. "Finally, I get to be with you…like on a *real* date," he says as we sit down side by side, our toes touching on the beach.

I smile playfully. "Hate to break it to you, but a dream is not a date."

He dons his best smile, exposing a perfect row of sparkling white teeth.

"You're right. A dream is *so* much better." He places his arm around me and draws me in close for another kiss. I'll admit that I am enjoying this closeness with him. He murmurs into my hair, "We can do anything, and none of it will matter tomorrow. I won't even remember that you crushed my whole world when you stood me up tonight."

I push him away. "I didn't stand you up!"

The look on his face shows immediate regret for bringing this up now. Disappointment reaches his features. "Of course you did. *The dance*, remember? You went there with Nick, but you were supposed to go with me."

Flummoxed, I glare at him. "I called and left you a message to explain."

He shakes his head slowly. "I know. I heard it. But still, I wrote the song for you."

Oh yeah, the song. *God.* My voice breaks as I say, "I can't believe you did that."

The red sun reflects off the surface of his turquoise eyes in a way that completely melts me. He sighs, voice quiet. "Yeah."

"Oh well," I say in a breathy voice. "But what about all of those swooning girls?"

"What about them?" he says, smirking.

"Well, it's hard to take you seriously when you always have this long trail of pretty girls following you around," I say.

"Uh-huh, right," he says, eyes glistening and playful. "I'm not the only one with that problem."

"What?" I say in surprise. "Not me! No, I don't have—"

"Really?" he says defiantly. "Now I know about Nick, but who else is out there? I know at least five other guys at school who think you're hot." He smiles widely. "And despite all of my efforts – our dinner, the song – I trusted you with my feelings about my mom…and my secret at Agora." His mood shifts to annoyance. "After all of that, the only thing I get is you inside of a dream!"

"But I thought you just wanted to be friends," I whisper, biting my lip.

"Wha…? No!" He's incredulous. "How could you think that?"

Guilt overwhelms me. It's as if he took a knife to my gut and twisted it. "Okay, I screwed up! Is that what you want to hear?" I pull away from him.

"I don't want to hear anything but the truth," he says softly. "Do you care about me at all?"

For a moment, I'm totally swept away by the mournful look in Ever's deep liquid turquoise gaze. It makes me want to run somewhere far away with him and never look back. The truth is that I care way too much about him, but there's no way I can admit it. These feelings are too deep, too awful scary for me. If I go there, I'll never recover. Not ever.

"You know I do," I whisper, pulling him close to me again. He reaches up to push a strand of hair behind my ear. Very endearing. His eyes reflect the magical light of the setting sun as he starts to sing to me.

Feel the way I feel and be with me…

He runs his finger along the nape of my neck, and chills run down my spine. Something about this moment is almost too much. I'm overwhelmed with emotion. I pull away slightly.

"What is it?" Ever says, concerned. In a flash, the sweetness he showed me just a moment ago is gone, as if a defensive mask now shrouds his true self.

The look in his eyes reminds me of…of…oh yes, when he left me so abruptly at the site of Agora because of the text. Suddenly, I feel upset.

"That text…who was it from?" I ask, pushing him away slightly.

"What text?" He looks confused, acting as if he has no idea what I'm talking about.

"You know what text! It was *so* not cool of you to leave me there at Agora all alone in the middle of the night."

"You said it was fine!" He pushes me away, folding his arms across his chest.

"So what? Actions speak louder than words. After all that we shared at the hospital and Agora, you just up and left me there. I thought you said you weren't spoiled!"

I'm waiting for him to get mad, but instead of anger, he laughs – a big hearty, bellowing laugh – which makes my blood boil. When he calms down, he pulls me up close against him, crushing my body against his. His mouth hovers dangerously close to mine, sending my heartbeat into an insane frenzy. I inhale his intoxicating scent but then struggle against him to recover myself.

Ever guides my chin up so that I meet his gaze. "Just because everything doesn't go exactly as you think it should doesn't mean that I'm spoiled." His blue-green eyes sparkle mischievously. Then he adds in a low, husky voice, "Believe me, I know how to treat a woman."

I am totally stunned, frozen in place. My breath stops in my chest. *Holy sweet Jesus! He is so hot.*

I attack him without abandon, pulling him closer. Our lips meet. I feel an insane urgency for him, as if I want him to devour me like a wild animal, and he returns the energy. The feeling is incredible. We pull apart temporarily. I whisper, "I guess we had a misunderstanding."

He says, "I guess so," but then pulls me back into a fierce embrace, now drawing the length of my frame under him onto the warm sand next the water. I feel his body pressing into mine, which takes my arousal to a whole new level.

I feel his hands travel over my skin, sending insane tingles throughout my frame, softly down to my chest and under my shirt. Lost in the depths of his stunning blue eyes, I see sweet adoration there.

I wake up with a start as my body slams hard onto the floor and I cry out.

What just happened?

Harsh reality hits me as I realize that I just fell out of bed. I wrap my arms around my leg, inspecting my knee where an angry bruise has formed. Oh, man. My body is completely drenched with sweat.

God, was that a dream? It felt so real.

Conflicting emotions muddy my mind. I'm aroused, perplexed, overwhelmed, and annoyed, all at the same time.

But Ever?

So much for my trying to forget about him.

31 – THE STRONGHOLD

"What's all the commotion in here?!" Janus comes stomping out of his room, rubbing his eyes.

Good God, did I talk in my sleep? I grab the sheet and pull it up over myself. The bruise on my leg smarts as I remember crying out in pain as I smacked the floor. That's all it was. Janus has no idea about the dream.

"Oh, I fell off the bed," I stammer in a raspy voice, my body still trembling all over. There's no chill, yet I shiver as if I'm sick. Maybe I am.

"What are you, a little child?" he grumbles. "For crying out loud, maybe we need to buy some restraints for you. You woke up the whole neighborhood!" He complains on and on as he pulls out a pan and a bowl, then places a carton of eggs on the counter. "May as well make breakfast. Have you ever had tiganites?"

I shake my head no. I don't dare talk, paranoid that the strained tone of my voice may somehow betray me. I can't stop thinking of Ever and, *ahem*, that dream.

Janus looks up, lost in thought, thankfully oblivious to me and my indiscretions. "Tiganites are Greek pancakes. So much better than what you have in America. You'll see!" He's way too enthusiastic for me at this early hour as he busies himself, scurrying like a madman all around the kitchen. My stomach growls in anticipation as I'm accosted by a savory montage of nutmeg, cinnamon, and vanilla. *Oh, yum.*

As we're sitting quietly at the table eating together, Janus takes me by surprise. "Happy birthday," he says softly. With all that has happened, I totally forgot that today is my birthday!

He wasn't kidding earlier about these pancakes. They're

sumptuous, fluffy, and stuffed with Greek yogurt. "Wow!" I say with delight. "This is amazing. Thank you!"

Janus smiles, revealing a whole row of his decrepit, yellowing teeth. "Since it's your birthday, I have a special gift for you." A gift? This is a surprise. "My gift to you is that I'm going to forget that you completely disobeyed my orders and went to the dance anyway. Believe me, this is quite a gift because – oh my Aether – I was hopping mad last night!"

Crap. I'd hoped he wouldn't notice! Well, at least he's trying to be reasonable now. This moment could have been miserable hell, but instead, we're celebrating my birthday! Stranger things have happened with Janus. I keep waiting for the usual swing in his mood, which should happen any minute now.

"Uh, Janus…what's the Aether?" I ask.

"The what?" He seems caught off guard.

"The Aether. You just said it. But also, I heard it discussed at your book club meeting."

"Oh yeah, okay," he says, his finger on his chin, thinking. "With all that you already know, I'm sure it's probably fine to tell you now." His eyes assume a faraway look. "For thousands of years, the Aether was a spiritual construct, the foundation for all major religions on Gaea. Over time, however, scientific discoveries led to a new, more sophisticated understanding of the metaphysical world."

His voice is steady and calm, eyes glistening as he continues. "Today, our view is that the Aether is 'alive,' existing at the quantum level in the form of invisible energy that connects everything, living or not, across all universes. It's kind of like the dark energy that you know from the theories of quantum physics on Earth, except our more advanced version of the quantum sciences suggests that the Aether is sentient, like a collective consciousness."

"Oh, kind of like a divine spirit," I reply. I'm so curious. The more I learn about Gaea, the deeper the rabbit hole feels.

"Kind of." Janus smiles. "But try to think about it from outside the 'box' of religion, be it one or many gods."

He hums to himself as he goes back into the kitchen, reaches up into the cabinet, and brings down a small purple packet that looks like a vitamin supplement. Very carefully, he opens the packet and empties a white powdery substance onto the counter.

Cocaine. *Really?*

I watch in horror as Janus uses a small tube to inhale the contents up his nose.

My mouth hangs open in disbelief. I can't believe he would do this in front of me. "Seriously, Janus! Can you take your coke habit somewhere else?" I say with disgust.

Instead of responding indignantly or defensively as a normal person should, Janus starts to cackle. "Oh gods, now that is funny!" He quirks his brow at me, smiles wryly, and asks, "Cocaine? That's what you think I do? Really?"

His lack of regard for my feelings makes me frown, but I feel compelled to respond. "Well, yeah. You snort white powder up your nose. What else could it be?"

That's when Janus does something altogether unexpected. He lifts his finger up into his right eye and pops out what looks like a contact lens. And there, suddenly, I can't believe it, but his real eye color is...*purple.*

"What the...!?" I say, jumping back a few feet, freaked out.

His grin grows wide with excitement. Then finally, he explains, "It's not cocaine! This is the Elixir!"

I'm still fixated on his exposed purple eye. "This color...I've seen it before. The gods on Gaea...Ares, Poseidon," I stammer, trying to remember.

Janus nods enthusiastically, then explains that the Elixir is a compound that the gods have taken for thousands of years to maintain what we think of as immortality. The purple eye color is an unfortunate side effect.

Whoa. I was kind of wondering how the gods could still be alive on Gaea, even if time does seem to pass at a different speed from here. Intensely curious, I ask, "How does it work?"

"You know about the mineral lumite, right?" he asks.

I nod, totally rapt.

"The dust from lumite is harvested on Gaea to create the Elixir. Any humanoid that consumes it can harness the Aether, which enables rapid healing and regeneration, but not to the point of causing cancer. We age, but extremely slowly, which provides the illusion of immortality."

I'm not even sure what to say, so I just sit there and stare at him. At long last, I feel that he's being honest with me, and it's about time.

An alarm beeps on Janus's watch. "Blasted Drakon dung! I'm late!" He runs out of the room, slamming the door behind him, leaving me here to digest it all.

I sit still for a minute before I jump up and start my search for Bastet's collar. Where could he be hiding it? I comb through the entire apartment with absolutely no success. *Argh!* I throw my hands in the air. We've been through so much together, yet Janus doesn't trust me! It infuriates me...and hurts! But more than that, I feel helpless.

As the day wears on, panic and desperation grow within me. What if I can't find it?! There's no point in even trying to figure out how to use the Catalyst if there's no way to get back to Gaea in the first place!

On top of this, just having the Catalyst in my possession terrifies me. I can't be responsible for ending the world! Once I learn what I need to know from it, I can't wait to be rid of it, to return it to my mother's room under the school...the Stronghold.

I pick up my cell phone and scan my missed calls. Nothing. Then I look at texts. Nothing. I have a confession. As much as I want to forget both Nick and Ever, I'm having trouble with it. Knowing how much time it takes for Nick to process things, I'm sure I won't hear from him for a while, and frankly, that's a good thing for me. Melina is not my problem. He needs to get over it.

I guess I hoped I'd hear from Ever, especially since he knows that today is my birthday. Of course, I can't get that dream with him out of my mind...of us...*ahem*...yes, doing that. It's not as if we went all the way, but it felt so very real, as if it truly happened.

The reality is that I'll have to let him...*both* of them...out of my mind, *now*. A tear rolls down my cheek as this sinks in. I won't be distracted anymore until I find my mom. Time to move on, and fast.

Bastet rubs on my leg, her tail twitching erratically. "Meow!"

"Yeah, girl, I'm going to be fine," I say.

I swear that if a cat could smile, I'd see one on her face.

"Maybe I'll just call in sick to school tomorrow," I sigh, my resolve wavering.

Bastet's ears quirk up, tail twitching. Her tail points to the picture of my mom. I have a mission.

"Yeah, yeah," I say in a resigned voice. "No more messing around. I'll go!"

***

The next day, on my way to the bus stop, I feel strong and capable, ready to tackle whatever comes my way. Even so, I'm not looking forward to running into Ever. I remind myself that it was only a dream, a trick of the mind. My dreams belong to me. Abruptly, I bury these thoughts deep inside the recesses of my mind.

I feel a vibration through my backpack. The Catalyst. Something about having a device that could end the world in my backpack changes my perspective. Onward and forward.

A cracking sound startles me. As I turn, I see a man standing across the street. A sick, twisted grin tells me that this is bad. Vorlage. My pulse rises in anxiety, so I remind myself that I'm stronger than they are. They are just normal people, nothing special. Still, if there is one, then others are nearby.

The bus stops in front of me, blocking the sneering man from my view. As I step inside, take a seat, and look outside, the man outside has disappeared. Good.

As the bus takes off, I sigh in relief. Twenty minutes later, as we're approaching the front gates to the school, I look up towards the driver. Through the rearview mirror, I see him look up. His eyes meet mine, and he smiles wide. Disgusting yellow teeth gape inside his mouth. Vorlage...here...on the bus.

"Nice to see you, Helene," he sneers, eyes locked on mine.

I panic as I look around. The other kids are completely oblivious to what's happening.

The bus doors open, and I rush out past the driver, out onto the pavement, chest heaving. Entering the school gates, I run as fast as I can up the winding road and don't stop until I reach the safety of the school.

As I rush down the hall to my first class, I consider that it wasn't that bad. I can easily take on one Vorlage. It wasn't an attack. They were trying to scare me. But why?

Before I know it, I'm sitting in mythology class, doodling on a notepad, when Ms. Petraki calls on me.

"What?" I ask, startled.

"Your ring...it's *interesting*," she says as she stands over me. She reaches down to my hand. "Do you mind if I take a closer look?"

"I...I don't know." This takes me off guard with no time to think as she brings the ring on my hand up closer to her face.

"Interesting indeed. Thank you," she says with a smile, then turns to face the class. "In 1943, at an excavation site here in Greece, archaeologist Dr. Spiros Rigatos came across an interesting finding. Instead of the usual sixteen-point star associated with the Vergina Sun or the Macedonian Star that appeared on Greek relics from the sixth to second centuries B.C., he found some ancient objects with a twelve-point star engraved on them. It was never substantiated and hasn't been backed up by any other findings so far but is quite relevant in this case. Helene, how many points do you count on the star on the face of your ring?"

I look down and count. "Uh, twelve," I say hesitantly. I'm a little freaked out to be so openly discussing my mother's ring, the ring of Artemis. This line of questioning seems suspicious.

"Right!" Ms. Petraki says. Her face is filled with passion, as if this is of great personal interest to her. "According to a lesser known theory inspired by Dr. Rigatos's findings, the twelve points on this particular star represent the twelve gods and goddesses of Olympus. Allegedly, the symbol served as their emblem, like a personal seal signifying their divine status within the hierarchy of society. Legend has it that there were only twelve such rings in existence."

The color drains from my face as I realize just how accurate Dr. Rigatos was with this discovery.

The teacher continues, "Each god or goddess was given a ring forged from a magical silver metal. The ring served as their key to the city of Olympus. To enter the front gates, they had to insert their ring into the proper place and tap it three times."

The bell rings, leaving my mind in a daze as class abruptly ends. I make my way out into the hallway and down to my locker. It's time for siesta, so the crowds clear out quickly, leaving me alone. This is my chance to get into my mother's secret room so I can finally figure out how to use the Catalyst!

When I open my locker, though, there's no sign anywhere of the twelve-point star that was my entry into the secret room earlier. I slam my hand into the locker, totally forgetting my otherworldly strength, causing a huge dent in the metal door. *Agh!* I sink to the ground and bury my head in my hands. That's when I see it. Hidden in the side wall of the locker is a tiny imprint of a twelve-point star the size of my ring.

Elated, I insert my ring into the imprint. Nothing. Panic starts to consume me, but then I remember what I just learned in mythology class. The gods tapped their ring three times when it served as a key to the city. Of course, that's got to be it!

I hold my breath as I tap my ring...one, two...three. Nope. Nothing happens.

This can't be happening! In a rage of sheer frustration, I slam my ring into the indentation, this time with extreme force. What if I can't get in there?

I do it again. *Slam!* What will I do?

And one more time. *Click.* The back of the locker opens. Sigh. Thank God!

I make my way down to the secret room and start my search for anything that can help me figure out how to use the Catalyst to locate the Lone Cypress Tree. There must be something here. My eyes travel up to the photos on the wall and to the ancient books on the shelves.

As I scan the titles, pull out a few, and leaf through them, I start to feel frustrated as nothing seems to relate to the Catalyst. What a waste of time!

Suddenly, I feel a vibrating sensation emanating from my backpack. I yank it off and swiftly unzip it, but of course, I already know what it is – the Catalyst. It feels hot, alive. A bright red light flashes on the top of the device. What have I done?

The screen remains blank, but the red light transforms to bright white as it triangulates with two other crystal prisms in the ceiling of the room. A three-dimensional holographic image in vivid color fills the room while a cacophony of sound permeates the space around me, fully immersing me in this lifelike artificial reality.

The image before my eyes is Gaea, out in the far reaches of the desert, somewhere between the crumbling ruins of old Olympus and the menacing volcano where I saw the Drakons. I see an enormous mazelike structure that juts up from the massive sand dunes. Deep crevasses fill the surrounding land with acrid smoke rising forth from within. This must be Tartarus, the deep abyss that was said to exist in the Underworld, the prison for the wicked.

I've seen this place so many times before in my dreams.

Three icons suddenly appear on the small screen of the Catalyst…first the sun, then the moon, and then the clouds. A cursor blinks in wait. I need to make a selection. But which to choose?

I have no idea, so maybe I'll just close my eyes and randomly pick something. But no, I must put some thought behind this. Since this is Mom's secret room, what I need to ask is, what would she choose? Umm…my mother is Artemis. I scan my thoughts to recall which symbol is associated with her in mythology. Another name for Artemis is Selene, which means "the moon." Artemis would choose the moon.

The next screen displays twelve icons, each representing one of the twelve astrological signs. My heart rate quickens as the pressure builds. Which one do I choose? Again, I consider my mother. She's a Sagittarius. I press that icon.

Immediately, the screen goes blank, and the holographic image surrounding me shuts down, completely dark. I must have made the wrong choice.

Now what?

Just as I start to panic, a new holographic image lights up the room around me. This time, it is Gaea, but in the deep of night. The blackened sky above me is filled with millions of glistening stars. The most prominent constellation looks like a huntsman or an archer. On Earth, this would be the constellation of Sagittarius!

The bottom-most star of the constellation almost touches the horizon. As I reach my index finger out to swipe at this star, the hologram zooms in to better view of the desert, and as I trace my finger along the trajectory of the Huntsman's arrow and out past the volcano, I see a tree standing all alone, surrounded by the vast sands of Gaea.

The Lone Cypress Tree.

Elation surges through my veins at this revelation. This is it. I know where Mom is hiding!

Urgency surges through me. There is no time to spare. I need to get back to Gaea now. Unfortunately, though, Janus has Bastet's collar, so there's no way for me to get back through the Gate.

What will I do now?

32 – ANOTHER WAY

I hit the button on the top of the Catalyst, and immediately, both the device and the hologram power down. The light on the top flashes twice, then stops. I should return the Catalyst to the safety of the glass box here, but now that I know how to use it, I can't just leave it behind. I'm sure I'll need it once I get to Gaea. So, I throw it into the back of my pack and head up and out of the secret room.

I have no idea how much time has passed. I exit the locker with extra care, slowly creaking open the metal door to peek outside. Kids fill the hallway. Not good. How long will I have to wait here until the halls are empty again?

I peek out into the hall two more times until finally all seems completely silent. I slowly start to inch my way out when I hear a noise behind me. Someone is there. Of course, Samantha.

"Did you just get locked inside your locker?" she asks in shock, flipping her perfectly coifed hair over her shoulder.

"Uh, no," I say, brushing off my clothes. "I thought the lock was broken, and the only way to fix it is to tackle it from the inside. I wasn't *locked* in there."

Samantha sneers but then tries to cover it with her usual contrived smile. I can tell that she's not sure what to do with my explanation; it's obvious to me that she's never fixed anything in her ridiculous fairy-tale life.

"Right...*whatever*," she says. She then lowers her voice as her expression shifts. "Look, you should know that Ever and I are back together now. I know you were spending time with him, but that's all over now."

She flips her long, silky blond hair off to the side again, smirking. "See, the thing is, Ever would never go out long term with a *freak* like

286

you. He never commits to anyone, and he always comes back to me. At the end of the day, I'm the only one who really matters to him."

Normally, her words wouldn't bother me, but considering how upset Ever was with me after the dance, they cut deep. It's true that he was hanging out with Samantha after I left him at the dance. I cross my arms. If he's back together with her, then fine!

Samantha stalks off down the hallway, so I head towards the gymnasium to meet Vani before econ class. As I turn the corner, I stop dead in my tracks, my heart racing at the sight of him. Ever.

At the far end of the hallway, he stands surrounded by his friends, lounging casually together on the lockers, laughing and carrying on. With his dark tousled hair and tattered black jeans, Ever is quite the rebellious bad boy today. Not that I mind. Not at all.

Staring at him like this, I lose control of my thoughts and allow my eyes to travel down his torso and...*oh!* My face flushes bright red. *Enough!* The dream is still so alive in my mind that I can't seem to help myself.

But then, suddenly, everything changes. Nestled in the center of Ever's belt buckle is an amber-colored cat's-eye stone. No way! How this can be?

When we were at Agora, Ever made the book of *Theogonia* light up and I wondered if there was something special about him, if he knew about Gaea. He acted so nonchalant about it that I totally dismissed it. But now I'm not sure. Maybe I'm not alone in this. Whenever we touch, I feel such an intense surge of electricity. It seems entirely plausible that this cat's-eye stone on his belt is special, just like the one on Bastet's collar, that it will open the Gate.

All I need to do is get that belt from Ever. But how? First and foremost, I know I'm going to feel weird with him after that dream. Second, he's probably still mad at me from the dance. He might not talk to me. Third, if I can get him to talk to me again, I need to ask him to borrow his belt. But if I ask, I know what he's going to think...that I want something else from him.

Never mind! I throw my hands up, exasperated.

Now that I know where to find Mom on Gaea, I'm not going to

give up easily. There's got to be a way. My mind spins through various scenarios, all ending badly, when a crazy idea hits me. What if I let Ever think I want "something else," just enough for him to give me the belt? It's not like I have a boyfriend. Nick isn't returning my calls. Besides, the truth is, after that dream, I wouldn't mind if something more should happen with Ever.

First things first. I'll need to get him to talk to me. I have no choice but to apologize about what happened at the dance, even if I don't feel it was my fault. If, as Ever said in the dream, he thinks that I stood him up on purpose, then it's time to clear the air. Somehow, I need to get him away from his friends so I can talk to him alone.

I fight to steady my pulse as I saunter over to Ever and his friends. I'm having trouble looking directly at him, so I try staring at his eyebrows.

"Hey," I say, smiling as nicely as possible. I'm not nervous. No way. Not me.

"Hey," Ever says, his expression reserved and cool.

We all stand there in awkward silence until finally he rolls his eyes at his friends. "Uh, Phil, Theo? Why don't you guys go run some drills out in the gym or something?"

They exchange strained glances. Finally, Phil slugs Theo on the arm. "Uh, yeah. Great idea." They walk away, leaving Ever here with me all alone. Perfect.

"I...uh..." I start, twisting my hair around my finger.

Ever cuts me off, forcing my gaze up to meet his. "I finally heard your voice mail." His eyes are pensive but light up when they meet mine. A good sign. "Look, I had no idea that Nick was in the picture. Had I known, well...."

Uncomfortable silence ensues. What to say next? I don't know, so I just say what I'm thinking. "I haven't heard from him, so I have no idea what's going on there."

"Oh," Ever says, trying not to sound too happy about it, but then his true feelings betray him when he says, "Okay, good." He must realize that he said the wrong thing because he frowns and backpedals. "No, what I meant to say is that I'm sorry to hear that."

I stare at him, quirking my eyebrows as if he's making no sense at all. This seems to fluster him more. He looks down and shifts his feet. Is he actually being shy? I don't know, but I need that belt.

"So…" he starts to say, but I swiftly cut him off.

"I just wondered, where…did you get your belt?"

"My *what?*" he asks. Any shyness is gone.

"Your belt," I repeat.

"You were looking at my belt? Hmmm," he says, clearly pleased.

"Just answer the question. Where did you get it?" I ask, this time more firmly.

"Well, if you must know, my mom gave it to me as a Christmas gift. It's my absolute favorite. You like it?"

"Yes, I do…especially that stone. It's a cat's-eye, right?"

He beams, fully enjoying this attention. "Yeah, I guess this color is pretty rare."

While this is all nice and fun, it's time to cut to the chase. Before I can think too hard about it, though, the words flow out. "So I was wondering…can I borrow it?"

A look of surprise crosses his face. "Right now?"

"Well, no. Later. After school," I say mysteriously.

"Uh, okay, because I kind of need it right now." He quirks his eyebrow at me, suddenly skeptical. "Why do you need it?"

I try my best to lie, which is difficult with Ever. "Uh, well, I want to buy one like it for my godfather as a gift, and I need to have it in front of me when I look it up on Amazon."

Almost immediately, I realize how stupid that is. He sees right through me, two steps ahead. He scoffs, "You're not going to find this belt on Amazon. It's one of a kind!" He turns his wrist over to show off his Apple watch. "But I can Google it to see if there's a knock-off that you can buy."

I can tell that Ever is thoroughly enjoying this. Nothing with him can ever be easy. I shake my head insistently. "No, I can't buy it now. I need more time to compare alternatives."

He knows I'm up to something. He gives me a frustrated, perplexed look. "Uh-huh, right. Well, then, you can do your shopping on your own time…without my belt." He turns on his heel to leave.

That was unexpected. I grab his arm. "Wait!" Inadvertently, I pull him over to me, causing his body to crush up against me slightly. "How would you like to meet the real Hermes?" I say earnestly, batting my eyelashes at him. I've never tried to flirt like this before, so I'm sure I look ridiculous.

"Okay, now you're not making any sense at all." He doesn't seem to be taking my bait. I try again, but this time I push him up against the locker with a little force. His turquoise eyes lock onto mine as I hear a slight intake of his breath. A look of recognition fills his face, which makes me think he's remembering the time I took him down during fencing in PE. Hot flush travels up to my face as I think of him lying there underneath me. This gets his attention.

He grins. "Did you sleep okay last night? Or is this all just a big…" – he winks at me, mischief in his eyes – "…misunderstanding?"

OMG! He knows about the dream! But how?! Not possible! I flush about five shades of red, totally mortified. I need to regain control of this now. What to do? There's nothing left but honesty.

"Look, I wasn't quite telling you the truth before. I have another *secret* need for that belt, but I can't tell you about it here. I'll have to show it to you." My voice is urgent now. "I need you to come over to my house and look at something in my basement, but you need to bring that belt. Do *not* forget the belt."

By the look on Ever's face, he totally thinks that I'm coming on to him now, which excites him. His expression is full of that charm and charisma that I can't resist. "Hmmm…." He lowers his voice to a sultry whisper. "What time?"

I struggle to contain myself as I try to maintain my composure. "Tonight, after Janus is asleep, around midnight. You'll have to sneak in through the window using the outside stairway. It's the main window on the second floor. That's where I sleep."

Just then, Samantha walks by us and says, "Ever, are you coming out with us later?" She sneers at me, clearly enjoying my discomfort. God, I hate her.

Ever looks up, startled. "Huh? Oh, maybe."

Samantha saunters off with her friends.

I forgot all about Samantha. All the progress I thought I had made with Ever disappears just like that. There's no way I can go through with the seduction if he's back together with her.

I whisper to him through clenched teeth, "Jesus, are you and Samantha back together...*again*?"

He frowns, seeming confused for a moment. "Uh, yeah. I mean, no, no." He looks distracted, like his mind has been taken away to another place. I see a hint of the vulnerability that I witnessed just a week ago flash across his face, which makes me remember that his mother is sick in the hospital. This must be weighing heavily on Ever's mind right now. Instantly, I feel awful trying to manipulate him, even if it's for a good cause.

"How's your mom?" I ask quietly.

"I don't know. I want so badly to go to the hospital to see her, but my dad doesn't want me to go. He's afraid I'll get sick just from visiting," Ever whispers.

Sadness overtakes me for a moment. I wish that I could do something to help. But of course I can't. "You know how you trusted me with your secret at the ruins of Agora?" I ask.

He nods slowly, his eyes wide and rimmed with melancholy. I decide to take a leap of faith and trust him with a tiny shred of hope.

"I need that stone on your belt for something important, something that might help me..." – my voice is urgent as I plead with him – "...find my mom."

Ever's demeanor shifts as he fully takes in what I just said. "You know where she is?"

"Maybe," I whisper.

He thinks for a moment, but then his eyes light up. "Okay, yes."

Relief fills me. I think I might just pull this off!

His smile is warm and sweet as he turns to leave. "See you later, American Girl."

I watch him as he walks down the hall and almost smacks into Vani, who is rushing towards me, just as he disappears around the corner.

Seconds later, Vani grabs my elbow. "Sorry I'm late, but…" – her eyes grow wide with concern as she points back to where Ever just was – "what was that all about? Didn't you get enough of him at the dance?"

I try to act as if I don't know or care. I shrug, saying, "Who knows?"

Vani seems satisfied. "Good, because Nick was pretty upset. I had to have a talk with him."

"Oh?" I say. It's nice to hear that Vani has my back with Nick, that there's hope of salvaging things with him. She doesn't offer any more details though, so I let it lie.

As she shifts to other topics, I tune Vani out. My mind drifts back to my earlier plan to get back to Gaea. The image of me and Ever lying on the hot sand there fills my mind. It will take unbelievable willpower for me to not move too fast with him.

But Mom's words of wisdom echo through my mind: *Sometimes you can't have what you want right now. It's better to wait.*

I must be strong and do the right thing for her… and for *me*.

33 – LONE CYPRESS TREE

I consider the possible repercussions if Janus or Athena were to find out that I am going through the Gate again. Not good. But it's a chance I must take. Elation fills me as I realize just how close I am to finally finding my mom.

Bastet rubs her long body against my leg and meows. As I reach down to stroke her back, I am startled by the sudden sound of a knock on the grimy window next to my bed-that-is-a-couch. Ever. My heart rate quickens. He can't know that I feel this way about him. I need to keep the upper hand here.

I need to make sure that the coast is clear before I open the window. Gingerly, I place my ear to Janus's door to listen. I hear a sound…*snort!* A good sign that he's deep in sleep. I walk back over to the window and slowly lift the glass pane upward, trying not to make any noise.

There is Ever, beautiful as usual, but with a crease between his brows. He's clearly annoyed as he asks in a clipped tone, "What took you so long?"

His voice is so loud that I'm scared he will wake Janus, and then my whole plan will be blown. "Shhhh…you're going to wake up the whole neighborhood. We have to whisper!"

He has the nerve to laugh.

I sock his arm. "It's not funny!"

"Okay, okay!" He lowers his tone to the softest whisper that he can muster, which is still too loud by my standards.

I motion to him with a finger to my lips for him to lower his voice even more.

"I can't!" he whispers more quietly, now totally frustrated.

A sound in the other room causes both of us to jump, then freeze.

Janus grunts loudly as he turns over in bed before the slow, steady snoring resumes once again.

"Now, *that* is loud!" Ever says, smirking.

I shake my head, then take his hand. He gives me a sly grin as I slowly, very quietly lead him away from the window, out and down the stairs, then into Janus's shop below.

"Okay," he whispers, his look uncertain but curious. "Now what?"

My plan is simple. Ever needs to give me the belt and wait here. I'll go down to the basement by myself to see if the cat's-eye stone in the belt will open the Gate. If yes, then I need to get rid of Ever since there's no way that he's going with me to Gaea. I wouldn't want to put him in any unnecessary danger. Besides, he would slow me down too much.

First, though, I need him to somehow give me the belt.

At the top of the basement stairs, I use my finger to open the hidden bookcase with a *zap! Click.* The door opens.

Ever's eyes widen "A secret entrance."

I whisper into his ear, "I need that belt now."

He steps back in surprise but then seems amused.

Oh, no. What is he thinking now?

He grins, swiftly moving in close to my ear. "You want it?" His eyes light up mischievously as he moves my hand down to cover the top of his belt buckle. "Come and get it."

He brushes his lips softly across mine, causing raw energy to pulsate through me.

My eyes widen as I suck in my breath and tremble. I can't breathe. God! I must keep my focus. Remember Mom. Focus. I draw in a slow, steady breath, in and out.

I push Ever away, but he thinks I'm playing some sort of game.

"This is not a romantic venture," I declare.

"It's not?" he says, his voice small and disappointed.

"No!" I say. "Remember? I told you this was an important mission to find my mom."

"Yeah, but I thought…" His voice is tight, exasperated.

"Just *give me the damn belt*."

"Okay, fine." He pulls off the belt and hands it to me, glancing over at my laptop, as if he expects me to take the belt somewhere near the computer. "You know I would have given it to you no matter what. I told you that I will always understand when it comes to family…especially your mom."

"Really?" I whisper.

"Of course," he says softly. He moves in close, kissing me gently above my ear. It's an incredibly sweet gesture, like he genuinely cares.

"Oh," I say, sighing as I try not to let his actions distract me from what I need to do. So much of me longs to stay here, to experience more with him, but I have no choice. I have to go, and I need to do it alone.

"Wait here." I pick up my backpack off the floor, slip the straps through my arms, and start to head towards the basement stairs.

Ever falls in step behind me and grabs the belt out of my hand. "No way! You can't just leave me here by myself. What if Janus wakes up? What will I say?"

I spin around to face him, totally annoyed. I sigh but then try to defer to his ego. "Are you really afraid of him? Technically, he works for your dad! You can order him to go back to bed."

"Ha-ha. No way. I don't care! I'm not giving you the belt unless you take me with you. I want to help you find your mom," he says with wide, round turquoise eyes.

"But this is dangerous!" I exclaim in frustration. Good God, he makes me crazy. Can't he just do what I ask just once?

"I'm not afraid of danger. I can handle it, whatever it is."

"Fine!" I hiss in his face.

"Good," he says tersely, then moves in close to me again. His deep blue eyes are locked on mine as he puts the belt back on, buckling it firmly in place. I sidestep him to avoid crushing into him as I start to head down the stairs. He grabs my hand, but I yank it swiftly out of his grip, shaking my head no. He sighs loudly, swearing under his breath as he follows close behind me down the flight of stairs.

I turn the corner into the basement and my pulse quickens with giddy hope at what I see. At the top of the mirror, the cat's-eye stone glows brightly, just like the stone on Ever's belt. He looks down at it in shock.

"It's working," I call. The mirror comes to life as the brilliant blue waterlike sheen slowly consumes its face. A few seconds later, I hear the pitter-patter of Bastet scurrying down the wooden stairs. She races past us and leaps through the Gate in a graceful arc.

Stunned, Ever says, "What the…?"

In the excitement of the moment, I completely forget everything. Without any further thought, I step through the shimmery, glowing mirror. As so many times before, my vision spins, the world around me swirling into the blur of colors and lights, all racing forward to merge dynamically into the epicenter of the now-familiar vortex.

I land effortlessly on Gaea's soft, silky sand and throw down my pack onto the ground next to me. A few seconds later, I turn to see Ever jump through the Gate and hit the ground hard with a loud *thud*. He passes out cold on the sand.

The land beneath my feet trembles in fury, shaking and shuddering, as the face of the watery substance that is the portal flickers and dims, but after a moment, it reemerges in all its glory. Janus was right! The Gate must be growing unstable.

Bastet, as my giant mountain lioness, sidles up to me, nuzzling her large head against my hand, the whole time glaring anxiously at Ever's splayed-out body on the sand.

"I know, I know!" I try to explain to the large cat. "But I had no choice!"

As Ever starts to awaken, the lion licks his face. "Ugh. What the…?" As his eyes adjust, they widen in terror as he realizes that he is face to face with an enormous mountain lion. "Agh!!!" He scrambles backward and trips back down onto the sand.

I burst out laughing – a deep, hearty belly laugh – and it feels so good. "She's a bit scary at first," I explain calmly, "but she's a friend of mine. Her name is Bastet. You'd better not get out of line, though, or she'll let you have it."

Ever sits there, eyes unfocused. He's completely disoriented.

Suddenly, he bursts into hysterical laughter, like he can't believe how absurd this is. He's lying on the hot sand, limbs splayed out in all directions, with a gargantuan wild lioness staring him down. Not something you see every day.

He smiles. Crinkles form adorably around his eyes. "So much for getting to second base with you tonight."

I chuckle softly at this as I make my way to the arched open doorway that leads out into the far reaches of the desert. Just as I step forward, my foot smacks into something solid – an invisible barrier. My shoe sizzles as smoke singes the rubber bottom. A force field. Of course! Since Minios isn't here, this must be some sort of guard to keep Dregs like me from traversing any farther.

Ever looks around at the crumbling ruins surrounding us and through the open window wells out to the vast dunes and the enormous red sun. "I feel like I've been here before," he says pensively, "like maybe in a dream."

"I highly doubt that," I say.

He shrugs, then gives me a wry grin, as if it's an inside joke. "Maybe I'm mistaken."

Of course he is! How could he dream about Gaea if he's never been here before? Unless... But it was *my* dream!! He can't visit me in *my* dreams. No way!

"So, what is this place?" he asks, his face alive with childlike awe.

I'm about to tell him when the ground beneath us starts to tremble again. The intensity grows, so we grab onto each other, trying to maintain our footing on the slippery sands. Bastet lets out a loud bellowing *roar!* as she rams her body into both of us, sending us tumbling to the stone wall closest to the arched doorway that leads out to the desert.

Suddenly, I hear her voice call out, clear as day inside my mind, *"Watch out! Drakon!"*

The walls begin to crack as stone and rubble fall around us. The ground buckles and seizes up, sending us higher and higher on the pile of sand. The trembling intensifies until an enormous snakelike beast bursts out of the ground right in the middle of the crumbling structure where we stand, forming a gaping crevice in the land. The towering beast roars and bellows, fire blazing from its mouth. The land continues to churn and quake violently as the creature snakes in and out of the crack he just created.

I hear Bastet in my head again. *"Move away from the door! I'm going to try to lead it away from here!"*

Bastet roars again, this time nipping and biting at the Drakon as she leads it towards the doorway. Drakon surges its enormous head up and forward, headed for the open doorway, when…*smack!* Each time the Drakon smacks its ugly head into the invisible barrier, there's a loud crunch, then a sizzle. A foul burning stench permeates the air. The brown-scaled beast gets angrier and angrier with each failed attempt.

After a few more tries, the Drakon hits the arched doorway with such impact that it catapults backward, sending the creature sprawling into the far end of the structure. It smacks into the wall right next to the Gate. A chunk of stone tumbles down from the archway just above the Gate. Luckily, it was not the stone that holds the cat's-eye, which still glows bright.

Finally, the Drakon blows out all its fury by creating a blazing firestorm, sending its body flying into the invisible barrier. This time, though, the beast is stuck, its head trapped within the barrier. Electrical shocks zap it repeatedly, causing the Drakon to thrash its body back and forth violently, but its tail continues to lash out at the stone wall behind it. We'll have to do something fast or it will destroy the Gate.

"Now what do we do?" I call to Ever.

"I don't know, but we need to go *now!*" he yells to me over all the noise.

Bastet's voice fills my mind. *"Helene, if you can hear my voice, you can communicate with any animal. Quiet your mind."*

Even with all the chaos that surrounds me, I close my eyes and breathe in deeply. My heart rate slows as I reach my mind out to the Drakon. I envision its thrashing body as the blood pulses through its veins. Its heart rate accelerates to a chaotic panic. Then I see the inside of its tiny brain. I hear its thoughts, but it can't speak like Bastet. It feels only raw emotion. Pain. Anger. Fear. Terror.

"Helene!" Ever yells. "What are you doing?"

I ignore him. Bastet coaches me. *"Focus. Feel it. Love it. Talk to it."*

I envision a long tube connecting my soul with the Drakon's and send it pure, unaltered love from my heart. Instantly, it stops thrashing. I send it visions from my mind of the blissful serenity of the Aegean Sea. It closes its eyes and its breathing slows. I connect with a bird flying in the sky above. I project that feeling of soaring high through the wispy clouds, of the peaceful calm of this experience. I hear a snort, a sigh, and then the Drakon's whole body relaxes into a deep slumber.

"You did it!" Bastet praises me.

I open my eyes to see Ever standing there, incredulous. "What just happened?!"

Now is not the time to explain that I can communicate with animals. Ever has had enough of a shock for one day and his first journey to Gaea. I don't want to totally overwhelm him, so I shrug.

When I don't answer, he gets annoyed. "Okay, whatever." He looks around the room. "I guess we're not leaving that way..." He gestures to the doorway where the Drakon's enormous body completely fills the space. "...with that thing in the way."

I look around. We can go back through the Gate to Earth, but otherwise, we're stuck here.

Bastet's voice echoes through my mind. *"You're not stuck! You can go out through the crevice that the Drakon made. There should be a tunnel down there. Take the sand boards from behind the Gate."*

"Sand boards?" I *do* remember Xonos talking about "boarding" during one of my early visits through the Gate.

Bastet's voice booms in my head. *"Yes, the twins use them to travel over the dunes. It's not hard. Kind of like surfing."*

Oh, Jesus. I don't know how to surf!

Ever is staring at me. I must have been talking out loud to Bastet. I'd better be more careful or I'll have to explain it to him. I'm not sure I'm ready for that yet. I take Ever's hand to lead him over to the edge of the crater. As we peer over it, we're accosted by a putrid stench that makes us gag. The entire interior of the Drakon tunnel is coated with a fresh coat of brownish-green slime. *Ugh.*

I turn to Ever, pointing him back towards the Gate. "You should go back to Earth."

His face and hair are covered with glittering flecks of sand. His voice is solid, resolute, as he declares, "If you stay, then so do I!"

I sigh. "Okay, fine. Just remember, I gave you the choice." I pull two sand boards out from their hiding place behind the Gate, then toss one over to him. "Take this board and let's go!"

"Board?" he asks, intrigued.

"Yeah, sand boarding. It's like surfing but on the dunes," I say, as if I know exactly what I'm talking about.

As we slop our way through the goo in the tunnel, I notice that the sandstone has been carved with almost perfect symmetry. It reminds me of what the twins told me about how the Drakons are responsible for breaking up the land to extract the mineral lumite, which is used as a power source on Gaea. It's also the source of the Elixir.

Bastet trots in from behind us. Ever and I walk side by side, almost touching. I take some time to explain what I know about this incredible place. He listens intently, reacting at times with a childlike glee that I've never seen before in him. I'm surprised that he's not more shocked or startled because it's a lot to take in, but he seems to adjust to it just fine. When I finally get around to describing why I'm here...why *we're* here...to locate the Lone Cypress Tree so we can find my mother, his eyes light up.

"I knew you were searching for your mom, but this goes way beyond anything that I could have imagined!" he says, bubbling with emotion. He turns serious. "I can understand why you can't tell anyone about this place. A normal person wouldn't believe that any of this could be real," he says resolutely. His blue-green eyes sparkle like the sunlight shimmering across the waves of the sea, so beautiful that I'm lost for a moment. "But I'm not just anyone...and I'm definitely not normal."

"Look, I understand if you don't want to continue on with me," I say, giving him another out. "This is my journey, and it's likely to be even more dangerous than what we've just been through. You can still head back through the tunnel and the Gate."

Ever shakes his head in exasperation. "I told you, I'm not leaving! Now that I'm here, I want to help you. It makes me happy to be here for you." His eyes glisten, growing wistful. "You know how much I love my mama, so I can relate to your need to find yours."

"*We should reach the end of the tunnel soon,*" I hear Bastet say.

I answer her out loud. "Oh, good, because I've had enough of this claustrophobic place!"

"Uh, Helene?" Ever asks. "Who are you talking to?"

My eyes snap to meet his. "Uh, no one."

"You are so lying," he says, shaking his head. "I'm not stupid, you know!"

Bastet and I exchange glances. "*You may as well tell him,*" she says.

"Okay, fine," I say.

Ever moves between me and Bastet. "You…you can hear her?"

I look away for a minute, thinking but not answering.

"You think I didn't know?" he says, exasperated. "I figured it out a while ago!"

"Really? How?"

"Ummm, I kind of guessed it when we were dealing with the Drakon, and you miraculously found this tunnel," he says, grinning.

"Okay, fine! Yes, I can hear animals talk inside my head!" I exclaim in frustration. "I'm a freak. Isn't that what Samantha and everyone else thinks?"

Ever's voice is quiet as he gently places his hand on my arm. "You're not a freak. You're extraordinary."

A few minutes later, we pop out into the open desert. We must have walked quite a distance. From here, we can see the giant red sun slowly starting to set over drifting sand dunes that stretch almost as far as the eye can see. At the horizon, we can see the smoldering volcano, and next to it, smoke rises out of deep, jagged crevasses in the ground. We've reached the mines and prison called Tartarus, just like the 3-D image I saw down in the Stronghold and in my dreams.

On the other side of the mines, there's a vast red sea with an enormous power plant sitting on its shores alongside a magnificent, shimmery gray pyramid, which reaches up so high up into the sky that it appears from here to be almost the same height as the massive volcano.

"The pyramid city, New Olympus," I whisper.

"Is that the fully enclosed, sustainable city you told me about?" Ever asks.

"Yes," I explain. "The home of the gods."

We sit down on the hot sand, watching the giant red sun set in the distance. Glorious rays of blue, gold, and violet radiate from it like a fiery inferno.

"What's next?" Ever asks quietly.

"We wait until the stars come out and then look for the Huntsman's constellation. Your sign – Sagittarius," I say.

Ever smiles, but then a faraway look comes over him. "Wait, what did you just say?" he finally asks.

"We need to find Sagittarius…the constellation."

His eyes appear to glow an almost eerie shade of sky blue against the backsplash of billowing clouds floating behind him. "But how can that be? If we're on Gaea, which is another planet in a different universe, then how is it that we can see the exact same constellations here that we can see on Earth?"

That's a good point. "You're right! It wouldn't be possible, unless…" I feel like a brick just hit me as it dawns on me what this could mean. "Wait, for that to be the case, Gaea would need to be located exactly where Earth is in proportion to an exact copy of our universe, right?"

Ever's face lights up with excitement. "Yes! But if that's true, then Gaea must be an exact copy of Earth but in a different universe."

"But that can't be because in that case, Gaea should be identical to Earth, which it isn't," I say, frowning.

"Okay, yeah," he says, thinking.

I think of the subway tunnel under the ruins of Old Olympus where Bastet told me that the Gaeans were like us but from the future.

"I've got it! Gaea could exist in a different point in time, several thousand years in the future."

"Which means that the 'gods' would be advanced copies of us," Ever proclaims.

Our eyes light up as I finish his thought. "From the future in an alternate reality."

Ever shakes his head, totally blown away. It's incredible to see all the pieces finally come together.

He catches my gaze. For a moment, I'm transported back to his singing to me so sweetly at the dance, and then to the image of our bodies entangled on the sand in my dream. I'm lost in the depths of his intense blue eyes as my gaze slowly falls to his full lips. No, no, no. I turn my head away. This can't happen now.

We're both quiet. I turn back to Ever. We stare into each other's eyes. Slowly, he moves in, this time reaching over to hold my hand. I draw in my breath as he moves his hand to my chin, cupping my face, still looking deeply into my eyes.

Before I can say anything else, his lips graze my mouth, softly at first, but then he shifts to fully embrace me, his lips taking mine. Overwhelmed by his scent, the passion, and his desire, I remind myself that this is not a dream. This is *real.*

As we pull apart, both of us breathing hard, he rests his forehead on mine. "I wanted to do that for a *very long time.*"

In this moment of pure bliss, I try to remember all the reasons before that I didn't want this to happen, but nothing comes to mind.

Just then, Bastet raises her voice inside my head. *"If he tries anything you don't like, I will knock him on his ass!"*

The thought of Ever being knocked out by a cat makes me laugh out loud.

We look out over the desert. Darkness has overtaken the lands. I feel my breath catch as I stare upward. Above us is a vast darkened sky lit up with millions and millions of stars. In the middle, we can even see the semitransparent white, shimmering outline of what would be this universe's version of the Milky Way. Towards the coast of the red sea sits the moon, with its soft light dancing like magic across the surface of the lapping waves.

Ever takes my hand and holds it up, studying my ring in the moonlight. Suddenly, he turns his arm over. Holding his wrist out next to my ring, he slowly traces his finger over the star on the surface of my ring. The ring of Artemis. On his wrist is the golden tattoo. A perfect match for my star – the twelve-point star, the symbol of the gods.

I suck in my breath. "Ever, is it possible that…" – my voice breaks – "…that you're from Gaea?"

"No." He sighs loudly. "This has to be a coincidence. I don't see how it could be." He is quiet, contemplative, while he considers this further. "I don't remember anything about my life before I was eight. It's all so vague. I just feel emptiness from that time." Some deep-seated understanding seems to hit him. "I guess it's possible."

My mind is reeling as I consider what this could mean. If Ever is from Gaea and my mom is Artemis, also from Gaea, then who else is involved? How far does the rabbit hole go?

"*Ahem. Sorry to break this up between you two, but look up.*" Bastet's amber eyes glow.

I follow her gaze up and to the left. High in the sky is the constellation of Sagittarius.

"Look!" I point it out to Ever.

His eyes light up. "The Huntsman!"

"Yes! We need to find the stars that make up the arrow, which will point our way to the cypress tree," I say.

As we scan the sky, I hear Ever's sharp intake of breath. "There!" He points to near the bottom of the cluster of stars.

My eyes follow the stars that make up the Huntsman's arrow down to the horizon, past the mouth of the smoldering volcano, but there's nothing there. How can this be? All the clues have led me to this point. We can't have come all this way for nothing!

"I don't see anything," Ever says quietly. He must be coming to the same conclusion that I am. We sit in silence, muted frustration passing between us as I search the horizon one more time. The moon suddenly starts to be obscured by a dark shadow.

"Is that an eclipse?" I gasp.

"It can't be! Total lunar eclipses are extremely rare," Ever exclaims. The shadow grows until I see what it is: an enormous golden eagle. Could it be? No way. But why not? If Greek mythology is real, then so could be Aetos Dios, the giant golden eagle, Zeus's magical messenger. His magnificent wings shimmer in the moonlight.

In the partially obstructed moonlight, I see it. Off in the distance about halfway between the volcano and the pyramid city, I spot a jet-black silhouette that stands out in stark contrast to the soft light of the moon. As my eyes adjust further, I finally see the faint outline of a tree standing alone in the desert.

The Lone Cypress Tree.

34 – REVELATION

"Helene…your necklace!" Ever points at my chest. Searing heat burns my skin. Startled, I reach down and touch the rose-gold edge of my mother's cypress tree necklace. I jerk my hand back in scorching pain. The skin on my chest is raw and blazing hot where the cypress tree charm comes to life, casting an eerie green glow. A few seconds pass before it cools enough to touch it.

"Oh!" I say breathlessly. "It belongs to my mother. This must be a sign that we're close." I'm filled with excitement, anticipation, and fear. What if, after all of this, she isn't there? What if I'm too late or I never find her? What then? I can't think like this now.

Ever snaps me out of my funk. "So, what now?" His expression is alive and vibrant. Tiny flecks of sand glitter in his hair under the moonlight.

"We need to figure out how to use these." I plop the sand board down on the dune next to him.

"Awesome!" he exclaims. His expression is one of pure joy. Of course, he thinks it's awesome. Mr. Super-Athlete is probably an expert surfer. I follow him as he rushes up to the top of a gigantic dune, maybe as high as a hundred meters.

He gingerly steps onto the board. But then…*slam!* He tumbles down, landing flat on his back, his body covered head to toe in sand. "Oh God. I love it!" His blue eyes twinkle when he smiles, almost giddy. We both laugh as he comes back up the dune to try again.

"Well, I guess you aren't perfect at everything you try."

"Sand boarding, cleaning…and *girls* are my challenges." He grins. "It's having the courage to get right back up and try again that makes one truly great."

"Aren't you full of wise words?" I tease. He nods, winks at me, then takes off down the vast dune, leaving me all alone. This time, his form is perfect as he takes on so much momentum that he boards down one dune, then most of the way over to the next dune on the other side, then shows off with a full flip, landing flat on his butt at the top. A triumphant smile covers his face as he yells to me, "Your turn!"

The steep slope drops below me at such an extreme pitch that I feel dizzy. I'm totally freaked. But here I am, in a different world. I've been through so much and come so far to find my mother, I'm not going to let a little fear stop me. Besides, I have super-strength. This should be easy.

I close my eyes, step on the board, and *go.*

Oh God. My heart surges with adrenaline. I feel so free, so alive as my board surges down the sand at an insane velocity. And as my board travels up the other side of the hill, I take a nosedive directly into the sand, filling my nostrils with minute crystals, which makes me snort....hard. Still sprawled out on the sand about ten feet away from me, Ever bursts into laughter, and of course, I can't help but join him.

Now confident that we can do this, I take the lead as Ever follows. We surf over the towering sand dunes, adrenaline soaring, pure exhilaration surging through our veins at the joy of feeling so utterly free. The unknown danger ahead further fuels the excitement of this euphoric experience for us.

Bastet sails past us, racing to the top of the next dune, when suddenly she stops cold in her tracks. Her eyes grow wide and anxious, her plush fur standing on end as she scans the desert below her.

Her voice in my head is fierce and urgent. "*Stop!*"

The sound of thousands of men chanting in unison accosts our ears before we see them, but instantly, we sense the danger and freeze, quickly dropping down to the sand on our bellies. We leave the boards behind and arm-crawl up the side of the dune to peer over the side.

We've reached the edge of a vast plateau that overlooks a wide, desolate stretch of plains between the volcano on one side and the enigmatic shimmering pyramid city on the other. Directly in the center lies the Lone Cypress Tree. And, between us and the tree, stand a contingent of marching men.

A rush of fear surges through me at this staggering sight. Could this be Zeus's army, the Vorlage? I remember when Athena told me that on Gaea, they are gold-plated robots, not human. But the army below does not look gold-plated from here. They look like men.

As Ever takes it all in, I'm surprised to see him so quiet. He's deep in thought, which makes me concerned that this may be too much for him. This is his first time through the Gate, after all, which is a lot for anyone…and now to add the danger of a thousand-man army is way more than I think even I can handle.

"Are you sure you're up for this?" I ask him softly.

He solemnly nods. I've never seen him so serious before as he says firmly, "I am if you are."

I'm still not convinced. "No, you don't understand. I've been here before, but this is your first time. I totally understand if you aren't up for this."

He says vehemently, "I said I'm good."

"Okay, fine," I say. "But how will we get past them?"

"Good question," he says. The moonlight dances across the surface of his glistening blue eyes, making them appear mysterious and endless.

Bastet bursts into my thoughts. *"You'll have to traverse around the volcano to reach the back side of the tree. On sand board, that could take a week."*

No way! The wind blows out of my sails. With the cypress tree so close and in plain sight, we can't wait an entire week.

"Can't we just wait for them to leave? Surely they can't stay there forever!" I cry out, forgetting for a moment that Ever is here with us.

The procession of men, their eyes the haunting red color of blood, marches together in perfect synchronization. It takes me back to when I first came to Athens, to the dream I had on the airplane. Thankfully, they shift direction at the cypress tree and march off towards the smoldering pit and blackened castle-like structure that must be Tartarus.

"The coast is clear," Ever says, pulling away. "You ready to find your mom?"

"Yes!" I'm trying to psych myself up.

Time to shift gears and do what we came to do. Excitement builds in me as we make our way over to the cypress tree. We search up and down its rugged trunk and every space around the base for some sign of Mom. *Nothing.*

"I can't believe it!" I sigh, sinking to the ground to rest under the tree.

Ever sits down next to me. "Let's just take a break. Maybe something will turn up."

But I'm not so hopeful. My mind spins in anxious misery. Was all this for nothing?

"Agh!" I slam my hand onto the side of the tree, totally exasperated. We've combed over the same areas again with absolutely no success. Now what?

Ever is still on the other side of the tree searching when a sliver of moonlight casts itself onto the side of the tree just under where my hand rests. I'm about to give up all hope when I see something unusual in a crevice in the tree. As I move in closer, I probe this area with my finger and feel some sort of notch hidden in the side of the tree. It's the twelve-point star! The indented area feels about the same as what I found in my locker at school, which allowed me entry into my mother's secret room. This is it.

"I think I found something."

Ever joins me. The ray of direct moonlight shines down on the tiny section of the tree. I fit my ring into the groove, tap three times, and *click!* A large section in the trunk suddenly slides open to reveal a dimly lit winding stairway leading down into the ground.

Elation fills me. I jump up and down and shout, "Yes!"

Ever's smile is wide, his sea-blue eyes dewy and alive at our triumph as we embrace in a victorious hug.

"I'll go first," he offers. "Ha ha," I say, brushing past him to lead,

"I don't think so."

He shakes his head. I don't think I surprise him with this anymore. As we make our way to the bottom of the stairs, we find ourselves inside a cavernous room with a dirt floor, filled with various pieces of equipment and other stored items. At the far end of the chamber is a wall covered with sophisticated technology and data scrolling over a semi-transparent screen, which appears to offer surveillance of the entire surface of Gaea.

On our right is a metal tank. It looks like a coffin attached to a long tube filled with an iridescent purple liquid flowing through, which snakes from the surveillance wall down to the back of the tank. A low, steady hum is barely perceptible. I run my hand over what looks like a fogged-up window in the top of the tank. As the fog clears, I can't believe my eyes. *It's Mom!*

"Ever, look!" I call. "My mom! She's in here!"

I feel him behind me as he wraps his arms around my waist and peers over my shoulder. "Is she...asleep?" he asks pensively.

"I...I don't know," I say, wondering what this tank – which appears to be some sort of machine – is doing to her. It looks like she's in a coma! Tears come to my eyes. What to do now?

There's a dusted-over section on the top of the machine. A panel. There are five multicolored buttons with no symbols or signs nearby to indicate what they do. The button in the middle is red. I push it.

Instantly, the hum wavers as the machine starts to power down, the liquid in the tube drains out, and the whole top section starts to open. I'm terrified that I've done something wrong, that somehow, I might hurt Mom.

"What did you do?" Ever asks, incredulous at the sight.

Before I have the chance to answer, I see my mother's eyes flutter and her hand twitch. "She's waking up!" I say as I rush to the side of the machine and watch. My mother opens her eyes. She seems disoriented, but as her vision clears, her eyes come to life when she catches sight of me.

"Mom," I whisper. I can't believe it. After all this time, it's really her.

A large smile consumes her pale face. She tries to talk. "He...Hele...Helene," she sputters, as if trying to speak causes her a great deal of pain.

I reach my hand out to her and help her sit up. Ever helps me lift her frail body out of the machine and down to the ground to lean up against the wall. Her body is broiling hot, yet she's shivering, teeth chattering as if she has a serious fever. Ever runs off and comes back with a pile of blankets, which he wraps around her. I settle in next to her, trying to warm her with my body heat. Soon her body relaxes and her voice returns.

She speaks slowly, as if still in pain. "Where are we?"

"Under the Lone Cypress Tree," I tell her, as if this is the most normal thing to say, "on Gaea."

"What?" she asks, incredulous, as fierce intensity consumes her features. "But how?"

If she doesn't know where she is, then she must not know anything about how she got here. But I'll bet she knows why.

"I know how I got here but not you, Mom," I say, my voice steady and even. But then a wave of raw emotion floods my mind, and I can't contain myself. I need answers, and I need them now. "What...what happened to you, Mom? *Why* did you leave me?" I ask, anguish filling my voice.

She looks stunned, cheeks flushed as if someone slapped her. Her voice is low and quivering, full of remorse. "Oh, honey, I would never leave you on purpose! I had no choice." She lifts her finger slowly towards Ever, asking, "Who is...this?"

Ever lifts his brow at me, wondering how I will answer. I weigh my words carefully as I say, "Ever Sarantos."

My mom's face grows deathly pale, mouth dropping open in surprise. "No...."

"I'm sure that you must have met Ever's father, Georgios?" Now that I know about the crush that his father once had on my mom, I'm dying to know her response.

She's silent, contemplative for a moment, then says, "I mean, of course I've known Georgios a very long time." She grins at Ever.

"Somehow, I doubt your dad knows that you're here, right?

Ever smiles sheepishly, as if he thinks he is about to get in trouble. "Well, no."

"Uh-huh. Don't worry. I'm not telling him unless you do." She smiles easily, which makes him instantly relax. I can tell that she likes him.

She looks at me. "What were you doing in Athens, Helene?"

Ever sits to my left, stroking my back patiently as I recount the story from the time she disappeared to the point where I met Ever's dad…skipping over that…to Gaea and all that has happened for us to arrive here. Her expression is incredulous, stunned, but then changes as if careful to reveal too much.

I recount how I was attacked by Ares and his thugs on Earth. Her eyes grow wide in concern. Her voice is hushed as she whispers, "Vorlage?"

"Yes." I nod slowly. "Now, tell me, what happened to you?"

Mom's voice is low and quiet. "In California, they found me at the labs and tried to kill me. There was an explosion, my body was covered in fire, and I must have passed out because I have no idea how I got here." Her voice is raspy and urgent. "But Zeus can't know that I have a daughter!"

"Why not, Mom?" I ask with fierce intensity. "I know who you are!" I tell her, still crying. But suddenly, my tears dry up as I feel my own power return. I am strong, just like my mother. "Artemis," I say, breathless.

Ever's mouth drops open. "Whoa! What?" He's been so quiet, I almost forgot that he can hear everything. He grasps my shoulder.

Mom's eyes are wide. We both ignore Ever. So many unanswered questions fill my mind. I want to know it all.

At the very least, though, it's about time that Mom tells me about the Prophecy. I deserve to know. It's time. "And Mom, I keep hearing about some sort of prophecy. What is it? No one will tell me. Only you can tell me!"

Mom looks down at her hands. "Okay." Her voice is quiet as she gathers her thoughts, then starts. "Of course, you've heard of the

Oracle at Delphi?"

Ever and I exchange glances, nodding in agreement.

"Well, after the Gaean plague – the Scourge – ravaged our planet and killed most of the population, times were dire, grave here. There wasn't a lot of hope. Zeus inflicted enormous pressure on the Oracle to tell him how to solve his problems, but instead she delivered a grim warning. The Prophecy foretold of a child who would be born from a virgin goddess with the blood of the Elixir, who would one day rise up out of the dust, rally the people, and overthrow Zeus to bring peace and harmony to all worlds."

Her voice is breathy, mysterious. "We call this prodigy the Protogena."

"Since the Oracle was under so much pressure at the time, we couldn't be sure if the Prophecy was true or not, but Zeus took it seriously. Immediately, he had all three virgin goddesses – Hestia, me, and even his beloved Athena – arrested and sentenced to death. Of course, as we were taking the Elixir, it was impossible to immediately execute us, so we were sentenced to the prison at Tartarus while the Elixir was drained from our bodies. But that gave us the chance to escape."

I feel a chill and shiver, totally overwhelmed to finally hear the truth. Ever wraps his arm tighter around my shoulders as we both continue to listen.

Mom's eyes are animated as if on fire. "While we were incarcerated, the Rebellion went to work to fulfill this Prophecy, to utilize advanced bioengineering and genetic manipulation to 'create' the Protogena. This meant that a virgin goddess needed to give birth to a child with the blood of the Elixir, which to us literally meant inserting the Elixir directly into the child's DNA inside of a test tube. Once on Earth, we utilized an archaic technology called in vitro fertilization along with a surrogate, and nine months later, you were born."

As the last piece of the puzzle falls into place, I can't even find the words to describe how I feel. It's overwhelming. My whole existence flashes before my mind's eye in an instant, and I know that it's all true.

"I'm the Protogena." I can barely say it. It's so outrageous, even more so than anything else I've heard or seen, that it's like I'm not hearing it.

Mom nods enthusiastically, as if I should be excited about this. "Yes!"

Ever, who has been listening quietly this whole time, cuts in. "So, if Helene is the Protogena, how is she supposed to defeat Zeus?"

"The gods don't have real magical powers, but the Protogena, with the Elixir directly in her bloodstream, can harness the power of the Aether to manipulate space with her mind and body."

This is all so crazy! I can barely think straight. My backpack vibrates. Oh, crap. I forgot that I had it. The Catalyst. When I pull it out, the light on the top starts flashing and beeping loudly. What is it doing this time?

When she sees the Catalyst, Mom is furious. "No!" She swiftly snatches it out of my hand.

"What is it?" Ever asks.

"A tracking device." Mom's voice is tight. "A beacon!"

35 – BELIEVE

My mother's face is a stern mask of concentration as she swipes across the Catalyst several times. The beeping sound stops, but the light still flashes. Then finally, after more effort, the light ceases, and the screen goes blank.

Mom turns to us, anxious. "It may be too late. He may already know where we are." She tries to stand. "Help me!" Ever hoists my mother up to stand, then I guide her painstakingly to a nearby console. "Athena...I have to call Athena...*now!*"

Athena's holographic image pops up in the middle of the room. When she sees Ever and me standing in the same room as my mother, her whole face falls in anger. "How...is this possible? Janus had explicit instructions to keep you away from the Gate."

No one says anything. My mother holds up the Catalyst. "We have other, much more pressing matters to handle, I'm afraid."

"How...how could you bring the Catalyst here?" Athena seethes, her eyes boring into me like daggers.

"There isn't much time for explanations," my mother says. "The beacon was activated. Zeus will know how to get here now. The safe house has been compromised." My mother has transformed right before my eyes into the consummate professional. I can't help but feel proud.

She turns to Ever and me. "You need to leave here now." Her face is lined with worry, yet her voice is steady, strong, and commanding. "Go back to Earth and home to Georgios."

"No way, Mom. You have to come too," I tell her.

Athena cuts in, her voice harsh. "Your mother is too sick and weak to trek across the desert with you. She'll never make it."

"Bastet brought us here. She can take us back too," I plead.

Mom shakes her head. "Bastet can carry only you and Ever, not all three of us."

"I can walk back by myself," Ever offers, holding his hands out.

My mom shrugs. "No, Ever, you can't make it that far on foot without water. And if you don't die of thirst, then the Cyclops will get you."

We argue back and forth, with Athena chiming in. I can't take much more of this.

"But Mom, I need you! You can't leave me again. I just found you!" I plead with her, my face growing red with angst.

Athena intervenes. "Enough! The greater good is at stake here. Sometimes sacrifices must be made. Helene and Ever, time to go! I have already sent people to your location to retrieve Artemis. She'll be home as soon as possible."

Just then, a loud crashing sound interrupts us. The noise is from above ground, outside of the cypress tree in the desert. Someone is here!

My mother screams as she flicks on a screen. "They're already here!" Bastet has pinned a Vorlage soldier to the side of the tree. Behind her sits an empty land cruiser. No doubt more Vorlage are nearby, but no others are in sight yet. "You need to leave *now*!"

"There's no way I'm going anywhere without you!" I raise my voice in defiance. Ever stands in silence next to me but in clear support of what I want.

Athena turns to my Mom. "You know what you have to do."

My mother stands with her mouth slightly open as she thinks about this for a moment but then disagrees with Athena. "No, I can't. I can't do it. What if something happens to her? She's not ready...my little girl! I can't!"

Athena's blue-green and golden eyes are mesmerizing as she grows more persuasive. "Artemis, you have to let her spread her wings and fly. It's time for her to fulfill her true destiny. My son too! I did what was necessary so many years ago for him! Now it's your turn."

I can't be without my mom, not after all of this. "I'm not leaving you, Mom!"

Athena nods to my mother, who nods back in agreement. Athena is talking to my mom in her head! Suddenly, my mother grabs a dagger from the table and aims it at her side. "Helene, don't make me do this. I will if you won't leave."

How could she do this to me? Ever tries to grab the knife from my mom, but Athena yells at him, "*Stop!*"

Somehow, this makes Ever cower, and I can see from his confused look that he's not sure why. My mother makes me promise not to come back through the portal again unless they ask me to. The portal is too unstable for travel. There's a real risk that it could just shut down and collapse from overuse, just like the Olympic Gate thousands of years ago. She commands us, "You have to go *now!*"

We hear an explosion from above. Artemis and Athena exchange devastated looks as Athena says somberly, "It's too late. They're here."

Ever isn't giving up so easily. He grabs my backpack and takes my arm. His ever-changing eyes assume his mood like a chameleon...*my* chameleon. Right now, his irises appear an intense steel blue that reflects the backbreaking stress we both face. "It's never too late to try! Come on! We're leaving!"

Athena's hologram fizzles out with the rest of the electronic equipment in the room. Only the dim red emergency lights remain.

Ever rushes over to where my mother is sitting when four gold-plated robot men rush at us from above. The Vorlage. Just before they reach us, Ever shoves me aside with him under a table and holds his hand tightly over my mouth, restraining me. I try to thrash around to break free of him so I can help my mom.

He whispers urgently in my ear, "I need to look out for you first, Helene! If you go out there, they will capture all of us. Is that what you want?"

The Vorlage surround my mom with large gold-plated weapons, then push her up the stairs and out of the room under the cypress tree into the desert above. After a moment, Ever and I tiptoe up the stairs, following behind them.

As we reach the desert, the door to the tree slams shut. There's no going back now. I hear Bastet roar in warning when three more Vorlage suddenly pass by us from behind the tree. We shrug back and away from them just in time to avoid alerting them to our presence. I look up and am relieved to see Bastet sitting tall at the top of the sand dune overlooking the plateau where we stand. For the time being, we hide out in safety behind the tree.

My mother, her body frail, is on her knees, surrounded by Vorlage, when I hear a familiar laugh. Ares…he's here, this time in the flesh. His black trench coat floats out behind him in the slight desert breeze. "Artemis! Nice to see you again!" His face is twisted into a cruel sneer. "Zeus will be so happy to see you, too."

Raw adrenaline pulses through my veins in panic as I struggle against Ever's firm grip on me. Suddenly, the scene in front of us takes shape. I notice that the entire procession of red-eyed men we saw earlier is once again marching in our direction. After several minutes of their synchronized chanting, they halt in front of three men, each impeccably dressed in business suits.

I recognize two of the men as Poseidon and Hades, but there is something different about the man in the middle. With his imposing stature and stern demeanor, he is clearly their leader. Zeus. His face, though, is all wrong. It's blurred as if someone has applied an eraser to it, and it's shadowy, so what remains seems the emanation of pure evil. I can barely make out his shifting features, but the combined effect of it all…is totally creepy.

Just like in my dreams…

Ever whispers in my ear, "Wow, that golden monocle is cool. Looks like Google Glass…totally high-tech."

I try to see what Ever is talking about, but I can't. "I don't see anyone with a monocle."

"C'mon, of course you can! The ugly guy with the massive scar on his face who just shot the lightning bolts? Pretty sure he's Zeus."

I strain my eyes, blinking twice more. Still, Zeus's face is completely blurred, but it seems alive with a menacing fury. For some reason, Ever can see Zeus, but I can't. From the look of all the people here, I'm guessing that they can all see him too. Why not me?!

As Zeus addresses the army before him, my eyes fall to his hand, where he wears a ring made of solid gold. The twelve-point star is engraved on its surface. It's an exact copy of my ring, only larger. He lifts his left hand up to the sky. The quick flash of static lightning shoots out of his hand, up into the heavens. The sound of thunder vibrates in the ground. The procession of men bow down onto their knees with their eyes aimed at the ground.

They chant, "Zeus!"

36 – SMOKE AND MIRRORS

But not everything is as it seems. As the lightning streams from Zeus's hand into the sky, part of the current of electricity accidentally flows downward, zapping him in the middle of his foot. "Argh!" He curses, hopping around in pain.

He tries again, lifting his hand upward. But this time, the bolt zaps him in the head. A tuft of his perfectly manicured jet-black hair falls out onto the ground. "Aaaggghh!" he screams, heaving what looks like a flesh-colored metal mechanical device from his hand onto the ground. "All of our equipment is dying, just like this forsaken planet!"

I stand in silence, piecing it all together in my mind. It's like *The Wizard of Oz*, where the gods use technology and gadgets to deceive the masses. Like Clarke's Third Law. It's not magic, it's advanced technology.

Ever whispers, "It's just a bunch of smoke and mirrors!!"

I place my finger over his lips. "Shhhh."

Hades, who stands to the left of Zeus, begins to laugh, his red-purple eyes dancing with bizarre mania. A three-headed Chihuahua lies on the ground near his feet, all three heads resting on the ground, eyes closed, as if sleeping. Hades is preoccupied as he studies what looks like a helmet that he holds in his hands.

The man on Zeus's right is Poseidon, which I know from when I saw his "ghost" at the Temple of Poseidon. With his tailored suit and salt-and-pepper cropped hair, he looks like he could be anyone on Wall Street, except for the violet eyes. There's an air of boredom about him. Or maybe it's apathy. Not sure. He coughs into a rag he holds. "We'd better get our masks on soon or go inside. Well, except for you, Hay."

Hades's head snaps up at the sound of what must be his

nickname. He wobbles a bit and weaves as he walks, as if he's perpetually drunk. "Wha…? Yeah," he says, slurring his words. "Me" – he points at the red-eyed men standing quietly in front of them – "and the Draakkonnn riders."

"Let's get this over with, then," Poseidon says in a clipped tone.

Hades chuckles as he places the helmet on his head, and *poof!* He vanishes. Only his hysterical cackling can be heard. A few seconds later, his body reappears, but he's holding the helmet again. He turns in a circle, giggling. Helmet on, he vanishes. Helmet off, he reappears.

"Will you cut that out?" Zeus screams. "Time is of the essence here."

The Vorlage lead my mother in front of Zeus and throw her onto the sand at Zeus's feet. She appears to be passed out. My heart feels as if it is beating out of my chest. What can I do? Ever was right. We are vastly outnumbered. If I try to save my mom now, not only will my life be in jeopardy but also Ever's. I can't do that to him.

Zeus commands, "Awaken the prisoner."

"Gladly." Ares shakes his head. An overzealous smile consumes his face. With a wave of his hand, the Vorlage kick my mother repeatedly until she stirs.

Pain sears through me until I can no longer stand it. "My mom!"

My feet start to move before I even have time to think, but I'm unable to move because Ever has wrapped his long arms around me to restrain me. He whispers harshly in my ear, "You'll just get yourself killed, which helps no one."

His words slice into me like a whip. I stop dead in my tracks. But I feel a tear run down my cheek as I continue to watch my mother suffering like this.

With my mother now fully awake and on her knees at Zeus's feet, he addresses her. "Ahhhh, Artemis! I have a little present for you. I know all about your daughter…our little Protogena-to-be."

My mother's stoic expression suddenly shifts to utter shock and panic. While we were fully aware that Zeus knew that my mother had a daughter, Ares didn't say anything about me being the Protogena when I was attacked in the alley back in Athens.

The Vorlage pass a new apparatus to Zeus, which he affixes to his left hand. He aims it outward to test it. *Zap!* The harsh streak of raging electricity flows outward, zapping one of the red-eyed men. He falls to the ground.

Zeus calls out, his voice booming, "Helene Crawford! I know you have the Catalyst. Bring it here to me or else your mother will be next."

My mother stares wide-eyed in terror as Zeus extends his arm towards her, sending a loud, cracking jolt of electricity to zap the ground only a few centimeters from her body.

The Drakon riders start to chant, once again perfectly synchronized. They hold their arms out in front of them, then slap their chests once and yell, "Zeus!"

The sound of the chanting drowns out the sound of my cries, as Ever struggles to hold me back from running towards to my mom. I turn to face him, tears flowing freely down my face as he holds me close, stroking my hair to comfort me. I pound his chest in my grief.

His eyes are red-rimmed and pained as hestrokes my back and kisses my hair. His face is pensive, full of empathy. "I'm so sorry."

Zeus is not dissuaded. "This is your last chance! Bring me the Catalyst!"

He extends his device towards my mother again, and my mind spins out of control. Then a totally wild idea comes to me. Maybe I can use the Catalyst to construct a Gate to get Mom, and all of us, out of here…to Earth.

I press and hold the button on the top of the Catalyst, just like the last time at Janus's apartment, when I almost constructed a new Gate. The screen displays two pictures, one of Gaea and one of Earth.

Ever looks over my shoulder, concern etching his face. He whispers, "Helene, what are you doing?"

I'm not sure what comes over me, but I've had enough of this. Ignoring him, I look down at the screen on the Catalyst. The two icons of Earth and Gaea are still there. My finger hovers over the Earth symbol. I press it.

The image of the two planets joined by the portal shows on the lit-up screen and starts counting down: 10…9…8…

If I create a new Gate here now, doesn't that allow Zeus to go back to Earth too? That would screw everyone.

My God, what have I done? *Armageddon!*

I feel light-headed. I start to waver on my feet, but Ever holds me steady. Focus, Helene. There's got to be a way to fix this. I try slapping the Catalyst on my leg.

The countdown continues: 5…4…

Ever has figured out what I'm doing. "What the…?!"

"Shhhhh!" I whisper to hush him. There's no time to explain.

A tiny symbol, a clock, appears in the upper corner of the screen. What could this be? There's no time to think. I press on the icon.

The screen screams to life as words fill the screen: Permanent or Temporary?

Suddenly, I recall Janus's words back when he told me about Orion's Key: *"The Catalyst creates an actual wormhole, either a temporary or permanent 'Gate,' between realities."*

3…2…

Ever's eyes are wide with terror. He's reading the screen with me, totally freaked.

Oh God! I slam my finger down on "Temporary."

…1…

Countdown paused.

We sag against each other in sweet relief. But this isn't over yet. Not even close.

Enter operation time: 30, 60 or 180.

Panic fills me. I can't think. What do these numbers mean?

Well, it can't be minutes, so I'm guessing seconds. Ten seconds is too short, but the other choices are way too long. Zeus could follow us through.

Zeus's terrible voice booms, making me jump. "Helene, you're out of time!" He aims his menacing hand at my mother's head.

Time to take action. I hit the icon: 30

A new countdown resumes: 30…29…

I break free of Ever's grip and rush out from behind the cypress tree to my mom's side, holding the Catalyst out in front of me towards Zeus.

"Look!" I taunt him, moving in closer to stand between him and my mother.

Zeus gasps in shock at the sight of me. "You're way too stupid to be the Protogena. That was far too easy! You're just a little girl while I'm the god of all gods. You were going to take me out?" His cackling laugh echoes through the desert.

Out of the corner of my eye, I see the screen of the Catalyst counting down: 17…16…

My mom turns to me, speaking in a calm, even tone. "Helene, listen to me…"

Ignoring her, I yell to Zeus, "Do you know what has caused the demise of most great men and civilizations throughout history?"

He seems totally taken off guard by this question.

I yell, "*Hubris!*" as I throw my mother the Catalyst.

"Sorry, Mom, but you're going back to Earth." 3…2…1… A flash of the shimmering blue appears in the wall just behind my mother. A huge explosion knocks out all the Vorlage around us, like an electromagnetic pulse. And *poof!* My mother and the portal disappear as the Catalyst clatters to the ground, sizzling and burned out. Totally dead.

Poseidon picks up the charred remains of the Catalyst, shaking his head as he examines it. "The Catalyst is destroyed."

Zeus screams out in a horrendous rage, "Nooooooo!"

When he calms down, he turns his anger to me once again. "I'm going to kill you for this, little girl!" But looking around, he quickly realizes that all the Vorlage were knocked out by the electromagnetic explosion.

Ever comes running out from behind the cypress tree to my side. Unfortunately for us, though, the red-eyed Drakon riders move in to surround us, grabbing us with an intensity that even I'm surprised by. They are incredibly strong.

I can see the frustration on Ever's face. I've never seen him this scared before, but this could be it. Our lives could be over now.

I hear Bastet's voice inside my head. *"Remember your power."* She must be hiding somewhere behind the tree. My power? Of course! Just like my mother, Artemis, goddess of the animals. But what animals are out here in the desert? Birds...no. I rack my brain. I don't know!

I recall the scene from before when I entered the Drakon's mind to lull him to sleep. The Drakon! I know what to do!

I sink to my knees, startling the rider, who shoves the butt of his weapon into my back. I can hear Ares's cutting voice speaking to Zeus. "I promise that she'll die in the *worst* way." I drown out the sound of his voice as I close my eyes, slowing my breathing...in and out...ah....and sink into a deep, meditative state. I imagine the Aether...the collective consciousness...the unseen energy that flows through all things...and there I see a Drakon. It's deep in sleep in a chamber under Tartarus. Its eye pops open. "Help me!" I cry out to it.

In an instant, the Drakon's enormous body roars to life. Without any thought at all, its primitive brain propels it up against his restraints with so much force that it breaks all its bonds. Fire emanates from its gaping mouth as it blasts the metal wall next to it. Slowly but surely, the metal starts to melt, rolling down the wall into pools on the floor until only bedrock is exposed. The creature bellows in insane fury. Suddenly, I hear hundreds of other Drakons awakening all around it, breaking out of their restraints. Intense feelings of unrestrained joy fill their bodies at this sudden taste of freedom.

My eyes pop open. Nothing seems to have changed with our predicament except that Ares is taunting Ever. "And who are you?" he asks with a sneer.

Ever won't look up at him, so Ares lashes out with a kick to his side. Groaning, Ever rolls over, holding his side in anguish. *No!* I feel a rush of rage. The only thing holding me back is knowing that help is on its way...soon.

Suddenly, the ground starts to shudder, quake, and groan. Ares's eyes grow wide. "What the...?" The next moment, it seems to dawn on him what this could mean. "No!! Riders, control your Drakons!!"

The ground beneath us cracks open as my Drakon bursts its

massive head out of the ground next to us, knocking Ares and Zeus off to the side. Two of the riders fall into the gaping depths of the abyss created by the Drakon.

I feel the familiar rumble, then sense the consciousness of the Drakon that I summoned...*my friend*. It's coming back for me. The image of a Drakon rider fills my mind, and within seconds, all the knowledge of how to mount and ride a Drakon floods into me. I know what to do.

I motion to Ever. "Grab the Catalyst and my waist. Don't let go. I've got this!"

"But it's useless...dead!" he says, shaking his head at the burned-out Catalyst.

"Just do it!" I shout, frustrated. There's no time for arguing.

"Fine!" Ever's face is ashen with disbelief, probably still in shock over all of this, but he nods as he picks up the Catalyst and moves in behind me, wrapping his arms tightly around me.

The tremble in the ground intensifies to where I'm not sure I can continue to stand. Then my Drakon bursts out of the ground from under us. Instantly, I grasp onto the horn in the center of his neck and swing myself up into the saddle, pulling Ever up behind me.

I yell back to him, "Hold on tight!" I project the image of the Gate into the Drakon's mind, and off we go, sailing across the desert dunes at insane speed. The image of Zeus and the Vorlage fade fast behind us. I feel the heat of Ever holding me tight, and it fills me with calm as we make our escape.

The Drakon drops us off just outside of the Old Olympus ruins where the tunnel leads down towards the Gate. Ever and I hop off. I place my hand on the nose of the Drakon and stroke him softly, projecting the image of my love and gratitude to him. He rears his head up and takes off back towards the volcano.

I'm worried that Ever's ribs are broken, but when he lifts his shirt to show me his side, the skin is flawless and unblemished with not even a bruise. We laugh in surprise, and keep laughing so hard we're almost crying.

He moves in close to me, wiping the tears from my cheek. "I knew

you were hard to get, but this is so much more than I bargained for."
He grins, his sea-green eyes sparkling mischievously.

As I step back a moment, I notice that Ever has changed. His
muscles are much more defined, his skin a deeper tan, almost
glowing. He's breathtaking. And now that I feel I truly know him, that
he would do anything for me, I appreciate his beauty even more. Ever
is amazing, inside and out.

Bastet arrives behind us, panting hard as she must have tried to
keep pace with the ridiculous speed of the Drakon. As she rushes up
to me, I feel her rub her head under my hand and hear her say, "*You
had the power all along. You just had to believe it for yourself.*"

"Okay, Glinda," I say to with a wink. But she's right. I'm totally
floored by my capabilities and maybe a little nervous about what else
I might be able to do. All three of us start the long walk through the
underground tunnel that leads to the Gate.

"Who's Glinda?" Ever asks. "What was that about?"

"Uh," I say, "just a joke about a girl from Kansas."

As we come up through the other side of the tunnel, the cat's-eye
stone on Ever's belt glows intensely. As we pop up far enough to see
the Gate, its brilliant blue sheen is ready for us. Time to go. I motion
to Ever. "You go first."

He steps through. The ground shudders, making stones tumble
down around the sides of the Gate.

Bastet is concerned. "It's grown unstable. I doubt it will support
all three of us at once. You go. I'll stay behind with Athena."

I should be upset, but I know Bastet will be fine here with Athena.
And the truth is, they probably need her more here than I do on Earth
since she is just a cat there and can't communicate with me. For once, I
don't try to argue with her.

"*Thank the gods!*" she says in my head smartly.

I give Bastet one last hug as I step through the Gate back to Earth.
This time, though, I close my eyes, and it's like stepping into the next
room.

37 - TRUTH

"What took you so long?" Ever takes me in his arms. I try to catch my breath. I turn to meet his gaze. He reaches up to dry my eyes.

I attempt a small smile, but my voice is shaky, unsteady. "You...you saved me back there."

"Of course," he says softly, kissing each of my eyelids. "There's no way I would let you sacrifice yourself, for your sake...or *mine*." He pulls me in close to him again, and I lay my head on his chest. It's warm and comforting. I wish I could stay here forever. "I need you," he whispers tenderly in my ear.

Tenderness surges through me. *I need him too.*

As my eyes fully adjust, I see Janus standing wide-eyed behind Ever. He's tapping his foot loudly, clearly annoyed. As usual, his rainbow headscarf is has fallen off slightly to reveal his shiny bald spot.

I tell Janus and Ever that I had to leave Bastet behind with Athena, but Janus assures me that I made the right choice. Athena can use her help on Gaea. "Besides, it will be nice to be rid of that damn cat around here. She's a pain in the as—!"

"Janus!" I interrupt him. "Enough!" We all laugh together before I grow quiet. Suddenly, I'm worried about my mom. Where did I send her with the Catalyst? What if we can't find her?

Ever notices. "What is it?" he asks me.

I shrug. "Is my mother...*here*?" I ask tentatively.

Janus shakes his head as he starts to stomp up the wooden steps. "Come on upstairs. You'll see."

Why can't Janus just tell me now? I pull Ever off to the side. "I'm worried about my mom. The Catalyst indicated that she was going to Earth, so she should be here."

"Really?" Ever jests. "Because Earth is a pretty big place!"

I sock him on the arm. This is no time for joking. "You're not helping!"

"Right," he says, shrugging. "Sorry."

He leads me up the steps and into Janus's shop. Janus is nowhere to be found. There's no sign of my mother either. We're about to go up the stairs to the apartment when we hear the abrupt slam of a door.

Georgios Sarantos is standing in the front doorway. His piercing blue eyes are alight with fire, blazing at us as the fierce and angry storm clouds in the sky outside behind him swirl around him. He is silhouetted in a menacing fury. It's an incredible sight to behold. His arms are folded sternly across his chest, with Dimitris and Yannis standing expressionless on either side of him.

Clearly, we're in trouble.

"Where the *hell* have you been?" Georgios says, his intelligent, intense blue eyes focused on me and Ever. He turns to Dimitris. "Can someone please explain to me where these kids have been for the past four days!?" He slams his hand down on the desk.

I hear a sound behind us, and standing just inside the door to the Tranquility Room is Janus. As Georgios's stern gaze locks onto Janus's eyes, I see something rare in them: fear. How will Janus explain to Georgios where we've been?

Ever steps in front of Janus, trying to save the day as he explains to his dad, "I took Helene away on a short holiday."

Georgios's face turns bright red. "You did what?!" Just then, Janus steps up to Georgios and whispers something into his ear. "Oh." He smiles wickedly and then begins to laugh.

"Really? It's been four days and you just now noticed!?" Ever says, frustrated. My heart goes out to him. I mean, it's a little sad that his dad didn't care enough to notice before now.

"Oh, believe me, I noticed." Georgios chuckles.

Georgios's intense blue eyes sear into me. "No more lies or games. Give me the Catalyst."

How does Sarantos know about the Catalyst? He doesn't know about Gaea...or does he? Something is going on here. Janus must have spilled the beans. I turn to him, my tone accusatory. "Janus, you weren't supposed to tell anyone about this! You said it yourself. What about Prometheus?!"

"What about him?" Georgios interrupts, his voice firm, his smile intense as his brilliant blue eyes bore into mine as if he's mocking me. This isn't funny. Why is he acting like this?

Janus turns towards me, also smiling, but in a strained, ridiculous way. Very uncharacteristic of him. But then I discover why.

"Helene, I'd like to introduce you to…Prometheus."

My mouth falls open in amazement. "My God," I whisper. "But…but…" I stammer, not finding the words to say. According to the myths, Prometheus was supposed to have died after being tortured by Zeus in punishment for bringing the gift of fire to mankind. He was a thorn in Zeus's side then and apparently still is now.

I hear Ever sharply draw in his breath. When I look over at him, total disbelief has overtaken him. "No," he whispers under his breath. He stares at his dad in shock, eyes wide and his mouth gaping open.

Sarantos grins as he pinches out one of his contact lenses. His eyes are a deep violet, much darker than the bright purple eyes of Janus and the other gods. "Yes, that's literally true. I am a god."

Ever stares down at his hands in greater shock than before. I'm afraid that he's going to faint.

Georgios pops the blue lens back into his eye and holds out his hand. "The Catalyst?"

I sigh as Ever and I exchange glances. In many ways, it will be a huge relief to no longer be responsible for hiding it, but then it dawns on me that this may be my only bargaining chip. If it's true that he's Prometheus, then he must know where my mom is.

Of course, I know this is wishful thinking. It's also possible that no one knows where Mom is. The Catalyst wasn't supposed to self-destruct like that. It's possible that my mom is gone…and this time for good. The surge of emotions I feel at this threaten to overwhelm me. But I must be strong. There's still hope.

"First, tell me where my mom is!" I demand.

Georgios smiles defiantly at me. "That's easy." He points to the door to the Tranquility Room. "She's resting in there."

What?! Insane relief courses through me as I rush over and throw the door open. My mother lies asleep on a plush bed, safe and recovering. A tube of the now-familiar glowing purple liquid flows into her body from an IV. I praise God, the heavens, the universe, and the Aether...anyone who will listen. *Thank you!*

As I reenter the room, Sarantos once again extends his hand to me. "Give me the Catalyst...*now.*"

I nod to Ever, who pulls the device out of what remains of my tattered backpack, then hands it to his father.

For a moment, Sarantos is quiet as he attempts to bring the Catalyst to life. The room is totally silent, so much so that it's like all life has frozen in its tracks.

Sarantos screams.

He throws the Catalyst across the room. I hear the metal crunch as it hits the wall with so much impact that it leaves a small crater where it hit.

After Sarantos calms down, he's still upset and seething. "Well, I sure hope that the Cat's-Eye Gate holds because now we have no way to create a new one!"

My mother must have come in behind us because no one realized that she was standing there until we heard her voice call out, "At least Zeus can no longer get it back. Georgios, they saved my life!"

Sarantos shakes his head at us. Janus cowers in the corner, too upset to look at any of us, probably afraid of what he would do to us right now if he had the chance. A moment later, something catches his eye. Slowly, he makes his way across the room and begins fidgeting with the knobs on an old dusty TV set, probably some relic from the 1950s. It must have been running in the background at a low volume while we've been here. Janus adjusts something, and the sound comes to life.

I see an image on the screen that makes my heart lurch. It's a young boy spewing up blood. His body is sickly white, marred by a vast web of tiny red veins, as if out of a horror movie.

A look of dramatic concern sweeps across the faces of Janus, Georgios, and my mother. The news anchor appears quite dire as she stands in front of the Parliament in central Athens.

"A mysterious illness has been officially identified in Athens, and with many victims hospitalized, concern is growing that this disease has the potential to become a pandemic. As the outbreak was only first identified a few weeks ago, the mortality rate is still unknown; however, as of this morning, seventeen people have died.

The world is on alert and carefully watching Athens for signs of the spread of this unknown illness. At the Greek government's official request, the United States has sent the Centers for Disease Control and the World Health Organization is here to monitor and assist.

Some groups within Greece speculate that refugees may have brought this mystery virus here, and thus the police are on high alert against possible rioting among fringe groups."

Janus shakes his head, seeming particularly distraught about this news. He's muttering something as if he's talking to himself, but then I hear him say, "Are you hearing this?"

My mother shakes her head and says, "The Scourge?"

Georgios shakes his head abruptly at Janus. "No way. It can't be."

What are they talking about? The Scourge. The plague that wiped out Gaea.

My attention shifts back to the TV. An important-looking man in a white lab coat, a genetic scientist specializing in nanoparticle science from the Lawrence Livermore Labs and University of California at Davis, is speaking:

"...particularly concerning, this virus is genetically different from anything we've seen before..."

Ever's mom is sick in the hospital. They said she had a severe case of the flu, but what if it's this mystery virus instead? My heart aches for Ever. His face falls in agony. "Dad, Prometheus – *or whoever you are* – what about Mom? Does she have this virus?"

Sarantos looks unconcerned. His voice is low. "I doubt it. She's alive and recovering. I'm sure it's just the flu."

Ever's eyes light up. He's clearly happy, but he's not done with his father quite yet. "Dad, we need to talk."

Sarantos dismisses him, seeming to think they shouldn't discuss anything more in front of us. "Later."

But Ever challenges him. "Just tell me this…" His eyes grow wide. "Am I from Gaea?"

"I said later, Ever," Sarantos says in an annoyed tone.

"No, Dad! No more lies!" Ever insists. "Just tell me the truth!"

Georgios sighs as he turns his wrist over and places it side by side with Ever's. He then rubs it vigorously until it looks like some makeup has come off. On Georgios's wrist is a yellow-gold twelve-point star, an exact match to the star on Ever's wrist. "Need I say more?" Georgios says.

Ever nods as if he had been expecting this but then demands in a mocking tone, "I don't understand. So, what…what should I call you? Prometheus?"

"Nooo." Sarantos's smile is back, as if Ever's question is somehow funny. "Call me what you've always called me: Dad." At that, he turns and walks out.

My mother comes over to sit by me on the couch. We share a rare moment alone. My eyes glisten with love for her. "I know now why you had to do what you did at the cypress tree," I say. "It's all starting to make sense for me now."

Mom hugs me in close to her. "Oh, baby, I'm so proud of the amazing and strong woman you've become." Her dark hazel eyes grow serious. "You don't even need me anymore. Just imagine what is yet to come for you."

The realization of what is expected of me is overwhelming. I am the Protogena. It's enormous. How can I, just a regular girl, be the one who saves everyone? I'm not sure that I can live up to this responsibility. Besides, what if they were wrong about this Prophecy? What then? I can't think even another moment about it right now. It's just too much.

I feel a hand wrap around my waist, pulling me in close. Ever whispers softly in my ear, "Can we get out of here? I think we need some space."

My mom nods in consent, smiling. "Yes, go! You deserve to relax for a while. Enjoy the calm before the storm."

Dimitris must have heard our conversation because he's already preparing for us to leave, but Ever takes us all totally by surprise when he says to Dimitris, "Give me the keys. I'm driving."

"You know how to drive?" I tease him, eyebrow raised. I've never actually seen Ever drive a car before. He's always had a driver.

"Of course!" he says, eyes blazing with a fervor I haven't seen since…oh yeah, that dream of us together on Gaea, the mirage. "I'm an expert driver. But I'll warn you; I like to drive fast."

He extends his hand to me. "Let's go!"

38 – PANAXIA

Ever whisks me away in the big black Mercedes through the twisting streets of Athens. Angry, dark gray thunderheads gather above us high in the sky. We finally slow down when we reach the sign that tells us we've reached the town of Vouliagmeni. A few minutes later, we pull up in front of an ornate and stately Mediterranean mansion nestled into the hillside overlooking the gorgeous bay. This must be Ever's house.

Just then, I feel a buzz on my hip. My phone. When I look down, I see a missed text. It's from Nick! "Helene, we need to talk....Call me!"

It feels as if the dance and all that happened there was so long ago now and insignificant compared to what just happened on Gaea. I finally found my mom!

Nick's text makes my heart ache. As strong as my feelings are now for Ever, I can't so easily forget what I felt for Nick. Sometime soon, I know that I'll have to think more about him, but right now, I'm just so exhausted. All I want to do is relax and enjoy this peaceful moment with Ever.

I feel a firm hand on my back and I jump. Quickly, I stash my phone. Ever smiles sweetly at me and invites me to join him outside.

Something jumps onto my lap. Bastet? No: It's an adorable medium-sized tan dog. His face is wrinkled with a big black nose and cute little ears, like a shar-pei. I feel him slobber all over my leg as his curled tail flips around with excitement.

"Your dog!" I laugh as I recall the picture of this dog that Ever had on his phone back when we had that amazing dinner near the site of Agora on the night he shared so much of himself with me, including his secret ability to light up Hesiod's *Theogonia*.

"Yeah." He smiles. "This is Hampos, my guard dog."

I smile, but suddenly a wave of melancholy sweeps over me.

"What is it?" Ever says, suddenly concerned.

At first I don't know, but then it hits me. I know exactly what's bothering me: Samantha. She told me that she and Ever were back together. Now that I'm back here on Earth, all the old feelings I had before come rushing back to me. I know that I shouldn't believe a word of what Samantha says, and besides, I shouldn't care about it at all.

But I feel angry and hurt.

"What about Samantha?!" I ask Ever.

"What about her?" he says playfully. I scan his eyes for some explanation, but all I see is amusement there. "You're jealous," he says, grinning mischievously.

"No…I'm…I'm not!" I raise my voice at him in frustration. "What is so darned funny?"

"*You* are," he says with a twinkle in his blue-green eyes. We stare at each other for a moment. My eyes are wide, unblinking.

Understanding sweeps over his face. "I knew it! You feel something for me!"

"I need you to answer my question," I say, ignoring him. "Are you back together with Samantha or what?"

"I could ask the same of you about Nick," he chides me. "Isn't he your boyfriend?"

"No!" I say in surprise. "I told you the truth before. I haven't heard from him. I don't know what's up." Samantha's warning before about Ever's inability to commit continues to bug me. "But at least he's willing to make a commitment." I regret saying this as soon as it leaves my mouth.

"What's that supposed to mean?!" Ever asks, taken by surprise. He swiftly moves in close to me, so near that my senses are overwhelmed by his delicious scent. It drives me crazy. He reaches over to stroke my cheek. "How would you know?"

How can I avoid answering this question directly? "Well, we kissed."

Ever laughs. "Oh, so if I kiss you, then I can claim that you're my girlfriend? That's the qualification?"

"No! I told you that he's not my boyfriend! Besides, you can't kiss me because you're with Samantha. I need to be the only one," I say, sure that this will stop him from continuing this line of questioning. "I want to be *cherished*. A kiss would *never* be enough."

Before I have time to react, he grabs my hand, draws me in close to his body, and whispers in my ear, "You *are* the only one."

He can't do this to me. I have some dignity, after all. I wriggle free of him, refusing to meet his gaze. "No...hey! Samantha told me that you never commit to anyone."

Without warning, Ever sweeps me up into his arms, forcing me to look at him. "She said that only because I won't commit to *her*." His eyes come alive in bold defiance. "I take things slow because when I make a commitment, I mean it."

Ever strokes the inside of my palm, making little circles with his finger. "Do you see now that you really are the only one for me?"

"Uh-huh," I whisper.

He takes my hand and leads me out onto the lawn, his dog trailing behind us. As rain starts to fall, we get caught in the storm, laughing in each other's arms and enjoying the warmth of the rain as we get completely drenched, watching the usually calm bay transform into a frenzy as huge swells and waves consume the sea.

As the storm clouds roll in over the bay seemingly out of nowhere, a barrage of surfers – all clad in black wet suits, holding surfboards in a variety of colors – come out from all directions, hopping the fences that separate the exclusive private beaches from the less-manicured public beach. It is truly a sight to behold to see so many black-clad bodies floating on surfboards out in the middle of the bay as the ferocious swells bob them up and down in the middle of the storm. The rain dies down again to a light drizzle, and we see the clouds in the sky open to let the sun peek through.

And that's when I see it...

A gorgeous rainbow in a perfect semicircle forms over the bay.

I stare up at it in awe, so grateful for this moment of perfection. The rainbow reminds me of the story of Noah and the Ark. Almost no one believed that his against-all-odds mission to save what was left of mankind was real. I feel that the rainbow was a sign sent from God to remind Noah to keep his chin up and to know beyond doubt that with enough belief and perseverance, miracles are possible. I can so clearly understand now how he must have felt and wonder if this rainbow is here today to send me that message, one I definitely need right now.

Ever leads me back up to a covered veranda, where we lounge on a white wicker couch and watch the sun set. We stare as orange and pink rays of sunshine peek out sporadically through dark gray thunderclouds. Ever lifts my hand up to his mouth, slowly kissing each finger, starting with my thumb. Then he sings that sweet song to me softly:

On a night like this, the stars above are shining.

His mouth caresses my index finger. Chills run down my spine.

As a chameleon, I'm changing in your eyes.

His lips move to my middle finger. Heat starts to grow within me.

I will be yours till the sunrise.

My heart rate quickens as he moves onto my ring finger.

I want you now, don't you see?

Burn your boundaries and come with me.

This time, he looks up into my eyes longingly.

I want forever and this night…

It's the song that he sang to me at the dance, which he wrote just for me and so deeply affected me. The intense melodic sound of his voice, so sweet and emotional, stirs the inner recesses of my heart. I can't help but turn around and gaze deeply into his stunning, mesmerizing eyes. He stands, pulling me up close to him.

"While I sing to you, dance for me, ballerina…my American girl," he says, smiling sweetly, holding his hand out in a sweeping motion.

As Ever starts to sing again – "*Eternity begins tonight, come hold me tight…*" – he pulls me around to him, and we sway together. I feel my body respond and move to the rich, soothing sound of his voice. I pull back from him and sweep around in a gorgeous arc of my body. He wraps his arm around my waist, spinning me around and around, ending with me swept into a deep back bend.

He pulls me up and, moving slowly behind me, begins kissing my neck just under my ear, sending shivers up and down my neck and spine. His hands encircle my waist, caressing me just above my belly button.

Ever turns me around to face him, then gently moves a strand of my hair away from my face, tucking it behind my ear. He guides my chin up as his full red lips meet mine...but this time, his kiss is incredibly slow and sensual. He takes his time and makes it last. Every move he makes tells me that I am the *only* one...I am cherished.

While I rest peacefully within his arms, for the first time since my mother disappeared, I feel safe and happy. Pure bliss fills me, warming me inside.

A monarch butterfly lands on my arm, which startles me. For a moment, I'm transported back home to California, where my butterfly friends would land on my arms, fluttering about in greeting when I came home from school. I guess I'm a little surprised to see a monarch butterfly here in Greece.

"Panaxia," Ever whispers, "from the Valley of Butterflies on the island of Rhodes."

I lightly stroke the gorgeous creature's delicate wings, admiring their intricate pattern. There's a vibrant energy from my little friend resting under my finger. This must be another sign of encouragement from above.

I am the Protogena.

I can do this.

EPILOGUE

I don't get it. Three weeks of complete and utter silence from Nick since he sent that text. I called, texted, e-mailed. Nothing. That night back at Ever's house, Nick's text message was so urgent that now his silence seems completely wrong. Finally, I decide the only thing to do is to go next door to see him in person.

My heart races erratically as I climb the stairs of Nick's apartment building. I'm not sure I should do this. I mean, I looked it up on the Internet. There's a name for it when someone completely cuts off all contact with someone they're dating. It's called *ghosting*. All the advice I've read says that Nick's just not into me if he's not taking the time to call me back. Not that I need him to be "into me" since Ever and I are going out now. I do miss Nick's friendship, though. More than that, I'm worried about him.

As I'm about to knock, the door opens. I almost run smack into Nick's mother, Anastasia. "Helen, uh, what are you doing here?" she asks in surprise. She looks worn out and completely different from how I remember her. Gone is her heavy makeup and gold jangly jewelry. It feels as if it's a colossal effort for her to talk to me.

"I came to see Nick," I say weakly. My heart is beating like crazy as the butterflies roll around inside my stomach.

Anastasia sighs loudly. "You don't know, then?"

"Know what?" I ask in surprise, not expecting her reaction.

"Nikos and his father are in the hospital...horribly sick with that awful virus, Helen. He's not doing well." Sadness consumes her features as a tear drops down her cheek.

God...no!

FOREVER AND TONIGHT

Original Song by Kostas Martakis*
Find out more at www.foreverandtonight.com

On a night like this, the stars above are shining
As a chameleon, I'm changing in your eyes
I will be yours till the sunrise
I want you now, don't you see?
Burn your boundaries and come with me
I want forever and this night
Take me in your arms and hold me tight
I want you now, don't you see?
Feel the way I feel and be with me
I want forever and this night
Eternity begins tonight, come hold me tight…
Clarinet Solo
On a night like this, the world becomes our heaven
And we chameleons who fall in love with light
Fallen' in love with forever
I want you now, don't you see?
Burn your boundaries and come with me
I want forever and this night
Take me in your arms and hold me tight
Se thelo tora pio poly (I want you now, even more)
Feel the way I feel and be with me
I want forever and this night
Eternity begins tonight…
Clarinet Solo
Se thelo tora pio poly (I want you now, even more)
Oooohhhhh…
I want forever and this night…
I want you now, don't you see…?
Feel the way I feel and be with me
Se thelo tora pio poly (I want you now, even more)
I want forever and this night
Eternity begins tonight, come hold me tight…

* Produced and recorded by Panik Entertainment Group Ltd with Kostas Martakis, Marios Psimopoulos and Vicky Gerothodorou.

MORE BOOKS COMING SOON

From the *Protogenesis*™ series:

Book 2: First Cure (2018)
Book 3: Protogena
Book 4: First Uprising
Book 5: First Competition
Book 6: Protogenoi
Book 7: Before the Origin

Sign up here to receive updates, special offers and to follow the blog:
www.protogenesis.com

Footsteps in Athens
Follow Helene's Footsteps through Athens, Greece through six short movies narrated by Greek musical star, Kostas Martakis, and learn more about the characters and magical world of the *Protogenesis*™ series at:
www.footstepsinathens.com

Find out more about Alysia and her real-life adventures in Greece, including a US reality-based TV series under development, at:
www.alysiahelming.com
www.meetmeingreece.com

EXCERPT FROM BOOK TWO
PROTOGENESIS: FIRST CURE

PROLOGUE – THE ESCAPE

Planet Gaea – Earth Time 1998 A.D.
POV – Helene's Mother, Diana (goddess Artemis)

If I were a typical victim, my current reality would se em quite bleak. I'm hanging precariously from a rusted-out chain in a moldy dark room being tortured within an inch of my life. Strong women aren't simply born. We are forged through the fires of life. I am a woman who has weathered the storm and harnessed the thunder to not only survive, but to thrive. Frankly, I'm shocked that my captor could be so stupid as to underestimate me.

My heartbeat is faint and weakened from the torture, but survival is not an issue. I draw on my breath, deep and steady, in and out...in and out. After a moment, the chaos in my mind clears as a magnificent memory materializes there - bold, vivid and beautiful – of me and a Cypress tree. It stands so stately, alive, lush and green...such a stark contrast to the dire horror I currently face. A long time ago, when the forests thrived here, the one place where I could always find solace and inner peace was under the canopy of these towering trees. It is this image in my mind now that allows me to gather my physical strength, which I need to execute the plan.

Chained up next to me, but not within reach, is my oldest and most cherished friend, Athena. Even more than my own pain, I can't stand to see her like this...so worn down, a shadow of the magnificent beauty that she once was...but even in this gods-awful weakened state, I know that her inner light still shines...strong and vibrant. I know this because we've been plotting our escape plan for the past two weeks. Thankfully today, not a moment too late, Aetos Dios – the Golden Eagle – arrived outside our window screeching at the top of his lungs. We were waiting for the sign that the black box has been placed. This is it.

"Artemis...it's time," I hear her voice clearly inside my head.

Athena has a special ability...telepathy. Not a good idea to underestimate her either. Our plan should work without a hitch, assuming my other friend, Hestia, survives. She hangs limply from a rusty wire, tattered and frail. Her long wavy blond hair and pale ivory skin still remain, reminiscent from her days of glory.

All three of us likely are necessary to overtake our executioner and his 'pets', although to be honest, we have the definite advantage, knowing his greatest weakness: *hubris.*

My executioner - a maniacal man with red-purple eyes and lopsided hair - laughs hysterically, giggling loudly. His only answer is the snap of his whip as it slices across my neck. He mocks me, "A few more hours and you'll be human...torture will overtake your mind as you slowly slip into insanity. Then...off to the Aether!"

As long as the Elixir is still in my blood, I cannot die, at least until there is no Elixir left. He's standing a little too close to my face, the foul stench of his breath hot on my neck, as he continues his rant, "...and since we've been friends for so long...what has it been?"

I don't even open my eyes. He's not worthy of any attention from me.

"Hey!" He grabs my arm, twisting it hard. "Talk to me! How long has it been??"

The pain in my arm overwhelms my resolve, so my eyes fly open. But there's no way I'm giving him the satisfaction of conversation with me here.

"Over twelve thousand years!!" he yells right in my face, but I just stand there as fierce defiance fills my eyes. Of course, I've known him my whole life...we grew up together, but that makes almost no difference to him. He's always been a cutthroat bastard, but at least back then, he at least pretended to care about his friends. Now, I barely recognize this twisted demon of a man who insists that we call him by his real name: *Hades.*

"Very well, since you've been such an old and dear friend to me for all of these years, I have a gift for you. You get to choose...which way do you want to die? Whip...?" he holds up the black serrated whip of which I'm already familiar, "...or Fork...?" He points to the wall where his weapon of choice - a two-pronged fork – is resting. I instantly recognize it as a gravity disrupter. If he activates it, everything within a five-foot radius his target destabilizes into dust. Probably the more pain-free option.

"I'm going wrap this chain around your neck, and snap it in two!" I scowl. My voice ragged and short as I struggle to breathe, but it still comes out loud and clear. "C'mon Hay! You're better than this!" I goad him. I'm not taking his crap, not for a second.

"What did you just call me?!" he screams into my ear, making me jump. The restraints cut into my wrists as he slams his fist into the side of my head, "what's my name??"

I'm chained to the side of the wall or I would fall to the ground from the force of the blow. The cobblestone walls are stained a deep burgundy from the blood of thousands of other victims through the centuries who must have long perished by now. The overwhelming stench of rancid mildew drifts through the air to me, irritating my senses, although I've become used to the rats scurrying between my ankles.

I slam my forehead into his face, forcing him to fall back and clutch his head in shocked pain. As he draws his hand back from his face, his eyes are wild, filled with fury.

"Agggghh!! I'm bleeding, you filthy witch!" he screams, "You'll pay for that!"

Just then Athena makes her move, calling out to him, "C'mon sweet thing. Do you really want our blood on your hands?"

His head whips around to glare at her as his hands rush up to cover his ears. He shakes his head in a frenzy, as if to knock out something this is lodged in his brain. "Get out of my head, Athena!!! I know what you're trying to do!"

She's relentless, not giving up, "I'll make you a deal. Just give me the Elixir and you can have the one thing that you've always wanted…"

This gets his attention, making him sidle over to where Athena hangs on the wall across from me, "and what exactly would that be..?" he says as he strokes a strand of Athena's hair behind her ear.

"You know…" she smiles seductively at him, charm and lust oozing from every pore.

"You lie!" he screams, "You'd never give up your precious virginity!"

"What do I have to lose…? You want me, you always have…"

I scream at Athena in disgust, "Athena, how could you…?! How *dare* you turn on us?"

This just amps up Hades more. He grabs the back of Athena's head, then plants a big sloppy wet kiss on her lips. She plays her role flawlessly, deepening the kiss with fervor.

"I need my hands free if you want more," she smiles at him sweetly. He takes the key and unchains her arms. She falls to the ground, wrapping her arms around his waist as she stares intently into his eyes.

Just then, a dog starts yipping. At Hades' feet, stands a feisty little creature. This ridiculous freak of nature…what looks like a Chihuahua with three heads and a snake's tail is the unfortunate result of genetic engineering gone horribly wrong. That, or perhaps someone's idea of a harsh joke.

I wince as I peer down the length of my legs where scores of blood-crusted welts cover my legs and ankles. Ceberus Jr. may look small and harmless, but make no mistake, he is pure evil…just as twisted and insane as his owner. Fifteen pounds of sheer anger and ferocity. The original Ceberus, a gigantic three-headed monstrosity, was once one of the most fearsome of all creatures…at least until he met his untimely demise.

The obnoxious barking distracts Hades enough for Athena's spell to dissipate. His eyes grow wide in sudden fury as he roughly grabs Athena's face with his hand. He laughs, then says in a mocking tone, "Did you really think you could best me when you're tied up?

Hades face reddens, eyes red-rimmed and bulging slightly as his rage starts to build. "You always did think you were smarter than anyone else…Zeus' little pet," he says with a sinister smile, baring a row of yellow crooked teeth, as he raises the whip up into the air, ready to strike.

"No, only *you*," Athena replies, regarding him with her cool, ice blue gaze. Her voice is sarcastic, but from her clenched posture, I can see that she is bracing herself from the impact of his whip.

Instead of striking Athena, though, he turns at the last minute, swerving towards Hestia. As the whip darts outward wicked fast, it leaves a gaping wound on her once beautiful face. I hear a weak moan emanate from her frail, hanging body as she writhes in pain and her head lolls from side to side from the impact.

Hades takes in Athena's look of horror with a large obnoxious grin. He knows that Athena's love of her friends is so strong that this is the worst imaginable punishment for her…far worse than if she were to take the blows herself. "Still feeling smart?" he says, with a terrible cackle.

"Hades…!" he whips his head around to me, a little annoyed to be distracted from Athena, as I chide him in a loud voice, "Do you really believe that crap about the *Prophecy*?" My voice laced with sarcasm as I continue, "What a load of dung. The Oracle is spinning more nonsense, as usual… 'A virgin will give birth to a child that will end the Zeus' tyrannical reign and bring peace to the people'. Wow, I think I've heard that story before…uh, the Virgin Mary?"

My intense brown-purple eyes are as alive and defiant as ever, in my best effort to bait him. "You know that the Oracle is making up tall tales just to gain favor with Zeus, right…? You're just a stupid pawn in a game you'll never win!"

He becomes irate. The whip descends. I feel pain seer through my body as the tiny barbed rope slashes across my thigh, leaving a deep gash and blood running down my leg. I close my eyes and send a message to the only thing that can protect me. A rat lunges in Hades direction.

"What th-…?" Hades screams in agony, "that vermin bit me!!"

"Thank you, my little friend," I think silently. I still have some of my powers left from what remains of the Elixir in my blood, but they are fading quickly. He raises the whip again, but it cracks against the wall, breaking in two.

"Damn me to *hell*!" He scoffs. In an insane fury, Hay throws the whip down onto the hard stone floor, scowling in a full out tantrum.

Just then, my precious little rat scurries over to Athena, depositing a small purple glass vial into her hands…Elixir! Just enough to revive Hestia. *Well done!*

A violent landquake shakes the room. Hades looks around frantically, wild panic in his blood shot eyes. When he looks away, a ferocious look overtakes Athena…she's tough. A true survivor. The land beneath Hay's feet begins to quake again, forcing him to recede to the other side of the room.

Before I can register what is happening, Athena uses the key she stole from Hades earlier during their 'kiss', releases herself from her bindings, and throws me a dagger and the key. I use it to release my restraints.

Once I'm free, I allow my mind fall into a hypnotic meditative state as I sense some minute remains of the elixir in my blood, allowing the energy life force – the Aether - to consume me. That's when I call out to them in my mind…the troops.

Off in the distance, I hear a loud mournful *roar*, like that of a wounded lion. The sound is so startlingly familiar. I am filled with hope.

I hear the sound before I can even open my eyes. The ground quakes again, but this time I know why. A stampede of different animals led by my beautiful white Stag rushes into the room, quickly overtaking Hades, throwing him down onto the ground.

Athena scowls, throwing her arms up in frustration, "It's not time for the animals yet! You're supposed to focus on Hestia first!"

The truth is that I had expected it to take a little more time for my 'troops' – a herd of exotic animals, each uniquely regal, majestic and lethal - to arrive. With so little Elixir left in my system, I'm frankly surprised that they came at all.

"I don't exactly have the level of control over things that I used to!" I retort. My giant lioness roars loudly, making me turn. Hades has stabbed her with a sword as she pins him down underneath her enormous paw, claws dug into his writhing arm.

Athena and I use the key to free Hestia from her bondage. Once unrestricted, Hestia falls to the floor, lying in a heap. I feel my forehead crease as I try to feel for Hestia's pulse…fading and weak, it's barely there.

"Hestia…?" Athena picks up the glowing purple vial, cradles Hestia's head in her lap, and pours the shimmering liquid down into her mouth.

Suddenly, Hestia sputters and coughs, sitting straight up with a start. As her eyes fully open, she struggles to lift her gaze up in our direction. "I…I'm not going to make it…"

"No…" I stifle the pain in my voice, not wanting to show her how much I believe her.

"No way!" Athena commands, "Don't talk like that. Now that you have the Elixir, you're going to be fine." She pulls Hestia up to her feet, a mischievous smile filling her face as she says, "Let's go!"

As we take off through the large stone arched doorway, I see Hades run over to the wall, to where a black box is nestled into the wall. What in the hell fire could he be up to? Whatever it is, it can't be good.

We pause for a moment to survey the vast maze of tunnels in front of us. Which way is the exit? *"This way!"* I hear Athena scream in my head. Glad she knows the way. It would be so easy to get lost here and never find your way out. This prison, called Tartarus, is notorious for this.

As we run down the middle corridor, my hope is quickly dashed when just up ahead of us comes a crackling, hissing sound. When I see what it is, my breath stops short in my chest...it's *Medusa*.

Not the old Medusa that was killed and now resides on Athena's shield...this is the new and improved version...half machine, half genetically altered creature...a cyborg, yet more twisted and devious than before. I had heard rumors about her resurrection, but had never seen her face to face...never wanted to either.

Cyborg Medusa's hair consists of slithering poisonous snakes just like in the old days, but now, they are silver and metallic. Her body is a repulsive green with her expansive barbed wings folded behind her as she glides effortlessly across the narrow opening of the tunnel ahead towards us.

Rarely do I experience real fear anymore, but right now, I am *terrified*...especially when I catch a glimpse of her face...it's more hideous and repulsive than I could have imagined...and her smell is repugnant, like rotting flesh. I try desperately to avert my gaze from her eyes, which from here, appear deep burgundy, like old blood. As she approaches me, she comes so close to me that I feel her rancid breath hot on my face as she sniffs up and down my whole body. I stand still as a statue. Maybe if she thinks I'm already made of stone, she won't bother me.

A second later, Ceberus Jr, who must have run in behind us, now runs past us and starts yapping, working himself up into a ridiculous frenzy. Not smart. At the speed of lightning, Medusa whips around, directing her eyes onto the obnoxious barking creature. In a split second, thousands of tiny needles shoot out of her eyes at him, hitting him like darts. Instantly, his eyes gloss over and he crashes down to the ground, paralyzed...almost as if he's been turned to stone.

"I'll take care of Medusa," she yells in our minds, *"You get out of here!"* Athena runs over to the side of the tunnel closest to the monstrous cyborg.

"Anapsyta!" Athena she yells. Medusa's head snaps around and moves so fast that I barely track her as she flies over to where Athena now stands behind a large stone column. They chase each other around the column. I pick up the dagger that Athena just dropped, we turn around and run down the tunnel back towards the torture chamber we just left.

I hear a shriek behind me...a terrible, horrible high-pitched wail, which makes me turn back and look. Somehow, Athena has stabbed Medusa in both eyes with what looks like Hay's dagger, disabling her ability to paralyze anyone. *Yes*! A small victory!

When I turn back around, though, I'm horrified to see Hay's fanatical grin as he stands behind a panicked Hestia, holding his dagger at her neck. Where are the animals...? I can see the lioness, still bleeding from an earlier wound, stalking in behind Hades...

Suddenly, I hear a scream which makes me turn, "Aghhhh!!!" It's Athena. She's in trouble. Cyborg Medusa cackles in a screeching cacophony of sound as she pins Athena in the shoulder with a razor-sharp talon from her wing.

I throw Hades' dagger to Athena, which shoots out from my hand quick as a whip, landing with a dull thud in Medusa's wing. Athena grabs it and slashes out at Medusa's face, drawing blood as the knife slices through her cheek.

But Medusa is pissed as hell. Fast as lightning, her silver tongue whips out of her mouth, clipping Athena around the neck, slowly choking the life out of her. This can't be how it ends! Athena's eyes widen as her face turns a ghastly white. Perhaps death is our destiny after all...

Then suddenly, I hear Hades' cry and I turn to see Hestia standing strong and tall behind me, her eyes now a vibrant shade of purple, alive with the Elixir. There in her outstretched palm, I see a small flame. Slowly, steadily, it grows larger and more voracious, until the fire is a raging inferno.

A mixture of defiance and strength fills her face as she aims and shoots the sparking blaze outward, slicing through Medusa's tongue with flawless precision. She shrieks in a wild rage, snakes hissing as her head thrashes around and her tongue swiftly retreats.

Just as Athena is freed, Hestia summons a much larger ball of flame, this time aiming into the heart of Medusa's thrashing body. Almost as swift as the flame hit Medusa, the cyborg staggers, then crumbles to the floor, the electric circuits inside her clearly shorted out as they simmer and crackle. The rancid smell of burning flesh makes me gag. Only the jagged end of her black barbed tail twitches as an after effect.

Athena runs to me, "Time to go!" as she summons my lioness. As the lioness releases Hay, I hear a bizarre sound…he is laughing in a fit of outlandish hysteria. But why…?

I turn and suddenly understand. He aims the gravity fork in our direction. One blast and we're all dust. I close my eyes, bracing myself, but feel nothing…yet. I'm still here.

I see Hestia moving towards Hades.

"Hestia, no!!!" I yell.

She shakes her head as a lone tear slips down her cheek, "I'm sorry…"

Just as Hay's finger hits the trigger, Hestia leaps out in front of us…and just like that, her body is instantly consumed by the gravity, transformed into a fine mist of dust.

I scream, "Noooo!!!"

Hades gears up to hit the trigger again, when we hear a sudden noise behind us. Athena grabs my arm, pulling me down to the ground…just in time, as the serrated tip of cyborg Medusa's tail darts out, only inches from where we lie on the ground, pinning Hades in the shoulder into the wall behind him. Medusa is back!

The murderous smile that once consumed his face is now a mask of fury, as he screams at her, "Not me, you idiot!" Her metallic tongue lashes out at him, choking him around the neck. With his free hand, he points the gravity fork at Medusa and hits the trigger. This time, there is no return for Medusa. *Zap*...she evaporates into nothingness.

With not a moment to spare, Athena shoves me up onto the back of my giant lioness and we deftly make our escape, but just barely, as we can feel repeated blasts from the gravity fork as it hits the walls around us, causing rock and stone to fall down all around us. Just when the tunnels threaten to consume us, we burst out into the vast expanse of desert nighttime. My vision is shrouded by tears as the wind whips our hair on our faces.

There is no time to spare as we reach the decrepit remains of the old city, which back in the glory days was the crown jewel of the planet. The drifting sands of endless desert dunes and hot red sun have long overtaken this place, now giving it the vacant feeling of emptiness, nothing more than a dusty graveyard.

Just ahead, we halt just as we reach the edge of the ruins at the old city. Athena gets down on to her hands and knees, digging into the sand with her bare hands. She emerges a moment later with the black box in her arms. A look of satisfaction comes over her, as she finds what she's looking for inside. She grabs my arm, thrusting a thin glass vial filled with a glowing purple substance into my blistered hand.

I raise an eyebrow as I ask, "The Elixir...?"

"Yes...and no," she says as fierce determination fills her eyes, "something much better...take this. You know what to do."

Time to go. I pull Athena in close to an emotional embrace, like I might never see her again. I love her dearly. My closest friend. "Will I see you again...?" I ask her.

"If the Prophecy is true, then of course. It is our destiny."

ABOUT THE AUTHOR

Alysia Helming started writing her own short stories and plays for school in the third grade, and throughout her life has never forgotten her passion for writing. In 2000, Alysia coauthored a pilot for a TV series, "One Degree of Separation" and in 2006, she coordinated the local premiere of the feature-length movie "*The Great Warming*" starring Alanis Morissette and Keanu Reeves, assisting with the nationwide release of the film. As a former student in Screenwriting at **University of California, Los Angeles**, Alysia wrote a full-length feature film screenplay, "The Green Warrior", in 2009-2010.

"*Protogenesis*" is Alysia's first novel, which is book one in a seven-novel series. She travels regularly between her home in the San Francisco Bay area, and Athens, Greece, the primary setting for her novel series.

Protogenesis was self-published in 2016. Within the first month, it rose to best-seller on **Amazon** for three consecutive weeks and was featured on the **Reuters** feed at **NY Times Square**. While writing this novel, she visited Athens, Greece 13 times where she met over 500 people who helped her research and develop her novel, including the real-life inspiration for one of her characters, Greek star **Kostas Martakis.**

When she isn't writing, Helming is considered a 'Clean Energy Guru'. She was the former CFO and now, is a majority investor/owner in **Pristine Sun**, a major solar independent power producer in the United States, which she co-founded with her husband.

Helming is the primary shareholder and President of **Protogenesis Media,** the Executive Producer of the short film series *Footsteps in Athens,* and the Creator/Executive producer of the new American reality-based TV series *Meet Me in Greece.*

Find out more at www.alysiahelming.com

AUTHOR OF THE SONG

Kostas Martakis is an accomplished Greek singer, TV host and actor, having released four studio albums, all of which went Platinum in Greece, and numerous singles that reached the Greek top charts. Currently, he is recording his fifth album and preparing to release the theme song *Forever & Tonight* for the best-selling American novel: *Protogenesis.*

During his 11-year career, Martakis has collaborated with almost every famous Greek singer in live concerts and shows. He was selected as the opening act for the **Jennifer Lopez** concert in Athens in 2009 – the same year that **E! Entertainment** included him in their "**25 Most Sexy Men in the World**" ranking. He has also participated, twice, in the Greek national final for the **Eurovision** Song Contest.

In addition to music, Martakis is an accomplished dancer and TV persona, which he demonstrated when he participated in the Greek

TV shows *Dancing with the Stars* and *Your Face Sounds Familiar,* and then co-presented the second season of *Dancing with the Stars* and the very first Greek music-fashion show, *Mad Walk.* He was also the host of the Greek TV-game show *Super Buzz* in 2015, and co-host in the Greek prime-time morning TV show *Kalimeroudia* from 2015-16.

In 2013, Martakis stunned audiences with his breakthrough role as an actor when he starred in the successful Greek adaptation of the musical *Rent.* He also starred the musical *(Den) Se Thelw* in 2015. In 2016, Martakis starred in an American short film series, *Footsteps in Athens,* which is promoted by the largest Greece tourism website (1 million+ followers), *Discover Greece.*

Martakis is an active owner in **Protogenesis Media Inc,** and a driving force on the creative team as a Producer for the new American reality-based TV series *Meet Me in Greece.*

Find out more at www.kostasmartakis.com

ACKNOWLEDGEMENTS

There are so many incredible people that helped me through the process of writing my first novel, but I want to start by thanking the Universe and God for bringing together all of the right people into my life at exactly the right moment to provide me with the research and life lessons that I needed in order to write this incredible novel. The journey has not always been easy, but the result here is so amazing that I am grateful for all experiences and people who touched my life through the creation of this novel series.

In the beginning, this was a collaborative effort with my teenage niece, Hannah Emerson, who first inspired me to begin writing this series. Ultimately, we both wrote our own stories, fell in love with those stories and decided to part ways to write separately. I am looking forward to the day when Hannah publishes her first novel.

To my incredible husband, Troy. Thank you for being so supportive and understanding through my writing journey and my many trips to Greece without you, for trusting me when I'm sure it felt so difficult to do so, for believing in me that I could follow and achieve my dreams.

To my son, Xander. Thank you for creating the "secret room under the school" and other creative ideas that came from your dreams. Thanks for letting Mommy go to Greece without you on a regular basis. I am so excited that you are now inspired to create your own book series.

This novel would not be possible without my literary agent, Johanna Maaghul at Waterside, and my publisher, Reagan Rothe at Black Rose Writing, and my core team of editors including story/structural editor: Copy/Line/Story editor: Kelly Luce (Harvard Fellow and Award Winning Young Adult Fiction Author and Editor) Story Editor: Kelly Fullerton (UCLA screenwriting lecturer and Young Adult Hollywood TV writer), Greek cultural editor: Denia Metaxa,

Young Adult editor: Hannah Emerson, Content editor: Deborah Cohen, and to my test readers in the US, Greece, Australia, UK and Germany.

Special thanks to Greek musical artist, TV host, actor and former model, Kostas Martakis, for inspiring my character, Ever Sarantos; and for transporting me regularly back to Greece with your gorgeous voice and mesmerizing music. Of course, I am most grateful to Kostas for his gift to me of the song "Forever and Tonight" which was written and produced in collaboration with Panik Entertainment Group, Ltd, George Arsenakos, Marios Psimopoulos, Vicky Gerothodorou and Jazz/Clarinet musician, Thanasis Vasilopoulos.

Also, thanks to Kostas for being a great friend, advisor and for narrating a series of short movies for www.protogenesis.com to help Protogenesis bring the magic of Greece to the world. To renowned Director, Vassilis Antoniadis, of Filmskin and scriptwriter, Betty Saradinou, for all your amazing work on the movies and promotion efforts. Thanks to Vally Agiropoulou and George Arsenakos at Panik Entertainment Group for PR collaboration and Kostas Martakis' management company. Also, I have been inspired by the music of Greek music star, Demy, and by her sister, a lyricist, Romy Papadea.

I am especially grateful to my team at Protogenesis Media Inc., an entertainment and media company. Denia Metaxa is the Executive Director for our book division. Thanks to Denia's sister, Bessie Metaxa, for being test reader #1 and her mother, Eleni Metaxa, for her advice on Greek cuisine.

Extra special thanks to Sonia Rodiadis, who is our PR & Communications Director, and outside public relations experts Brittany Bearden and Dea Shandera. Thanks to Markos Kamfonas for his support as Kostas Martakis' internal manager.

Thanks to Lia Papadopoulou for allowing me to use her Shar-pei, Hampos, as inspiration for Ever's dog, and Maldiva the Abyssinian and my mother's cat, Sophie, for inspiring Bastet.

Incredible thanks to my friend, renowned designer and Househunters International Reality TV host, James Charles. His company Kinari Design is an international design and architecture firm located in Athens, Los Angeles and the UK. Architect Nasia Kalokerinou designed many of the incredible scenes depicted on my website www.alysiahelming.com and www.protogenesis.com, as well as the map of Gaea included in the book.

Thank you to my Greek research contributors: Pantelis Panos from the American Classical School in Athens, Desi B. Desi, VIP Destination Manager Greece, Anastasia Rigatou, Greek Archaeologist and Tourist Guide, Voula Tsouna, Professor of Philosophy and specialist in Socrates and Plato from the University of California, Santa Barbara, Richard McKirahan, Professor of Philosophy and specialist in Socrates and Aristotle from Pomona College, John McK. Camp II, Director of the Agora Excavations.

For insights into the Greek financial and refugee crisis, many thanks to Epameinondas Farmakis, Exec Director of Solidarity Now and the Minister of Foreign Affairs for the Netherlands, Bert Koenders.

For the design of the fictional mystery virus, which starts in this novel and plays a major role in the next book, I am thankful to Sha and Matt Coleman, both biomedical genetic scientists from the Lawrence Livermore National Laboratory.

I am grateful for the advice and guidance provided from a variety of advisors from the Entertainment Industry, including George Zakk, KO Creative, Jeffrey Rose, Kelly Fullerton, Peter Mallouk, Manos Gavras, and many others.

Much thanks to KO Creative for website and graphic design, my main driver in Greece, Dimitris Kapetanakis, to everyone at the Margi Hotel in Vouliagmeni, including Theo Agiostratitus and Afroditi Sol, for providing me with an incredible home away from home when I stayed in Athens. I will always remember The Farm Experience and Billy the Donkey.

I am certain that J.K. Rowling has inspired me, as I read out loud the entire Harry Potter series to my son while he was learning to read. Other writers that have influenced my writing journey are Stephenie Meyer, Suzanne Collins, C.S. Lewis, George Lucas and Judy Blume.

Many thanks to the late Wayne Dyer for introducing me to the Tao Te Ching, to Oprah Winfrey and Deepak Chopra for teaching me how to manifest energy through their meditation series, and my spiritual guides, Jon Rasmussen and Ben Oofana.

Also essential to this whole journey and my sanity were my

parents, Ron & MaryLou Carlson, my sister, Jennifer Rafferty, Anne & Jim Cadwell, and my wellness team: Tracey Stone, Sam Rhame D.C., Carrie & Dr. Tony Waechter, Danielle Boucher, Holly Wallis and Karen Dishmon from Reactive Movement. Thanks for keeping me sane and healthy!

Lastly, thanks to *Ballet North* and Laura Luzicka Reinschmidt for so many years of training in classical ballet; and to Jennifer Stahl Weitz from the San Francisco Ballet for reviewing and loving my book, and starring in the "Forever & Tonight" music video.

View other Black Rose Writing titles at www.blackrosewriting.com/books and use promo code **PRINT** to receive a **20% discount** when purchasing.

CPSIA information can be obtained
at www.ICGtesting.com
Printed in the USA
FSOW04n1824311017
40437FS